Among the Shrouded

Sevens Prophecy Series
Book One

Among the Shrouded

AMALIE JAHN

BERMLORD PUBLICATIONS

ISBN-13: 978-0991071302 (BERMLORD)
ISBN-10: 0991071301

Library of Congress Control Number: 2013918765
BERMLORD, Charlotte, North Carolina

Second Edition, January 2015

Typeset in Garamond
Cover photograph by Brigette Werner
Cover layout by Amalie Jahn
Author photograph courtesy of Mary Ickert of Mary L. Photography

For Mrs. Jacqueline McCosh
(and English teachers everywhere)

Thank you for encouraging me to love the written word.
I can only hope the writing I do today honors the memory of the lessons
you taught so many years ago.
If you were still here, I would hope you might read this
and it would make you proud.
But then again, maybe you've been with me all along.

Acknowledgments

As an author, technology is a beautiful thing. I would especially like to thank Google and their amazing map program which allowed me to walk the streets of Kiev with Kate at all hours of the day and night from the comfort of my couch wearing only my pajamas.

To my editor, Anne Zirkle, thank you for accepting the invitation to go along on this journey with me, for saying the hard things that needed to be said, and for taking *Among the Shrouded* from a fledgling manuscript to a cohesive novel. I enjoyed every minute of working with you.

And to Drew, thanks for putting up with my own special brand of crazy. No one else in the world does it better.

"Borromean rings are three rings which are interlocked in such a way that removing one ring causes the entire structure to fall apart. This is an illustration of what is known as a Brunnian link, a situation where no two loops in a figure are directly connected.

Borromean rings are extremely ancient. They appear in Buddhist art from thousands of years ago, for example, and they can be seen on Viking rune stones, in Roman mosaics, and in an assortment of other places. People appear to have an enduring fascination with the phenomenon of Borromean rings, and they appear especially frequently in religious artwork from a variety of cultures.

When used in religious artwork, coats of arms, logos, and crests, Borromean rings are meant to symbolize strength in unity, a living illustration of what happens when one link in a united element is removed. The rings are named for the Borromeo family of Italian nobles, who famously used them in their family coat of arms, popularizing the three interlocked rings."

Source: www.wisegeek.com

Among the Shrouded

CHAPTER

1

MIA

Mia looked through the one-way glass into the room of men. Each was of similar height and build, about five and a half feet tall and moderately overweight. She'd spent so much of her life looking into the lineup room that by the time she officially became a part of the police force, she'd been given her own spot. There was a sign taped to the wall of the room. It read, 'Stay out of Mia's spot.'

She began coming to the lineup room just after her seventh birthday, several years after she revealed her gift to her father, the Chief of Police, Carlos Rosetti.

"Who do you think did it?" her partner Jack whispered.

She wrinkled her nose and squinted, pushing closer to the glass in front of her.

"I don't know exactly. Two have dark auras, but one of them is darker than the other. He's probably our guy. Whatever he's done is recent." She didn't take her eyes off the possible suspects as the door to the lineup viewing room opened.

"Ma'am," Jack said to the elderly woman who joined them in front of the window, "I need you to look carefully and tell me which of these men you think you saw breaking into your home on the night of the 17th."

The woman hesitated, scanning the row of men before her.

"The second one, there on the left. I believe that's him," she responded at last.

Jack scribbled feverously onto the page tacked to the clipboard in his hand. "Okay. I've marked him down," he said. "Thank you for your time today." Then he spoke into the call box. "Send in the next group, Pete."

He escorted the elderly woman out of the room and returned with a middle aged man in a well-tailored suit.

"Good morning, Mr. Franklin," Jack said, shaking the man's hand. "All I need you to do is take a look at the next group that will be arriving and let me know if you see who was vandalizing the storefront on the night in question. Take your time. There's no need to rush."

In the adjacent room, the line of short, fat men filed out and another group shuffled in. The men in the second lineup were just over six feet tall with thin, muscular physiques.

Mia gasped audibly, causing both men to turn. Jack raised an eyebrow in her direction.

"It's nothing," she remarked. "I was just clearing my throat."

The men turned back to the lineup and she remained silent for the remainder of the process, although she was unable to take her eyes from the last man in the row. He was attractive, almost strikingly so, but his face could not hide a sadness lurking just beneath the surface. However it wasn't the man's features she found so alarming. For her, there was something even more unusual about the man.

Mr. Franklin quickly identified who he believed to be the vandal and was immediately ushered from the room.

Once they were alone, Jack could no longer curb his curiosity.

"What's the matter? Did he pick the wrong guy?" he asked.

"I don't know," she responded, still unable to comprehend what she had just seen.

"You don't know?" he said incredulously.

"No, Jack. I don't know," she replied, her voice rising.

He fished a stick of gum from his pocket and continued to pry. "Why don't you know?" he asked, popping the gum in his mouth. "You never 'don't know.'"

She paused, biting at her nail. "One of the men. I couldn't see his aura."

"Why not?" he asked. "Was there a glare? Is it too bright in here?"

"No," she replied, shaking her head, "he just didn't have one."

He cracked his gum to irritate her like a pesky brother. "How could he not have one? Everyone has an aura. That's what you've always said."

Instead of responding to her partner, she turned on her heel and left the room without further explanation. The door slammed behind her and she nervously scanned the hallway for the lineup detective, Peter Winchester. She spotted him coming around the corner at the far end of the hall.

"Pete! Hold up! I have to talk to you," she shouted.

Pete stopped walking and headed back down the hall in her direction.

"The last group…" she began, before he interrupted.

"The vandal?"

"Yeah. Do you have the list of participants with you?"

He handed her the clipboard from under his arm. She scanned the list. "Who was on the end? The last one?"

"Uh, he's here," he said pointing to a name on the chart. "Thomas Pritchett. He was a plant though. He just signed up to be designated as a regular. Do you think something's up with him? You know we get a lot of trash walking in here looking to make a quick buck."

She paused. "No. Nothing like that. I thought he looked a lot like an old classmate of mine, but I guess not. Thanks, Pete," she lied, unwilling to disclose the truth about her inquiry.

"No problem. Anyway, have a good weekend, Mia. I have tomorrow and Sunday off. First time in months," he said.

"Have fun," she replied absently as she headed in the opposite direction, down the hall toward her office.

She was grateful to be alone as she sat at her desk, and hoped Jack would be occupied elsewhere in the station for a while. She held her head in her hands, trying to understand why she had been unable to see Thomas Pritchett's aura. For the first time in over twenty years, her confidence in her ability was shaken. She recalled the only other time in her life when the validity of what she saw had been brought into question.

The auras had been a part of her life for as long as she could remember. For many years as a child, she had wrongly assumed that everyone saw the world as she did, with each person surrounded by a veil of light or dark. In the beginning, she didn't know what the difference represented.

When she was four, her mother took her to visit her father at the police station for the first time. Until that point in her life, she had only seen people with auras that were light. There were some that were noticeably dimmer than others but everyone she came into contact with had radiated some form of light. However, as they'd entered the building that fateful day, an officer walked past her escorting a man in handcuffs. The detainee was cursing and screaming as he was led into the booking area. She was shocked to see his aura had no light and instead he appeared to be shrouded in a veil of darkness.

She had immediately questioned her mother about what she had seen and repeatedly asked what had happened to the man's light.

"Good girls don't make up stories or tell lies," her mother had scolded as she swatted her on the bottom for being an embarrassment and causing a scene.

That night, she had trouble falling asleep. From under her blankets she laid awake listening to her mother and father arguing about her outburst at the station. Her mother was convinced Mia was either possessed by an evil spirit or had some kind of psychiatric disorder requiring immediate medical attention. Her father, on the other hand, felt a 4-year-old could not be trusted to tell the truth and that her outburst had simply been the result of an overactive imagination.

At some point, no longer able to listen to their fighting, she had crept down the stairs and joined her parents in the dim light of the kitchen. That night, she understood for the first time that her parents did not see what she saw. They were unable to see the auras. She realized no one could. She tried in vain to explain to them how everyone appeared to her, bathed in a wash of luminosity, but they didn't understand. It would be many years until her father would open his mind to the promise of her gift, and sadly, her mother would never accept there were parts of the world that were beyond her understanding.

Mia was roused from her thoughts by a presence in the room. "Jack said I might find you in here," said Major Rosetti from the doorway.

"Hi, Dad," she smiled.

"He said something spooked you. What's going on?"

After she revealed her gift to him, her father eventually accepted and embraced her unique view of the world. However, he had always encouraged her to keep her visions private so others wouldn't be able to take advantage of her abilities. Out of respect and love for him, she had done just that, sharing her secret with only a handful of people in her life.

What he didn't know however, was since the day she discovered that her ability was unique, she had been

7

searching for both a cause and a purpose for her gift. Isolated by her secret, she sought out others like her – people with the ability to see the world in different ways. By the age of eleven, she'd expanded her search beyond the people she knew to include a worldwide audience, scouring the internet for stories of people with extraordinary capabilities. She discovered people with incredible strength, those who claimed to speak to the dead, and even a few whose stories rivaled her own in strangeness, but despite her loneliness, she'd never worked up the courage to correspond with any of them.

She attempted to explain what happened in the lineup room to her father. "One of the plants in the lineup, this guy named Thomas Pritchett... I couldn't read him. He had no aura."

"Is that unusual?" he asked.

"In twenty-four years, I've never seen a person without an aura. So yeah, it's unusual."

Rosetti sat in the chair at Jack's desk and ran his fingers through his thinning hair.

"So you saw a kid without an aura? So what? So that's it for the day? Pack it in?"

Mia shook her head at his single-mindedness. "No, Dad. No. I'm fine. I'm working on my case load. It's just... I don't know. I thought I had this thing all figured out. The light, the dark, the shades and variations. But this? This nothing? It's new. I don't do well with new," she said, looking at her father solemnly across the room.

After a moment he got up to stand behind her, giving her shoulders a gentle squeeze as he planted a kiss on the top of her head. "I'm sure you'll be fine, my Mia. You always rise to the occasion. I've got one more meeting this afternoon about the new commissioner's visit next week and then I'm headed home. Give your grandmother a call if you get a chance sometime and don't stay too late, okay?" he said as he headed out the door. "Love you."

"Love you too, Dad," she said, rolling her eyes and smiling at his ability to brush her concerns aside so easily.

Once he shut the door behind him, Mia wasted no time retrieving a manila envelope from the bottom drawer of the file cabinet she and her partner shared. She slid her casework to the side and emptied the contents of the envelope onto her desk. Newspaper clippings, printed copies of internet searches and her master list sat before her.

She scanned the list of names scribbled in various colored inks on the yellowing piece of wide-ruled paper, torn from her seventh grade social studies notebook. Many of the frayed spiral edges were still intact. Somewhere between disappointment and relief, she discovered Thomas Pritchett's name was absent from her list of psychics – people who were gifted just like her. Her pen hesitated above the page as she was unsure whether to add his name to the group.

She chewed on the plastic pen cap. Was the reason she couldn't see his aura due to his own peculiarity or was something going terribly wrong with her own ability?

After finally deciding to add his name to the list in pencil, she returned her file to the cabinet just as Jack appeared in the doorway.

"Heading out?" he asked, tossing his keys on his desk.

She glanced at the wall clock. Her shift had ended hours ago. "Yeah. I guess so. You?" she asked, slipping her jacket off the back of her chair.

"Not yet. I still have to log the evidence inventory from the assault in Fells Point on Tuesday. What a mess that's been. It's always the drunk guys, right?" he laughed, winking at their inside joke.

"Always the drunk guys," she confirmed, as she passed behind him on her way to the door.

"You okay? About earlier? The lineup?"

"I'm fine." She shrugged. "It just took me by surprise."

"I'm sure it was a fluke. See you in the morning," he called as she headed into the hallway.

"Bright and early," she said.

After leaving the station, she drove to the Parkville apartment she shared with her best friend Chelsea. The two grew up living across the street from one another, and Mia had always been drawn to her because of the brightness of her light. Chelsea radiated goodness and she found herself inexplicably drawn to people with the brightest auras. So although their lives had taken different paths career wise, she found she functioned better with Chelsea in her day to day life, especially considering the darkness she was surrounded by at work. After graduating from the police academy, she reconnected with Chelsea, who spent four years earning her degree in education. The plan was for them to share an apartment for a while, until they both established themselves financially. Two years later, they were still living together. She was relieved to see Chelsea's subcompact parked in front of their building as she pulled into the parking lot.

"Rough day?" she asked as Mia came through the door, tossing her sidearm and belt on the table.

"Not until the end. But we caught the jerk that beat those women behind the loading docks, so that was good. How about you?"

"I had three IEP meetings this afternoon and not a single parent showed up. I don't know how I'm supposed to help these kids singlehandedly. It's pretty bad when I can't even get the parents to show up. Makes me sick for the kids," Chelsea said as she pulled a bottle of wine and two glasses from the cabinet. "So what happened at the end of the day?"

"Nothing really. There was just this guy in a lineup…"

"A guy?" Chelsea asked, raising an eyebrow in her direction.

"Yes. A guy," she replied, rolling her eyes at her friend. "It was nothing. He was just… unusual."

"Unusual like 'I'm in a trailer for a horror flick' way or unusual in an 'I'm totally interesting and you should get to know me' kind of way?"

Mia uncorked the bottle of wine. "Neither. What are you doing tonight?" she asked in an attempt to change the subject.

"Nothing. I'm beat. Tyler is working late, so he won't be over. I picked up a movie if you want to watch it with me."

"Yeah. Let's do that. Let me change and I'll help with dinner."

She spent the rest of the evening trying desperately to forget about Thomas Pritchett and his missing aura, but her mind kept wandering back to him. She wasn't sure if it was the missing aura or the sadness she saw in the lines of his face, but she was convinced there was more to him than met the eye.

Thomas took the ten dollar bill he made from the lineup and put it in his pocket, adding it to the $186 he had already cashed from his paycheck at the restaurant. He hopped a bus to the Inner Harbor where he hoped to add a little more money to his wallet, giving him enough for the mortgage that was due by the following afternoon. If he didn't, it was going to be a ramen noodle kind of week.

It was getting late and he was happy to be leaving the more dangerous area of the city where the police station was located. He always felt anxious around high crime areas but not just because it gave him a general feeling of malaise. There was always the risk of being mugged or shot or attacked in some way, but there was more to it for him. For a reason unknown to him and for as long as he could remember, he could sense when there was the potential for danger and, for this reason, he was relieved to be heading into the relative tranquility of the hotel lobby right in the heart of the city.

When he arrived, he made his way into the spacious entrance of the hotel, giving a nod to Bill at the concierge desk. Bill, a friend of a friend, had been kind enough to get him an interview at the hotel when money had gotten tight, and for that, he had always been grateful. The baby grand piano was located directly beside the check-in counter, which he was glad to see was teeming with guests. Friday nights were typically great for tips, especially if he arrived in time to catch the dinner crowd.

As he sat down on the bench, he placed his tip jar from his backpack on top of the piano. Beautiful music poured from his fingertips and the two story lobby was filled with a spirited rendition of Rachmaninov's Piano Concerto No. 3 in D minor.

Within moments, a hotel guest strolled over to place a five dollar bill into his jar.

"Where did you study?" he asked.

"Here and there," Thomas replied, a small smile on his lips.

"I'd guess Peabody or perhaps Julliard," the man continued.

Thomas only smiled and thanked him for his kindness. The reality of his playing was he had never paid for a single piano lesson. He had, however, spent almost every afternoon of his childhood with his elementary school music teacher. Sadly, he hadn't chosen to stay at school long after the dismissal bell because of an intrinsic pull toward musical appreciation. He had done so to avoid the alternative to staying at school, which was going home to his foster father. Even at a young age, he had sensed the danger around him and sought to avoid it at all costs.

To her credit, his biological mother could have done worse. Drunk and high, she could have left the baby, who fell from her loins at the rest stop bathroom. She could have placed him in the trashcan as her boyfriend had suggested. But she hadn't. Even in her frenzied state and despite the fact she had been unaware of the pregnancy, she had felt compassion toward her son. She convinced his father to drive her to the closest fast food restaurant where she left him just outside the entrance, wrapped in a Mega Metal concert t-shirt, in the middle of the night.

After that, he had become a ward of the state, moving from orphanage to orphanage and eventually foster home to foster home. Each placement had been worse than the last and he had found ways to avoid his foster families. In elementary school, instead of going home after the final bell rang, he would hang out with his music teacher, Mrs. Lawson. She had been drawn to his sweet spirit and happily took him under her wing. It was Mrs. Lawson who had inspired his love of music and taught him to play the piano. But it was also Mrs. Lawson who reported the bruising on his arms and torso to the Department of Social Services. After he was removed from the first abusive home, he never saw his music teacher again.

He had lived with a total of four different foster families during his childhood. Sadly, the second and third had been no better than the first. In alcohol induced furies, the foster fathers would often attempt to use him as a punching bag, but somehow, he was always aware of when the men were ready to strike and would manage to avoid any serious or permanent injuries. By the time he was thirteen, he was fortunate enough to be taken in by Howard and Mildred Pritchett, an older couple who had been unable to have children of their own. Encouraged by a flyer in their church bulletin about the benefits of adopting older children, the Pritchetts were quickly enchanted by him and saw to his care for the remainder of his teenage years.

After high school, no longer wanting to be a burden on the Pritchetts, he had moved out, convinced he could provide for himself. But when Howard Pritchett died of a sudden heart attack only three months later, Thomas had moved back in to help support the only real mother he had ever known. It was Mildred to whom he would deliver his tip money at the end of the evening. It was Mildred to whom he dedicated each of the evening's songs.

CHAPTER

3

MIA

Mia woke to the sound of rain dripping off the gutter just outside her bedroom window. She hated the rain, and a sense of foreboding followed her around as she readied herself for the day. She tiptoed out of the apartment, leaving Chelsea sleeping peacefully in the adjacent room.

Her drive to the station was uneventful, but the moment she arrived, she hit the ground running. She found Jack, already in their office pouring over cases assigned to them overnight as she walked through the door.

"How bad is it?" she asked, picking up the mug of coffee he'd placed on her desk.

"We've been assigned three shootings, two rape cases, and a murder in a pear tree," he replied, attempting to infuse his own brand of humor into the situation. "The sergeant wants me to take the shootings and you to take the rapes. We're working the murder together."

She took a sip of the coffee. "That's fine. Are the girls here at the station or are they still at the hospital?" she asked, picking up the files.

"They're already downstairs with Sanchez."

"So they've been processed?"

"Yeah. Rape kits were done at the hospital and they were brought back here about half an hour ago to finish with their statements."

She took off her coat and draped it across the back of her chair before heading back out the door. "Okay," she sighed, "I'm on it."

He grabbed her arm as she slid by his desk. "There's one more thing. I heard the one girl is young. Really young."

She took the stairs down to the basement of the building where the rape victims were waiting in separate rooms. For some reason, she didn't seem to mind the special victim's cases. Although many of her colleagues avoided them at all cost, she felt strangely compelled toward the women who were brought to her, stripped of their dignity by the men who objectified them. As she made her way down the hall, she mentally prepared herself for what she was about to see. It was never the same and it was never easy.

The first room housed a nineteen year old college student who was slipped Rohypnol while she was at a bar the night before. Unlike the many women who never reported being drugged and raped, this woman was brought in by a concerned roommate. She spent just over an hour taking the victim's statement, as well as the description of the man she believed assaulted her. The auras around both the victim and her roommate were bright and it disturbed her to know the woman's assailant would probably never be found. After suggesting to the woman that she seek counseling as a way to come to terms with what had been done to her, she said her goodbyes and returned to the hallway.

In the second room, she found a child. Eleven-year-old Janelle had been found by a police officer patrolling the streets of her west Baltimore neighborhood at three in the morning. She was discovered sitting on a street corner, bleeding and incoherent. At her initial hospital interview, she was unwilling or unable to provide the doctor with any information about what had happened to her.

Mia opened the door cautiously and was horrified by the sight of the child who was curled into the fetal position on the far side of the room. The girl was filthy and clearly malnourished. The aura surrounding her was very, very dim, and she was in danger of leaving the light in favor of the darkness that was obviously a large part of her everyday existence.

She sat in a chair beside the girl and introduced herself.

"Hi, Janelle. My name is Mia and I'm a police officer. I want you to know I'm not going to hurt you. And I promise not to get you into any trouble. Do you understand what I'm saying?"

The girl raised her head from between her knees to make eye contact and looked skeptically at her. She did not speak.

"I'm sure you know who did this to you. I bet he may have done it before. And I bet that you might even think he's a friend."

"He ain't no friend," Janelle interrupted.

"Oh! Good! I'm glad. You know a real friend would never do something like this, so I'm glad it wasn't someone who told you they were your friend." She paused, studying the girl again. "Is your mom around?"

"Yeah," Janelle replied.

"Was she around last night?"

"Yeah."

"Did she know this happened?"

Janelle sat with her chin thrust forward stoically, her expression unwavering. She did not answer.

Mia leaned toward her, purposely invading her personal space and spoke to her in a low, quiet tone. "Janelle, I know you love your momma. And I know you feel like you're responsible for making sure she's okay. But that's her job, not yours. I know she had something to do with what's happened to you. Maybe she's trading you for drugs. Maybe just cash. I don't know. But what I do know is I've met other girls just like you before. And sometimes the best place for special young women, the ones who've been in your shoes, is not with their mommas."

She paused, gauging the girl's expression to see if she had succeeded in penetrating her armor. Janelle's shoulders sagged and she cast her eyes toward the linoleum floor.

"There's this place I know," Mia continued. "It's just for girls. Some are younger than you. Some are older. The girls live there, together. They learn. They eat and sleep and play. And it's safe. There are no drugs. There are no guns. There are no men. If you want, I could take you there, just to see. You wouldn't have to decide right away, but if you wanted to give it a try, I could make that happen."

Neither one said anything for several minutes. Janelle ran her fingers up and down a deep scar on her right arm. Mia waited patiently.

"Momma got clean once. For a little while. She was nice to me and she didn't keep any men around. But then this new guy comes around. And he got Momma back on meth. Since then…" Janelle paused, furrowing her brow. "I try to stay away. Stay at a friend's or somethin', ya know? But I have to check on her to make sure she still livin'. Went back last night and she turned me right over to him. She took the meth first though."

Mia swallowed back the urge to be sick and prayed Janelle would agree not to go back. "So, do you want to go see the place I'm talking about? I promise I'll check in on your Momma. I'll make sure she knows you're safe. And happy."

Janelle closed her eyes, pondering her options. "Yeah. I'll go."

She wanted to wrap the girl in her arms and feel her warmth but knew better than to attempt any physical contact with someone in Janelle's fragile condition.

"It'll take me a couple days to fill out the paperwork and get the process going. Until then, I'm going to call a friend of mine who has a place where you can stay. You can go there tonight. Okay?"

Janelle fixated on a spot in the corner of the room and refused to make eye contact. "Okay."

"And I'll check in on you before I leave for the day. Are you okay here?"

"Yeah."

"Good. Then I'll see you later." She stood up but was hesitant to leave.

Janelle reached across the space between them and grabbed her hand. "Thanks," she said.

"You're welcome," she replied, squeezing her fingers tightly.

Back in her office, she struggled to breathe as she splashed water out of the plastic bottle on Jack's desk onto her face. It took several minutes to regain her composure before she was able to make the phone call to the director of the Girl's Rescue Alliance of Baltimore. By the time she put down the receiver, she was emotionally drained. She was relieved the wheels were set in motion to secure Janelle's future along a safe and happy path, as long as Janelle chose to continue to walk along it. However, she had found over the years she could only offer to help those in need. Help was not something that could be forced upon people who were unwilling to accept it.

She rocked on the two back legs of her chair and forced herself to think about something other than the rape victims she had just encountered. As her mind wandered, she immediately thought of Thomas Pritchett. Since Jack was still preoccupied with the shooting cases, she allowed herself a few minutes to scan the police database for information about the mysterious aura-less man.

The first thing she discovered was that she and Thomas were born on the same day in the same year. Disquieted at first, she quickly brushed it aside as a bizarre coincidence. There was no record of him in any of the criminal files and she was surprised to find she was relieved. Another quick search revealed he lived with a woman named Mildred Pritchett in Overlea, just a short drive from her own apartment. A property search showed the house was purchased by a Howard Pritchett, who was deceased.

A picture of his life began to unfold and suddenly, any intrigue she'd been feeling disappeared. She surmised Mildred was his mother and therefore, Thomas was a grown twenty-four-year-old man still living at home with his mom. Even worse, he was in such dire straits that he was willing to participate in police lineups with the hope of earning a mere ten dollars apiece. It seemed unlikely that he was one of her psychics given his financial situation, since most of the people she found were using their abilities to earn a living. Working as a faith healer, clairvoyant, or medium often proved to be a lucrative career path.

If he isn't one of us, then why can't I see his aura? she thought. *Perhaps something is going wrong with me.* A coil of anxiety began tightening in the pit of her stomach.

"Who's Thomas Pritchett?" Jack asked as he leaned over her shoulder.

She jumped out of her chair, startled by Jack's presence. "How many times have I told you not to sneak up on me!" she scolded him.

"A million," Jack laughed. "So, who is he? Did you meet him on some online dating site?"

"No," she replied, "he was the guy. The one from the lineup yesterday. The one with no aura."

"So, what'd you find?" he asked, collapsing into his chair.

"Nothing. He's just another guy. I thought I might find something that would explain why I didn't see anything, but there's nothing there. I need to forget about it."

"I'm sure it was nothing. He's probably just some thug looking for drug money. I wouldn't give him another thought."

She shut down her computer and picked up her coat. "I'm going to head downstairs to check in on Janelle, the little girl, and I'll take the murder file to read at home tonight. Were you able to deal with the shootings?"

"Yes. SSDD. Are you still meeting Stella and me for brunch tomorrow? She wanted me to make sure I reminded you," Jack said, rolling his eyes.

"Yes. We can compare notes on the murder investigation then, if Stella lets us talk shop."

He threw a wave over his shoulder. "Fat chance. See you tomorrow."

"Bye, Jack."

After confirming that Janelle would be well taken care of for at least 24 hours, she left the station and drove home. After stopping to pick up two orders of General Tso's chicken at the Chinese restaurant down the street from her apartment, she found Chelsea stretched out on the sofa dressed in yoga pants and a hoodie, surrounded by stacks of term papers.

"Dinner is served," she called as she breezed into the kitchen.

"Thank goodness!" exclaimed Chelsea. "I'm starving! I literally haven't moved from this sofa all day. If I have to grade one more paper tonight I may gouge out my own eyes!"

"I got General Tso's and egg rolls, just for you," she said as she set the bags of food on the kitchen counter.

The girls recounted the events of their day over dinner. Although Chelsea was usually able to find the silver lining in the work Mia did each day, she was unable to come up with anything positive in response to the story of Janelle's rape.

"So senseless. So brutal. I don't know how you do it," Chelsea commented as they cleared the dishes together.

"I'll be honest, it's really starting to get to me. And I can't stop thinking about that weird guy from the lineup yesterday."

Chelsea looked up from the plate she was drying. "What does he have to do with anything?" she asked.

Mia hesitated. "I couldn't see his aura," she replied finally.

"You didn't say anything about that yesterday. Why couldn't you see it?"

"I don't know. I don't want to admit it, but I think maybe I'm starting to come unhinged a little bit. Like maybe being around all the darkness is starting to change me. I feel like this could be just the beginning," she said, unable to control the frustration in her voice. "Maybe I'm starting to lose my sight."

"No, Hon, I'm sure it's nothing," Chelsea consoled her, crossing the kitchen to give her a hug. "I'm sure it's him. There has to be something wrong with him that his aura doesn't show. You are so strong and so courageous. This can't have anything to do with you."

"I looked him up today," she said, gritting her teeth as she pulled away from Chelsea. "I didn't see anything unusual. He seems like an average guy. If I can't see his aura, the problem is probably me."

"Don't buy trouble," Chelsea said wisely. "Just wait and see. I bet that will be the end of it. And if it isn't and something else is strange... well, you'll deal with it then."

CHAPTER

4

THOMAS

His mother was already finishing her English muffin when Thomas arrived at the kitchen table on Sunday morning.

"Good morning, Tommy," said Mildred as he poured himself a cup of coffee from the pot already brewing on the stove.

"Hi, Ma," he replied, giving her a kiss on the cheek.

"What time do you have to be in to work this morning?" she asked.

"Nine-thirty." He sat beside her at the table and watched as she finished her breakfast.

"I miss sitting in church with you," she commented.

"Me too, but we need the money and the tips are good at Belinda's. Especially from the Sunday brunch crowd."

She turned her mug in her hands which were skeletal and knobbed with arthritis. "I know you're right, but I hate seeing you having to work so much. You work all the time." She sighed dramatically. "How are you ever going to find a nice girl to settle down with if you are always worried about making money to look after me?"

"I already have a nice girl, Ma," he laughed.

"I'm way too old for you! And I'm serious Tommy. You're young. You should be out having a good time. Going to school. Sowing your oats. I'm a huge burden on you."

He wondered just how many times they were going to repeat the same conversation. "I've told you a million times, you're no burden. You saved my life, remember? It's an honor to be able to help you." He paused, smiling at her. "But enough of that. You have to get to church and I have to get to work, so no more dawdling."

Mildred gave his arm a squeeze and stood up to wrap her scarf over her head and around her shoulders. "I'm making spaghetti tonight," she called as she headed through the back door, "maybe someday you'll invite a girl home to join us for Sunday dinner."

He shook his head at his mother. She genuinely wanted the best for him and to her that meant being young and in love. Sadly, he didn't recall a time in his life when he had ever felt young. Or in love for that matter. Staying alive had always been his biggest concern. Finding happiness was never really part of the equation.

After breakfast and a quick shower, he dressed in his uniform and took the bus into Towson where he worked as a busboy at Belinda's Bistro. Since there was no money for car payments or insurance, making public transportation his only means of getting from place to place, it was a good thing riding the bus didn't bother him. In fact, most days he quite enjoyed it. Sometimes he would bring a book to read or he would listen to music, but mostly he just watched the other people around him, going about their day. He tried to imagine what their days were like, where they were going, and what greater purpose their lives served.

On Sunday mornings the bus was usually empty, but on this particular morning, there was a haggard looking man slouched low in a seat as Thomas made his way down the center aisle. The man appeared to be intoxicated and was talking jibberish to himself. The muscles in Thomas' jaw tightened involuntarily and he was overcome with a familiar sense of dread. He chose a seat toward the back of the bus, far from the man, and yet he found the tension that pulled at his stomach would not release. He knew not to ignore what he was feeling because his apprehension had saved him from significant pain and grief throughout this life.

He gave a sideways glance at the man.

"What're you lookin' at?" the man slurred, turning around in his seat to face him.

He did not respond and kept his eyes down, pretending to pick at a bit of dirt on his pants leg.

"I said, 'What are ya lookin' at?'" the man yelled a second time.

He was suddenly aware of the knife holstered in the man's boot, and he could feel the drunk's anger, which wasn't necessarily directed at him, but at the world in general. Thomas knew immediately he was in the wrong place at the wrong time and that he needed to get away immediately to avoid getting hurt. He stood up, scooting quickly to the front of the bus.

"Can you let me off here, please," he asked the driver, his voice full of urgency.

"This isn't a stop, Son," the aging driver replied.

"I know. I don't feel well," he added. "I'd really like to get off."

The bus pulled off to the side of the road at the next intersection and he stepped off. He watched the plume of exhaust dissipate as the bus drove away and felt the tension in his muscles release. It was a six block walk to the next stop, but he knew he'd made the right decision.

By the time he punched in, he was thankful to be only eight minutes late for his shift. The restaurant, however, was already full of patrons enjoying Sunday brunch. Hash browns, omelets, quiche, and bacon rolled out of the kitchen. He quickly tied on his apron and grabbed his sanitizing spray and rag.

As he made his way out of the kitchen, a news story on the radio caught his attention. Accounts of a stabbing on an MTA bus were being reported. He stopped mid stride to listen to the details, certain the incident could have only taken place on the number 55 bus into Towson. The announcer confirmed police were just arriving on the scene where a middle-aged man had been stabbed repeatedly by an unknown assailant witnesses described as 'drunk and homeless.'

He held his breath as the broadcast ended with confirmation that the stabbing had indeed occurred on the same bus he opted to get off. He leaned against the wall for stability as the reality of the fate he avoided set in. Although he felt awful for the stabbing victim, he was thankful his instinctive anxiety had saved him once again.

After several minutes of deep breathing, he composed himself and finally made his way into the dining room to begin his rounds. He was careful not to interrupt those who were eating but aware of those who needed glasses and plates removed from their tables. During the course of his employment, he learned to be invisible, observing empty glasses, table trash, and patrons who were paying the tab and getting ready to leave. He moved stealthily, quickly turning over tables so new customers could be seated. The familiar repetition of his work took his mind off the morning's bus ride and after several hours, he was feeling significantly better.

Just before noon, he was placing linen napkins and bread plates on a table which had just been cleared. Out of nowhere, the hair on the back of his neck bristled and he felt as though he was being watched. He continued to set the table but attempted to glance around the room inconspicuously. There were several older couples seated beside the windows. A family with four well-behaved children was at a booth by the kitchen. There was a group of boisterous women at the large circular table in the center of the room, and to the far left, by the entrance at a four top, was a party of three - two young women and a man. One of the women was looking directly at him.

He quickly finished his task and carried his bin of dirty dishes into the kitchen. He sensed the woman was interested in him for some reason, but he couldn't imagine her intent. He peered through the kitchen door to get a better look at the woman who now consumed his attention.

She was attractive, her long dark hair lying in gentle waves across her shoulders. Her skin was warm and bronze and he surmised she was probably of Italian descent. She was laughing with the couple sitting across from her at the table. While he watched, the other woman handed her a small sheet of paper. They stood to hug one another, reaching above the plates and glasses on the table below. The man, beaming with pride, placed his hand against the abdomen of the woman beside him. He understood at once what had transpired - the couple had announced they were expecting a baby.

"Quit daydreaming, Tom. Table nine needs to be cleaned and the family at eleven are overflowing with dishes," snapped one of the servers impatiently.

"I'm sorry. I'm on it," he responded.

Back in the dining room, he tried to avoid the woman and her companions, but as he cleared the table beside them, he continued to feel as though he was being watched. He stole a glance over his shoulder as he wiped the table top and was surprised to see the woman staring at him once again. He gave her a sideways grin. She seemed to hesitate for a moment. His heart stopped as he waited for a response.

Finally, mercifully, she returned his smile. He finished the place settings and returned to the kitchen with the bin of dirty dishes he had cleared. By the time he returned to the dining room, the woman and the couple were leaving through the front door, and he was left with an unexpected sense of disappointment.

CHAPTER

5

KATE

Yekaterina Malinov trudged through the snow in her well-worn boots and ill-fitting coat. The frigid air blew beneath her collar and seemed to invade every cell of her body as she crossed Kiev Polytechnic Institute campus.

Yekaterina, known to friends and family as Kate, enjoyed learning. Her dream was to become a physician, like her father, but with the recent economic downturn throughout the Ukraine, there was little money for higher education. During the six years since graduating from secondary school, she had completed just over half of her university requirements. The subsidies from the government did little to ease the financial burden, so she took classes as her family could afford them, usually one at a time.

As she walked the half mile from the university to the small downtown apartment she shared with the rest of her family, she contemplated the reality of her latest struggle. In less than two months, her younger sisters, twins, would be graduating from secondary school. They were both far more intelligent than she was and deserved an opportunity to attend university as well. The unfortunate truth was that even with the government stipend her sisters would receive, her family could not afford to send all three girls to university at the same time. It was time for her to leave school and pick up a second job to help put her sisters through college.

Along the walk, she stopped in a handful of retail stores to inquire about job openings. As was always the case, none were hiring. She was frustrated with the lack of opportunities for her generation. After the country gained its independence from the Soviet Union, times had been tough. Eventually, the Ukraine had found its place in the world and experienced economic success at the turn of the century. In those years, she had convinced her mother to open a bakery and her father had developed a thriving medical practice. However, since the global economy had recently declined, life had taken a turn for the worse in the country as a whole and in her family as well. Her mother had scaled back the bakery workers to a skeleton crew, and although her father still saw patients, many of them could no longer afford to pay him for his care.

Since times had gotten tough, she had begun to rely more and more on her gift to help her family get by. As a child, she had learned early on that she could manipulate the people in her life into doing the things she wanted them to do. And although she could have spent her childhood persuading her friends and family into giving her toys and candy, she found she was happiest when she was using her ability in the service of others.

During the summer when she was seven, her family had taken a much anticipated trip to the countryside for a three day vacation. During their travels, they happened upon a small town with a gelato shop. Her father had treated her and her sisters each to a delicious cup of icy goodness which they enjoyed while sitting on the front stoop of the shop. While they ate, a large group of farm children passed by, hot and tired from a day spent working in the fields. Watching them trudge down the street, she remarked to her sisters that she thought the farm children looked as though they would like some gelato too, if only she could buy some for them.

At that moment, the shopkeeper emerged from the store and announced the cooling unit of the main freezer had suddenly shorted out and the gelato would need to be eaten immediately before it melted and caused a mess. He began passing out bowls of gelato to everyone on the street, including all of the farm children. It was at that moment she began to fully understand the power of her gift. She realized she only needed to acknowledge her own conscious desires, and somehow, her abilities would help to take care of the rest.

She thought of this day and how to use her gift now to help pay for her sisters' college tuition as she climbed the four flights of stairs to her family's apartment. After weeks of brainstorming, she still didn't have a feasible idea and as she opened the front door, her mood, which was as grey as the snow laden sky, did not improve.

Her mother was already home from the bakery, a sure sign it had been a slow day for sales. Both of her sisters, Natalya and Tetyana, were seated at the small kitchen table engrossed in their studies. The only positive sign was that her father wasn't there. She hoped he was seeing patients at the clinic. Patients who could pay him in hryvnia instead of bartered goods.

"Hello, Katerina," said her mother who was sitting in the living room folding laundry as she walked through the door. "How was your class?"

"It was good. We began studying embryonic development. It was fascinating. Cell division is a magical thing," she said. "And what about you, Mama? Why are you home so early?"

"Ah, we sold out of the few pastries we had early this morning, but there were no supplies to bake more. I sent Yuri to purchase flour and sugar from the wholesale market, but I don't know how much he will be able to buy. We will just do the best we can tomorrow."

"Mama," she began, sitting beside her mother on the threadbare cushion of the sofa, "I don't know if doing the best we can is going to cut it anymore."

"What are you talking about, child?" her mother responded.

She lowered her voice to a whisper, "I'm talking about my sisters. I know their stipend was awarded, and I know it won't be enough."

"We will manage. We always have," her mother said stoically as she smoothed the collar of the shirt she was folding.

"No, Mama, we won't. We've always managed to have food on the table and clothes on our backs, which is a lot more than some. But now, three schoolings to pay for?" She shook her head. "No. It's impossible. We will starve."

"Yekaterina! You disrespect your father and you disrespect me. Who is putting these thoughts in your head?"

Kate glanced over her shoulder at her sisters. "No one, Mama. But I'm not a child anymore. I see what is happening. And I am old enough to help."

"You have a job."

"I do, but I can get another."

"You will not have time for your studies if you get another job."

She squared her shoulders in a gesture of defiance. "Then I will give up my studies."

"No," her mother said flatly.

"Just for a while," she explained. "Just until the girls are done. Then I will go back."

"No. It will be too late for you then. Just like it was too late for me. You will never go back."

She began pairing the socks that were piled at her mother's feet. "Then I will become a baker like you," she said brightly.

"You are not a baker!" her mother said, raising her voice. "You are a doctor, like Papa."

She folded a pair of her father's worn socks together. "I'm not a doctor yet and maybe I never will be. But that's okay. I want the girls to have a chance."

Unable to conceal her anger, her mother snapped the wrinkles out of the pants she was folding, causing Kate to flinch. "We will find a way. No more talk of second jobs. Go sit with your sisters and do your work so when your father arrives he will see you are grateful. We will not speak a word of this to him, do you understand?"

"Yes, Mama," she replied, retreating hastily to the kitchen.

True to her word, she remained silent about her intentions at dinner, and when her father reported to the family that he had been approached by the chief of staff at the Isida Hospital about a position – a position that would be salaried, she knew her gift was working once again to provide for her family.

"What did you tell them?" Natalya asked as she dipped her bread crust into her stew.

"I told them I would have to think about it."

"What!" Kate exclaimed. "What is there to think about? With a guaranteed salary, there might be a way!"

"A way for what?" her father replied. Her mother glared across the table, causing her to hesitate.

"Nothing. Nevermind. That's great, Papa. I just think, for my opinion, that you should take the job."

He used his napkin to wipe a splatter of soup from his moustache. "It would mean closing the clinic. The clinic I worked so hard to establish. And what of the people I serve? What happens if I am no longer there to care for them?"

"Papa, they never pay! You take care of them for what? For the eggs they give you? The two-day-old fish?"

"Yekaterina, I take care of them because I can. Because I took an oath."

"But what about us? What about Natalya and Tetyana? University will not accept fish as payment for their education!"

No one spoke. Her mother held her spoon in midair and the twins held their breath. She stared at her father who held her gaze with a look of disbelief and shame.

"Go," he said finally.

He said nothing more. Just go.

She rose from the table and took her coat from the back of her chair where she'd placed it earlier in the evening. She quickly wrapped her shawl around her head and neck and left the little apartment, out into the cold and quiet of the night with nowhere to go and no one to help her. Her gift could only present her family with opportunity. It could not make them take it.

CHAPTER

6

MIA

After brunch with Jack and his wife Stella, Mia spent Sunday afternoon alone in her apartment, stewing about all that had transpired. She was shocked by the news that Jack was going to be a father. Knowing what she did about humanity and seeing the things she saw every day, she couldn't imagine bringing a child into the world. She tried to wrap her head around how Jack's life was going to change now that he was going to be both a father and a cop. She didn't envy his position.

In addition to the baby news, she also found herself preoccupied with thoughts of Thomas Pritchett, the aura-less man, who had now come into her life not once, but twice in a single week.

She'd been surprised to see him working at the restaurant. She assumed, because of his participation in the lineups, that he was the type of man who wouldn't be able to hold down a steady job. As Jack pointed out, most of the people who were willing to do a lineup for ten dollars were not typically the salt of the earth. However, as she had watched him during brunch, she was impressed by the pride he took in his simple actions – folding napkins, picking up trash, and clearing dirty dishes. He seemed to take his job very seriously and she found she was both surprised and pleased by her discovery. However, one fact remained that both concerned and intrigued her. For a second time, she had been unable to see his aura. And for a second time, she found she was unable to get him out of her head.

After a restless night's sleep, she was exhausted Monday morning. Her mind swirled with thoughts of her crumbling abilities and unstable future, and she hadn't fallen asleep until after two in the morning. She was relieved when Chelsea met her in the kitchen with a fresh pot of coffee already brewed.

"What would I do without you?" Mia asked, taking the first warm sip from her mug.

"Walk around like a zombie." Chelsea's head lolled to the side and her eyes rolled into her head. "Give me your brains!" she teased.

"I feel like a zombie. Maybe it's the weather. What's the forecast for today?" she asked.

Chelsea grabbed the remote to turn up the volume. "Don't know. Just turned on the news a couple minutes ago. The new commissioner is the big story. Do you think you'll get to meet him today?"

Panic immediately surged through her body, and she silently cursed herself for foolishly focusing on Thomas instead of her job. "Oh, God! I completely forgot about that! The one day I need to look sharp and instead I look like I've been run over by a bus!" Mia cried as she tore out of the kitchen. "I've got to get ready. Thanks for the coffee," she called over her shoulder.

One shower, four ibuprofen, and two cups of coffee later, she arrived at the station feeling only slightly more human. Most of the officers on her shift had already arrived and were milling around, waiting for word on when the commissioner would arrive. Her father came around the corner as she was entering her office.

"Morning, Sunshine," he said, walking up behind her.

"Hey, Daddy," she replied. "You nervous?"

He leaned against the doorframe. "Nah. I've seen so many commissioners come and go. But I'll tell you this, I think this one's got some staying power. I think he's a good man. Gonna lead this city in the right direction."

"I hope so. We could use some support from the top."

"That we could." He stopped speaking and motioned toward Jack's desk. "Where's that no-good partner of yours?" he teased. "He told me he was going to tell you his news this weekend."

"Yeah. He told me. A baby. I told him I was excited for them."

"You don't sound too excited," he replied.

She tucked a loose strand of hair behind her ear as she checked her uniform in the mirror. "It's just... I know how hard it's going to be for him. For the baby. For all of them."

"We survived, didn't we?"

"We did, Daddy. We did," she said remembering how difficult it had been.

Rosetti gave her a playful salute and backed down the hall. "We're all meeting in the conference room in twenty minutes. Don't be late," he warned.

She shuffled paperwork around her desk while watching the painfully slow-moving hands of the clock on the opposite wall. Ten minutes later, Jack rushed in, carrying his duffle bag and what remained of a bacon, egg, and cheese biscuit.

"Hey, Mia!" he exclaimed, genuinely happy to see her.

"Hi," she replied, not surprised by his late arrival.

He threw a stack of files on his desk. "I spent a lot of time researching the murder investigation yesterday afternoon so I can bring you up to speed on that after the commissioner thing. I'd like to go down to forensics and take a look at what they found at the scene. There are a few pieces of the puzzle that just aren't fitting together for me."

"That sounds good," she said, rising from her desk. "We're supposed to be in the conference room in less than ten minutes. We can go together."

Without another word, they hurried into the conference room at the end of the hall. The room, which usually provided plenty of space for weekly meetings and press conferences, was filled beyond capacity with officers and news reporters interested in meeting the new commissioner for the first time. The only space available by the time they arrived was in the far back corner. At 5'4" tall, Mia had difficulty seeing over the heads of the other spectators.

"I can't see," she told Jack. "I'm going to try to wiggle up to get myself a closer spot."

She wove through the crowd until she found herself only a few feet from the podium in the front of the room. Her father was already situated beside the stage and was preparing to introduce the commissioner.

"Officers, ladies and gentlemen, it is my honor and privilege to introduce you to Baltimore's newest police commissioner, Roger M. Dalton."

A thunderous applause erupted from the crowd and she watched as Dalton was ushered onto the stage beside her father.

Unfortunately, she didn't hear another word the commissioner said. Not a word of the introduction speech given by her father outlining Dalton's prestigious history in law enforcement, extensive education, or awards bestowed upon him. She didn't listen to anything Dalton was saying about his plan to help eliminate crime in the city by getting illegal weapons off the streets and more officers on them. She heard nothing.

The initial shock of what she saw nearly took her down. She braced herself against the wall and struggled to keep her knees from buckling beneath her. As she concentrated on breathing, she could not tear her eyes from the commissioner, who was shrouded by the darkest aura she had ever seen.

Two theories immediately formed in her mind as she struggled to compose herself. Either she was indeed losing her abilities, which was causing her to see things that were untrue, or Dalton was actually a very, very bad man. Regardless of the reason, she was flabbergasted.

As the conference ended, she was relieved as the attendees began to make their way through the exits at the back of the room. She was slowly shuffling along with the rest of the crowd when she felt a hand grab her shoulder. She turned around.

"Commissioner Dalton, I would like you to meet one of Baltimore's finest, my daughter, Officer Mia Rosetti," her father said.

Dalton extended his hand and waited for her to respond. She stood transfixed, motionless. Her father gave her a gentle nudge and commented, "I believe she's a little starstruck, Commissioner!"

She cautiously placed her hand in the commissioner's. His handshake was firm. Strong. Powerful. Finally, she found her voice and both men looked at her expectantly.

"It's a pleasure to meet you, Commissioner Dalton. I look forward to serving you proudly," she said.

"And I you, Officer. I have a feeling your father and I are going to be spending a lot of time together, whipping this city into shape. I believe you and I will be getting to know each other well in the coming months."

"That sounds great," she responded feebly. "Now if you will both excuse me, I have a large stack of paperwork on my desk to attend to. It's been a pleasure, Commissioner."

"Goodbye, Officer Rosetti," he said warmly, a broad smile on his face.

As soon as she was out of their line of sight, she ran quickly to her office, slamming the door behind her. She closed her eyes and leaned against the door, using it to support her weight for she thought at any moment her legs would fail her.

"Boo," said Jack from across the room.

"Jack!" she screamed. "How many times…"

He held his hands in the air. "I know, I know. I just can't resist. But look at you. What in the world is wrong? You look like you're going to throw up."

"I think I might," she said.

"Maybe you're coming down with something," he said, crossing the room to take her arm.

"No, that's not it," she responded as Jack helped her to her chair.

She remained silent for several moments, contemplating how much information she wanted to disclose. Finally, she decided to tell him the truth. She trusted Jack implicitly.

"So, the new commissioner…"

"Seems fantastic! Don't you think?" he interrupted.

"He seems fantastic to *you*."

"And what? He doesn't seem fantastic to you?"

"No," she said flatly.

"Mia, we've never had a commissioner with such great credentials and such a stellar track record. This guy is the real deal. Just look what he did in Detroit!" said Jack enthusiastically. And then he stopped, looking carefully at her. "What did *you* see?"

She shook her head, unable to speak the words aloud.

"It's his aura?"

She nodded.

"It's not light?"

She nodded again.

"You're sure?"

She thought carefully before beginning. "Until last week, I would have been positive. Absolutely certain. But today? I don't know."

"It's that guy without the aura. He has you spooked."

She scribbled mindlessly on the back of an old memo. "Maybe. I'm starting to think I might be losing my ability. First, it's that Thomas guy, and now, the commissioner is dark? That's crazy. There's no way he could be where he is and who he is if he was dark. That would be impossible, wouldn't it?"

Jack booted up his laptop and logged in to the server. "It would be tough. He seems genuine. And honest. The dark aura must be a mistake. When was the last time you were wrong about someone?"

"Never."

He entered his secured password. "Never?"

"No, never. I see what's inside. What's streaming from the soul of a person. You can't mask it or change it. It just is what it is. And I've never been wrong."

"But you think you're wrong now?"

The thought of a corrupt commissioner was devastating, but not nearly as devastating as the prospect of losing her abilities. "I think I don't know what I think," she said. "So for now, let's just go down to forensics and finish this murder investigation. I need something solid to hold on to right now."

"Nothing like solving a murder to ground you in reality," teased Jack.

"Nope, nothing like it," she replied.

CHAPTER

7

THOMAS

"How much are we short?" Thomas asked his mother.

Mildred laid the cash from the envelope on the table. "About $200. We can take it from the grocery money. I haven't been hungry lately anyway," she sighed.

"No, Ma, I'll get it. I've got a couple of piano gigs tomorrow, and I'm going to head over to the police department now and try to get into a few lineups. It's been helping that I look like a pretty average guy," he told her.

She grunted disapprovingly. "I hate that you are associating with criminals to earn money. It just makes me ill. If Howard were still here, you would be off leading a normal life."

"I've never led a normal life," he laughed, recalling the years before the Pritchett's took him in. "I wouldn't even know what to do with a normal life if I had one! And for the record, I'm not 'associating' with criminals. I'm helping to stop them."

"I guess you're right," she replied. "But still…"

"Ma, you and Dad took care of me, and now I will take care of you. I'm happy to do it. I just wish I had a way to earn a more steady income."

"Someday you will."

After hugging Mildred goodbye, he slipped on his shoes and coat and walked three blocks to the closest bus stop. It was a cold day, but not too windy, so the sun was enough to warm him as he waited idly for the city transit. He daydreamed about his passion, music, and what it might be like to someday own his own music studio. In the future his goal was to inspire children to embrace music the way Mrs. Lawson had inspired him, but he had never been to college, and earning a teaching certificate seemed impossible given his current situation. He wondered how long he was going to be able to continue working as a busboy and lineup extra before he lost his mind completely.

As the bus pulled up and he climbed aboard, he was taken aback by the sight of one of the women on the bus. From the back, she looked exactly like the woman who took an interest in him at Belinda's. Without any hesitation, he approached her, but was disappointed when she wasn't the woman after all.

"Is there something you need?" she asked him rudely.

Her abrasive response caught him off guard and he took a step back, both shocked and disappointed. "No. Nothing. I just thought you were someone else."

"Well I'm not, so go sit down, Mister," the woman replied.

He shuffled to the back of the bus, angry at himself for causing a scene and dismayed by how upset he was that the woman was not who she appeared to be. He'd thought about her several times since Sunday, but admonished himself each time for romanticizing about something that would never come to be. The woman had been beautiful and clearly well-educated. He quickly convinced himself she would never be interested in someone like him.

When he arrived at the station and checked in at the lineup office, he was happy to discover he matched the description of three of the suspects in custody. He mentally subtracted the thirty dollars he was about to make from the total owed on the mortgage.

After being offered something to drink, he sat down in the waiting room with the rest of the lineup participants. Some of the men were appalling to him. A few were clearly addicts, looking for cash to supply their next hit. There were a couple of homeless men who looked as though they were just happy for the opportunity to be out of the cold. He shook his head at the irony of his situation, acknowledging just how easily he could have ended up addicted or homeless or both. And even though luckily his life had taken a better path, he was still sitting in the police station, just as they were, looking to make a few bucks. Life was a funny thing.

The door to the hallway opened and several of the men were called into the lineup room. As the door was closing behind the last of the men, he caught a glimpse of a petite female officer with long brown hair walking past the doorway. He was immediately on his feet, unable to stop himself. At the door, gripping the handle, he realized the ridiculousness of what he was about to do and stopped. He had no idea what was compelling him to follow the officer. After only a moment, he decided the worst thing that could happen would be that she wasn't the woman from the restaurant. By the time he entered the hallway and saw her turning the corner, he decided perhaps the worst thing would be if she was.

As he picked up his pace and quickly rounded the corner behind her, he was surprised to see she was now only a few feet in front of him. His pulse was racing, his hands were shaking, and all at once, he decided to turn back. However, at that exact moment, the woman stopped and turned around.

She gazed at him with a look of shock and wonder like a stargazer viewing the heavens with the aid of a telescope for the first time. As their eyes met, he was filled with a sense of peace. Somehow, he knew he should go on.

"You," she said.

"Me," he replied.

"You were here last week, doing a lineup."

"Yes." he confirmed. "And you had brunch at Belinda's Bistro on Sunday."

She smiled. "Yes."

They stood, inches apart, considering one another. He couldn't shake the feeling that something beyond physical attraction was drawing him to her. She was out of his league in every possible way but for some reason it didn't seem to matter. The same anxiety that always kept him safe now encouraged him to trust her. Without knowing why, he finally broke the silence.

"How long have you been in law enforcement?" he asked, attempting to sound casual despite the awkwardness of the situation.

"Two years" she responded. "I graduated from the academy two years ago."

"Do you enjoy it?" he asked.

She eyed him suspiciously. "Yes. Mostly. I love helping people," she replied.

He wasn't sure how to continue the conversation and blurted out the next thing that popped into his head. "My mother is concerned about me hanging out with criminals doing these lineups, but I feel like I'm doing my part to help make the streets a little safer. Do you think I'm helping, doing the lineups?"

He saw a look of amusement in her eyes and knew he was embarrassing himself. "Yes," she said, "I think you are."

He grinned at her in an attempt to salvage what was left of his dignity. "Was it a little weird that I just brought up my mother?" he asked.

She returned his smile. "Yeah, it was a little weird," she admitted. "But it's okay. If it makes you feel any better, I work with my dad."

"It helps," he said, excited by the fact that she was interested in connecting with him in some small way.

"Thomas Pritchett?" A voice called from the far end of the hallway.

"That's my cue," he said, backing down the hall in the direction of the lineup room. "So, I'll see ya."

"Yeah, I'll see ya around," she said.

He turned on his heel and walked briskly toward the lineup room. As he approached the corner, he paused briefly and contemplated turning around to see if she was still there. It occurred to him that he hadn't even asked for her name and before he could stop himself, he glanced over his shoulder.

She was still there. Standing in the exact same spot. Watching him. He waved at her.

She waved back.

He turned the corner and entered the queue with the rest of the men. The first time he participated in the lineup, he could only think about how to determine which of the men was the guilty party. However this time, as the group of men was ushered into the narrow room, he was completely preoccupied with the woman officer.

"Face straight ahead," came the voice over the speaker system.

He thought of her eyes.

"Turn to the left," the voice said.

He imagined what her hair would feel like against his cheek.

"Turn to the right," the voice said again.

He remembered the way she smiled at him.

By the time the men were asked to leave the room, he was already trying to figure out how he could arrange to see her again. The chips were stacking against him, especially since she was a confirmed college-educated law enforcement officer. This meant she was smart. It was easy to see she was also attractive. And, he admitted to himself with displeasure, there was a very good chance she was already involved with someone else. He, on the other hand, was a busboy with a high school diploma who still lived at home with his mother. He immediately acknowledged a more unlikely couple had never existed.

And yet, he couldn't get her out of his mind. He spent the rest of the afternoon standing against the wall just outside the waiting room, watching to see if she would pass by again.

She never did.

CHAPTER

8

MIA

Mia and Jack were playing 'good cop, bad cop' inside the interrogation room. Over the years together, they had perfected their technique to the point of being almost over the top, straight out of a TV drama.

And Mia was always the bad cop.

"If you weren't robbing the electronics store, then by all means, tell us where you were, Mr. Snyder," she growled at the surly looking man sitting across the table from her.

"I was at my brother's house," the man replied, as he rubbed the muscles in the back of his neck.

"And your brother was there with you? He'll be able to corroborate your story?"

"Yeah."

"You sure about that?" she asked.

"Yeah," Snyder said.

She started pacing the length of the room, her hands buried deep in her pockets. "That's really funny. You know why? Because I had the bartender in here earlier, and he said you left without your brother just after 11PM. And your brother was there until 2AM. The electronics store alarm went off at 12:17AM. So you know what that makes you? Busted," she said to the man, glaring daggers at him as she stopped in front of his chair.

"You can't trust that bartender!" Snyder yelled. "He's got it in for me!"

"Does his video surveillance have it in for you too? Because we've got a warrant for it and as soon as we review the footage, you will be without something very necessary."

"What's that?"

"An alibi."

"Mr. Snyder," Jack interrupted, speaking in a calm, controlled, almost soothing voice, "let me help you out here. Officer Rosetti, she's good friends with the district attorney. She's going to get a warrant for your home and your computer by the end of the day, and we both know what she's going to find. Even if you've stashed the stolen equipment elsewhere, your computer is going to seal your fate. It will have every invoice for every piece of electronic equipment you've sold online. You know it. I know it." He paused, for dramatic effect, and pointed to Mia as he whispered to the man, "And she knows it."

She pulled out the chair to sit beside the thief, allowing the feet to make an obnoxious scraping sound against the floor tile. "Not only do I know that, but I also know you have people above you pulling the strings. And I am going to make sure they know how badly you screwed this up when I bring them down too," she said, bringing her face so close to Snyder's she could smell what he had for lunch.

"Take it easy, Officer," Jack said, pulling her away from the table. "Mr. Snyder, like I said before, Officer Rosetti is good friends with the district attorney. But I happen to be married to her. So if you tell us what we need to hear, I am pretty sure I will be able to pull a few strings to get some time taken off your sentencing. You are going down for this I'm afraid, but you don't have to fall so hard. Please, let me help you out here."

Snyder looked from Jack to Mia and back again.

"How much if I get time for this?" the man asked.

"Eight to ten," Jack answered.

Snyder paused, obviously mulling over his options.

"I want a lawyer," he said.

Outside the interrogation room, they headed down the hallway toward their office.

"I thought we had him," she said, upset by what had just transpired.

"We've got him. Lawyer or no. You done good kid," Jack said, throwing an elbow into her shoulder.

"Thanks. I'm still feeling off kilter though. I could have done a better job if my head was fully in the game."

The pair entered their office. She sat down and laid her head on her desk atop a large stack of papers. Her mind was spinning and she had never been so confused and angry about her mental state. It was distracting and she hated feeling so vulnerable.

"What is it?" Jack asked.

She didn't answer.

"The aura thing?"

She grunted.

"The guy without the aura or the guy with the dark one?" Jack pried.

"Yes," she said, lifting her head at last, the stress of the situation written all over her face.

As they looked at one another, he was clearly waiting for her to open up. After being raised with six sisters, Jack was good at waiting.

She sighed loudly. "The aura-less guy, Thomas Pritchett, showed up for another lineup. I didn't say anything at the time, but I saw him at brunch with you and Stella on Sunday. He's a busboy at Belinda's. While we were there, he kept looking at me. Probably because I was looking at him. Anyway, I talked to him today."

"Here at the station?" Jack asked.

"Yes. He followed me down the hallway."

"Seriously?" he asked, furrowing his brow.

"Yeah." she paused. "He was nice in a dorky sort of way."

"'He was nice?' Mia! He's a busboy. He works lineups. And for some unknown reason, he has no aura!" Jack exclaimed.

She reflected on the sense of peace she felt when she encountered him at the station. It was all she could do to avoid the lineup area for the rest of the day. "Maybe he does have an aura and I just can't see it. He could be light. I'm really starting to think I'm the problem."

"You're not the problem," Jack concluded.

"If I'm not the problem, then why is the commissioner dark?" she asked, revealing the depth of her confusion.

He didn't respond.

"It just doesn't make any sense. None of it makes any sense. The guy without the aura, the dark commissioner... the only possible explanation is a glitch in my system."

She remained silent for several minutes while Jack logged on to his computer, waiting for him to correct her by affirming her gift's infallibility once again. When he didn't reply she finally asked, "Do you think I should say something to my dad about the commissioner?"

"Why would you? I thought you just said you have a glitch," Jack replied.

She beat her fists into her desk in frustration. "Because if I'm not the problem and the commissioner really is dark then my dad should know."

He stared at her. "I don't know what to say to you. You're all over the place. Is it you? Is it them? How the heck should I know?" He turned back to his computer screen. "I guess just do what you need to do."

She rose from her chair, suddenly feeling empowered and surprisingly confident in her abilities. She crossed the office without looking at Jack and walked swiftly into the hallway. She headed toward her father's office and was pleased to find him sitting at his desk. She knocked on the door and he waved her into the room.

"Hi, Dad," she said.

"Hi, Honey. How was your day?" he asked.

"Fine." She paused. "No, actually, not fine. Weird."

"Weird how?" he asked, motioning for her to sit down beside him.

She sank into the chair and composed her thoughts, remaining silent for several moments.

"Whoa. This is serious," her father commented as he waited for her to begin.

She stared at her father, commanding his full attention. "Dad, remember the day when I was nine and we saw the man in the museum?"

"Yes. Of course."

"Do you remember what you told me that day?"

"Yes. I told you I believed in you and your abilities."

"And do you still?" she asked.

"You know I do, Mia. What's all this about?"

"It's about the commissioner."

"What about the commissioner?"

She took a deep breath and closed her eyes. When she opened them, she looked directly at her father and willed him to understand. "Dad, I don't think the commissioner is everything he appears to be."

"How does he appear, Mia? How does he appear to *you*?" he asked, his voice wavering slightly.

"His aura is as dark as I've ever seen," she replied in a whisper.

He didn't respond to her for several moments. She had decided to leave and was halfway to the door when he finally spoke.

"How can that be?" he asked.

"I don't know, Dad," she replied. "But here's the way I see it... there's either something wrong with him or there's something wrong with me. Either way, it's a lose-lose situation."

"That it is," he acknowledged, pulling at his moustache. "Can I be honest?"

She stopped in the doorway. "You always are."

"I kind of hope there's something wrong with you."

"Me too, Dad. Me too."

By the time she returned to her office, Jack had already left for the day. She locked the door behind her and while her laptop was booting, she slid the well-worn file from its hiding spot in the bottom drawer of the cabinet. The sheet of notebook paper was a familiar sight, as were the names listed neatly in her own handwriting. There were 37 people, including Thomas Pritchett, whose name she added when she'd first seen him the week before.

She wasn't sure he belonged on the page, as every person listed was believed to have a psychic ability. All she knew about him was that she couldn't see his aura, which she hardly counted as an ability, especially when the others on the list had gifts including telepathy, telekinesis, precognition, divination, apportation, and biolocation. However, despite any proof otherwise, she felt compelled to leave his name along with the others. Perhaps blocking her ability was a gift in and of itself.

Her list began quite simply as a way to ease her growing isolation. Middle school had been especially difficult for a number of reasons, not least of which being her ability to see the state of a person's soul. Despite keeping her gift a secret, other children sensed that she was different, and at a time in life when everyone wants nothing more than to fit in, Mia found herself on the outside looking in. She tried ignoring what she saw and what she knew about the people around her, but she heard the whispers and malicious remarks. She was an outcast and there was nothing she could do about it.

Late one evening, she sat awake, studying for a test on the Ottoman Empire while she waited for her father to get home from work. The television was on for company, but she wasn't watching any show in particular. She happened to look up from her textbook as the local news ran a story on a man who claimed he could gain information about a person or event by touching a related object. The reporter described Frank Harris as a psychometrist, which Mia would later learn was also known as a token-object reader.

Mia fingered the man's name, the first one on the list she began that night, written in pink highlighter. Beside him was the name of his gift, as it was for all the names she added in subsequent years. There were adults and children, men and women, Americans and foreigners – all people who possessed abilities which were neither believed nor understood. She added people to her list, one by one over the course of 12 years, never corresponding with them in any way, just content with the knowledge that she was not alone.

And yet, even as she sat amid the incessant chaos of the police station, she had never felt more detached from the rest of the world. Perhaps, she reasoned, it was time to reach out to one of the psychics on her sheet of paper.

CHAPTER

9

KATE

"Does Father know you've come back?" Tetyana whispered to Kate as she allowed her older sister to crawl under the covers beside her.

"No," she replied.

Although it was still several hours until sunrise, she'd spent most of the night wandering the streets of Kiev trying to think of a way out of her predicament. Like always, she would find a way to use her power of actualization to get what she wanted, but she was still struggling with which course of action she should take. Finally, after her feet could carry her no further and her hands could no longer feel the coldness of the night, she had relented and returned home. Without a sound, she crept into the apartment and without taking her clothes off, climbed into bed with her sister.

"You're freezing," Tetyana said, wrapping her arms tightly around her.

"How mad is he?" she whispered, not wanting to wake Natalya.

"You know Papa. He boils quickly, but he cools quickly too. I heard him ask Mama if he should go looking for you before they went to sleep. He will be happy to see you at breakfast, even if he doesn't say so."

She felt her limbs slowly thawing out and she allowed herself to close her eyes. When she awoke several hours later, she was still wrapped in her sister's arms. As she stirred, Tetyana woke as well, stretching and yawning in the dim light of morning.

"Do you really think they don't have enough money for all of us?" Tetyana asked out of nowhere, clearly having thought a great deal about it while Kate was gone.

"I know they don't," she replied.

She pulled the sheets up to her chin. "Then we won't go to school. We'll just go to work with you."

"Tetty, no. That's not an option. You and Natalya must go to university. I promise you, I will find a way."

"Find a way to what?" Natalya asked from the twin bed beside them as she rubbed the sleep from her eyes.

"Find a way to pay for our school," Tetyana replied.

Natalya squinted into the darkness. "Oh, Kate," she exclaimed, noticing her sister had returned, "you're back!"

Natalya clambered out of her bed and jumped on top of her sisters, pushing all three of them into a pile on the floor. They erupted into a fit of hysterics, laughing and giggling like schoolgirls. After several moments of uncharacteristically childlike behavior, the girls settled themselves and returned to their beds. Tetyana sat crossed-legged at her sister's feet.

"What should we do?" she asked, serious once again.

Kate began loosely braiding Tetty's tangled hair as she shared her plan. "Last night, while I was walking, I remembered a flyer I saw in the student union building a few months ago. It caught my attention because it had an American flag on it. It said something about applying for an American to sponsor your tuition. I remember it seemed strange to me, but maybe it is something I should look into," she explained.

"Do you think it's real? Do you think Americans do that sort of thing?" Natalya asked.

She tied off the end of her sister's braid. "I don't know. But it was in the student union. I was going to head there before work today to see if the flyer was still there. I'm sure it will be," she said.

Tetyana nodded in agreement. "Are you prepared to face Papa this morning?" she asked.

She wasn't looking forward to confronting him but knew there was no way around it. "No. Not really. I guess I should probably do something to smooth things over with him."

"We can help you," Natalya said enthusiastically.

"Yes, we'll help!" Tetyana exclaimed, hopping up from the bed to retrieve her robe from the hook on the wall. "Let's go make him his favorite breakfast. It will make him forget all about last night!"

The three sisters worked quietly but efficiently in the tiny kitchen, preparing their father's favorite breakfast as best they could with the supplies that were available. They were able to prepare the blini with what little flour, sugar, and salt was in the pantry. Kate was happy to see they had just enough buttermilk and the single egg required to complete the recipe.

"Do we have some cheese?" she asked.

"A little. And look," said Natalya, opening the icebox, "here's some jam for the blini. And it's currant, his favorite."

The girls brewed a kettle of black tea and prepared the tray of food to carry into their father's room. She closed her eyes and envisioned her father's forgiveness, and as she walked confidently down the hall, she knew his anger didn't stand a chance against her abilities. At precisely eight o'clock, they entered the room.

"Good morning, Papa," she said cheerfully. "And good morning to you too, Mama."

"Good morning, Yekaterina. I am glad to see you are safe."

"I am fine, Papa. Thank you." She paused. "We made you breakfast," she said boldly, handing her father the tray of food.

"Blini! My favorite!" her father exclaimed. "How thoughtful of you all. Thank you."

"You are welcome, Papa. I hope you can forgive me for speaking out of turn last night," she ventured as her father took his first bite of blini.

"You are already forgiven, Daughter. How could I stay angry when I love you so very much?"

"Thank you, Papa. I love you too. Now, if you will excuse me, I must get ready for work," she said as she backed out of the room, thankful that she was able to change his mood so easily.

Exhausted but invigorated by the prospect of securing tuition for her sisters' education, she dressed in several layers in preparation for her journey to work. She planned to leave an hour earlier than usual in order to give herself enough time to stop by the student union to inquire about the flyer. She wrapped her scarf around her head and face, threw her messenger bag across her chest, and, after kissing her mother and sisters goodbye, headed into the morning.

She enjoyed her walk to the university. Even after walking for several hours the night before, her legs were fresh and strong. She rarely took public transportation and instead preferred to walk most places she needed to go. She strolled beside the Dnieper River along a well-worn, tree lined path. In the coldest winter months, it was frequently frozen solid, providing travelers the ability to ice skate to their destinations along the entire length of the river. During the summer, the beaches along the riverbanks were full of bathers and sun-seekers alike. As she made her way to the student union, there were neither skaters nor bathers. In fact, she found herself quite alone.

Upon arrival at the student union, she quickly made her way to the large corkboard where she had seen the flyer regarding the American investors. Her heart leapt as she spotted the flyer just where she had seen it several months before. She had known it would still be there, waiting for her.

It read, "American investor in search of students needing cash for tuition." She pulled a paper and pen from her bag and wrote down the information, including the name and number of the person to contact. She was pleased to see it was a local number but thought it was unusual for an American to have a Ukrainian exchange.

After leaving campus, she surrendered to the ease of the metro and quickly arrived at the National Museum of Literature where she worked several days a week cataloging books into their ever expanding library. After clocking in, she checked with her supervisor to see what she was expected to accomplish during her shift. As soon as she was permitted, she stole away to an abandoned office in an administrative wing of the museum. She quietly closed the door behind her and lifted the receiver of the phone on the desk. She heard a dial tone and dialed the numbers from the flyer. It rang only twice.

"Hello?" a woman's voice answered.

"Hello. My name is Yekaterina Malinov. I am a student at KPI and I came across your flyer on a board in the student union. I was interested in finding out more about your program."

"Miss Malinov, I'm so happy you've called. We are always looking for qualified young women for our program," the woman replied warmly.

"What do I need to do to apply?" she asked.

"We hold seminars once a week at our offices located by Poshtova Square. Are you familiar with the area?"

"Yes ma'am."

"Wonderful. I will email you a formal invitation and you can join us this coming Wednesday for an informational seminar. Do you have an email address you can share?"

She gave the woman her address and thanked her for her time. She replaced the receiver and suddenly felt as light as air. In an unusual show of emotion, she skipped down the hallway back into the main portion of the museum where she completed her assigned work for the day with renewed energy.

Her excitement in sharing the news of the seminar with her sisters was so great that when her shift ended, she found she couldn't wait another moment to get home to them. Instead of taking the hour to walk across the city as she normally did, she frivolously spent money on the metro for the second time in one day which allowed her to make it home in less than ten minutes. Both Natalya and Tetyana were preparing dinner in the kitchen when she burst through the apartment door.

"Hello, sisters!" she called to them.

"Hello, Kate!" they called back in unison.

She threw off her coat and scarf and laid her messenger bag on the kitchen table. She collapsed into the kitchen chair which creaked unpleasantly under her weight.

"You are going to university!" she announced.

"What do you mean?" Natalya exclaimed, turning from the fish she was preparing on the stove.

"I've been invited to a seminar on Wednesday with the American investor!" she explained.

"Already?" Tetyana asked.

"Yes! Can you believe it? I promise you I will convince them to invest in us, all three of us," she said.

"Are you going to say anything to Mama and Papa?" asked Natalya.

Dealing with her parents was always tricky, even with the power of gift. "No. I'm going to wait until I've been selected. Once the investors have promised me money, how will they be able to refuse?"

"How indeed!" Tetyana agreed.

She busied herself with her sisters, preparing supper for her family. As she finished scrubbing the potatoes, she couldn't help but smile to herself, confident, that like always, things were going to turn out just the way she had planned.

CHAPTER

10

THOMAS

It was a very good thing Thomas was a proficient pianist, for as he sat at the piano located in the atrium of one of the largest shopping centers in the city, the movement of his fingers was the last thing on his mind.

For several days, he had become preoccupied with the young officer he'd met at the police station. He returned to the station each afternoon, hoping to be chosen for a lineup, only to be disappointed when the officer in charge announced they wouldn't be requiring his services. In addition to the money he was losing out on, he was also dismayed that he wouldn't be able to linger by the hallway door on the off chance she would pass by once again.

Each piece he played flowed seamlessly into the next and he closed his eyes. The composition he was playing, the Piano Sonata in B Minor by Franz Liszt, was a piece he had learned during his brief stay with his second foster family.

After being removed from his first family by the Department of Social Services, he had initially been content with the second family into which he was placed. The most exciting part for him, when he arrived with two small bags and the coat on his back, was seeing the piano against the far wall in the formal living room of the house.

Several weeks after settling in, he had cautiously approached the piano. He pulled the bench out quietly, taking special care to avoid scratching the feet across the hardwood floor. At first, his fingers seemed to have forgotten their place on the keys. He plunked out a simple tune that echoed throughout the house. After several minutes however, he found he was able to remember much of what Mrs. Lawson had taught him. He surrendered himself to the music and was surprised when minutes later, his new foster mother, Beatrice, appeared beside him on the bench. She urged him to continue and began playing harmonies at her end of the keyboard. He enjoyed a few precious months of peace playing the piano with Beatrice. Until the drunken beatings began.

As an adult, he acknowledged he was never meant to stay with his second family because, of course, then Mildred would have never become his mother. However, it was a shocking blow as a child when Beatrice's husband, Frank, began using a belt on him whenever the opportunity arose.

At that time, he was just beginning to understand what the voice in his head was suggesting when it woke him at two in the morning and urged him to hide from Frank, who was arriving home quite inebriated from the local bar. He had initially ignored the nagging feelings of anxiety that began cluttering his thoughts. However, after several unprovoked lashings, he began listening to the fear that boiled up inside his gut. Hiding and avoiding confrontation became a way of life for him. And, on the handful of occasions when he suppressed the anxiety and attempted to stand up to his foster father, he discovered he was no match for Frank physically as he was unable to protect either himself or Beatrice from her husband's rage.

If Frank had taught him anything, it was to listen to the protective counseling his gift provided. It was a lesson he carried with him every day.

As his next selection wove its way through the noisy chaos of the atrium, he couldn't help but wonder what had happened to Beatrice in the years since he'd been removed from her home. He hoped she was safe, wherever she was.

His tip jar was reasonably full and he was debating about heading head home when he noticed a young woman standing on the far side of the atrium. She bore a striking resemblance to the woman from the police station, but he was cautious about approaching her after what had transpired with the woman on the bus the week before. He waited to confirm she was actually the officer before chancing another awkward confrontation. His fingers continued to play, but he watched the woman standing patiently outside the jewelry store. After several moments, she turned so he could see her face, and he slowly released the breath he was holding when he recognized her as the officer from the station. His fingers hurried to complete the song he was playing, as he was unwilling to cut off the piece before its end. He hoped he would be able to finish before she moved out of sight.

And then, with only several measures to go, a man came out of the jewelry store and placed his arm around her shoulders. She returned his ridiculously large grin and they began walking together out of the atrium. He was carrying a small bag, and it was obvious they had just purchased jewelry together.

His heart sank and he felt as though he had been punched in the gut. He conjured up the most melancholy song in his repertoire and began to play, without regard to the listeners of whom he was requesting tips. He was angry at himself for the way he was reacting, but found he could do nothing to suppress it. Like it or not, he was heartbroken at the sight of the officer with another man.

After packing up his belongings, he took the number seven bus home. Although Mildred often waited up, he was especially happy to see the kitchen light on as he entered the tiny row home they shared.

"Well, goodness, who died?" she said as soon as she saw him coming through the door.

"Aw, Ma, it's so stupid," he said. He threw down his backpack and sat beside his mother at the kitchen table, resting his head in his hands.

"Did you get dinner?" she asked.

"A little. Not really. No," he replied.

She moved toward the large pot on the stove. "I made soup. Would you like some? You can tell me what's going on while you eat."

"Sure, Ma. I'd love some," he said. He hesitated to go on, fully aware of how his mother would react to anything he had to share concerning a woman. He waited until she placed the bowl of homemade corn chowder in front of him before he began. The steam from the bowl warmed his cheeks and the familiar aroma seemed somehow to calm his weary soul.

"So I met this girl…"

"A girl!" Mildred exclaimed.

"Yes, Ma. A girl. But don't get too excited yet. I saw her tonight. And she was with someone else."

"No!" she said, genuinely devastated by the news.

He shrugged in a *what-are-ya-gonna-do* sort of way. "Yeah. Like I said, it's stupid. I don't really know her. I don't even know her name. All I do know is she's a cop."

"A cop? Did you meet her doing those lineups?"

He blew patiently on a hot spoonful of chowder. "No. That's the weird thing. I first saw her at Belinda's the other morning. She was having brunch with some friends. I felt her staring at me while I was bussing tables. She kept looking at me like she knew me. And I got this feeling. I don't know how to describe it. It was like she was pulling me toward her. It was as if I was supposed to meet her for some reason."

"Well, did you talk to her?" Mildred asked impatiently.

"No." He ate another spoonful of soup. "Not at Belinda's. But then, I couldn't stop thinking about her. She's been right here," he said, pointing to his forehead, "and I can't get her out."

"But you did talk to her?" she interrupted again.

"Yes, Ma, I'm getting there." He paused to wipe a bit of soup that was dribbling down his chin. "So I didn't say anything to her at Belinda's, but later in the week, while I was at the police station doing another lineup, I saw her walk by the door to the waiting room."

"And she saw you?"

"No, I followed her down the hallway like some crazy stalker."

"And then you talked to her?" Mildred asked anxiously.

"Yes! Then I talked to her!"

She beamed with pride from across the table. "And what did you talk about?"

"Nothing. It was ridiculous. I had nothing important or interesting to say. I told her you were upset about me doing the lineups."

"Well, that was truthful."

"Terrific. At least I'm a *truthful* 24-year-old who still lives at home with his mom…"

Mildred deflated, her shoulders slumping beneath her.

"Aw, Ma. I'm sorry. I didn't mean it that way. You know I want to be here with you. But this girl, she doesn't know the circumstances. It just makes me look like a failure."

"So what happened tonight?" she asked, composing herself and taking his hand in her own.

"I played tonight at the atrium in the mall and I saw her standing outside the jewelry store. I was just about to walk over to her when a guy came out of the store and put his arm around her and they walked out together. It was stupid of me to think she wasn't already involved with somebody else. It was even stupider of me to think she would be interested in me, even if she wasn't with another guy."

She squeezed his hand with a surprising amount of strength. "Thomas Pritchett, I don't ever want to hear you say that again. Do you understand me? That is the silliest thing I've ever heard. You are a wonderful young man.

Honest. Hardworking. Faithful. Any woman should be honored to know you."

"Thanks, Ma," was all he could reply.

"So this girl's not the one. So what? When I met Howard, I knew. When the right girl meets you, she'll know too. Have a little faith."

Sensing Mildred was on the verge of breaking into one of her famous impassioned monologues, he quickly changed the subject. "Well, the good news is, I earned enough tonight that we will easily make the mortgage payment this month. We might even have enough extra for that application to Peabody."

"Thomas! That's fabulous news! I just know your piano playing is going to be your bread and butter. We just need to get your feet through the right doors."

"I'm trying, Ma," he replied as he pondered everything he wanted to change about his life. "I'm trying."

CHAPTER

11

KATE

The email inviting Kate to the informational seminar arrived in her inbox the day after the phone call. Desperate to make a good impression, she raided both her sisters' and her mother's wardrobes in search of the perfect outfit. Each piece she tried on seemed too worn or outdated, and so, without her parent's permission, she borrowed a few hryvnia from the stash her parents kept in the jar on the top pantry shelf. She promised herself that once she was able, she would return the money, with interest.

On Wednesday afternoon, she was having difficulty concentrating during Biology. Her class was discussing meiosis and mitosis, but she was preoccupied with the seminar and the ramifications of the evening's events. As soon as the professor dismissed her class, she raced from the room, hoping to catch the 3:11 metro into Kiev's elite shopping district. Both of her sisters were planning on meeting her at oz.store, one of the trendiest clothing retailers in the city.

As she rounded the corner from the metro station, she spotted both Tetyana and Natalya waiting outside the entrance to the store.

"This is so exciting!" Natalya exclaimed, running to her as she approached the storefront.

"What are you going to buy?" Tetyana asked.

She held fast to the bills folded carefully in her pocket. "I don't know. I don't have much money. I need to find something that makes me look dependable. And hard working. Like I would be a good investment."

"You are a good investment, Kate," Tetyana said, smiling at her sister.

They walked into the store and started toward ladies apparel. "Well, I'm sure there are going to be other students there, so I need to make sure I stand out. I need them to notice me and remember me when it's time to give out money for school."

The girls wove through the aisles of clothing, each of them picking up pieces to show the other two. They finally decided she should wear a dress, but a professional looking one with a collar and full sleeves. At long last, they came upon the perfect choice.

"Get the blue," Natalya encouraged her.

"No, the green is better. It matches your eyes," Tetyana chimed in.

"I think," she said, holding the dress at arm's length, "I'm going to get the red."

"It is beautiful," Natalya said.

"And they will certainly remember you," Tetyana agreed.

"Then the red it is," she said, knowing at once it was the perfect selection.

By the time the girls made their way home during the busy rush hour commute, there was very little time left for her to prepare for the seminar. They had already agreed upon the story they were going to tell their parents regarding where she was going for the evening.

After changing from her street clothes into the form fitting red dress, she applied a layer of mascara to her lashes and put on a touch of lipstick. Satisfied she was as ready as she was going to get, she succeeded in slipping unnoticed out of the apartment.

Although she was upset about having to spend more money on another metro ticket, she was realistic enough to know she would never make it to the seminar on foot, especially given the impractical shoes Natalya had forced her to wear.

When she arrived at the address, she was confused by her surroundings. She had expected she would be meeting the investors in a business office or perhaps someone's home. Instead, the address she was given led her to a building which resembled a small, aging warehouse. There was no front entrance but, after exploring a side alley, she found a large steel door on the back of the dilapidated brick structure. Unsure about what to do next, she cautiously knocked on the door.

A heavyset man opened the door from within. He was dressed fully in black – a black oxford shirt and black dress slacks. His face was partially obscured by a beard and there was a noticeable scar down his left cheek.

"Welcome!" he said warmly, his voice in stark contrast to his outward appearance.

"Hello," she replied.

"Come in," said the man, "Who can I announce has arrived?"

"My name is Yekaterina Malinov."

The man led her down a narrow stairway into a cavernous room in the basement of the building. The ceiling of the room was low and the floor was made of concrete. There were a few scattered rugs positioned between several groups of mismatched chairs. The only light was provided by three industrial looking fluorescents which did nothing to soften the harshness of the space.

The burly man announced her arrival to the handful of other guests who were already mingling with one another around the room. She immediately picked out two distinguished looking men wearing business suits and what appeared to be very expensive shoes. It was obvious they were the American investors although she thought it was strange that one of them seemed to be extremely young. Regardless of their ages, they were the people she needed to impress, and as if drawn to her by some unseen force, they immediately approached her. She smiled, knowing her gift was once again helping her to get what she wanted.

"Yekaterina, a pleasure," said the older of the two men, taking her hand and kissing it gently. "My name is Henry, and this," he said, motioning to his companion, "is my business partner, Patrick."

"It's nice to meet you," she said, suddenly very grateful for the English classes her parents had forced her to take.

"No, it's nice to meet you," said Patrick. "You look absolutely exquisite!"

She felt her cheeks blushing to match the shade of her dress and averted her eyes, no longer able to maintain their gaze. "Thank you," she said modestly.

"Come, sit down," Henry encouraged her. "We are about to get started.

She crossed the room and sat beside another young woman who looked to be about her age. She scanned the room and saw there were six other young men and women in attendance. She assumed they had all responded to the same flyer she'd seen in the student union.

As soon as she was seated, Henry and Patrick began their presentation in the center of the room.

"Welcome," Henry began. "We are so glad you have come to join us this evening to find out more about what we can do to help you fulfill your dreams."

"We will start by explaining what the program is all about," continued Patrick. "It is actually quite simple. Henry and I are interested in the financial prosperity of this wonderful country of yours. We know the Ukrainian people have been hit hard over the past several years by a terrible recession. We believe one of the best ways to improve the prospects of the country is to improve the prospects of its people. And the people with the most to offer are college students."

Henry took over for Patrick, "And that is why you are here. Every month, we select several students to go to the United States. We provide work visas and all of your transportation needs. While you are in the states, you will be given high paying American jobs. You will live communally, which helps to keep living expenses to a minimum. Therefore, you are able to quickly save money that you will be able to use to complete your education when you return home. Our typical students are able to return to the Ukraine in as little as six months to a year with enough money to pay for the remainder of their studies. Then you can start your lives here as well-educated, debt-free adults who will help improve the financial stability of the country."

"All we ask is for you to fill out our questionnaire and spend some time with us tonight while we get to know you. Within several days, we will contact you to let you know if you have been selected. Are there any questions?" Patrick finished.

Each of the students looked expectantly around the room at one another. Kate took the opportunity to set herself apart from the crowd by speaking first.

"I have a question," she began. "I was unaware we were going to be asked to leave the country. I have never been outside of the Ukraine and have never been away from my family. Will we be able to communicate with them?"

Patrick beamed at her. "That is a great question, Yekaterina. Yes, of course. You will have telephone services available to you so you may keep in contact with your family throughout your entire stay."

"Why can't we just get jobs here?" one of the boys asked.

"As you may know, the job market here in the Ukraine is very tight. In the United States, jobs are more plentiful. Additionally, the pay in the U.S. is a great deal higher than the pay you would make for the same job here in the Ukraine. Great questions. Anyone else?" Henry asked.

The girl seated beside her spoke up. "What type of jobs will we be given?"

"Depending on what you fill out on your questionnaire, we will try to match you to a job that meets your specific qualifications and training. So to that end, it will depend on you. If you have a business background, you may be working for a Fortune 500 company. If you have a science background, you may be working in pharmaceuticals."

"Where will we be living in the United States?" asked a girl who was seated at the far corner of the room.

"Again, that will depend on the job you are assigned. We have apartments set up for you in many cities around the country."

The room fell silent. Each of the students looked carefully at one another, suddenly aware they were actually each other's competition for the few coveted positions.

"Well, if those are all the questions you have for now, let's move to the questionnaire portion of the evening. As soon as you have finished, you are welcome to speak with each other and get to know one another a little better. Who knows, perhaps you may be roommates sometime soon!" Henry said.

The two men passed out questionnaires and pens to each of the students and Kate quickly filled hers out. Most of the questions revolved around her educational background and skill set. There were a few personal questions which inquired about her family and the jobs each of her family members held. She was required to submit her tax identification number. She assumed they would be looking into her financial need. The final question asked what her goals were with regard to the income she would be making in the United States. She listed two - become a physician and assist in paying for her sisters' educations. She felt no one in the room would have more noble goals.

As the rest of the students were finishing their sheets, the girl beside her introduced herself as Lera. "Can you believe this opportunity?" she asked.

"No. These men must be angels," Kate replied. "I wonder how many of us will be selected?"

"I don't know. I wish they could take us all."

"Me too. I wish they would take my sisters. All three of us could use the money."

"Are they in college too?"

"No," she explained, "they will graduate from secondary this year and start university in the fall. But only if our family can afford to send them."

Lera appeared puzzled. "You have two sisters graduating at the same time?"

"They're twins," she explained.

"Who are twins?" asked Patrick as he approached the girls and joined in on their conversation.

"My sisters," she replied.

"Oh, and are they as beautiful as you?" he asked.

She found herself blushing again. Unaccustomed to the forwardness of the American men, she was unsure how to respond.

"My sisters," she began, "will be starting university in the fall and they would benefit greatly from this opportunity. Probably even more than I."

"I see," said Patrick, pausing briefly to think. "Here's what we can do. Why don't you fill out questionnaires for your sisters as well and we will keep them in our files. When they are ready, we will keep them in mind for our program. How does that sound?"

"That sounds wonderful!" she exclaimed, excited by the overwhelming effect her abilities were having on the investors. Her heart soared with the newfound possibility that her sisters might benefit from the program in their own right thanks to the power of her gift.

"Fabulous," said Patrick. "Let me find you a couple more questionnaires."

He walked over to the far corner of the room where he and Henry began having an intimate discussion. Both men glanced over their shoulders at her while she tried to avoid making eye contact with either of them. After a few moments, Patrick returned, handing her several sheets of paper.

"Henry is excited to hear about your twin sisters. We think they sound very promising and we would love to add them to our list of prospective students."

"That's wonderful!" she exclaimed. "Thank you both so much for presenting all of us with this opportunity. I truly appreciate it."

She filled out a set of forms for each of her sisters and returned them to Henry and Patrick who were saying goodbye to the guests as they made their way out the door.

"Thank you again. I look forward to hearing from you soon," she said as she handed the papers to Patrick.

Henry leaned in so his face was only inches from hers and whispered in her ear. "I can assure you we will be in contact. In fact, you may want to begin packing."

As she rode the metro back home, she couldn't stop smiling. She settled into the uncomfortable plastic seat and allowed herself to relax for the first time in weeks. It occurred to her that every piece of the puzzle was coming together for her family, and she was amazed by the fantastic opportunity her gift had provided. Sadly, as the train clattered along, doubt crept in as she reflected upon the one obstacle she would still need to overcome - her father. For a moment, she worried he would forbid her to participate in the program. And then, as quickly as it had come, she pushed the thought aside, trusting her abilities would not bring her so close to a solution only to allow her father to stand in her way. She spent the remainder of the ride home concentrating on one thought... convincing her father to allow her to go to the United States.

CHAPTER

12

MIA

"Hey, Mia?" Pete said, as he peeked his head into her office.

"Yeah," she replied, looking up from her computer screen.

"That guy you asked about? He's here."

Her stomach turned over involuntarily. "Oh. Oh good. Okay. Thanks, Pete. How many lineups is he doing?"

"Just two."

She glanced at her watch. "About how long until he's done?"

"Fifteen, twenty minutes tops."

"Thanks," she said.

"No problem. You gonna tell me what all this is about?" he asked.

"Probably not," she grinned.

Pete disappeared back down the hallway and she tried to complete the report for the missing person she was filing. However, the news of Thomas Pritchett's arrival had officially derailed any progress she was going to make on it for the rest of the morning. She logged off the precinct's server and closed her laptop. At the doorway of her office, she paused, checking in both directions for her father. Since her revelation about the new commissioner, their conversations had become strained and she had taken to avoiding him whenever possible. Neither one of them wanted to believe what her vision indicated about the state of the commissioner's soul, so as was their typical approach to such things, they just avoided the topic and one another altogether. There was no sign of him so she made a beeline for the lineup room.

As she took her spot behind the one-way glass, she peered into the adjacent room at the line of women before her. It was unusual to see a group of women and the guilty party was immediately visible to her. Of the six women in the lineup, only one was shrouded in a veil of darkness. The others, although dim, were bathed in light. Each of the eye witnesses that were brought in to choose the culprit from the lineup did so quickly and correctly.

When the witnesses were finished, the row of women in the lineup was replaced by a row of men. Her eyes were immediately drawn to the man in the center of the row - the one without an aura. Like every other time she had seen him, Thomas continued to defy her perceptive abilities.

Mia watched him carefully. He couldn't see her behind the one-way glass, and she used the opportunity to study his behaviors. She tried to determine what type of aura he would have if there were one for her to see by studying the movement of his hands, the tightness in the muscles of his face, and the look in his eyes. He carried himself completely differently from the man beside him, whose aura was heavy with darkness. Although sadness haunted his eyes, they did not possess the anger of the man to his immediate left. And yet, she remained skeptical of believing what she could not see.

She watched as he was removed from the room. Moments later, he returned as the member of yet another lineup. As the witness was brought into the viewing area, she was once again unable to look away from the aura-less man. He turned to the left and then the right. His profile was handsomely chiseled and for the first time, she was struck by just how attractive he was. She was immediately overcome with a desire to understand the origin of the man's sadness as well as determine why she was unable to see his aura. As the lineup ended and Thomas filed out of the room, she fled from the viewing area into the hallway, nearly knocking over the witness beside her in the process. She hurried down the hall and around to the back side of the building in an attempt to reach him before he left. As she turned the final corner leading to the back entrance of the station, he was there.

"Thomas!" she called out, surprising herself with her boldness.

He turned immediately and she watched as a look of joy spread across his face. She slowed her pace and walked toward him. He began walking in her direction and as they met, she found herself at a loss for words. Luckily, Thomas quickly found his voice.

"Hi," he said.

"Hi," she replied.

"I never got your name."

"It's Mia. Mia Rosetti."

"Officer Rosetti," he laughed.

"No, Mia is fine." She paused. "How was the lineup?"

"Oh. Good," he said offhandedly. "One of the guys in the last group made me a little uncomfortable though, but I guess that comes with the territory."

"Yeah, we get a lot of unsavory types around here," she laughed. She scanned the hallway, suddenly self-conscious about their lack of privacy. She looked at her watch.

"It's almost lunch time," she said. "I've got a little while until my next meeting. Do you want to grab something to eat? Assuming you don't have somewhere else you need to go, of course."

He hesitated. "That would be great. Where do you usually eat?"

"Oh, anywhere. There's a little sub place just down the street that's good. If you wait here, I'll go grab my wallet."

Although it was risky reaching out to Thomas, especially given that she had no way of positively identifying the state of his soul, she'd decided it was time to connect with someone from her list. Regardless of whether he was gifted, finding out more about him might shed some light onto the problems she was experiencing. If he was in possession of a gift which kept her from reading him properly, it would lend credence to the theory that she wasn't experiencing problems and that the commissioner might actually be bad. On the other hand, if he turned out to be an average man, it would help to confirm that she was probably only experiencing an anomaly and that the commissioner was fine.

She was glad to see that he was still waiting for her when she returned as there was a part of her that expected him to be gone. They walked silently together on the three block walk to the sub shop, but she found she wasn't disquieted by their lack of conversation. She was pleasantly surprised when he held the door for her as they entered the building.

He encouraged her to order first and before she could pay, added his order to hers. *Of course,* she thought, *I'm picking up the tab.* She was shocked, however, when he insisted on paying for both of their lunches. She noticed he chose the least expensive sub on the menu and she immediately felt bad for having added a fruit cup and iced tea to her order.

They sat together at a secluded table in the corner of the shop. She sipped her tea while he watched her from across the table.

"I saw you again the other night," he said carefully.

"You did? Where? At the station?"

"No. At the atrium in the shopping center downtown."

"Oh," she said, slightly unnerved by the prospect of being followed, "why didn't you say something?"

"I was busy and then…" he paused, taken a long sip of his water.

"And then what?" she pried.

"Well, then I saw you with your boyfriend and decided I didn't want to risk making you uncomfortable."

"My boyfriend?" she said, wondering who he had seen with her, because she hadn't dated anyone since joining the force. She was beginning to wonder if he was a little crazy.

"Yeah, you were with him at the jewelry store," he explained, sensing her confusion.

She laughed loudly. "Oh, Thomas! That wasn't *my* boyfriend! That was my roommate's boyfriend! He's asking her to marry him and I went along to help him pick out the ring."

"Oh!" he exclaimed, noticeably relieved. "I guess I should've said something after all."

"You couldn't have known. You probably did the right thing." She was curious as to why they were in the same place at the same time on so many occasions. It seemed as though it was more than a coincidence. "So, what were you doing at the mall? A little retail therapy?"

"Uh, no. I was working."

"Oh," she said. "Which store do you work at?"

He took another sip of his water. "No store. I play the piano," he replied.

She remembered the amazing piece that drew her out of the store and into the atrium. "That was you?"

His cheeks flushed. "Yeah. That was me."

"Thomas, you play beautifully! Your music is why I stepped out of the jewelry store. I heard you playing over the junk they were piping through the audio system and had to come out of the store so I could hear. Your playing... it was divine."

"Really?" He seemed genuinely surprised.

"Yes, really. You have a gift, Thomas. I remember thinking that whoever was playing was wasting their time at the mall. You should be playing concert halls. Truly."

"Thanks," he responded humbly.

She regarded him across the table as she took sip of her tea, thinking perhaps there was more to #37 than she first imagined. "Where'd you study?"

He laughed and shook his head.

"What? Did I say something wrong?" she asked, suddenly afraid she offended him.

"No, it's just that I've never had a formal lesson."

"You're kidding," she said, awestruck.

"No. I took up the piano after school with my first grade music teacher, Mrs. Lawson. She would sit with me after everyone else had gone home for the day and she taught me the scales and simple tunes. The more I played, the more she taught me, the more I learned. I haven't seen her since I was nine, though."

For some unknown reason, she suddenly felt compelled to know everything she could about Thomas Pritchett. He was different. Perhaps he was exceptionally different. "What happened when you were nine? Who taught you after that?" she asked.

The woman from the lunch counter brought their subs and set them on the table. He thanked her and continued his story. "When I was nine, I had to move," he said cautiously.

"Did your father get transferred?" she pried.

"Well, the man I was living with wasn't my father, and I guess he did sort of get transferred, in a way. Does being moved to prison count as a transfer?"

She froze, her sandwich hanging from her mouth in mid bite. After composing herself, she finished chewing, swallowed, and laid the rest of her sub back on the plate. He, on the other hand, continued eating without missing a beat.

"Thomas?" she said.

"Yes," he replied, his mouth full of turkey club.

"You don't know me, so you don't have to tell me things if you don't want to," she assured him.

"I'm all grown up, Mia. It's part of my past, it's part of who am I, but it doesn't define me. So," he sighed, "what do you want to know?"

"Who got incarcerated?"

"My foster father."

She hesitated to ask the follow up question, knowing in her heart she already knew the answer. "Why did he go to prison?"

"He beat me," Thomas replied. He had stopped eating and was looking at her as if to gauge her expression.

Before she could stop herself, she reached across the table and put her hand on top of his. "I'm so sorry," she said.

Instead of reacting, he simply finished off the last bite of his sandwich. She was suddenly afraid she had crossed a line and he was going to stop talking to her altogether. That was the last thing she wanted. She pulled her hand away and quickly changed the subject.

"So, after Mrs. Lawson, who else taught you to play?" she asked.

She was relieved when, after wiping his mouth with his napkin, he finally responded. "At the second foster home, the mother played. She didn't really teach me, but I had access to all of her sheet music and I just kind of taught myself. She would play with me most evenings. Playing the piano was an escape. For both of us."

Mia suddenly remembered their first conversation. "The other day, at the station, you told me your mom was concerned about the lineups. Is that the mom you were talking about?"

"No."

Her heart sank. "Oh, Thomas. I'm so sorry."

"You don't have to be sorry. None of what happened to me is your fault. And anyway, by the fourth foster home, I finally landed in a good place. When I was thirteen, Mildred and Howard Pritchett adopted me. I've been with Mildred ever since."

"And she's the mother…"

"She's the mother. She's sixty-four. We lost dad years ago. Right after I graduated from high school. It's been me and her ever since."

She suddenly understood so much about the man before her. Without seeing his aura, she was beginning to see on her own that he was a man of the light. And yet, there was still a veil of skepticism related to the fact she couldn't know for sure. Regardless of what she had discovered, she was still no closer to understanding whether his missing aura was because of a glitch or if perhaps Thomas had a gift of his own. The only way to find out for sure was to spend more time getting to know him.

She looked at her watch. "Thomas, I have to get back to work."

"Okay," he replied, although she thought she detected a hint of disappointment in his voice.

After finishing his glass of water, he took their trash to the garbage can, and she met him at the door. They walked down the street together in relative silence once again. As they approached the station, he cleared his throat.

"Mia, I really enjoyed lunch."

"Me too," she said, surprised by the truthfulness of her response.

"I would love to see you again sometime. Outside of a lineup, of course."

"Yeah. I mean, absolutely. I'd love that."

"Would you like to come to dinner sometime? To my house?"

She hesitated, wavering between accepting and declining his proposal. He seemed awkward and perhaps a little immature, and he certainly wasn't the type of man she typically dated. Not to mention her experience as an officer made her cautious of the stranger beside her. She wished silently that she was able to see his aura and confirm her intuitions. She reasoned that accepting his offer would be less of a date and more of a fact-finding expedition, but deep down, she knew there was more than just a reconnaissance mission at stake. Something in her heart compelled her to accept.

"Thomas, you know, that would be great. But…" As she said the words, she watched his face fall. Unable to cause him any pain, she continued. "But, I may be working a few night shifts over the next week. So, can we meet for lunch again?"

A smile spread across his face. "Lunch, huh?"

"Yeah, lunch. Is that okay?"

"Of course," he laughed. "Lunch is good. How about a picnic? In the park."

"That sounds wonderful!"

"When are you free?" he asked.

"I'm free tomorrow."

"Then so am I," he said smiling.

They stood together outside the back entrance of the police station.

"So, how about if I meet you right here, tomorrow, at noon?" he asked.

"I'll see you then," she replied.

Mia returned to a desk full of difficult assignments made far easier by the prospect of lunch with Thomas the following afternoon. She was confident that with enough snooping, she would get an opportunity to discover whatever secrets he was hiding.

CHAPTER

13

KATE

It was late. Kate slipped her key into the lock and turned. To her surprise, the deadbolt did not disengage. In fact, it had not yet been set for the night. She returned her key to her pocket and opened the door to the apartment, allowing it to swing slowly into the room. The dim light of the pendant hanging above the kitchen table flooded the exterior hallway. She walked inside.

"Where have you been, Yekaterina?" her father asked in a low, authoritative tone.

She glanced around the room, unsure about what had transpired while she had been gone. Her sisters were seated side by side on the living room sofa and her mother joined her father at the kitchen table. She made eye contact with Natalya in an attempt to understand what had been shared with her parents, but Natalya averted her gaze and began picking on a loose thread pulling from the sofa cushion.

"Your sisters are terrible liars," her father declared.

Once again, she had gotten herself into trouble with her father. It was a place she was quite used to being and a place she was quite used to getting herself out of as well. She quickly decided she would need to be honest with him if she had any hope of salvaging her plan. She closed her eyes and willed him to be understanding about what she was about to say.

"Papa," she began, "do not be angry with the others. They had nothing to do with this. It was all my idea."

He ignored her pleas. "Where have you been? I will not ask you again."

"I have been offered a job," she replied.

Both of her sisters perked up and the light returned to their eyes.

"What sort of a job?" her father asked.

"A very good, very high paying job. I will make enough money to finish putting myself through school in only six months!"

Her father remained skeptical and his eyes bored through her, but she could see from the expression on her mother's face she was softening.

"Go on," said her father.

"There was a flyer, in the student union, and I responded. Tonight, I went to a seminar regarding the logistics of the arrangement. I was offered the position."

"And what are the 'logistics of the arrangement?'" her father asked suspiciously.

"The job is not here," she replied.

"Not here in Kiev? We cannot afford another apartment," her mother said.

"No, not here in Kiev, but my housing will be provided. As will my transportation there and back."

"What sort of transportation?" asked her father.

"Airfare."

"Airfare!" her mother exclaimed. "Where are you planning on going?"

"The United States," she replied.

A silence fell over the family. She felt the bones in her legs beginning to soften and she wondered whether they would continue to support her as she waited for a response from her father. The seconds ticked past. She concentrated on her breathing. Slowly, in and out. She focused her energy on getting what she wanted while she stared at the patent leather shoes that pinched and rubbed her toes. She dreamed of the moment when she would be allowed to remove them. And then her father spoke.

"When will you leave?" he asked.

CHAPTER

14

THOMAS

Thomas lied to Mia. When she suggested meeting for lunch instead of dinner, he knew he wasn't free the following afternoon since he was scheduled to work at Belinda's Bistro all day. But in that moment, waiting more than twenty-four hours to see her again had seemed far too long. At the same time, he knew she had declined meeting him for dinner because she was wary of him. She was smart and had been trained well. He found he liked that about her. And so, as the sun crept over the horizon the next morning, he was faced with a dilemma.

In addition to being scheduled to work, he was also extremely short on cash. After buying both of their lunches the day before, he didn't have nearly enough money to purchase food for the picnic he had promised. In fact, he had only $4.18 in his pocket.

It was time to get creative.

In order to save what little cash he had, he decided to take a different route to work which required him to walk almost a mile between two of the bus stops along the way. It was an area he avoided most days due to the gang related violence that often broke out. He kept a brisk pace, holding his backpack tightly with both hands while keeping his head down.

In addition to the nagging anxiety that accompanied the danger in his life, he had always felt as though he was being protected in some way, as if he was shielded from peril by some unseen force. It had kept him safe over the years, and as the bus stop came into view, he breathed a sigh of relief. When the gun fire broke out behind him as the bus pulled up to the curb, he knew this particular morning his gift had protected him once again.

Despite the extended route, he arrived early to work and was waiting outside the back delivery entrance when Belinda herself showed up with the key. She was a handsome woman. In her mid-fifties, with a head of tight grey curls, Belinda was a baker by trade, but had managed to expand her tiny breakfast bakery into a café that served both breakfast and lunch to its lucky patrons. She had hired him as a bus boy when he was eighteen on the recommendation of her sister, who was, at the time, his high school English teacher. Belinda had offered him promotions into the kitchen or as a part of the wait staff on countless occasions, but he had always refused, content with his position cleaning and resetting tables.

"Morning, Thomas," she said with a smile.

"Good morning, Belinda!" he replied.

"Up with the birds this morning, are you?" she laughed.

"Yes, Ma'am. I've got a big day ahead of me!"

"Oh?" she said, leading him into the kitchen.

"I actually have a date," he disclosed.

"Anybody I know?" she asked as she disarmed the burglar alarm and turned on the lights.

"Probably not personally, but she's been to the bistro before. She's a police officer. Her name is Mia."

"Oh!" Belinda replied. "That's exciting!"

"It is," he said, "but I am having a bit of a crisis."

She wasted no time getting to work, hoisting a 30 pound bag of flour onto the counter. "Can I help?" she asked.

Thomas lifted the second bag. "That's kind of why I'm here."

He explained his double booking for the lunch hour and his lack of funding to supply food for the picnic.

"I feel awful asking, but I know the leftovers usually just get thrown out anyway. And I'm happy to come back right after lunch and do the full cleaning for tomorrow," he explained.

Belinda thought for a moment. "Thomas, I appreciate your resourcefulness, but I will not have you taking yesterday's leftovers on your date this afternoon. I can do better than that. How about if I whip up an extra portion of quiche and muffins and you can take them fresh?"

"Belinda, I can't pay for those. I'm happy to take whatever is going to get tossed, really."

She shook her head decisively. "You are not going to pay for it, Thomas. It's a gift and it's the least I can do. I want to do this and I will not be talked out of it. As far as finishing your shift this afternoon, I think you've put in plenty of overtime over the past six years that you've earned a couple hours of paid leave."

"But Belinda, I can't ask you to do that…"

"You didn't ask. It's a vacation. You've earned it."

He sighed and resigned himself to accepting charity from the kindness of others. It was something he had grown accustomed to throughout his life, but he still didn't like having to do it.

"I'll make this up to you," he promised.

She patted him affectionately on the chest. "I'm sure you will," she replied.

Belinda tied her apron around her waist and opened the walk-in refrigerator in search of ingredients for the items on the day's menu.

"Can I help you?" he asked, peeking into the refrigerator. "At least that way I will be able to tell her I made our lunch, even if I leave out that I didn't do it on my own."

"Pick up an apron, Loverboy," Belinda said, handing him several crates of eggs. "It's going to be a fun morning!"

Together, they baked seven varieties of muffins, four types of scones, six trays of quiche, and sliced enough fruit to feed a small army. As the rest of the kitchen staff arrived, he was relegated back to the dining area, preparing place settings and sweeping the floors. Belinda approached him as he was placing water goblets on each of the tables.

"Thanks for your help this morning," she said, handing him a large paper bag.

"No, thank you," he replied. "What's this?"

"It's your picnic lunch. I've packed it all up for you. And I'm also sending you home."

"Home? Why?" he asked.

"Well, I've got John coming in to bus and I just don't need the both of you here today. So take your lunch and head on home. Get fancied up for your big date this afternoon. I'll see you tomorrow and you can tell me all about it then."

"Really?" he asked.

"Really."

He stood up from the bistro table and took the bag from her hands. He bent down over her squatty frame to give her a squeeze.

"Thanks, Belinda," he said.

"Get outta here," she replied, giving him a gentle shove.

He took off his apron and clocked out. Carrying the bag of food in his arms, he gave Belinda a nod as he left through the back door. The bag seemed especially heavy for just two slices of quiche and a couple of muffins and he was curious about what else she had placed inside.

When he arrived home, the house was empty. It was Friday and his mother was working at the senior center across town. He sat at the kitchen table and emptied the contents of the bag. There was an entire quiche, four muffins, two scones, a large container of fruit and a bottle of wine. He read the label. It was the most expensive vintage Belinda's served, worth well over fifty dollars. Next to the wine, wrapped in linen napkins, were two wine glasses. He was immediately torn between being grateful for her generosity or resentful for the fact there was no way he was ever going to be able to repay her. He shook his head and repacked the picnic lunch carefully back into the bag.

He had planned on wearing his work uniform on his date with Mia since he assumed there would be no time to change. However, since he was now in possession of a fifty dollar bottle of wine, he decided he should probably change out of his uniform and into something more appropriate.

After trying on the entire contents of his closet, which amounted to several pairs of jeans and a handful of shirts, he finally decided to wear his darkest wash jeans with a vintage Woodstock t-shirt he happened upon at an outdoor flea market over the summer. He threw on his only coat, a leather jacket given to him by Howard and Mildred on his sixteenth birthday, picked up the picnic bag, and headed out the door to the police station.

CHAPTER
15

MIA

Mia's morning had been particularly slow. If there had been more criminal activity in the overnight hours, the time between breakfast and lunch may have passed more quickly as there would have been more cases in need of attention. However, it seemed to her that the universe was conspiring against her. On the one day she had something interesting she was looking forward to, many of Baltimore's repeat offenders had managed to stay out of trouble and all of the day's large cases had been assigned to other officers before she arrived for her shift.

Without any active cases to research, she decided to use the time before Jack clocked in to investigate her own pressing issues. She woke just before her alarm with an idea to research anomalies in psychic phenomena to see if there were any recorded instances of people losing their abilities. She was hoping to find documentation to support that what was happening to her was normal, or at least normal for gifted individuals.

She quickly found various articles supporting the notion that some people's abilities wax and wane, especially during times of stress or emotional shifts. Initially excited by what she found, Mia became more disenfranchised the longer she read. Most of what she discovered didn't apply to her specific abilities, and unlike other people who experienced frequent changes in strength, her gift had never wavered. As she was about to give up on the idea of finding solace on the World Wide Web, the title of page caught her eye. She clicked on the link and was presented with a strange prophecy.

Seven Light - Seven Dark - Seven Sins
The Sevens Prophecy (With Regard to the End of Days)
There will come a day when seven psychic children of the light and seven psychic children of the dark will be born. From the moment of their birth, strong powers will be in place to bring the seven light together and the seven dark together to form two separate but equally powerful groups. The first seven to gather all in one place will seal the fate of the world – dark for hell, light for heaven. At that point the seven deadly sins will take over the planet or cease to exist.

It was rare for her to find information acknowledging the reality of light and dark. Conferring with the dead was relatively common, as were some forms of telepathy, especially between twins, but she had never come across any articles referring specifically to light and dark.

She reread the prophecy a second time and then a third. The idea of two gifted groups deciding the fate of the world seemed ridiculous, another preposterous lie to fuel the fires of misunderstanding and hatred between psychics and regular people. She was just about to close the screen when she decided to print the page, just in case.

She slipped the copy of the prophecy into her file just as Jack appeared in the doorway with his brown bag lunch. He greeted her warmly and sat down across from her at his desk, laying a large stack of files between them.

"Did you get to update the sex offender registry?" he asked.

"Yup."

"What about running those fingerprints from that break-in two days ago through the national database?"

"Yup."

"Any hits?"

"Nope."

"Bummer. We'll have to go at it from another angle. I've got an eyewitness in that case, but he's pretty mentally unstable. I don't know how he'll hold up in court. I was hoping those prints would come through with something. Maybe we can work on a warrant this afternoon."

"Yup."

"Speaking of warrants, did you hear anything about the one for the meth house?"

"Yup."

"And?"

"It came through."

"Hmmm." Jack paused. "Did you hear about the drive-by last night?"

"Yup."

He stopped again and looked directly at her, raising one eyebrow. "What's with the short answers?"

"Don't know," she responded.

"Well, that was two words," he laughed. "Is there something going on? I usually can't shut you up."

She hesitated. She had no intention of sharing the findings of her research, especially about some unbelievable prophecy. "I have a date," she blurted instead, before fully considering the ramifications of disclosing the information.

"A date?" Jack exclaimed loudly.

"Shh. Yes. A date. For lunch."

Jack slapped his hands on his desk. "I can't believe you've been holding out on me! When in the world did this happen? Who's the lucky guy?"

She hesitated again. "I don't want to tell you."

"What?" he said. "Why not?" He looked at her from across the desk and she could tell he was trying to read her expression. She attempted to appear resolved. "Fine," he continued. "Don't tell me. I'll find out soon enough. I know people."

She stood up and grabbed her coat from the back of her chair. "Well, good luck earning your Junior Detective badge on this one, but I'm not sharing any information with you. At least not this minute. But if I'm not back by two, please come looking for me," she said as she walked through the door into the hallway.

"That doesn't sound good. Mia! Mia, stop! Does your dad know about this?" Jack yelled after her as she continued toward the back of the building.

She smiled at Jack's persistence. He always knew just which of her buttons to push to get what he wanted.

"The guy is Thomas Pritchett. He's the one from the lineup," she called over her shoulder, throwing a casual wave in his direction as she turned the corner.

She pushed open the back door of the station and was blinded momentarily by the brightness of the day. As her sight recovered, she recognized Thomas leaning casually against the wall of the building across the alley. She smiled at him and quickly crossed to his side of the street.

"Have you been waiting long?" she asked.

"Just a few minutes," he replied, his face lighting up as she approached, putting her at immediate ease.

"Where are we headed?"

"Well, I'll leave it to you," he said. "We can just go across to Fayette Park, or if you don't mind a little walk, we can head over to the Shot Tower."

The sun was warm on her face and she like the idea of getting further from the prying eyes of the station. "It's a beautiful day and I could use the exercise. Let's walk over to the Shot Tower."

They walked together, side by side, Thomas carrying a large bag which she assumed contained their lunch. He also had a blanket draped over his arm.

"Did you have a good morning?" he asked as they crossed the expressway.

"Yeah.   Good.   Not too busy.   I had trouble concentrating though," she confided.

"Why's that?" he asked innocently.

"I was anxious about another lunch date with you," she replied, unable to keep the smile from her face when she realized it was true.   "I don't get asked out very often.   I think most guys are turned off by the fact that I'm a cop. Men like to be the macho one in the relationship."

"I'm perfectly okay if you want to be the macho one," he laughed, "because I have a feeling you could probably hold your own against anyone who tried to cross you."

"You think so?"

"I think so," he said as they reached the park entrance. "Do you want to sit over there under the tree?"

"Perfect," she agreed, eager to begin grilling him for information.

They spread the blanket over the ground. It was lumpy and more dirt and weeds than grass, but she couldn't help but feeling happy about the company she was keeping, regardless of the setting. He began to empty the contents of the brown paper bag. She had no idea what type of meal awaited her, but she certainly hadn't expected the feast he provided, especially given his meager occupations. The last things he took from the bag were a bottle of wine and two glasses.

"Oh Thomas, this looks amazing!" She picked up the bottle of wine. "This is fabulous! A merlot! My favorite! But I have some bad news."

"What?" he asked.

"I'm on duty, technically, so no wine for me," she explained.

"Oh! You're right!" She could tell he was embarrassed. "I don't know what I was thinking! I'm so sorry."

"It's no big deal. You can just save it for another time," she said. "But look at everything else. I want some of everything. Did you make all of this?"

"Yes. No. Well... I helped," he explained. "I can't lie to you. Belinda, over at the bistro, she and I made this together this morning. It was mostly her, but she let me use a knife and the oven, so I felt pretty important."

"Well, it looks amazing," she said, grabbing a fork and taking a bite of the quiche. "Oh, Thomas, it's so good."

"Belinda is an amazing baker and chef," he said. "She's tried to get me to work in the kitchen with her over the years, but it's way too stressful back there for me. Lots of rushing and bumping about. No thanks. I'll stay in the dining room where I can enjoy the guests instead of the chaos that goes on behind the scenes."

"So, let me get this straight," she said, taking another bite of quiche. "You bus tables at Belinda's Bistro in Towson?"

"Monday, Wednesday, and Friday, seven until two. Saturday and Sunday, nine until two.

"*And* you do lineups at the station here in the city?"

"I've been stopping by after Belinda's every afternoon, just to see if they need me."

"*And* you play the piano at the atrium in the shopping district at night?"

"Only twice a week there, but I also play at the Tremont Plaza Hotel two to three nights per week."

"Holy cow! Am I missing anything?"

"Yeah, sometimes, if I have time on my mornings off, I go to the senior center where my mother works and I give piano lessons to the residents. But I don't earn any money doing that. It's pro bono," he said smiling.

She reevaluated her opinion of him as he surprised her once again. "You are a force of nature, Thomas Pritchett," she said, finishing off a chocolate scone.

"Maybe, but I'm not out in the world saving people like you are."

"I'm not really out there saving people either. I fill out a lot of paperwork every day," she laughed.

"Well, paperwork or no, the city is safer with you in it."

"Thanks," she replied, humbled by his kindness.

She paused to take a strawberry from the bowl of fruit and met his gaze. Since his confession about being raised in the foster care system, she kept thinking about how difficult his formative years must have been. She couldn't figure out how he had managed to survive such a horrible childhood without more psychological scarring. It appeared however, as she looked at the handsome man before her, that perhaps he had been able to after all. It was almost as though he was immune to the pain of his experience.

"So, tell me about the piano thing."

"What about it?" he asked.

"Why aren't you studying at Peabody or something? You're obviously very gifted."

He shrugged nonchalantly. "I've never applied."

"Why not?"

"Because the application fee is $115."

"Ouch."

"Yeah, ouch. But that's only a tiny part of the problem. When my dad was still alive, my mom and dad tried to convince me to apply, but I didn't want to waste the money. And I'm glad I didn't, because since he died, my mother and I can barely afford the mortgage, much less a tuition payment."

"How much is tuition?" she asked.

"Almost $40,000 a year."

"Double ouch."

"Yeah. So, that's why I'm not studying at Peabody."

She savored another strawberry. "What about scholarships?"

"What happens if I waste the money to apply and then don't get one?"

"What happens if you *do* get one?" she responded.

"Touché," he said. "Really, it's fine. Maybe someday I'll be able to pursue my dreams, but for now, I'm happy right where I am. I like doing what I do, even if I'm just scraping by." He paused, giving her a sideways grin. "Should I be telling you that? That I'm only just scraping by?"

She laughed, "No, probably not! But at least I know what I'm getting myself into!"

He took a bite a quiche and was suddenly serious. "Are you getting yourself into something?"

She was annoyed at herself that she hadn't thought through her words more carefully and was embarrassed by the implication. "Uh, maybe. This is something, isn't it? Lunch, two days in a row?"

"Yes. I mean, I thought it was something. But I didn't know whether you thought it was something. I was hoping it was something, but then again, I'm always sort of cautiously optimistic."

"I'll make a note," she said, using her fingers to write on an imaginary tablet. "Scraping by. Cautiously optimistic. Anything else I should know?"

"I think you are beautiful," he replied.

"Thinks I'm beaut..." she began, before cutting herself off midsentence. At that moment, something strange caught her eye from across the park, just beyond a small grove of trees. "Thomas, stay right here. Don't move. Promise me."

In an instant, she was on her feet, her hand on her firearm, sprinting across the park. As she ran, she watched as a man dressed in filthy fatigues approached an older couple walking toward him from the opposite direction. The darkness surrounding the man was unmistakable, and he was only seconds away from causing harm to one or both of the pedestrians. She hesitated to call out to him for fear he would take off, and yet she knew the couple's safety hung in the balance. Just before she was close enough to apprehend him, he struck, pulling a knife on the woman and slicing her arm as he cut the purse from her shoulder. The woman screamed, Mia called out, and the man took off in the direction of a back alley.

With her weapon drawn, she sprinted across the busy intersection behind a building in the direction of the mugger.

She gained on him quickly, calling repeatedly for him to stop and drop his knife. She knew there was a strong possibility he was also carrying a gun, which made her nervous because she wasn't wearing her vest. As she rounded the corner, she saw that he was trapped at the end of the alley. Predictably, the man attempted to scale the fence which was preventing his escape, but she had already made up too much ground. She pulled on both of his legs with all of her strength and wrestled him to the ground. Her small frame and quick movements made it easy for her to avoid being caught. She maneuvered into position behind him where she was able to force him to the ground by shoving her knee into the small of his back. Grabbing both of his hands, she cuffed him securely before allowing him to stand.

With adrenaline coursing through her veins, she escorted the cursing, bloodied man back onto the street. She was quite surprised, however, by the scene that greeted her. Instead of the mayhem she expected, the injured woman was lying calmly on the ground with Thomas and her husband kneeling by her side. She was shocked to see that Thomas was naked from the waist up and as she drew closer, she saw his shirt wrapped tightly around the woman's wound. She reached for her phone to call for back-up and an ambulance just as two squad cars, lights flashing, pulled up beside her. Four officers from her station hurried out of the cars to assist her with the arrest.

"The woman on the ground needs an ambulance. I was just about to call it in," she told the closest officer.

"Somebody already did. It should be here in less than two minutes," he replied.

The mugger was quickly placed into the back of one of the police cars so he could be taken to the station for booking, and the ambulance arrived with record speed. After briefly giving her statement to her fellow officers, she made her way over to the woman as she was being loaded onto a stretcher.

"Thank you, Officer Rosetti," she said weakly.

"It's my pleasure, Ma'am," she replied. "What's your name?"

"My name is Ethel. Ethel Huggins. And this here is my husband Ray."

"Pleased to meet you, Officer," Ray said, extending his hand which she shook firmly. "I don't know how you got to us so quickly, but thank goodness you did, or that man would have gotten away for sure!"

"I'm just glad you're going to be okay," she said patting the woman on the arm and sidestepping the question behind the compliment.

"And if it wasn't for this kind man here," Ethel continued nodding toward Thomas, "the paramedic said I would have lost a significant amount of blood. It's just a miracle you both were here for us."

The paramedic appeared from within the ambulance. "Time to get you to the hospital, Mrs. Huggins," he said.

After they said their goodbyes to the Huggins, Thomas packed up their lunch while Mia spoke with the officers remaining at the scene. They offered to drive her to the station but she opted to walk back with Thomas instead.

As they made their way across the expressway, she was surprisingly at ease with him, alone for the first time since their lunch date ended so unceremoniously. Something was definitely unusual about the mild-mannered busboy.

"You were pretty amazing back there," she said, giving him a playful nudge on the arm.

"Me? You chased down a mugger!"

"Yeah, but it's my job. You on the other hand... somehow you knew exactly what to do to help Mrs. Huggins. You talked her down, stopped the bleeding, and completely defused the entire situation."

"You learn a lot growing up in places where abuse is a daily event."

"I guess you do," she said. It unsettled her to think of him in an abusive situation.

Neither of them spoke for several minutes as they made their way down the street. Finally he commented casually, "Well, that was an interesting lunch."

"Yup. I've only known you two days and you're already taking your clothes off," she quipped.

He blushed. "You never know what you're gonna get on a first date with me," he said.

"Second date," she corrected.

"How is this our second date already?" he asked.

She kicked a rock down the street in front of them as they walked. "Did you pay for lunch yesterday?"

"Yeah."

She caught up to the rock and kicked it again. "Well, then, it counts as a date. And if yesterday was our first date, then today was our second date."

He paused, stopping to look at her. "Gonna be hard to top this on a third date."

She contemplated the possibility of a third date, immediately reasoning that she still hadn't gotten a chance to press him for information about why she couldn't see his aura. However, if she was being honest with herself, the real reason to accept had nothing to do with solving her own issues - it was simply because she enjoyed spending time with him.

"It's gonna be really hard," she agreed.

He sighed heavily and chewed his bottom lip. "Maybe we should just end it here," he suggested. He feigned disappointment but his eyes were smiling.

She shook her head, unable to believe what she was about to suggest. "Not a chance. I know you've got that merlot in the bag, and after today, I could really use a glass. Let's do dinner."

"Dinner?" he said skeptically.

"Yes. Dinner. And since you're 'scraping by,' we'll have it at my house."

"Dinner at your house, huh?"

"Dinner at my house. Take it or leave it. But you bring the wine. Shirt and shoes are optional," she said as they reached the back entrance of the station.

"I'll take it. I can't do tomorrow, but I can do Sunday."

The anxiety she felt about her inability to judge his character based on his aura was beginning to fade. In fact, being around him made her forget it was even a problem. Still, she was surprised by the confidence she felt as she took out one of her business cards and quickly added her personal cell number and home address. She handed it to him.

"Sunday it is then," she said. "See you at seven."

16

KATE

In the aftermath of her father's acceptance, Kate was thrown headfirst into a whirlwind of preparations. Although she was excited her father had given her his blessing, she wasn't at all surprised by his decision. She had always trusted that the power she possessed, allowing her to manipulate situations so she was able to get what she wanted, would never let her down. She was counting on it now that what she wanted more than anything was a future for her sisters.

Natalya and Tetyana were initially devastated by the news she would be leaving them, but when she shared the news the investors intended on extending the same offer to them, possibly within the coming weeks, they quickly joined in the excited preparations.

As they promised, Henry and Patrick notified her via email two days after the seminar of her acceptance into the program. She was given instructions on what to pack as well as when and where she was to meet the others for her flight to America. She was also informed that her sisters were accepted into the program as well, and could join her as soon as they were able.

Over the course of the subsequent weeks, she finished the assignments required to complete the biology class she'd been attending. She arranged to have her meager government-issued stipend deferred until she returned from her trip and put in for a leave of absence at the museum where she worked.

The morning of her scheduled departure to America, Kate had never experienced such little control of her emotions. She was crying one moment and giddy with wild anticipation the next. It took her ten minutes to compose herself so she was able to join her family in the kitchen for breakfast without breaking down.

Her mother prepared a special meal of fish, rye bread and a particularly expensive cheese that was a rare treat for her family. As she sat silently eating the last of her cheese, she felt the full weight of her family's expectations resting heavily upon her shoulders. Not only were they counting on her to earn enough money to finish her schooling, but she was also responsible for paving the way for her sisters to do the same.

After breakfast, there were only a few minutes to complete the last of her preparations. The zipper on her mother's secondhand bag refused to give as she attempted to shove one last pair of socks into the side pocket. Frustrated and close to tears once again, she was dismayed when her father called to her from the kitchen.

"Yes, Papa?" she said as she dragged her suitcase from the room to set beside the front door.

"Sit down. I have something for you," he said.

She was taken aback by the emotion she heard in his voice. Her mother and sisters were standing expectantly by the stove behind her father. She pulled out the wooden kitchen chair and sat beside him.

"Generations ago, when your great grandmother moved here from Mother Russia, she brought these with her," he began, handing her a velvet trinket box. "You are the first of our family since then to leave this country to go to another. And so today, I," he paused and turned to look at her mother, "*we* would like you to have them. To take to America. For luck."

She took the box from her father's hands and opened the lid carefully. Inside the box was a pair of ornamental hairpins. The head of each pin was formed from enamel and painted with a tiny bouquet of flowers.

"Oh, Papa," she said, picking them up to touch their delicate beauty.

"Your grandmother's mother claimed they were given to her on her sixteenth birthday by a member of the royal family. I doubt the truthfulness of that origin, but nonetheless, they have traveled many miles with the Malinov's through the years. And today they will travel many more miles with you, my Yekaterina."

"Thank you, Papa. I promise I will keep them safe and bring them home to you," she said, placing the box in her coat pocket.

"I know you will. And now," he said, checking his wrist watch, "it is time to go."

It was a rare occurrence for her entire family to travel anywhere together, so it felt particularly strange as they all piled into the taxi waiting for them outside their building. At some point, it had been decided they would all make the drive to the airport to see her safely off. She had tried to convince them she would be fine on her own, but her father had insisted that the whole family should be there to say goodbye.

She sat with her parents in the back of the cab, while her sisters sat beside the driver in the front. The international airport was on the far east side of the city and it took them over half an hour to get there. It was a quiet trip which made her apprehensive. She had expected her sisters to be full of excitement and chatter, but they remained stoic in the front seat, gazing silently out the window at the scenery speeding past.

Upon their arrival at the airport, her father paid the driver and loaded her baggage onto a trolley. Natalya and

Tetyana took her hands and they walked together into the terminal. Her mother and father followed closely behind, pushing the trolley in front of them.

"Where are you supposed to go?" Natalya asked.

She carefully pulled her paperwork out of the side pocket of her luggage and began rifling through the pages.

"It says I am supposed to take my passport and my bags to the far end of the terminal by the customs office to obtain my ticket and boarding information."

"That should be this way then," said Tetyana, pointing in the direction of the customs sign.

"Are you scared at all?" asked Natalya as they made their way through the throngs of travelers hurrying in every direction.

"A little. I'm afraid of being without you both. Afraid of being on my own. But we have to remember it's only for a little while. Hopefully you will be joining me soon and before we know it, we will all be back home together again."

"And then we will never have to worry about how to pay for school. We will have plenty of money," Tetyana said.

It sounded almost too good to be true. "All good things have their price. And all things worth having require sacrifice. In the end, I know this will all be worth it."

"Did they tell you about your job yet?" Natalya asked.

"No. Nothing yet. I guess I'll just have to wait and see. Whatever they have me doing, I'm sure it will be fine," she replied.

They came to a gate where only travelers were allowed to proceed. She squeezed both of her sisters' hands tightly.

"I guess this is it," she said.

"I guess so," said Tetyana.

Behind them, her parents caught up with the trolley of luggage.

"We can't come any further?" asked her mother peering past the gate.

"No, Mama. We will have to say goodbye here."

"But do you see anyone you know?" her father asked anxiously. It was obvious he wasn't ready to see her off.

She scanned the area for anyone she recognized from the seminar, but there was no one she knew. Not even Henry or Patrick.

"No. Not yet. But I'm sure they are here somewhere. I'll be fine. Please don't worry," she added as she watched the tears building in her mother's eyes.

In an effort to keep from crying herself, she gave a quick round of hugs to each of her family members and took the trolley from her father's hands.

"I will call as soon as I can. They said it could take a while to get everything established once we get there, so don't worry if you don't hear from me right away. I will be fine."

Natalya rushed at her, nearly knocking her over with the force of her embrace.

"I love you, Kate," she said, her voice barely a whisper.

"Love you too, Nata," she replied.

After releasing herself from her sister, she carefully maneuvered the trolley beyond the gate into the customs area. She turned one final time to wave goodbye to her family and then headed down the corridor in search of the other students.

Around the corner, some hundred yards beyond the gate, she came across a man holding a sign with her name on it. She approached him cautiously.

"I'm Yekaterina Malinov," she told the man, who was tall and lanky with a wave of greasy black hair on the top of his head.

"Oh, good," he replied. "Henry and Patrick sent me. I have your paperwork. Come with me, please."

"Where are the others?" she inquired, pushing the trolley wildly as she attempted to keep up with the man.

"They're already here, on the plane," he replied.

She followed the man for what seemed like miles through countless hallways of the airport terminal. They finally arrived at an exterior door, which the man opened and encouraged her to go through.

"You can leave your bags here," the man said. "I will have someone load them for you."

She found herself on the tarmac, surrounded by dozens of cargo planes. The closest one, far smaller in size than the others, was equipped with a mobile staircase which led into the belly of the bird. The lanky man appeared beside her.

"Follow me," he said.

She followed the man up the staircase, holding carefully to the railing. The engines of the plane, already running, were terribly loud and she was forced to cover her ears with her hands as she reached the door of the plane.

The cargo bay was filled with crates securely fastened to the sides and to one another with large canvas straps. To her left, in the direction her guide was heading, were several rows of seats which were bolted to the floor. Two very frightened looking students from the seminar were already seated together in the seats closest to the door.

"Sit down with the others. Be sure to buckle up. You'll be taking off shortly," the man instructed.

"Sir," she called as he was turning to leave, "what's going on? Why aren't we on a regular plane?"

"It saves money to fly you to the United States on a cargo plane instead of taking a commercial flight. This way there is more money for your accommodations once you get there," he replied. "Have a good flight."

The man closed the hatch behind him and she stood dumbfounded in the hull of the cargo plane. She walked over to her traveling companions and chose the seat beside them.

"You're Yekaterina, right?" asked one of the women, an attractive blond.

"Yes, but please, call me Kate," she replied.

"It's good to see you again. I don't know if you remember me. I'm Lera," the woman said. She was petite and had the delicate features of a child. Her blond hair was bleached, but her roots were barely noticeable.

"And I'm Anya," said the woman who was seated on the end. She was the tallest of the three women and also the sturdiest. She was thickly built, but was not overweight by any standards. Kate was struck by her beauty but believed she would have been far more attractive had she chosen to wear less makeup.

"It's nice to see you both," she said genuinely, imagining how frightened she might have been if she was traveling alone.

"So," Anya continued, eyeing the others uncertainly, "just the three of us were selected?"

"It appears so," said Lera. "I thought for sure they would have chosen Pertuso. We've had several classes together and he's extremely intelligent. I can't believe I was chosen over him. We really lucked out."

"We did," she said, although she was beginning to feel unconvinced. She buckled her harness and tried to get comfortable in the seat. "Did either of you find out what job you are going to be assigned when we get there?"

"No," both women said in unison.

"Me neither," she confirmed. "How about Patrick or Henry? Have you spoken to either of them?"

"No," said Lera.

"I haven't either," said Anya added.

The engines of the plane, which until that moment had been running in neutral, sprang to life unexpectedly. The plane lurched backward, forcing the women forward in their seats.

Anya cried out in pain over the sudden din of the turbines.

"It sounds like it's going to be a noisy ride," Kate yelled to the others as they repositioned themselves in their seats.

"Have either of you flown before?" Lera asked excitedly.

She thought about how sheltered her life had been and wondered just how naïve she was as a result of her upbringing. "No," Kate said. "I've never been outside of the Ukraine."

"Me neither," Lera said.

"I have," Anya boasted. "When I was a little girl, during the good years, we took a plane to Paris to see the Eiffel Tower. It was nothing like this," she said sadly.

Kate tried to imagine what it would be like to go to France but had only memories of pictures in her history books as a reference. "What was it like to take a plane to Paris?" she asked.

Anya tipped her head back and closed her eyes. "It was quiet. And warm. And the seats were comfortable with lots of padding. We were brought food and drinks by the flight attendants. My mother even let me get a soda with a little umbrella," she reminisced.

"It sounds lovely," said Lera, scrunching up her nose. "So much better than this."

Kate decided she was done listening to the others feel sorry for themselves. "Well," she said, "this horrible plane is only temporary. Before we know it, we will be in America and we will be living in our wonderful new apartment."

"I sure hope it's going to be amazing," said Anya, "because truthfully anything will be better than this."

The plane, positioned for take-off at last, began gaining speed down the runway. Within seconds, the wheels left the ground, and the three women began their journey to America - the land of opportunity.

17

THOMAS

"Thomas?" Mildred called cautiously as she opened the back door of the row house.

"Yes?" he yelled from the second floor.

"The door is unlocked. Why are you home already?" she asked, her voice thick with concern.

He ran down the stairs two at a time and helped his mother into the house with her armload of groceries.

"I didn't do any lineups this afternoon," he explained, taking a gallon of milk from under her arm.

She hung her purse on the back of the kitchen chair. "Why not? I thought you said you were getting chosen for quite a few of them."

"I am. But I didn't have time today," he said as he began emptying the contents of the grocery bag into the pantry. "Instead of heading to the station, I went shopping because I needed a new shirt. Or at least one that is new to me. I found a nice one at the thrift store on York Road."

Mildred pulled her head out of the refrigerator where she was rearranging the contents to make room for a head of lettuce. "A new shirt! You haven't bought any new clothes since I forced you to buy a new pair of jeans a year ago. You wore that holey pair for months! What's the occasion?"

"I ruined a shirt today," he said cryptically.

"How in the world did you ruin your shirt?" Mildred exclaimed, closing the refrigerator door.

He finished stocking the pantry and folded the paper bag into thirds. "I used it to save someone's life."

"Thomas!" she responded, nearly dropping a loaf of bread on the floor, "what on earth are you talking about?"

He explained what had transpired at the picnic lunch that afternoon. "Mia invited me to dinner at her place Sunday night, so I figured it was as good of an excuse as any to get a new shirt," he concluded.

Mildred found her way to the kitchen table and carefully lowered herself onto one of the chairs. He didn't know how to respond to her silence.

"Ma?" he said crouching beside her and taking her hand in his. "Are you okay?"

"As I live and breathe, I never thought I'd see the day. But here we are. It's happening."

"What's happening?" he asked with genuine concern.

"You are going to fall in love. And get married. And I'm going to have a grandbaby after all," she said, tearing up.

He began laughing aloud. It was true – he'd never had much time for dating, especially since assuming the role as man of the house. Despite his work habits and although he thought Mildred's tearful display seemed a little over the top, he couldn't resist gathering her into his arms just the same.

"Let's not get ahead of ourselves," he said, smiling at her. "It's just dinner. No one's proposed. And the shirt's not all *that* great, so don't get your hopes up just yet."

On Sunday evening, he kissed a gleeful Mildred goodnight before boarding the bus running service to Parkville. He was wearing his new shirt, a 1970's yellow and brown plaid oxford with snaps instead of buttons. He carried a brown paper bag containing the bottle of merlot, a small bouquet of carnations, and one of his father's old novels about J. Edgar Hoover's involvement in the formation of the FBI he thought Mia would enjoy.

As the bus approached the stop closest to her apartment, he found that in addition to being excited to see her again, he also felt as though he was being drawn to her by some unseen force. It was a feeling he had never experienced before.

When she opened the door, he presented her with the flowers, and she seemed genuinely touched by the somewhat archaic gesture. She reached up to place a kiss tenderly on his cheek, and the warmth of her touch was still lingering as he followed her hesitantly into the apartment.

"Did you know that no one has ever brought me flowers before?" she commented as she rummaged under the kitchen sink in search of a suitable vase for the carnations.

"I find that hard to believe," he replied. "But for what it's worth, you're the first girl I've ever given flowers to."

"And I find that hard to believe." She emerged from beneath the sink with a large mason jar. "This will have to do," she said, placing it on the counter.

"It looks perfect," he said. "I brought you this too," he added, handing her the paperback from the bag.

"Oh," she said, scanning at the back cover, "this looks fabulous! Have you read it?"

"I just finished it the other day. Because the storyline is about the FBI, I thought it might be something you'd be interested in."

She flipped to the first chapter. "I love crime dramas," she said. "I love them because, unlike in real life, they usually have happy endings."

"Don't most people's lives end happily?"

"You *are* cautiously optimistic, aren't you," she laughed, setting the book on the counter. "I suppose they do end happily sometimes. But not for a lot of the people I see every day."

"I can imagine," he said as he watched her taking a homemade lasagna out of the oven. The intoxicating smell of cheesy pasta quickly took over the room, making him wonder why someone who clearly had so many career options would decide to become a cop. "What made you want to become a police officer and subject yourself to all that sadness? You should have become a chef instead."

She blew on a small bite of the lasagna before tasting it to make sure it was done. "I didn't want to at first," she replied. "It was hard, growing up with my dad as a cop. He was gone a lot. Worked weird hours. Drove my mother crazy with worry. And he brought it all home with him, you know? It's hard not to I suppose. I know I do. It's difficult to watch the worst of the world day in and day out and not let it start sticking to you."

She pulled a small bowl of salad out of the refrigerator and handed it to him to set on the table. She followed behind with a basket of bread.

"When I started college, I chose pre-law as my major. During high school I decided I wanted to become a judge. I thought the best way to help the good people of the world was to make sure the bad ones got convicted."

He couldn't imagine her being a judge, especially after watching her chase down a mugger. "So what made you change your mind?" he asked, as he opened the bottle of wine and began filling their glasses.

"I couldn't do it."

He nodded supportively. "It's a tough major."

"It is, but the studying wasn't the problem. It was the waiting. I couldn't fathom having to wait for the bad guys to get to me. As a judge, I was going to be the end of the road for the criminals. I began to understand that many of them would never even get to me, behind the bench in the courtroom. As much as I hated to admit it, I recognized I didn't have the patience to be a judge. I wanted to get the bad guys right away, at the source of the problem. I needed to become a cop."

"Just like your dad," he commented.

"Just like my dad," she said, taking a sip of wine. "This is delicious, Thomas.

"I'll tell Belinda when I see her," he smiled.

She rose from the table and brought the lasagna from the kitchen. As he watched her crossing the room, so obviously comfortable in her own skin, it occurred to him that he could very easily fall in love with Mia Rosetti.

"It smells so good. I love lasagna," he declared.

"I'm glad," she said. "I almost didn't make it. You know, the Italian girl making lasagna to impress a boy ..."

"Oh! Are you trying to impress me?" he teased.

"Only if it's working," she laughed. "I thought it might be a little cliché, but for some reason I didn't think cliché would bother you."

"If cliché always tastes this good," he said, taking his first bite, "I'll have it at every meal."

"Thanks," she replied. "It's my grandmother's recipe".

The two ate without speaking, just the scraping and clanking of forks on their plates, though he did catch her glancing curiously at him several times. He wondered what she was thinking and hoped her silence didn't indicate he'd said or done something to offend her.

"What is it?" he asked finally when he caught her staring at him for the third time. "Is there something on my face?"

"No. Nothing that doesn't belong there," she joked. "I was just thinking about yesterday and how kind you were to Mrs. Huggins. It was really..."

"Motherly?" he asked, remembering the way a former girlfriend had described him.

She smiled. "Refreshing. I was going to say refreshing. Most of the men I'm around all the time are so busy being tough, they forget to be kind." She finished the last of her wine and began clearing the table.

"I'm not very tough," he replied, joining her in the kitchen with his empty plate.

"I think you're a lot tougher than you think you are. Especially where it counts."

"Oh really?" He rinsed his dishes in the sink. "And where exactly does it count?"

"On the inside," she said. "To live through what you've lived through and come out the other side so grounded and, for lack of a better word, normal... that requires some serious toughness. I can't quite understand how you didn't end up like so many of the kids I see who fall through the cracks. The system fails so many of them. They turn to drugs and alcohol and crime. You didn't do any of that. You just... overcame. There's something special about you, Thomas."

He felt the warmth of her compliment but was hesitant to acknowledge it. Instead, he sidestepped around it with a compliment of his own.

"Well, it's a good thing you're a lot tougher on the outside than you appear. I would've never guessed you'd have been able to take down that mugger like you did the other day. That was amazing."

"It was okay," she said modestly.

"It was more than okay and you know it," he continued, beaming at her across the kitchen.

Based on the easy back and forth of their conversation, he assumed things between them were going well, so he decided to ask her about the strange timing of the attack. Her unusual reaction to what appeared to be a harmless situation continued to perplex him.

"What I can't figure out is how you knew," he said.

"How I knew what?" she asked, loading the last of the dishes into the dishwasher.

"How you knew that the guy was going to attack Mrs. Huggins."

He hoisted himself onto the countertop and watched as she made him a to-go plate, placing the leftovers into the refrigerator. When she finished, she surprised him by crossing the kitchen to lift herself onto the counter beside him.

"I didn't know," she said resolutely.

A beautiful wisp of a woman, sitting so close he could smell the crisp fragrance of her shampoo, he cautiously reached out to place a tendril of her hair behind her ear and was pleased when she didn't recoil. "That's bull," he said. "You knew. When you told me to stay put, that guy was nowhere near them. I had absolutely no idea what you were doing. There was nothing to indicate he was going to attack them."

She stared at the linoleum tile. "There was to me. It's just good training."

He could sense she was hiding something and couldn't stop himself from continuing to press her for the truth. "What do they train you in at the police academy? Seeing into the future?"

"No. Nothing like that," she said, clearly avoiding eye contact with him as she wrung her hands in her lap.

His question caused a palpable change in her demeanor, from confident to concerned, and yet he sensed she was getting close to sharing the truth.

"Then what?" he asked.

"Thomas, can I trust you?" she asked, finally looking him in the eye.

"Yes, of course."

She took his hand and pulled him gently from the countertop. She led him into the living room where she sat on the overstuffed couch and invited him to do the same. They sat, side by side, and he reached out tentatively to hold her hand.

"I'm all ears," he said, giving her a grin. He assumed her explanation would involve something as simple as seeing the man's face on some police rap sheet which alerted her to his proclivity for crime. If that was the case, he had no idea why she was making such a production over disclosing that information.

"I have this gift," she began. "It's an ability, sort of. I figured out when I was a little girl that I could see people's auras."

"People's what?" he asked.

"Auras. At least that's what I call them. It's hard to describe, but when I look at people, I see them under a veil. It's like a shroud of light or dark. Most people's auras are light because most people are inherently good. But some people have dark auras. They don't have the light inside of them that encourages them to do the right thing. And so instead, a lot of times, they do bad things. Very bad things. When I saw the man yesterday, at the park, his aura was very dark. Because his darkness was so close to the surface it indicated to me he was about to do something bad right then. That's how I knew."

She was looking at him expectantly, clearly waiting for a response, but unfortunately, he was unable to react. As she was speaking, he had been unwillingly transported back to his third foster home and the family into which he'd been placed when we was eleven years old. His "mother" made a living reading tarot cards to unsuspecting, vulnerable people. She was a liar and a fraud and she preyed upon her client's hopes and fears in order to fund her very expensive pill habit. It was by far the most traumatic of his foster experiences, and among other more painful lessons, she unknowingly taught him to be wary of believing in things he couldn't see.

He certainly couldn't see the auras Mia was describing.

As she finished describing her affliction, he couldn't bear the thought of continuing his evening with her. On top of unknowingly dredging up uncomfortable memories, the idea of spending any more time with a woman who thought he would believe such utter nonsense was unimaginable. She clearly wasn't the woman he thought she was.

"Thomas?" she said, breaking him from his trance.

His mind raced, searching for an excuse that would free him from the apartment and the aftermath of her strange revelation.

"I know all about people with special powers," he blurted, still rattled by the memories of his past. "And I completely forgot," he added, "I have to be in early to Belinda's tomorrow. I need to go."

He sprang from the couch and crossed the apartment without waiting for her to accompany him. When he opened the door, he paused briefly to call over his shoulder.

"Thanks for dinner. It was delicious. Goodbye, Mia." With that, he shut the door behind him and walked out into the night without so much as a backwards glance.

CHAPTER

18

MIA

Thomas' abrupt departure left Mia stunned and somewhat irritated. Chelsea was gone all night with Tyler at a Justin Timberlake concert, so after he left, she was completely alone.

She rattled around, and after cleaning up what was left of dinner, sat down in front of the television. The novel Thomas brought sat on the couch beside her, but she was too annoyed to open its cover. Instead, she fumed, allowing the frustration of the experience to dig at her.

At the forefront of her concerns was Thomas' strange comment regarding his experience with gifted people. She wondered if it was the indication she was searching for – proof that he was one of her psychics. If this was the case then her line of reasoning led her to believe that it was the commissioner's true nature and not some glitch in her abilities which caused her to see his dark aura.

Aside from the oddness of his disclosure, she was also disappointment that she had felt what could only be described as a strange connection to Thomas. Although his tokens were hardly extravagant, she assumed the simple gesture of an inexpensive bouquet of carnations and a used book spoke highly of his character. Because she relied solely on her abilities, she had never learned to properly assess another person's integrity and she was disillusioned by his reaction to her truth. Based on his generosity, she expected him to be more accepting of her abilities and it infuriated her that she had judged him so poorly.

The worst part, she acknowledged reluctantly, was also the most unexpected – she was upset by the prospect of losing Thomas as a friend. Although she only connected with him out of sheer curiosity, a simple means to an end, the sadness she felt at his hasty retreat could only be attributed to a weakness of her heart.

Over dinner, she had finally been able to ignore his missing aura. She was just beginning to accept the idea that her gift wasn't infallible and that perhaps Thomas's aura was light even though she couldn't see it with her own eyes. But then, after his abrupt departure, she was surprised by how exasperated she felt, and doubt about what was truly going on began to creep into her conscious mind once again.

After a restless night of fitful sleep, she was relieved to return to work in the morning, if only to surround herself with other people and their problems as a means of forgetting about her own. As soon as she entered the station, she headed toward her father's office in search of solace for her anguished mind.

"Morning, Sunshine," her father greeted her as she came through the door. "Except you don't look so sunny. What's the matter?"

She collapsed into the chair beside him. "Do you want the long version or the short version?" she asked.

"I've got time for either one," he said, scrolling through his email.

She yawned and rubbed her eyes.

"Well, ever since we discussed the commissioner and how he appeared to me, I've been living under the pretense that the problem is me. And not just because of the commissioner."

He looked up from the computer, giving her his full attention. "Oh really?"

"Yeah." She paused. She was hesitant to share personal information with her father, especially when it came to men. "Dad, I've sort of been seeing the lineup guy. The one without the aura."

He slapped his forehead with the palm of his hand.

"You're kidding."

"No. I'm not. I introduced myself because I thought meeting him might help me make sense of what's going on with my powers, but after last night I'm even more confused than ever," she said.

"You've lost me. Maybe I need the long version," Rosetti said, leaning back in his chair.

"Okay," she said, beginning again. "After you and I talked, I decided there was no way the darkness I was seeing around the commissioner could be a true indication of the state of his soul. That also suggested to me that the reason I was unable to see an aura around Thomas Pritchett had nothing to do with him and was probably also because of something going on with me. We ran into each other a few times and began spending time together. I figured if I could prove that he was just a nice, normal person it would confirm that the reason for his missing aura was just a glitch. On the other hand, if I discovered something weird about him, then I was gonna let you know that we might need to look into the commissioner more closely."

Her father scratched the back of his hand on the stubble under his chin. "We're still talking about the lineup guy, right?"

"Yes, Dad! And I was starting to believe he was a nice, normal person. At least until last night."

"Mia. What happened? If that man laid a hand on you so help me…"

"No, Dad, no. It was nothing like that." She paused, hesitating to continue with her story.

"Then what did he do?" Rosetti asked, his voice heavy with concern and dread.

"I told him."

"You told him what?"

"About the auras."

"Oh, Mia," he replied, shaking his head. "What did he say?"

"He said he knew all about people with special powers and then he just got up and left. That was it. He didn't even ask for an explanation. He just ended the evening without another word."

Her father looked at her indifferently. "I'm sorry. But I can't say I'm surprised. That man is probably trouble."

"Well, I was surprised. And it got me thinking. Maybe I was right about Thomas after all. Maybe the reason I can't see his aura *is* related to him and maybe that reason has absolutely nothing to do with me. Maybe I was wrong to have discounted my abilities."

"Maybe you were," Rosetti confirmed.

"But," she continued, "if I was wrong about him then maybe I was right about the commissioner."

"Aw, Honey, not this again."

"Yes, Dad, this again. You don't know what I know. You don't see what I see. I think it might be worth looking into."

"Officer Rosetti," he said, his voice suddenly authoritative so it was clear to her he was no longer addressing her as a parent, "I have been a police officer for thirty-one years. I pride myself on the work I've done and the work I do every day. Do you think for one minute I would support someone who I thought had any chance of being a less than honorable man?"

She remained silent.

"Do you?" he asked again, his voice rising as his composure began to crumble.

She focused on her shoes. "No, Chief."

"No is right! So I don't know what you think you've seen or what story you've concocted in your own mind regarding the commissioner, but I've heard the last of it. The commissioner comes highly regarded from the top echelon of the law enforcement community. If he's good enough for them, he's good enough for me."

He paused momentarily. As she stood from her seat and turned to leave the room, Rosetti spoke once more in the same authoritative voice.

"And Mia, as for the lineup guy… stay away from him."

She left the room without responding. Instead of returning to her office, she headed to the women's restroom where she braced herself against the aging pedestal sink and gazed into the hazy, patinaed mirror. Although she felt as though she wanted to explode, she was surprised to see her outward appearance revealed none of her internal turmoil. Until the recent developments with the commissioner and Thomas, she had always been confident in herself and her abilities. But now, she felt the entire foundation of her self-assurance collapsing beneath her, and for the first time since her isolated childhood, was discouraged.

She splashed her face with cool water and dried off with a paper towel. She wished there was someone she could talk to about her powers, as what she really needed was a sympathetic ear, and as she considered the people in her life she could turn to, she found herself thinking of Thomas. Strangely, in the short span of time she'd known him, she had already begun to feel he would be someone safe to confide in. Unfortunately, after the events of the night before, she now knew that wasn't the case.

That meant the only person left was Jack.

Back in her office, she found him in the middle of logging evidence into the police database from yet another meth house. He didn't move his eyes from the computer screen as she entered the room.

"What's shakin' bacon?" he asked.

"Not much," she replied. "Do you want some help?"

"Yeah. Sure. If you read them out to me, I'll be able to log this stuff faster," he replied. As he handed her the file, he finally looked at her face.

"You're pissed," he said.

"I'm not," she replied.

"Mia, I grew up in a household of sisters. I'm married to the most emotional woman on the planet. I know when someone's upset. You don't have to talk to me about it, but don't lie to me and tell me you're not angry about something."

"Fine," she acknowledged. "I'm angry. Are you happy now?"

"No. I'm not happy you're angry. But I am happy you aren't lying to me anymore."

"Fine."

"Fine."

She began reading out file numbers and their corresponding articles to be categorized in the database. Test tubes, burners, chemical solutions, weapons, meth… the list seemed endless. After twenty minutes of logging, she couldn't keep her mouth shut any longer.

"I told Thomas about my aura thing and he bailed because he says he knows all about people like me. I thought he was a nice, normal guy, and that I was just being glitchy, but maybe I was wrong. Maybe the fact he doesn't have an aura is actually because he's hiding something. If that's the case, then maybe the commissioner's dark aura is real too."

Jack took a deep breath and pushed his chair away from the desk, stretching his back and legs.

"Okay," he said. "Well, all that sucks. But which part of it has you the most upset?"

She thought for several moments, knowing she should be more upset about the commissioner than she was about Thomas because clearly, the ramifications of having an evil man at the helm of the entire Baltimore City Police Department were huge. However, if she was being honest with herself, losing Thomas was a far more devastating blow.

When she didn't speak, Jack interjected. "That's what I thought," he said.

She scowled. "What did you think?"

"It's the guy."

"You think you know me so well." She tapped a pencil angrily on her desk. "So what if it is the guy?"

"Nothing. So what if it is?"

She threw the pencil at him. "I'm not looking for a boyfriend, Jack. It wasn't even like that. He's kind of a wuss and a little over sensitive, but he's hard-working and funny and I honestly thought we were starting to be friends." She rested her head in her hands. "But after last night, I guess not."

"He freaked out?" Jack asked.

"Yeah. Big time."

He chuckled. "Mia, do you remember when you told me about the auras?"

"Yeah."

"I freaked out."

"No. You didn't. You were fine."

"Mia," Jack said, "I'm telling you. I freaked out. I didn't say anything because, well, for better or worse, I was stuck with you for a partner..."

"Hey!" she said, throwing a second pencil at his head.

"All I mean is that it took me some time to wrap my head around it. Once I saw what you could do and how it worked, it became an easier pill to swallow. And you have to admit, it's weird, Mia."

"Yeah. It's weird I guess." She chewed at a hangnail on her thumb. "So what are you saying?"

"I'm saying, give the guy some time. Let him get a hold of it. From his perspective, you went from this nice, normal, girl next door to a carnival attraction in two seconds."

"Hey! Watch it, Buster!" she replied initially before stopping to assess his point of view. "I guess you're right though," she relented.

"I know I'm right. I've been in his shoes. I can't believe I'm saying this, but give your lineup guy a break on this one. He does anything else to you, I'll break his neck, but for this one, I'm on his side."

"Fine."

"Now, you wanna talk about the commissioner?"

"No. Not really."

"Okay then."

They logged half a dozen articles into the system before Mia set down her file.

"Do you want to talk about the commissioner?" she asked.

"Honestly?" Jack asked, looking up from the computer screen once again.

"Honestly."

"No," he replied.

"Oh." She was disappointed. "Why not?"

"Because, Mia, nothing good can come of it. Let's say you're right, and the guy is rotten to the core. What exactly can we do about it? We can't cry foul on your hunch. He'd actually have to do something illegal. On the other hand, let's say you're wrong and the commissioner is the salt of the earth but you go stirring up rumors he's a criminal. Then what? Best case, you lose your job. Worst case, you end up in prison for slander."

She slouched into her chair. "So what should I do? Nothing?"

"Maybe we can just keep our eyes open. See if we notice anything strange going on. Other than that, I think we do nothing," Jack explained.

"Okay. Then we watch and wait."

"Watch and wait," he agreed.

CHAPTER

19

THOMAS

His fingers moved across the keys in slow waves of black and white. Without thinking about which notes he was actually playing, his mind was squarely focused on Mia and her bizarre confession. He didn't realize his melody was winding its way through the house, into the back hallway and up the stairs. He was unaware he'd woken Mildred from her sleep.

She appeared behind him in her robe and slippers and placed her hands gently on his shoulders.

"What's the matter?" she asked, her voice thick with worry and fear.

"Nothing," he responded without removing his fingers from the keys.

"Thomas Pritchett, I have been your mother for eleven years and in all that time I've only heard you play this piece twice before. Once when you arrived and once when Dad died. So when I wake up this morning to this melody again, don't you tell me nothing's wrong."

He stopped playing and turned on the piano bench to face his mother. Although he had always been grateful for her well-placed concern, he was, at the moment, unable to explain to her what he was feeling.

"Is this about the girl? Mia? Did the date go poorly?"

He bowed his head, upset at himself for being unable to shrug free of his strange connection to her. As much as he had tried throughout the night, he found he was unable to unwind himself from her.

"Thomas?" Mildred said, lifting his face to meet hers.

"The date was good. Great even. She's an amazing woman. She's smart. She's funny. She's courageous. She's beautiful." He stopped, unable to go on.

"It sounds like you're really falling for this girl. So what happened?" Mildred asked, sitting on the bench beside him.

"She's a fraud."

"A fraud?"

"Yeah. A fraud. A phony. A liar."

"What would make you say that?" Mildred asked.

He frowned, furious at the thought of being lied to. "She told me she can see people's 'auras.' She says when she looks at people she can see if they are good or bad by what kind of light they have around them. It's so much crap. I don't know why she would say something like that to me. She's no better than Madame Freakshow." He ran his hands roughly through his hair. "They're liars, both of them."

Mildred was thoughtful for a moment as her fingers traced the veins in her aging hands. She was choosing her words carefully so as not to upset him. Finally, she spoke, quietly but with unwavering resolve.

"Why do you think she would tell you that?"

"Exactly!" he exploded. "Why would she feel the need to lie to me?"

"Has it occurred to you that maybe she's not lying? Or at the very least, that maybe she believes what she's saying is true?"

He regarded his mother beside him on the bench - a religious woman who had always warned him of being wary of those who claimed to have what she called supernatural powers.

"Are you suggesting she can actually tell if someone is good or bad just by looking at them? That's crazy! I won't allow people in my life that can't be trusted. Never again."

She placed a soothing hand on the small of his back. "I'm just saying that it sounds to me like she has no reason to lie to you. That's all. Nothing more. What do you think she was hoping to gain by telling you about this ability of hers?"

"I don't know? Maybe she wanted me to think she was special or something."

"Does that sound like something she would do?"

"No," he admitted.

"And before this admission of hers, did she give you any reason at all for you to believe she was untrustworthy in any way?" Mildred asked.

He recalled how peaceful he felt in her presence. "No," he said finally.

The two sat in silence for several minutes.

"Faith," Mildred said finally, "involves believing in things you cannot see. And sometimes it involves believing in people. So until this Mia of yours gives you a reason to believe she is not a trustworthy person, perhaps you should give her the benefit of the doubt."

"Really?" He was surprised by Mildred's acceptance of Mia's ridiculous claims.

"Yes, really. Thomas, you bought a new shirt for this girl for crying out loud. She's got to be pretty special," she said, smiling warmly at him. The sincerity of her smile crinkled the skin at the corners of her eyes and lit up her entire face. Slowly, he could feel that she was beginning to tear down his wall.

"She is, Ma. She's an incredible woman. But why in the world would she go all paranormal on me? You know what my life was like with The Freakshow. I can't go through that again."

"So have faith in Mia. She's not that woman. She's not. She's a girl who thinks for whatever reason she can do something that seems improbable but that you have no way of verifying one way or another. So, for now, for argument's sake, assume she's telling you the truth."

"Can I do that?" he asked pondering the possibility.

"Can you?" Mildred replied.

"Yes," he answered, surprising himself with his acknowledgement.

"Okay."

"Okay," he said, standing from the bench and walking toward the steps.

"Where are you going?" Mildred asked.

"If I hurry, I can still make it to work at Belinda's on time," he called over his shoulder, taking the steps two at a time. Halfway up he stopped, turned on his heel, and headed back down the steps to where Mildred was still perched on the piano bench. He bent down to give her a hug and placed a quick kiss on her cheek.

"Thanks, Ma," he said, "you're the best."

Mondays were always busy at Belinda's. He was happy for the distraction the steady flow of patrons provided. He passed from one table to the next, an invisible entity among the customers. As he cleared dishes and swept crumbs from the tables, people continued their conversations, oblivious to his presence.

He was always amazed by the discussions he was privy to over the course of the years. He heard women discussing intimate details of their sexual liaisons with men who weren't their husbands. He heard businessmen discussing illegal stock transactions. He watched patrons drink from other people's glasses and steal from their friends' wallets.

As he was clearing one of the last tables of the afternoon, he noticed a group of unfamiliar men sitting at a four top in the corner of the restaurant. Most of Belinda's weekday customers were regulars who he recognized by face if not by name, so it seemed strange that he had never seen this particular group of men before. They were laughing amongst themselves and had grown increasingly boisterous with each bottle of wine they had uncorked. By the time the bill was paid, he was relieved for the peace that was restored as the last of the men left through the main entrance. He quickly locked the doors behind them and reversed the sign which hung on the glass to 'closed.'

It was customary for him to finish his assigned closing duties, clock out, and then linger with Belinda and some of the other staff while they prepared the dough for the following day. On this day however, after he reset all of the tables for the following morning and emptied the trash, he punched his time card and headed out the door.

The bus ride to the police station would prove to be the longest twenty-five minutes of the day.

CHAPTER

20

KATE

The flight to America was long. And loud. And cold. There was no heating system on board and without their luggage, the three women had only the clothes they were wearing for warmth. Kate eventually convinced the others to risk unbuckling themselves from their seats so they could huddle together on the floor. However, their attempt at using one another's body heat to stay warm proved to be only moderately successful.

During the course of their ten hour trip, it was as if the girls had established an unspoken pact to ignore the strangeness of their situation. They chose instead to discuss the future their American adventure was going to provide.

"What do you think our apartment will be like?" Lera asked as she rubbed her hands together.

"I saw on an American television show that all of their apartments have stone floors and walls made of marble. And there are crystal chandeliers and huge bathrooms and rooms to put your clothes that you can walk inside! Can you imagine having a whole room just for your clothes?" Anya gushed.

"I can't imagine having so many clothes that I would need an entire room for them," Kate said. "My sisters and I have one wardrobe for all three of us."

Anya blew into her hands and stuck them beneath her armpits. "How many people do you think will be there?" she asked. "Do you think it will just be the three of us?"

"That would be nice, but I bet there will be others. To be honest, I was hoping there would be a few boys," Lera said smiling.

"Speaking of boys," Anya added, "I was hoping to meet an American boy to secure a green card so I will never have to go back. If I never step foot in the Ukraine again, it will be fine with me. My future is in America."

Kate was disappointed by Anya's poor attitude toward their country. "Henry and Patrick are expecting us to return home so we can improve the Ukraine's future," she said. "You won't be helping your family if you never go back."

"My family never helped me," said Anya frankly. "I don't owe them or the country anything. Everything in my life, I've earned on my own."

Kate shivered in her thin coat and slid closer to Lera. "Well, I'll be going back," she said. "My sisters and my parents are counting on me. And I owe everything I have to them. So, American boy or not, I'll be going back home."

"Me too," said Lera, pulling her arms into her sleeves. "I have three little brothers who need me. My father died six months ago. I was able to finish out this semester because it was already paid for, but without my father's income, there is no more money for school. There is really no more money for anything. I'm going to save everything I can to send home to them. And please don't tell, but I won't be using the money I earn for school. I can't. Not when my brothers need to eat."

"I'm sorry about your father, Lera, and I promise I won't tell," she said.

"Me neither," agreed Anya.

The girls struggled to keep warm and leaned against one another for support as the plane sped toward America at forty thousand feet. At some point during the trip, the adrenaline of the day having long since worn off, Kate found she could no longer keep her eyes open. Mercifully, she drifted off to sleep.

She was awoken by hunger in the form of stomach cramps and painful spasms, and it depressed her further when she realized twelve hours had passed since she'd eaten breakfast with her family. The cold seemed trivial as now all she could think of was food. She shifted her position in an attempt to ease her discomfort, but her movements roused the other girls.

"How much longer do you think it will take us to get there?" Lera asked, stretching her arms far above her head as she struggled to unfold herself from her crouched position.

"I don't know, but I'm hungry," groaned Anya. "Do you think there's any food here on the plane?"

"Maybe, but it's not for us if there is. I'm sure we'll be there soon," Kate said brightly, the tone of her voice masking the true feeling of desperation that was beginning to seep into her bones.

"I hope they will have a grand buffet to welcome us when we arrive," said Lera.

Kate's stomach churned. "I'd be happy with some plain toast and tea right now," she said woefully, huddled between the other two, trembling and ravenous as the plane lurched forward, jostling them uncomfortably into one another. She wished silently that their trip would soon be over.

"My ears are popping," Anya exclaimed suddenly. "Perhaps we are landing!"

Mercifully, the plane began its steady descent and the girls returned to their seats, buckling their safety belts in preparation for the landing. As the wheels of the plane met the tarmac, the girls held hands and braced themselves against the terrific force of the plane as it slowed. They sat together quietly as the plane maneuvered around the runway, none of them wanting to break through the silence which accompanied the heavy anticipation of the moment. When at last the plane came to a stop and the cargo door was opened, nothing about the strangeness of the situation improved.

Two men appeared at the opening, burly and unshaven.

"Let's go," the larger of the two called across the expanse of the cargo bay.

Kate hesitantly unbuckled and rose to her feet, unsteady from the many hours of sitting crouched together with the others on the floor. The men were certainly not the welcoming party she'd expected and she was immediately disappointed by their appearance.

"Quickly!" the man called again.

Kate made her way with the others out of the plane, down the steps and onto the ground. After having spent the better part of a day trapped within the dim confines of the plane, she squinted at the blinding sun, shielding her eyes with both hands. The noise of the surrounding planes was deafening and she yelled loudly to the closest of the men as they crossed the tarmac.

"Are Henry and Patrick meeting us?" she called.

She didn't know whether the man was unable to hear her or was simply choosing not to respond, so she increased her stride and caught up beside him, pulling at his arm to get his attention.

"Are Henry and Patrick meeting us?" she repeated.

"Yeah. Sure, Honey," he replied. "You'll see them when we get there."

"When we get where? To the apartment?"

"Yeah. To the apartment."

Kate turned to Lera and Anya and took their hands. They followed the men, weaving through the sea of cargo planes and shipping freights until they came to a van on the edge of the airport grounds. She stopped, not knowing what to do.

"Get in," came a voice from behind them. She turned to see that a third man had joined the group. Dressed in work overalls and a heavy hooded red sweatshirt, the expression on his face was less than welcoming.

"I believe there has been a mistake," said Anya cautiously. "We are students from the university in Kiev. We are here on a work visa and are meeting our sponsors to take us to our apartment."

"There's been no mistake. Get in the van."

The girls filed into the windowless van one after the other. There were no seats and they were forced to sit directly on the cold metal floor.

"Do you have our luggage?" Lera asked.

"We've got another van bringing it," said one of the men as he got into the front of the van.

The doors were slammed shut and locked. Within moments the girls were on the move once again. They sat in silence, unable or unwilling to acknowledge the graveness of the situation aloud to one another. Anya and Lera appeared frightened and Kate imagined that her face wore the same grim expression.

After several minutes, Lera whispered, "This is not at all how I imagined it was going to be."

"Me neither," said Anya.

"Me neither," she said. Her thoughts were racing, struggling to understand what was happening around her. Doubt was creeping into the recesses of her mind as she tried to piece together what she knew. Henry and Patrick had not yet made an appearance. Their baggage was missing. They had flown somewhere in a cargo plane and were now being taken in a van to another undisclosed location. They had not been offered food or water or an opportunity to use the bathroom. She decided it was time to ask for what she wanted so she crawled to the front of the van and knocked on the partition which separated them from the men. A small door slid open.

"What?" the driver asked.

"Sir, we are quite hungry. We haven't eaten in hours. Also, we need to use the restroom. So I was wondering if we could stop."

"We'll be there soon. There'll be food. And a bathroom."

"How much longer?"

"Soon," the man replied without hiding the annoyance in his voice.

True to his word, the van stopped five minutes later and she allowed herself to feel excitement for the first time since boarding the plane. However, as the door slid open to reveal the inside of a large abandoned warehouse, another man greeted them with a sneer, and her stomach lurched when she noticed he was carrying a gun.

Lera grasped her arm tightly and cowered behind her. Anya, on the other hand, moved swiftly to the doorway.

"I don't know who you think we are, but you are clearly misinformed. We are students. We've come here to work. You need to take us back to the airport at once so we can clear this up because there has obviously been a mistake."

"Feisty, that one is," said the man in the red sweatshirt who appeared behind the one leveling the gun in the girls' direction. "Listen up, Missy. Let me tell you how this is all going to go down. I need all three of you to turn around and put your hands behind your backs. We're gonna restrain you for now, in case you get any funny ideas. After you're in your rooms, we'll take off the ropes, but only if you do just as you're told. Nod your heads if you understand, but don't open your mouths again unless you have permission."

Kate and Lera nodded and turned around as they'd been instructed, but Anya inched closer to the open door.

"Take her," the man in the red sweatshirt said to the one with the gun. The armed man threw himself at Anya, easily pinning her to the floor of the van where he quickly bound her arms behind her back. Anya was led from the van down a staircase at the far end of the room, and Kate heard her screams echo through the warehouse as a rope tightened around her own wrists. As tears streamed down Lera's face, Kate watched her being lead from the van in the same direction Anya had been taken only moments before.

She turned to face the two men before her and willed herself to remain stoic. She avoided making eye contact and kept her head high as they closed the van door behind her.

"Good lookin' group this time," the man with the gun commented as they descended a set of concrete stairs into the basement of the warehouse.

"Yeah, too bad about the tall one's attitude. I hope she doesn't make trouble. Boss won't like that."

"This one though," the gunman said, poking the weapon into the small of her back, "she's a beauty. Steak dinners for everyone tonight!"

As they reached the foot of the stairs, she was overcome by the stench and the thickness of the air. She gagged, thankful for the first time since her trip began that there was nothing in her stomach. She looked around the dimly lit room. The ceiling was low, only a couple of inches above the heads of the men leading Lera and Anya in front of her. The walls were solid concrete, as were the floors. The room was divided into about a dozen cells, each with a small mattress on the floor and a makeshift toilet that was little more than a hole in the ground.

As she was led down the narrow walkway that ran between the two rows of cells, she looked into the eyes of each of the women who were already caged inside. She counted eleven in all and each one she passed caused her feeling of desperation to grow. The women were filthy, reeking of their own excrement. Several looked severely malnourished to the point of starvation. But it was their eyes that haunted her as she passed before them. Their eyes were hollow. Empty. Devoid of hope or desire.

"Stop here," said the man as they reached an empty cell toward the end of the line. He opened the door and without the need for any physical aggression, she entered the cage willingly.

Anya was being placed in the cell directly across from her. She continued to scream and flail, kicking her feet and throwing her head in all directions. Lera succumbed willingly to her keepers, entering the cell beside her without incident.

Once inside, she turned her back to the gunman who was still standing before her, getting ready to close the door. She held up her hands and turned her head so she could see his face. He met her gaze and without speaking a word, she willed the man to remove her bindings.

"You wanna take off their restraints?" he asked the other men.

"Let those two go," said the man in the red sweatshirt, pointing to her and Lera. "But leave the tall one tied up. Gonna have to break her down."

The gunman removed the ropes from around her wrists and closed the door to the cell. He did the same to Lera, who continued to sob quietly. When Anya was finally contained inside her cell, the men headed toward the staircase without another word.

"There's food," Lera whispered as Kate watched the last man disappear up the steps. "There. Look on the floor."

She turned around to see a sandwich and a water bottle on the floor behind her. It was far from the feast the girls had imagined, but at that moment, it was the answer to her prayers. Bland and stale but full of essential calories, she devoured the sandwich as she watched her friends doing the same. However, as the food hit her stomach, a sickening feeling settled over her that had nothing to do with what she was eating.

All at once, she realized what was happening to her was not a mistake. She acknowledged with a wave of nausea her fate had been decided from the moment she responded to the flyer that was hung in the student union. There was no apartment. No job. No money to be sent home. She knew without a doubt there was a reason she was locked inside the cell, but she couldn't begin to imagine what that reason was. As she finished off the last bite of her sandwich, a final revelation washed over her. With much regret and despair she realized that somewhere in Kiev, five thousand miles away, she had already doomed her sisters to the same fate. A fate she doubted even her miraculous power could undo.

CHAPTER

21

MIA

It had been a relatively uneventful afternoon as Mia and Jack returned from their patrol. They issued two citations for public drunkenness and picked up a teenage boy for drug possession, but as they pulled the squad car into the fenced lot behind the station, she was feeling unsettled. As much as she tried to put her worries behind her, she couldn't stop thinking about a way to mend her relationship with Thomas. So when she saw him leaning casually against the wall of the building directly behind the station, her mood improved immediately.

"He's here," she said to Jack as they pulled into their parking spot.

"Who's here?"

"Thomas."

He punched her playfully in the arm. "That was fast," he said.

She hesitated to open the door, unsure of what she would say or do once she was forced to acknowledge him standing across the alley.

"Just go talk to him," Jack said, sensing her apprehension. "I'll file the paperwork from this afternoon and you go get things straightened out with Mr. Lineup."

She sat frozen in her seat. "What if he's still freaking out?"

"If he was still upset, he wouldn't be here," he declared. "Now go, before I make a scene."

She pulled the handle and the heavy door of the police cruiser creaked open, alerting Thomas to her presence. She chanced a glance in his direction and saw him smiling at her. She waved, returning his smile and he began walking in her direction.

"Hi," he said as they met in the middle of the alley.

"Hey," she replied.

He rocked nervously on his heels. "I didn't mean to interrupt you at work."

"It's okay, my shift's almost over."

"Oh. Okay. Well, still, I'm sorry to just show up here like this. I was going to wait until you came out at the end of the day. I didn't know you were out on patrol. I just didn't want to miss you, even though now I look like a stalker."

"You have my number. You could have called."

He shoved his hands in his coat pockets and she could tell he was anxious. "Yeah. I know. But what I have to say I kind of needed to say face to face."

She felt a stone sink in her stomach, thinking that maybe what he wanted to say was goodbye.

"I can wait here until you're finished work, and then, if you're interested, I was gonna blow off my piano gig for a couple of hours tonight to see if you wanted to go grab something to eat together," Thomas said, his voice hopeful.

"Can you give me ten minutes to change my clothes?" she asked, excited by the possibility of setting things right.

His face brightened. "Of course. I'll wait out here."

She rushed through the station, nearly running over several fellow officers along the way. She stopped briefly by her office to grab the street clothes she kept stashed beneath her desk.

"Well?" asked Jack as she breezed through the door.

"He wants to go get something to eat."

"That's good?"

"Yeah. That's good. I hope. Then again, he might just be taking me out to explain why he never wants to see me again."

"I doubt that. He looked happy to see you."

"I guess we'll see. See you tomorrow, Jack," she said as she headed back into the hallway toward the locker room.

After changing, she hurried back outside to meet Thomas and they climbed into her civilian car.

"Did you have somewhere in mind?" she asked as she placed the key in the ignition.

"There's this diner just up the road that's really good," he offered.

She knew exactly where he was talking about – she'd eaten there with her father many times. "On the corner of Holliday and Saratoga?"

"That's the one."

"Sounds good to me," she said earnestly.

She made a three-point turn in the crowded parking lot and headed toward the interstate out of the city. She drove in silence, afraid of saying anything to upset him and disturb their unspoken truce. Finally, as they pulled into the parking lot of the diner, he spoke.

"Mia, about last night. I'm sorry. I acted like a jerk."

"No. You didn't," she replied. "You acted the way any normal person would react when someone tells you they can do something that's preposterous. It's my fault. It was too soon to say anything. I just felt like…"

"Like I would be more understanding?" he ventured.

"Something like that," she said, turning off the ignition and sliding around in her seat to face him. "Should we continue this conversation inside?"

"Sure. I'm starving," he replied, attempting to suppress a grin.

They walked into the restaurant and the hostess seated them in a booth at the far end of the building where they sat across from one another at the table. After receiving menus and giving their drink orders, she continued their conversation where they left off.

"Thomas, I don't know why you came to the station today. Well, I hope I know. But I want to tell you I'm sorry too. You asked about how I knew the man was going to attack Mrs. Huggins and for some reason that went against everything I've ever done in the past, I had to tell you the truth. I'm sorry I shared it without preparing you for it in a better way."

He looked at her with more compassion than she deserved. "Mia, first, you have no reason to apologize. Don't ever apologize to anyone for who you are, even if you are slightly…"

"Weird?"

"Unusual. A little unusual," he laughed. "I'd like to explain myself too, not to excuse my behavior, but in the interest of full disclosure, since it appears that's what we have going on here."

She hoped he was about to tell her about his gift – the reason he knew all about people with special powers.

"I'm all ears," she replied.

"Perfect." He took a deep breath. "My third foster family, between the ages of eleven and thirteen, was the worst. It was physically better than the previous two, but was psychologically disturbing for me."

She cringed at the thought of him being abused in any way and wondered what it had to do with his ability.

"The man and woman I lived with had three children of their own, but they weren't real parents in any sense of the word. For the most part, I took care of myself and just tried to stay out of the way. The woman though…" He paused. "I've never hated anyone. Not the men who beat me or the women who let them do it. But this woman, I can honestly say, I hated her."

"What did she do to you?" she whispered, reaching across the table to take his hands. They were warm. Strong. Solid.

145

"I called her Madame Freakshow behind her back because she pretended to be a medium. She would have customers in the house at all hours of the day and night for tarot card readings and séances. The four of us kids were at her beck and call whenever she needed us during her performances. We were in charge of creating the 'effects.' We hid under the floor and knocked when she asked for signs from the spirit world. We turned fans on so the curtains would move. We made the lights go on and off. It was ridiculous. She was a liar and a fraud. I hated her because she made me feel like a liar and a fraud too. I can never forgive her for that." He paused, and she could see the pain in his eyes. "The worst part was that these poor people would come to her for help and guidance believing she was really able to see things she actually couldn't. I learned as much from them as I did from her."

"Because the people who believed in her were idiots," she surmised.

"Sometimes. Mostly they were just naïve."

She suddenly understood that the reason he left so abruptly the night before had nothing to do with having his own ability and everything to do with a troubling past experience.

"So you learned you should never trust what you can't see," she said.

"Yeah. Something like that." He hesitated and looked her directly in the eyes, his hands still in hers. She could feel the intensity of his gaze and was powerless to look away. "But you aren't Madame Freakshow," he said.

"I'm not," she replied.

"I know that now, but last night..."

"I get it," she said lightly, releasing her grip on his hands as she absorbed the full ramification of what he disclosed. "Last night, I was just another woman selling you a load of crap."

"You are definitely not 'just another woman.'"

"The load of crap part then," she laughed.

A blush spread across his cheeks. "Maybe a little," he admitted.

"It's okay," she replied, suddenly remembering the Sevens Prophecy. "There are a lot of bogus stories out there. A lot of people pretending to have abilities they don't possess. It makes it hard for those of us who have genuine talents to be taken seriously. In fact, just the other day I came across this ridiculous prophecy online. Seven bad psychics, seven good ones, all born on the same day to stop seven sins from taking over the world. Stuff like that gives legitimate psychics a bad reputation."

Thomas stiffened in his seat and took a sip of his water. "The Freakshow used to talk about that. She believed in it. Said it would usher in the end of days."

Mia closed her menu. "See what I mean? I shouldn't be surprised when people have trouble believing me when I tell them what I can do. Some of the reports are just too much. I sift through a lot of garbage in search of the truth."

The waitress appeared to take their orders and they both quickly decided what they wanted to eat.

"So," he began, as soon as the waitress was gone, "tell me more about it."

"About the auras?"

"Yeah, about the auras. How does it work?"

She thought for a moment and tried to figure out a way to explain what she saw without sounding like a liar or a fraud.

"I have no idea what the rest of the world sees when they look at other people. All I know is what I see. When I was four, I realized that what I see is different from what others see. Apparently the rest of you don't see the auras."

"I definitely don't see any auras," he said. "Maybe if I did I would've had better luck with foster families."

"Perhaps," she said, happy with how calmly he was discussing her ability.

"So Madame Freakshow, for example. If you looked at her, what do you think you would see?" he asked.

"It sounds as though she would have been surrounded by a darkness. It's almost like a smoky fog. But instead of moving through it, it's almost as if the person is shrouded by the darkness."

"And the mugger who attacked Mrs. Huggins, how did you know he was about to do something?"

"The fog around him was dark. Thick. Almost opaque."

"So how was that different than it would have been if he'd had no intentions of harming anyone at that moment?"

"The darkness would have been more see-through. Less cloudy."

She watched him staring at her. The sadness that had been a part of him on the very first day still remained, and yet, he seemed at peace. He smiled at her.

"What?" she asked.

"What do you see when you look at me?" he asked.

She faltered. The smile began to fade from her lips, but she quickly regained her composure. She wavered momentarily between telling him the truth and telling him what he needed to hear. Although the truth would give her valuable insight into whether he possessed his own gift, she knew it might also destroy him.

"I see pure light surrounding you," she replied at last.

"Really?" he asked, visibly shaken by her admission.

"Yes," she confirmed.

"Then they didn't break me after all," mused Thomas, a crooked smile forming on his lips.

"No. They didn't."

Their meals arrived. She'd ordered a burger and fries and Thomas the chicken parmesan. They ate in silence for several minutes.

"You like Italian," she observed aloud.

"It's my favorite," he said, his mouth full of linguini. "I guess that means you're kind of perfect for me."

"I guess so," she replied, smiling at his admission.

He took a bite of bread dipped in sauce. "Can I ask you more?"

"Of course," she said, delighted that he was willing to discuss the mechanics of her gift.

"Do people change?" he asked, twirling his pasta around his fork. "You know, if you're dark, can you become light? Or if you are born light, can you turn dark?"

Mia was impressed by the astute nature of his question. "I don't know for sure. All the babies I've ever seen have been light. I don't know if babies are ever born dark, but maybe they are. I've never seen one though. So by that line of reasoning, if we assume all babies are born in light, then at some point, they would have to change to dark. I've never actually seen anyone change from one to the other. But I have seen people with lights that are very dim. I've always suspected that, if the light gets dim enough, it could eventually go out altogether. That's when the darkness takes over I guess."

"So do people ever surprise you or do you always know what to expect from them?"

She immediately thought of the commissioner. He was clearly an instance of someone who, by his actions, should be bathed in light. But she saw the darkness. If her ability was still fully intact, she could only assume his public actions masked his true intentions. Although she prayed this wasn't the case, it caused her to pause briefly while she decided whether to share information about the commissioner with him.

"What is it?" Thomas asked, sensing her hesitation.

"If I tell you something, it has to be just between you and me. Can I trust you?" she asked.

"I'm here, Mia. I'm sticking around. You can trust me."

She closed her eyes, filled her lungs with air, and breathed out slowly through her nose. She didn't know why she felt compelled to share her fears with him, but for some reason, she believed it was the right thing to do. When she opened her eyes and saw the compassion reflected back to her in his face, somehow she felt she could trust him with her life.

"I don't know if you've been following the news, but a few weeks ago, Baltimore got a new police commissioner."

"I think I heard something about it on the radio at work."

"Well, I've met him. He works closely with my father. He comes highly decorated. And highly recommended by high ranking people."

"And?"

"And there is no light surrounding him."

"He's a police officer. The head of the police department. How can his aura be dark?"

"I don't know. My father's convinced I'm short circuiting and that I'm wrong about him. And I'm starting to think he might be right." She popped her last fry into her mouth. "Honestly, I don't know what to believe anymore."

He set down his fork and gave her his undivided attention. "Have you been wrong about anyone before?"

She thought about telling him how she couldn't see his aura but stopped herself, remembering her earlier deception. "Not that I know of," she said at last.

"So why would you be wrong now?"

She shrugged dramatically. "I don't know."

They sat in silence as the bill arrived. He scooped it off the table before she had a chance to react and handed the waitress enough cash to pay for both meals and an ample tip.

"That was really good," she commented about both the food and the company as the waitress disappeared into the kitchen. "Thanks."

"It was and you're welcome," said Thomas glancing at his watch. "I hate that I have to leave."

"Me too. But it's Monday night so I guess you need to hurry down to the hotel."

"Yeah. There are a bunch of conventions in town this week, so I should do well. Have to wow the crowds for the big bucks now that I have a beautiful woman to woo."

"Is that what you're doing? Wooing me?" she laughed.

"What? Are you not sufficiently wooed?" he asked, feigning devastation.

She remembered how disappointed she felt when she believed he was misleading her. She didn't want to admit that despite her initial platonic motives, Thomas Pritchett was growing on her.

"I'm perfectly wooed," she replied. "In fact, I'm so wooed, I think I would like to be wooed some more."

"I would like to woo you some more," he said. "Are you free next weekend?"

She tried to recall her schedule. "I work the early shift Sunday. It's the worst one of the week. There're all the Saturday night idiots to deal with, so I would love something to look forward to after that. I'm off at three."

She could see he was pondering their options. "How about the zoo? Do you want to meet there after work? We can spend the rest of the afternoon with the animals."

The zoo was the last place she expected a grown man to take her on a date, but she was surprisingly okay with his choice. "That sounds wonderful. I haven't been to the zoo in years. And I can guarantee the animals will be far better behaved than the people I'll have spent the morning with."

"Even the lions?"

"Even the snakes."

Thomas laughed as he stood up from the booth. She was sorry the date was ending but was excited by the idea of seeing him again. As they left the diner, he reached for her hand. Each time she held his hands she was struck by how strong and sturdy they were. So different from the hands she imagined would be capable of playing such beautiful music on the piano. Her tiny hand was engulfed by his firm grip and it seemed as though he was holding onto her for dear life.

"Can I give you a ride to the hotel?" she asked as they approached her car.

"Nah. The bus stop is right across the street and gas is far too expensive to have you chauffeuring me around."

"It's no trouble."

"Mia, it's fine. Traffic downtown this time of night is awful. I won't have something happen to you on my watch."

"Thomas, I'm a cop, nothing is going to happen," she laughed.

He crossed his arms across his chest. "The answer is still no. Get home safe and I'll meet you at the front entrance to the zoo on Sunday. Can you be there around three-thirty?"

"Yes," she relented, disappointed at not having a few more minutes with him.

"Okay, then I'll see you Sunday, my mystical law enforcement agent."

"See you Sunday, Mr. Lineup Virtuoso."

Without warning, he stepped forward so he was only inches away from her. Since she was a full head shorter than he was, he slipped his hand gently under her chin to tip her face up to meet his. She caught her breath, fully aware of what was about to happen. For a moment, she hesitated, allowing the doubt she was still harboring in the recesses of her mind about him to bubble to the surface. She looked into his eyes and saw what his aura was unable to reveal. Thomas Pritchett was a good man. She closed her eyes and stood on her toes.

His lips met hers with a tender fierceness. The kiss was soft and yet it carried an intensity that traveled into her soul. When at last he pulled away from her, she placed her head on his chest and wrapped her arms around his waist.

"Goodbye, Thomas," she said.

"See ya," he replied. He kissed her once more on the top of her head and turned to walk toward the bus stop. She watched until he was out of sight and finally exhaled.

CHAPTER

22

KATE

Kate spent three miserable days locked in the tiny cell of the warehouse basement. During that time she made several discoveries. Of the thirteen other women being held captive with her, none of them were American and each of them were brought into the country under false pretenses. Most of them had at least a working understanding of the English language, but there were two Romanian women who spoke no English at all. She, Lera, and Anya were the most recent women to join the group, and she learned Svetlana had been living there the longest, 147 days by her own calculations. The rest of the women had trickled in in groups of twos and threes over the course of the past four months.

Within several hours of her arrival, she began to piece together the details which would reveal the reason for her capture. After settling Anya and consoling Lera, she took stock of her surroundings and began a discussion with the woman across the corridor in the cell beside Anya. She was a petite Asian she suspected was from Vietnam.

"Can you tell us what is happening?" she asked.

"Please don't ask me. I cannot tell you," the woman replied.

"You can't? Why not?" Anya snapped.

"I can tell you. But you will not want to hear."

153

"Are we here to work? Is this a labor camp?" Lera asked.

"Not work like you are expecting. Not with tools or mops or shovels."

"What work then?"

"The men will come for you," said a voice from several cells away.

"What men?" Kate called. "Henry and Patrick? Are they part of this?"

"I don't know any Henry or Patrick. I know only the men who take us to the others."

"What others?" Anya yelled, her voice reverberating off the cement walls. "You aren't making any sense! Just tell us what is going to happen to us!"

From the far recesses of the warehouse, the hinges of a metal door groaned and a slamming sound echoed throughout the basement. The women fell silent.

The footsteps of the men could be heard as they approached the cells. There were at least four of them and Kate held her breath as they came into view.

"Where are the new ones?" said one of the men. He was dressed in a three piece suit and was cleanly shaven, his hair slicked smoothly atop his head.

"Down at the end," replied the man who had come with them from the airport, still wearing his red sweatshirt. He was accompanied by the van driver and a second man wearing a suit and tie.

They started down the corridor and she cringed at the sight of them as they approached. She forced herself to look into the eyes of the man in the tailored suit. Strangely, she wasn't scared of him although somehow she knew she should be deathly afraid. He stood before her, his eyes scrutinizing every inch of her body. She felt violated, as if she were on display at some bizarre museum where people were the main attraction.

"This one's a find," said the man in the suit to the one in the sweatshirt. "She'll do well on Friday night."

"What do you think about the other two?" the second suited man asked.

"This one is fine," he said motioning toward Lera. "This other one is a little big. We probably have clientele for her but she won't bring top dollar, that's for sure."

"She's still better than that one they sent us last month," the sweatshirt man commented. "I have no idea why that brute was ever picked in the first place."

"I'm surprised we didn't have to pay to have her taken off our hands," the second suited man laughed.

As the conversation between the others went on, the man in the tailored suit continued staring at her. She returned his stare, matching his intensity with her own. She refused to succumb to his degrading expression by lowering her eyes in submission.

"Is Vancini in town?" he asked the others without taking his eyes from her.

"I don't know, Boss. I can find out."

"Get him on the phone. He's going to want in on this one. Good work boys."

With that, the men returned to the far end of the corridor. Three of them disappeared up the stairs, but the man in the red sweatshirt returned, passing small packages of food between the bars of the cells to each of the women. He spoke to her when he reached the end of the row, handing her the package.

"What's your name, Honey," he said smoothly.

She snatched her food from his hands and pretended to ignore him.

"I asked you for your name," he repeated, unable to contain the irritation in his voice.

She tore into the box and removed the rolls and crackers. She broke a small bite from the bread and placed it quickly into her mouth. It was stale and rough against her tongue but she continued eating it until she had finished every crumb. The man watched her critically as she ate, furrowing his eyebrows and licking his lips. When he finally realized she had no intention of engaging him in conversation, he headed down the hall and disappeared without another word.

"Tell us what all of this is about," Kate demanded of the other women as soon as they were alone once again.

"They will take us to the others."

"What others?" Anya growled. "Enough with the secrecy!"

"The other men. The ones that will pay."

"Pay for what?" Lera cried.

"For whatever they want."

The gravity of her situation settled over her during the course of the following day. The women spoke to one another but no longer dared to broach the subject of the reason for their imprisonment. They discussed their families and their homelands. And they discussed food - at length. They described for one another different types of food, amounts of food, and ways to eat the food. It was clear to her, with the exception of the men, that hunger would be one of the greatest obstacles she would encounter.

In addition to the lack of food, there were also the cold and the unsanitary conditions to consider. Although the women were being housed underground in a relatively temperate environment, there were no heating or cooling systems. Therefore, although the temperature in the basement hovered between 60 and 65 degrees, she spent an extensive amount of time balled up on the thin, filthy mattress in the corner of her cell attempting to preserve her own body heat.

Since her arrival, she had not been given the opportunity to bathe or perform any other acts of personal hygiene. On her third of day of imprisonment, she spent the morning obsessing over her desire to brush her teeth. She closed her eyes, concentrating on the simple pleasure of cleaning the residue from the surface of her teeth and walls of her mouth.

She was startled from her daydream by the familiar sound of the metal door at the top of the stairs.

Immediately alert, every muscle in her body became rigid. The man in the red sweatshirt appeared in the corridor, as he had on each day of her confinement, with the day's rations. After passing packages of food to each of the women, the man disappeared up the stairs, only to return moments later with a large box. Her heart leapt with the hope of additional food. She quickly finished her small sandwich and waited patiently by the door of her cell.

The man made his way down the hall, distributing items to each of the women. She strained to see what was being handed out but was unable to catch sight of the delivery. Instead, she began to hear wailing from the far end of the corridor.

"No!" cried one of the women. Her hysterical sobbing immediately pierced through the silence of the basement.

Within moments, the man appeared before her, a large paper bag in his hands. He handed her the bag, squeezing it carefully through the cell bars. Without a word, she opened it, unsure of what horror she would find tucked inside.

After dumping the contents of the bag on the mattress, she was initially disappointed to discover there was no extra food. However, when she saw the bottled water, toothbrush, and toothpaste, she couldn't keep from grinning. Once again her unspoken desires had been fulfilled, just as they always were.

Closer inspection of the remaining items unnerved her. There was a dress, tiny and sequined, as well as an assortment of cosmetics and a pair of heeled shoes.

"You have fifteen minutes," called the man as he disappeared again from view.

"Fifteen minutes until what?" she asked her companions.

"Fifteen minutes until they come for us," came a quiet voice from the far end of the hall.

"Who? Who is coming?" Anya demanded.

"There is no time," cautioned Svetlana. "Make yourself as presentable as possible. There are terrible consequences if you do not."

Without another word, she removed the clothing she'd been wearing since leaving the Ukraine days before. As she took off her coat, the gift her father gave her on the morning of her departure fell from her pocket onto the concrete floor. She picked up the box, opened the lid and ran her fingers over the length of the pins. The irony of the opulent life they represented was not lost on her and she knew she could never wear them in her current situation. Carefully, she closed the lid and hid the box under her mattress, hoping one day she would have the opportunity to wear them under better circumstances.

She folded her dirty clothes neatly and squeezed into the form fitting dress she'd been given. She used the bottle of water to wash her face and her hands as best she could and then attempted to brush her teeth. The minty freshness of the paste in her mouth was heavenly and she relished the feeling, rubbing her tongue carefully against the smoothness of her teeth. Convinced she was as clean as she could be given her lack of provisions, she opened the handful of cosmetics and began to make herself presentable as Svetlana had instructed.

As she smudged the ruby colored rouge across her lips she heard Lera praying quietly they would be taken to the job interviews they had been promised so many weeks before. She closed her eyes, unable to face Lera in her blissful naivety and unwilling to face the horror she suspected was lying just ahead.

Sadly, as she sat waiting for the men to arrive, she found for the first time in her life, she was beginning to doubt herself and her abilities. Never before had she imagined her gift would prove insufficient in the face of adversity. However, listening to Lera's appeals to God in the adjacent cell, she couldn't help but question whether her gift was powerful enough to assist her in escaping from hell.

CHAPTER

23

MIA

"Hey, Mia? I need to speak with you. Do you have a few minutes?" her father asked as she stood in her usual spot in the lineup room.

"Yeah. Of course. What is it?"

"There's someone I want you to meet," he said.

She followed her father to the basement of the station where suspects were held for questioning and witnesses gave their statements. He stopped abruptly just outside one of the rooms. The door was shut and yet he spoke to her quietly, as if what he was discussing involved a secret of some sort.

"The girl inside this room showed up here in the middle of the night out of her mind with some crazy story about being held captive by a group of men in a basement somewhere here in the city. She's foreign. Claims she's from Poland, but her English is good. She's emaciated and my bet is she's on meth and is delusional. We filed reports early this morning and the next thing I know, I've got a message from the commissioner about her. Apparently he's interested in what she has to say and wants to know why we aren't taking her more seriously. He's on his way and I wanted you to go in and talk to her before he gets here."

"So you want me to check her aura?" she asked.

159

"Yes, but I also need more than that. I need you to talk to her. I know when girls come in here, you're the one who usually takes the cases. Just see if you can get anything serious out of her that doesn't sound like some sort of fairytale she's cooked up. She says her name is Zocha."

Mia opened the door and was unprepared for the sight of the woman who was sitting in a chair facing the opposite wall. In addition to being filthy, her skeletal frame was draped in an ill-fitting cocktail dress. The juxtaposition of the fragile woman and the extravagant dress was disquieting and she tried to ignore the way her shoulder blades protruded awkwardly from beneath the material.

When the woman finally turned to reveal her face, Mia couldn't help but feel disturbed. She imagined that perhaps at one point the woman sitting before her had been beautiful, but with the garish makeup and sunken eye sockets, she looked more dead than alive. It took everything she had to look directly at the woman, who, despite it all was shrouded in light.

She sat beside her, placing her own chair close enough to Zocha's that she could reach her should the need arise.

"My name is Mia," she began. "They told me your name is Zocha. Is that right?"

"Yes."

"Zocha, I'm a police officer, and I am here to help you. I see you've already been given something to eat," she said, pointing to the empty vending machine snack wrappers before her on the table. "And I also know you have already spoken to some other officers, but if you can, I would like you to explain to me about where you came from last night."

"I came from Poland."

"Okay. That's good. I understand you came here to America from Poland. Do you remember when that was?"

"Three hundred seventy two days."

"You have been here in America for over a year?"

"Yes."

"And where have you been all that time?"

"Locked away."

"Locked away where?"

"I do not know. They do not tell us. I do not know this place," Zocha wept.

"Don't cry," she said, handing her a paper towel from beside the sink in the corner.

Zocha balled her hands into fists, refusing to accept the towel. "They don't believe me," she cried. "They think I am pretending, but what I say are true things."

Mia slid her chair an inch closer to the girl. "I'm not them," she said calmly. "I believe a lot of things the others don't. Just tell me what you told them."

She slumped forward as if she no longer possessed the energy to hold herself up, but just as Mia was about to call for a medic, she spoke.

"I told them that a few nights ago, the men came to take us to the place where we are sold. It was just the same as every time. But know this, the longer you are here, the beauty you have, it goes away. And so they pay less and less for you. I know my time is coming. The time when I will disappear, just like the others who don't come back. So that night, when no one would pay for me, I knew I had to get away. Almost everyone was gone and the ones that were left had too much to drink. So I made myself very quiet and I crept out while they were not looking. I ran and ran. I stayed for a few nights out on the streets, in the cold. I finally asked for help and one woman told me to come here to the police and so that is what I did."

She sat in silence as she tried to digest all Zocha had told her. Finally she asked, "What are they selling you for?"

"For sex of course. We are sold to the highest bidder."

Her mind raced, searching for just the right questions to ask as she was quite certain the woman spoke only the truth.

"Do you see the men who purchase you? Can you describe them to me?"

Zocha thought for a moment. "Some of the time we are bound and our eyes are covered. But many times, I saw the men. They were very confident. Strong. Powerful men."

Her blood boiled thinking of the anguish those powerful men inflicted on Zocha and the others. "Would you be able to describe them so we could draw a picture or do you think you could pick out their faces from photographs?"

"Yes," she replied without the slightest hesitation.

"Good." Mia paused. As she contemplated whether she wanted to broach another topic with the frightened woman, the door to the room burst open and the commissioner appeared before them. She immediately stood at attention and welcomed him.

"Good afternoon, Commissioner Dalton," she said. "How can I help you?"

"Officer Rosetti," the commissioner said, returning her salute. "I'm here to speak with this lovely woman."

"I see," she said. "We were just discussing the events that led her here to the station. I'll be sure to make a detailed report of our conversation, Sir."

"I'm sure you will, Officer," he said. "But for now, I would like to have some time to discuss the situation with her as well, so if you will excuse us…"

"Yes, of course," she said, backing out of the room. Before closing the door behind her, she made eye contact with Zocha in an attempt to convey that she would be safe and that everything was going to be okay.

As she took the steps to the first floor of the building, she met Jack on his way back to their office.

"What's up, Coconut?" he said, falling into step beside her.

She rolled her eyes. "I just saw the commissioner."

"What's he doing here?"

"Apparently he has some interest in a woman who found her way here to the station in the middle of the night. She claims she escaped from some sort of sex ring operation."

"Is she telling the truth?"

"You mean is she light?"

"Is she?" he asked as they reached their office.

"Yeah. She is. She's a shell of a human being, but the light is still there. I just don't know why the commissioner would be so interested in her."

Jack hung his hat on a hook behind the door and closed it behind them once Mia entered the room.

"You know it was one of his pet projects when he was in Detroit," he said, taking a seat at his desk.

"What was?"

"Human trafficking."

"Oh, really?" She tried to recall if she'd ever read anything specific about the commissioner working in a special victims unit.

"Yeah. It's part of his platform. He's super passionate about it apparently. I read in one of his briefings, before he was chosen to come here, that he was up in arms about the fact that there are many police departments around the country who don't want to deal with the women who are technically illegals. It's a grey area in law enforcement I guess."

She shook her head. "I don't know how there could be any grey area when it comes to basic human rights, regardless of the citizenship of the person," she said.

"You know that and I know that, but we have a constitution to uphold and it is technically only upheld for U.S. citizens."

"So sad," she said. "Well, at least that explains the commissioner's interest in Zocha."

She looked at the clock above Jack's head on the wall. It was almost three o'clock and a jolt of nervous excitement shot through her body at the thought of seeing Thomas once again. She pulled several files to take home with her for the evening, including the report on Zocha, and began packing her bag.

"You're watching the clock!" Jack admonished her. "That's not like you. What's going on? Another hot date with the lineup guy?"

She grabbed her duffle containing a change of clothes from beneath her desk. "He has a name, Jack. It's Thomas Pritchett. And yes, we are meeting at the zoo to spend the afternoon together, if that's okay with you," she said snidely.

"Jeez! Sensitive subject! It's fine with me, Mia. You're a big girl and I'm glad to see you so happy. Have a good time. Just be careful, okay?"

"Didn't know I worked with *two* fathers," she laughed as she breezed through the door on her way to the locker room. "See ya, Jack."

"Later, Mia," he replied.

Thomas was already sitting peacefully on a bench just outside the entrance gate as she pulled into the parking lot of the Maryland Zoo. She couldn't contain the smile that spread across her face and was humbled to admit she was eager to see him. How feelings could change in just a few weeks.

After parking the car, she made her way across the parking lot and as soon as he saw her coming, he rose from the bench to greet her.

"Have you been waiting long?" she asked.

"Only a few minutes, but it felt like a lifetime."

She blushed at his romantic innuendo.

"It's good to see you, too," she said.

He took her hand in his and they walked together into the zoo. Instead of taking the tram, they opted to make the lengthy walk to one of the zoo's most beloved exhibits, the polar bears. They laughed together as they watched Magnet and Anoki frolicking together in the icy waters of their tank. From there they explored the African Journey loop. In the chimpanzee forest, they stopped to observe the humanlike behaviors of the primates.

"It's fun to watch them taking care of each other," she said as a female chimp plucked bugs out of her baby's fur.

"It's amazing that they just know what to do, isn't it?" he mused.

Spending the afternoon with Thomas and his missing aura caused her conundrum to resurface. Instead of fully enjoying their time together, her mind kept wandering to the possibility of losing her abilities and the commissioner's dark aura.

"If only I was as intuitive as an ape," she commented, reflecting on her concerns.

He nudged her playfully with his elbow. "Who says you're not intuitive?"

"I say." She watched a large male amble across the enclosure toward a tray of chopped vegetables. "It's just that recently, it seems like I never know quite what to do."

"That's crazy. What don't you know about?"

She liked the idea of being able to confide in Thomas and decided to share her feelings about the commissioner with him. It was nice to bounce ideas off someone outside the force.

"Well, I thought I knew what to do about the commissioner…"

"The one you think is bad?" he interrupted.

"Yes. I thought I was right about him. Right about him being dark. But now things have changed, and I'm beginning to doubt myself again. I just don't know what to do."

"Why not? What's changed?"

She wanted desperately to tell him about his part in her analysis of the situation but knew better than to risk his trust. Instead she explained about her morning.

"A woman was brought in overnight. She claims to have escaped from some underground prison where she was forced to have sex with men for money."

His eyes widened. "That's horrendous! Do you believe her?"

165

"I do," she replied. "Her spirit was pure."

Thomas was thoughtful for a moment as they watched a chimp scampering up a tree. "Okay, so you believe her story, but what does that have to do with the commissioner?"

"Well, I've heard of a few other cases like this one over the years. Cells of human traffickers pop up from time to time. Unfortunately, too many times the police can't do anything about it."

He turned from the chimpanzees. "Wait. I'm confused. Why in the world can't the police do anything about people being sold into what amounts to modern day slavery?"

"I know. It's unbelievable. You wouldn't believe the number of women and children in this country that are being bought and sold for labor and sex. Most of the women come from eastern block nations or the Far East. They are lured into brothels under false pretenses and then enslaved. There are language difficulties and physical barriers. Many times the women are completely helpless."

"And the police can't do anything because…"

"Because technically the women are illegal immigrants. They are not protected under our laws per se because they are not legal U.S. citizens. Sadly, many times when women escape or are found, they are arrested for prostitution."

"Seriously?"

"Yeah."

He furrowed his brow. "So, what about the commissioner?" he asked.

She sighed and turned back to the chimpanzees. "The commissioner shows up out of nowhere this morning and breezes in to take the case. He was extremely interested in it. My partner Jack says human trafficking is one of his pet projects. So now I'm thinking, if he's willing to take on something so difficult, how bad can he be?"

"I see." He thought for a moment. "Can I make a suggestion?"

"Of course."

"I certainly don't mean to imply that I have any idea about how your ability works, but it seems to me that perhaps in this instance, you might just have to rely on your other abilities."

She scoffed. "What other abilities?"

"Mia! You have lots of other abilities! You think you're a good cop just because of the aura thing? I would bet you use a lot more than just that when you do your job every day. In the short time I've known you, it's easy to see how highly intuitive you are."

It was hard for her to think of herself in such a positive light. "You think so?"

"Of course! So maybe, in this situation, you're just going to have to play mortal like the rest of us and just go with your gut."

"My gut?"

"Yes. So what does your gut tell you about the commissioner?"

She examined him, his soulful eyes teeming with compassion for her well-being and she knew it was official. Despite her initial reservations, she could no longer deny how she felt about Thomas. She reached up and took his face in her hands, placing her lips upon his. He returned her kiss, matching her passion with his own. When at last she pulled from their embrace and opened her eyes, her legs were shaky and she needed to hold his arm for support.

"I don't know what my gut is telling me about the commissioner, but I do know right now it's telling me I'm falling for you. Either that or my blood sugar is low!"

He laughed. "Maybe it's a little of both. How about ice cream? We can share a cone and maybe that will solve both of your problems."

Hand in hand, they strolled along the winding path, pointing out a myriad of animals to one another along the way to the snack shack. As they sat together at the picnic table, she admitted to herself, over the dish of chocolate and vanilla swirl soft serve they shared, that being with Thomas seemed to have a magical effect on her soul. Somehow, being with him, she was able to push the dire thoughts of the commissioner and her wavering ability from her mind and concentrate on nothing but whatever bond was growing between them. And that was a very good thing.

CHAPTER

24

KATE

The telltale sound of the rusty door hinges alerted the women to their captors' arrival. Kate was neither pleased nor dismayed to see the two suited men return, both brandishing handguns. The taller of the two, whom she assumed was in the position of authority, spoke directly to the girls as he entered the basement.

"You know the drill, Ladies. Stand by your doors and turn around, hands behind your back. And no funny business." He paused. "I'm talking to you," the man said directly to Anya as he passed by her cell. "Does anyone need to be reminded about what happens if you don't do what you're told?"

Anya did not respond but returned his steely gaze with her own.

"Ladies, would you like to tell our newcomers about last week?"

No one spoke. She felt her heartbeat pulsing in the veins of her neck and could hear it reverberating in her ears. She closed her eyes in an attempt to block out the negative energy hanging heavily in the room. She attempted to summon her gift, invoking whatever power laid within her to somehow help her avoid whatever was about to happen. However, instead of strength, all she felt was doubt.

"No one? Fine. Then I will share. While you are here with us, you are expected to do as you are told. As long as you do, your families will remain safe. If you decide to disobey us, there will be punishments, both to you and to your families. Last week, when Wan here decided to attack a customer, we were obliged to punish her and her family as well. I can see from here that she's still recovering from her injuries. Most of you had the privilege of hearing the recording of her mother being beaten. So, as we leave today for the showings, let's all play nicely. Remember, the girl who brings in the highest bid at the auction will be rewarded with extra food this evening, so I suggest you do your best."

She struggled to keep from throwing up. The reality of what was about to happen hit her with the force of a freight train. She immediately did as she was told, turning her back to the door with her hands placed behind her back. She thought of her parents and her sisters and made a silent pact with herself to do whatever was necessary to protect their safety.

One by one, the cage doors were opened, and when the men finally reached her cell, she submitted to them willingly. Her hands were bound behind her with a large length of rope that dug painfully into her flesh. She winced.

They were led up the staircase into the warehouse where the same van that brought them from the airport was parked. As they stood together in a line, blindfolds were secured over their eyes, and they were corralled roughly onto the floor of the van.

For the first time in days, she felt the warmth of human contact as the women squeezed together in the cargo bed. Her back was leaning against the back of the girl behind her and she was overcome with emotion by the power of that simple touch.

"Who are you?" she said to the girl she was resting against as soon as the door was slammed shut.

"It's me. Anya. Is that you, Kate?"

"Yes. Lera? Where are you?" she called.

"I am over here," Lera replied from the far side of the van.

"Try to come over to us," Anya urged. "Quickly, before we start moving."

"You are foolish," said one of the women from the front. "Stay where you are."

"No," Kate said, "she needs us. You will make it, Lera. But please, hurry."

Lera could be heard shuffling across the floor of the van on her knees, bumping into the others until she finally reached Kate, collapsing into her lap.

"I'm so scared," Lera whispered.

"Don't be scared. Whatever happens, it won't change who you are. At the end of the day, you will still be Lera. They can't take that from you," she said.

"You are wrong," the same cautious voice from the front of the van declared. "It will change you forever."

"They can only change us if we let them," she replied.

"We will see."

The women fell silent for the remainder of the ride and she concentrated on matching the cadence of her breathing to Lera's. When the van finally stopped and the door opened, they were unceremoniously dragged from their confinement and instructed to stand where they were placed. Cold air blew through her thin dress, causing her skin to prickle. She tried to imagine how wonderful the cold would feel if it was blowing off the Dnieper along her favorite riverside path. However, at that moment, she felt as though Kiev was as far from her as the sun.

Once inside, her thoughts of home quickly faded and she was overcome by the pungent smell of cigar smoke. The cold air was replaced by the dry warmth of a roaring fire she could hear crackling softly in the distance. Music was being played, but she couldn't tell if there was actually a piano in the room or whether it was merely a recording.

She was shocked when the blindfold was removed from her eyes, revealing the scene before her. She struggled to remember having been in a room filled with such opulence. There were crystal chandeliers hung high above her head and beneath her feet was a thickly woven Persian rug in hues of navy and burgundy. The few windows she observed were covered in heavy drapery and the room was dimly lit, making it difficult for her to examine the faces of the men who were milling about the room, smoking cigars and drinking scotch. Only two of the men were familiar to her, leaving seven others she had never seen before.

She held her breath in guarded anticipation of what was to come.

"Gentlemen," began her captor, waving his arm with flourish above his head, "I hope you will be happy with this evening's selection. As always, take your time with the assessment period. When everyone feels they have spent a sufficient time examining each girl, we will begin the bidding."

She felt the acid from her stomach bubbling into her esophagus. Her legs, always sturdy and reliable, suddenly felt like twigs beneath her, on the verge of giving way at any moment. She kept her eyes focused on an imperfection in the mahogany paneling on the wall directly in front of her. She couldn't make out whether or not it was a knothole from a long removed branch or perhaps a chunk that had broken out during installation. Regardless of what it was, she held on to her single point of focus while man after man approached her.

The first, a handsome middle-aged professional, gazed upon her with great longing. He didn't hesitate to run his fingers gently through her hair and then continue down her body to harshly grope her breasts and thighs. It was all she could do to keep herself from kneeing the man in the groin but the threat to her family's safety kept her feet planted firmly to the floor.

The second man was shorter than the first and brought his pockmarked face so close that she could smell the liquor on his breath. He walked behind her and she could feel as he pressed himself against her before grabbing her backside with both of his hands. She closed her eyes and breathed out deeply, her skin crawling with disgust as she willed him to leave her alone.

Each man seemed to have his own ritual - his own routine of inspecting the specific attributes he was looking for in a girl. Some fondled. Others merely observed. But the look in each of their eyes was the same. Pure malevolence.

As the men finished their examinations, she strained to hear the conversations between those that were gathering in pairs in front of the fire. She could only make out what those closest to her were saying.

"A nice piece of ass, that one," commented one of the men, pointing to Lera. "But I don't know whether she'll survive what I have planned. Seems a little frail."

"What about the other new one? The big girl. She seems like she could take a licking."

"Maybe. You know how I feel about the brunettes though."

"The last new one on the end is a find. Almost too pretty to mess with."

"Are you saying she won't be that pretty when she's done with you?" the pockmarked man chimed in, laughing heartily. "We all remember what happened with that little Asian girl you took out."

She couldn't stand to listen any longer. She closed her eyes once again and began to hum softly to herself, a tune she and her sisters had sung together as children. Although she tried to concentrate on the tune, the glaring realization that there were people in the world who saw her as nothing more than a commodity to be traded could not be ignored. Although she understood her body was about to be sold to the highest bidder for the sole purpose of whatever depravity the man could conceive, she couldn't bring herself to accept it. She shivered.

God help me, she thought, *because I may not be able to help myself.*

"First up," called the suited man from the far end of the room, "this fine specimen. Shall we start the bidding at $500?"

"$500," called one of the men.

"$550," called another.

"$600."

"$625."

The crowd fell silent.

"That's all? $625? Gentlemen, perhaps you would like a second look?" He paused to look around the room. "No? Alright then, $625 to Mr. R."

Most of the bidding continued down the line in much the same way as the first. However, one of the tiny European women spurred a bidding war which she was sure would end in violence between the three men vying for her services. Lera drove up a high price as well, bringing in $3,650. By the time the auctioneer approached her, she wished only to bring in a high enough price to ensure she would earn the extra food.

The features of the faces of each of the men were warped and distorted by the shadows that danced around the room, formed by the light of the fireplace - each one more hideous than the next. She focused her energy as the bidding began and concentrated on using her gift to ensure she would bring the highest bid.

"$1,000," called the first of the men.

"$1,500," called a second.

"$2,000."

"$3,000."

"$3,500."

"$3,750."

"$5,000."

The final bid silenced the room and she turned to see which monster would seal her fate. The drunken pockmarked man stepped forward.

"I believe I will have the honor of being the first to experience our newest beauty," he said, eliciting a round of laughter from the others.

"Going once. Twice. Sold to Mr. V."

Without notice, the women were immediately blindfolded once again and corralled back out into the cold night air. They returned to the warehouse in silence, none of the women daring to speak of what had just transpired. After being led to her cell, her bindings were removed and the rations were allocated to all of the women. As promised, she was given a double portion of food for having produced the highest bid. As soon as the men disappeared up the stairs and the door latch scraped defiantly against its collar, she called quietly to Lera and Anya.

"Girls, come here. Take some of this and pass it to the others," she said, breaking the bread in her hands.

"But that's your food. You earned it on your own. You should keep it," Anya said.

"No. I'm still strong. I'll only keep a little. Pass the rest to the ones who are starving. We aren't starving. Yet."

She watched as Lera and Anya passed the bread through the metal bars of the cells. Each woman took a portion for herself and passed the rest down the corridor.

"Thank you, Kate," called one of the women from the far end of the row.

"Yes, thank you," called another.

Quiet thanks came from each of the women imprisoned in the basement. Finally, from the far end of the room, she heard the same voice that had spoken to her on the way to the auction. It was Svetlana, the woman who held the honor of having spent the greatest number of days in captivity.

"Perhaps I was wrong," she said.

"Wrong about what?"

"About being changed," Svetlana continued. "You are the first to share her extra rations with the group. Since you arrived, you have been kind. And after today, your kindness remains. I only wonder, will you still be kind after Mr. V has his way with you tomorrow?" Svetlana paused. "I suppose we will wait and see."

"I suppose we will," she replied, knowing in her heart she would find a way to use her gift to stop whatever brutality was coming her way. And then, she would use it to protect the others as well.

CHAPTER

25

THOMAS

Early Monday morning, as he finished folding the last of the napkins before the bistro opened for the breakfast rush, Thomas couldn't erase the image of Mia's smile from his mind. For the first time in his life, he endeavored to imagine a future for himself. A future that would perhaps include Mia.

When the front door was unlocked, patrons began flooding into Belinda's. He busied himself with his usual routine – refill, remove, restock. His mind quickly returned to Mia and with it, a whisper of doubt about himself and his worth. As he cleared the dishes from the large round table, he wondered if she could ever count him as a legitimate partner given his stagnant career path. He made a mental note to look into the cost of online education classes. Perhaps, he decided, it was time to start planning a more stable existence for himself, his mother, and if he was lucky, Mia as well.

He drifted through the dining room, a ghost among the living. As he refilled water glasses at the four top by the window, he overheard a conversation between two women describing how they shoplifted several hundred dollars' worth of merchandise from a large department store at the mall the night before. He heard a wife discussing her hemorrhoids with her disconcerted husband over their breakfast quiche. Finally, at the very same table he had witnessed Mia receiving the news of her friend's pregnancy, he overheard an extremely disturbing conversation.

The well-dressed men he'd seen at the table the week before had returned, each with a large platter of eggs, bacon, and waffles in front of them. Their boisterous laughter broke through the muffled conversations that filled the dining room. At first, he thought nothing of their behavior. But as he cleared several of their plates at the end of their meal, he overheard one of the men mention 'the newest women in the auction.' The comment was jarring to him so he lingered at the surrounding tables in order to listen further to their conversation.

"Five thousand dollars seems a lot to pay for one night. She must be somethin'," he heard one of the men comment.

"Joe said that group had three new Ukrainian women and she was one of them. I'm kind of partial to the Asian girls myself. I can get white meat at home."

The group laughed and Thomas felt revolted. Ordinarily, he would have just walked away, but with the information Mia shared about the girl claiming to have been held captive as a sex slave, he decided to keep listening. He hoped that if perhaps they were involved, they would reveal more incriminating information.

"Well, I'm gonna talk to the new guy and see if I can't get in on the next auction. The last couple I've been invited to have been less than impressive."

"There were those Romanian women a few weeks back. Did you give any of them a go?"

"Nah. Too feisty. I like 'em more submissive."

After listening to the men for several moments, he had heard enough. He finished clearing the table beside them and took the dishes into the kitchen. When he returned to the dining room, he approached the hostess stationed at the front door to inquire about the men. He discovered the group had reserved their table under the name Wayne Brookins.

They soon finished their meal, but not before he had the opportunity to commit their faces to memory. He watched carefully as one of the men passed the bill to the waitress. He noticed that, along with the bill, he also handed her his credit card. He followed the waitress to the register and casually sidled up to her.

"Hey Jen, I just heard table six mention they were ready to order. Why don't you head over there and I'll ring this in and bring it over to you?"

"You're the sweetest, Tom," she replied. "Thanks."

Afraid he would forget the name on the reservation, he quickly grabbed a piece of scrap paper from the drawer and wrote the name Wayne Brookins. He then added the name printed on the credit card, Frank Guthry. After swiping the card and printing the ticket, he returned them both to Jen as she finished calling the order from table six back to the kitchen.

For the remainder of his shift, he was unable to concentrate. Tables were left unattended and dishes began to pile up. Finally, mercifully, two o'clock arrived and Belinda assisted him in clearing the last of the customers from the restaurant.

"What's going on? You seem completely out of sorts this afternoon," Belinda commented as they swept the floor of the dining room together.

"I overheard a group of men here today. They sounded as though they might be involved in some illegal activities. I'm wondering if I should report what I heard to the police."

"What kind of activities?"

"I'd rather not say. I think I'm just going to mention it to my friend who's a police officer…"

"Your lady friend," Belinda interrupted.

"Yes. Mia. Maybe she'll know what to do."

"Well, here," Belinda said, taking the sweeper from his hand. "You're officially off duty, so go give her a call and get it out of your system. I'll see you in the morning."

"Thanks, Belinda," he said as he untied the apron from around his waist and picked up his backpack from behind the counter. "See you tomorrow."

He stood at the bus stop, not knowing where he was headed. He took out his phone and called Mia on her cell. She answered on the first ring.

"Hi, Thomas," she said brightly. "How was work?"

He was surprised by how much better he felt just hearing her voice on the other end of the line. "It was... interesting," he replied.

"Interesting good or interesting bad?"

"Both maybe. I think I heard something today that might be related to the story you told me about the woman who escaped from the sex ring."

"You're kidding. That would be a huge coincidence."

"Seriously huge. There were these guys today at the bistro..."

"Thomas, stop talking. Let's not discuss this over the phone. Where are you now?"

"I'm at the bus stop, but I don't know where I'm going. Home I guess."

"No. Come to my apartment. We can discuss what you heard once you get here. How long will it take you?"

"Towson to Parkville? Fifteen minutes tops once the bus arrives."

"Do you want me to come get you?" she asked.

"Nah. I'll see you in a few."

"Okay. See you soon. And Thomas, did these men know you were listening?"

"No. I don't think so. Why?"

"Just promise me you'll watch your back, okay?"

"I always do," he replied.

CHAPTER
26

MIA

Mia was relieved when she heard the knock at her door. She ran to answer it, banging her hip into the corner of the kitchen table on the way to the front hall. After opening the door, she ushered him quickly into the apartment.

"What in the world are you so worried about?" he asked as she peered into the hallway before shutting the door behind him.

"Thomas, I haven't seen these people you overheard and I've been imagining the worst since you called. I wish you could describe their auras to me, but of course you can't, so we have to assume they have the potential to do harm, and specifically harm to you if they realize you were eavesdropping."

"Mia, you need to calm down. I think you might be overreacting," he said, taking off his coat and placing it on the back of the kitchen chair. "I promise you, these guys didn't even know I was in the room."

"You can't be too careful. Come sit down. I want to hear all about it."

They passed through the den where Chelsea was sitting in the middle of the floor surrounded by paperwork. After lengthy introductions were made, she led Thomas into her bedroom where he explained exactly what he overheard at Belinda's.

"I can't believe the men were just talking openly about the trafficking at the restaurant," she said to him as she threw herself across her bed.

Thomas sat on the floor and leaned against the wall beneath the window. "You'd be surprise what people feel is appropriate to discuss when they think no one's listening. I could go on for hours," he replied.

"So tell me about the men," she said, taking a notepad from her nightstand. "What did they look like?"

He closed his eyes, remembering the details of their appearance. "They were all well-dressed. Business casual I guess. Slacks, oxford shirts, expensive shoes… you know the type. They all looked pretty generic. One of them had a mustache and one had a scar on his temple that looked like it was a pretty bad gash at one point. Another guy wore glasses. They were thick-rimmed, hipster-like. They all had brown hair with modern cuts, styled well. I'd say the youngest was in his early thirties and the oldest was in his late forties."

"Could you pick them out of a lineup?" she asked.

He grinned at her. "Absolutely."

"Good. So tell me more about their conversation."

"They were talking about different groups of women and how there were three new Ukrainian women in one of the groups. Apparently one of the girls sold for five thousand dollars last night. Can you imagine selling people? These guys were vile and made my skin crawl. I don't know how you surround yourself with people like them every day, Mia."

"It takes its toll sometimes," she replied. "What you heard helps to confirm the woman's story. It seems we have a thriving trafficking ring set up here in the city. Maybe you could see the sketch artist at the station to get their faces on paper. And meanwhile, we can search here at home through the police database for photos of known sex offenders.

Maybe we'll get lucky and one or two of them will already be in the system."

"I can do better than that," he said, beaming at her from across the room.

"How's that?"

He produced a scrap of paper out of his jeans pocket and tossed it on the bed. "I have two of their names."

She glanced at the two names scribbled on the sheet and could not deny how impressed she was by his resourcefulness. "That's amazing. How'd you do that?"

"I checked the reservation list and their party was listed under the name Wayne Brookins. One of the other guys paid and I checked the credit card. The name on the card was Frank Guthry."

She climbed off the bed and threw herself on top of him, pressing her lips firmly against his and nearly knocking the back of his head into the wall.

"You. Are. Amazing," she said, composing herself as she backed out of his lap. "Have you ever considered detective work?"

"No. Never," he replied, still recovering from her display of unbridled affection.

"Come on," she said as she grabbed the laptop from the floor in the corner of her room. "Let's see if we can find these bastards."

She quickly booted up the computer and logged in remotely to the precinct's database. They sat beside each other on the bed while she entered the names of the men Thomas provided and within seconds, Wayne Brookins appeared before them.

"That's him!" he exclaimed. "That's the guy with the scar!"

She read his file aloud. "Wayne Reginald Brookins, born July 18, 1971 in Gaithersburg, Maryland. He's got a string of solicitation citations as well as a battery charge that was dropped. He has two handguns registered in his name. And his last known address is in Owings Mills."

"Can you look it up?"

"Yeah, hang on…" She paused, waiting for the satellite mapping program to upload the address. "Here it is."

"Big place."

"Big place," she agreed.

Neither of them spoke for several minutes as she tried unsuccessfully to acquire any additional information about the man. Finally, she turned off the computer, knowing the machine would never provide her with the evidence she was seeking. There was only one way to get what she wanted.

"I need to see him," she said finally.

"That's him right there on the screen. I already told you that," said Thomas.

"No. I need to see him with my own eyes. Not a photo. Him. In person."

"Is this about his aura?" he asked.

She nodded thoughtfully. "I have to see it. I know what the reports say, but I still want to see for myself. I need to know what we're dealing with and the only way for me to do that is to see the condition of his soul."

"I can keep my eyes open at Belinda's and let you know if he shows up again," he offered.

"No. I don't want to be passive. I have to be proactive. I want to go to his house."

He backed away from her. "Are you nuts?" he exclaimed.

As she contemplated her next move, she loosened the elastic from around her ponytail and allowed her hair to fall onto her shoulders before piling it up on top of her head again. "I don't know. Maybe. But I feel like we might be onto something big here and before I go to my father with it, I need to have something more to go on than hearsay from my boyfriend. No offense," she said, turning to him.

"I'm not offended by the term boyfriend," he said grinning.

"Thomas!" she said, embarrassed by her blunder which she tried to defuse by punching him in the arm. "Be serious!"

"I am serious," he said. "And I don't like the idea of you going to that guy's house."

"I thought you were the one who was always 'cautiously optimistic.'"

He stood up and began pacing the length of the room. "I'm not at all optimistic about this. The idea of tracking down this guy makes me... whatever the opposite of optimistic is."

"Pessimistic?" she said, rolling her eyes.

"Yes," he agreed. "Very pessimistic."

"Then come with me," she suggested.

He stopped pacing and stood directly in front of her. "What am I going to do? I'm a pianist, a lineup plant, and a bus boy. I don't have a lot of training for this sort of thing."

Without any further contemplation, she pulled her sneakers out from under the bed and slid past him to grab a sweater from her closet. "You don't need any training. You can just be my back up."

"Don't you have a partner for this sort of thing?" he asked, obviously ignoring her preparations.

"Yes. But he hasn't seen the guy before and you have. I could use you there to identify him."

Although he hesitated, she could see the lines on his face softening. "Fine. I'll come with you. But only because I can't stand the thought of not coming with you. For the record, it's against my better judgment."

"I heard. You're pessimistic. Duly noted."

"So what's your plan?" he asked.

"Plain clothes stake out," she replied, rifling through a pile of files on her dresser.

"Not happening."

She was becoming frustrated by his lack of gallantry. She understood that his childhood left him with scars that would never heal and a cautious nature, but she really hated that he wasn't more adventurous.

"Come on. It'll be fine. Tonight, after dark, we'll drive to his house and park down the street. We'll see what we can see. If he's there, great. Hopefully I'll get a look at him. If not, then we can go back another time or try some other route. Okay?"

"Okay," Thomas relented, brushing her cheek with his fingertips, "but I'll never forgive myself if something happens to you."

She felt every nerve inside her body ignite at his touch. She suddenly had the desire to spend the remainder of the afternoon holed up with him, exploring every inch of his aura-less physique, but she hesitated. She wasn't ready to allow him into that part of her life.

"We've got some time before nightfall. How about some dinner?" she asked instead.

"I could eat." He extended his hand in a gesture of solidarity. "But how about if I whip up dinner this time? I make a terrific chicken marsala."

"That sounds wonderful as long as I can help," she said, accepting his hand as she followed him out of the bedroom.

They invited Chelsea to join them for dinner but she declined, citing a special dinner of her own with Tyler at the restaurant where they'd had their first date. Mia assumed he would be presenting Chelsea with the ring she'd chosen with him. It was a bittersweet feeling as she hugged her friend goodbye and watched her walk out the door.

As they entered the kitchen, she hoisted herself onto the counter and watched as Thomas picked through the contents of her pantry to find the ingredients he was looking for. She was impressed by how effortlessly he moved around the space. He didn't use a single measuring cup and instead threw, what appeared to be random foods, into the bowl. She stood in awe of him and was beginning to wonder if there was anything he couldn't do.

"How can I help?" she asked, as he was stirring the sauce.

"Do you have any vegetables we can put with this for a side? Like green beans or broccoli or salad?"

"Maybe," she replied. She began digging through the refrigerator and found half a head of lettuce and two zucchini. "Here's what we've got," she said, holding up the vegetables.

"If you slice up the zucchini, we can roast them in the oven."

"I can handle that," she said, pulling a knife from the drawer. "How'd you learn to do all this?"

"All what?"

"The cooking stuff?"

He tasted the sauce and sprinkled it with another dash of salt. "Mildred is a wonderful cook. Before Dad died, we had a lot more time and money and she would make the most delicious meals. I spent a lot of time in the kitchen watching her. You wouldn't believe how much weight I gained when I came to live with them," he laughed.

"For not having a biological mother, you've sure learned a lot from the women in your life," she commented.

He stopped stirring the sauce and lifted his head to study her from across the room. "I've never really thought about it before, but I guess I have. I like to think I'm still learning from the women in my life," he said, smiling at her. "What about you, did your mother teach you to cook growing up?"

"No. My mom left when I was eight," she replied, matter-of-factly.

"Oh, Mia. I'm sorry. How did I not know that?"

"I guess it just hasn't come up," she replied. He looked at her apologetically. "It's okay," she said, hoping to brush aside the awkwardness of the moment. "It was a long time ago."

He placed the chicken dish and the sliced zucchini into the oven and joined her at the counter. "Is it okay if I ask you what happened?" he said, brushing a lock of hair from in front of her eyes.

"Yeah. Of course." She paused, evaluating Thomas and the most straightforward way to answer his question. "It was me, I think. I happened. I don't think she could handle my... eccentricities. On top of that, Dad was gone all the time, at the station, working weird hours all day and night. One day after school, I came home and she was gone."

"Gone forever?"

"Yeah. Gone forever. I haven't seen her since."

"Do you know where she is?"

"No. But to be honest, I haven't even looked for her."

He turned to her and wrapped her in his arms. She laid her head against his chest and appreciated all at once how grateful she was to have shared her truth with him. Standing in the middle of the kitchen, being held by a man she barely knew, she felt whole. Not that he was some illusive missing piece that finally completed her, but instead, that he was unknowingly helping to put her own disheveled pieces back together.

It was a humbling admission.

"I guess that makes us kindred spirits in a way, since we were both abandoned by our mothers," he said at last.

"I was lucky enough to have my dad though."

"That's true. And now you have me too."

"And you have me."

"That I do," he replied.

CHAPTER

27

KATE

On the day after the auction, something amazing happened to the fourteen women imprisoned in the basement of the warehouse. They allowed Kate's hope to spread like an evening fog among them.

"Do you want to know about what is going to happen?" a tiny Chinese woman named Su asked her as they readied themselves for the arrival of their captors.

"No," she said reluctantly. "Unless there's something you can tell me that will make it better."

"Close your eyes," called a woman named Uma from the far end of the hall.

"Think about something else," said Svetlana. "Think about something peaceful, like a sunset."

"Or picking flowers."

"Or petting a cat."

"I feel sorry for them," whispered a woman three cells down from her.

"Why would you feel sorry for them?" Anya asked.

"They don't understand what it means to love. And I do. No matter what, that makes me stronger than they are."

"You're right," Kate said as she zipped up the slinky dress that had been delivered to her cell earlier in the day. "We are all stronger than they are because we have loved."

"And been loved," called another.

"I don't feel strong anymore," said a small voice she had never heard before. "They treat us like animals. Like we aren't even human. Most days, I don't even feel like I deserve to be alive. So how can you speak of hope when you have not yet felt the power of their hatred?"

She hesitated, unable to formulate a plausible response to the woman's pain. She knew, of course, the girl was right. She had been caged and starved, but she had not yet been brutalized. That would change in a matter of hours.

"You are absolutely right," Kate said. "But how about this? Tomorrow, after I have withstood the same horrors you have experienced, if my hope remains, will you let me help you remember that you are more than what they say you are?"

The cell block was silent. No one dared to move. She held her breath and felt as if the well-being of the entire group hinged upon this one woman's response.

"He will steal your soul tonight," the girl said at last.

"Maybe he will," Kate relented. "And so what should I do tomorrow?"

No one spoke.

"Tomorrow," she said finally, "I will take it back."

With that, the ominous door hinges alerted the women to their keepers' arrival. Within seconds, the man in the red sweatshirt and his lackey appeared, their side arms holstered visibly on their hips.

"Showtime, Ladies," he called. "You know the drill."

Kate watched as all of the women down the line turned their backs toward their cell doors. Her heart broke for each of them. And as she listened to Lera and Anya being bound, she tried concentrating on a way out of her situation, but her fear was too great and it overshadowed any attempt at rational thought.

Unlike the last time, when the women had been transported en masse by van, tonight, as they reached the top of the stairs, several large black town cars were parked inside the warehouse. Two by two, the women were loaded into the cars, but not before their bindings were secured and blindfolds were put in place.

Lera was taken from her side and as she was led away, Kate called to her in Ukrainian, "Remember you are loved." For her disobedience, she was kicked in the back of her calves, causing her to stumble forward and fall to her knees. She hastily returned to her feet and allowed Svetlana to lead her into their waiting car.

The women were silent on the drive to wherever it was they were being taken. She could think of nothing to say that would make either one of them feel any better about what awaited them at the end of the journey. When the car finally came to a stop, the women were led, still bound and blindfolded, through what sounded like an underground parking garage. Her ill-fitting stilettos echoed loudly indicating the walls around her were made of concrete and the ceiling was quite low. The sound of a small bell and mechanical equipment led her to believe she was being taken into an elevator. Once inside, she relished the sensation of being lifted into space. She imagined that she was rising above herself. Above her captors. Above the hell into which she was about to descend.

When the elevator came to a stop and the doors slid open, she was led a short distance before being taken into a room and given her instructions. She was told to stay put and do whatever was asked of her. Someone would return for her at the end of the night.

Her blindfold was removed but by the time her eyes adjusted to the sudden brightness and she turned to face her escort, she found that he was gone and she was alone, standing in the center of a lavishly decorated bedroom. She was disappointed to feel that her hands were still bound.

She took advantage of the fact that Mr. V had not yet arrived and quickly surveyed her surroundings. Although it was divided into several more intimate spaces, the room itself was larger than her family's entire apartment. There was a dressing area housing a tall wardrobe and closet to her left. A small refrigerator and bar stood in the far corner of the room. Behind her was a bathroom as well as a door she assumed was an exit. Without hesitation, she hurried to the door and tried awkwardly to turn the handle with her still-bound hands. Of course, as she had expected, the door was locked from the outside in.

Discouraged but not defeated, she continued to scan the room and noticed there was a large window on the opposite side of the room. The draperies were tightly drawn and she was unable to see outside. She contemplated moving the curtains aside to see if the window would provide a means of escape, but before she could move, she heard the sound of a key being inserted into the lock of the door.

She turned just in time to see Mr. V walking through the door.

She recoiled, taking several steps back and running her legs into the side rail of the bed, bruising her already painful calf.

"Yekaterina, a pleasure to make your acquaintance," said Mr. V in a voice that made her skin crawl. She watched as he carefully removed his overcoat and laid it on the pants rack beside the wardrobe.

She held her breath, trying desperately to think of something she could say which would convince the man she was undeserving of whatever his intentions were for her, but her mouth was dry and she was unable to speak.

"You don't have to be afraid of me," he said soothingly as he walked across the room in her direction. "This can be a wonderful experience for us both. I am really hoping it will be."

"I'm not afraid of you," she said finally, surprising herself with her boldness.

"Ah. She speaks. Well, I am glad you aren't afraid. That's good because I have quite an evening planned for us," he said, removing his tie and unbuttoning the top button of his shirt. "What shall we do first?"

"Please don't hurt me," she said, willing her desires into reality by using her gift, the only defense she had in her arsenal.

"Now why would you think I would hurt you?"

She remained silent.

"I won't hurt you unless you give me a reason to hurt you. You aren't going to give me a reason, are you?"

She shook her head.

"Good. Now, how about you let me have a look at you? You were quite the hot commodity last night. I really had to up the ante to assure I got you first. Couldn't take the chance that anyone else was going to snag you out from under me."

He moved closer, to within only a few feet, and she could see the many craters that marred his ruddy complexion. Her muscles tightened and her jaw locked. She stood resolutely before him as he brought his hand up to her face.

"So beautiful. So perfect in every way. I only hope what I haven't seen of you is as perfect as what I have. Now, take off the dress."

She couldn't move.

"I'll not ask you again, Yekaterina. Take off the dress."

"I would, except they've tied my hands behind my back."

"Ah yes. You haven't proven to them that you are trustworthy. Of course. Well," he said, grabbing a hold of her shoulders and turning her around, "we can fix that." He paused, studying her momentarily. "*Can* you be trusted Yekaterina?"

"Yes," she replied.

Mr. V easily untied the rope that restrained her movements. His hands lingered far too long on her wrists as he turned her back around to face him. She could smell the alcohol on his breath.

"Now," he said. "Take off your dress."

She massaged her wrists and concentrated on maintaining her safety. Slowly, she unzipped the side of her dress and allowed the garment to slide effortlessly to the floor.

"Lovely," he said. "Just lovely." He moved a step closer. She shuddered.

He reached out and cupped her breasts in his hands. In what should have been a pleasant, loving act, she felt only disgust. She lifted her chin, a defiant gesture to a man who paid highly for submissive women. He met her gaze and cocked his head to the side, unsure of what to make of her boldness.

"I believe I will allow you to watch what I'm about to do to you. I was planning on covering your eyes. I hate it when all of you look at me so pathetically. However, I think it would be better for both of us if you saw exactly how little control you have here this evening."

She chose not to respond. Neither did she avert her eyes. Strangely, in that moment, all of the fear and doubt that had been consuming her thoughts disappeared. She was suddenly able to pool the strength from every fiber of her being into one single thought. The man standing before her would not violate her. This she knew.

With much dramatic flair, Mr. V unbuttoned the remaining buttons of his shirt, revealing his paunchy midsection and a scar that ran the length of his chest. Next, he removed both of his shoes, unbuckled his belt and slid it from around his waist in one smooth motion. He cracked the belt in the air as if it was a whip half an inch from her face. She did not flinch.

Before she realized what was happening, he grabbed her squarely by the shoulders and shoved her backward so she fell heavily onto the bed behind her. He was immediately on top of her, using the weight of his own body to pin her beneath him so she couldn't escape. In an instant, he wrapped the belt from his pants around both of her wrists and secured her arms to the bedframe.

"Now, my dear, you will not close your eyes. I want you to see all I have to offer you."

"You will not hurt me," she said. It was clear to her assailant she was not begging for her safety and she could see by the heat spreading across his face that he was enraged by the fact that somehow, she still thought she had the upper hand.

He quickly checked the tightness of her restraints and the bedframe groaned as he climbed off the bed to remove his pants. Within seconds he was straddling her once again, only this time his flesh pressed firmly against hers. A wave of nausea washed over her and she swallowed back the bile that inched its way into her esophagus.

He began by running his hands along the length of her body. He groped and squeezed her breasts and thighs, all the while, rubbing himself against her skin. She mentally removed herself from the situation by concentrating on the beads of sweat that began to form on the man's forehead. She ignored his meaty hands which violated her most private areas and instead watched as one bead of sweat after another materialized on his brow.

At some point, she noticed his breathing was becoming more labored, which she initially attributed to his growing excitement. She allowed herself to refocus her attention away from his face so she could better assess her situation.

Surprisingly, what she saw above her was a man who was clearly furious for some reason. For a moment, she feared his anger would be too much for her to control. And then, in an ironic turn of events, she saw what was happening. She looked down to see his flaccid genitalia flopping around between his legs and knew immediately that his anger stemmed from his body's inability to do what he wanted to her.

She couldn't help but smile at the solution her gift had provided.

"Stupid whore!" he screamed at her, slapping her across the face with the back of his hand. "Look what you've done to me! This is your fault! You, with your defiance and your holier-than-thou attitude!'

Her face stung and although she wanted to cry out, she would not give him the satisfaction. If she showed an ounce of submission it would feed his ego enough to stimulate the erection that continued to elude him. And so, she remained stoic as the pathetic creature above her grappled with the mechanics of his own manhood.

"God-damned, bitch!" he spat at her, slapping her again across the face and kneeing her brutally in the crotch. She held her breath, willing herself to remain steadfast in the face of her adversary.

Mercifully, he rolled himself off of her body and threw his legs over the side of the bed. He gathered his clothing, cursing and screaming at her all the while. After he finished dressing himself, he stood above her, bringing his face to within inches of her own.

"After the others have broken you down, I will have my turn and you will give me what I want, do you understand? Some of the others will love your defiance and they will beat it out of you. And once they have, then you will submit to me, I promise you. And on that day, I will get my money's worth."

He spat in her face and left the room, without looking back and without releasing her from her restraints. After she watched the door close behind him and heard the lock click into place, she finally allowed herself to cry. Tears for herself. Tears for her friends. Tears for her sweet sisters, who were destined to the same awful fate without the benefit of her otherworldly gift.

By the time her captors arrived several hours later to return her to the warehouse basement, her eyes were dry and her focus was resolved. One way or another, she would find a way out of her situation. Either that, or she would die trying.

CHAPTER

28

THOMAS

Thomas couldn't help but smile watching Mia navigate the traffic on the northwest expressway as they drove toward Owings Mills. She turned the radio up and was singing along at the top of her lungs, bouncing in her seat to the beat of the music.

"How do you do it?" he asked, grinning at her from the passenger's seat.

"Do what?"

"Compartmentalize your life."

"Do I?" she asked, glancing over at him.

"You must. I mean, here we are, on the way to spy on people, people who could be dangerous, and you're acting like we're on the way to the grocery store to pick up a snack. I hope I don't sound like a wimp, but I'm freaking out a little bit over here."

"Don't freak out, Thomas. I do this every day."

"Every day?"

"Okay, not every day. But I have before."

"How many times?"

Mia hesitated. "Twice."

"Twice!" he scoffed. "You are this confident and you've participated in a total of two stakeouts? You are not helping me feel better, Mia."

"It'll be fine," she said, reaching across the center console to take his hand. "We're just going to sit and watch. There's nothing dangerous about sitting and watching, is there?"

"I guess not, but I might need you to take my mind off things while we are doing all this sitting and watching."

"What did you have in mind?" she asked, smirking at him as she took her eyes off the road for a moment.

"I don't know. We'll think of something," he teased.

They continued driving in contemplative silence. He found that the more time he spent in her presence, the more he was becoming enchanted by her. She carefully maneuvered the car through the upscale neighborhood and he was fascinated by the intensity on her face as she concentrated on which way the GPS was instructing her to go.

"I think we're almost there," she said, squinting in the darkness to see the street sign on the corner post. "I'm going to drive past the house first and then double back. We'll park a good bit away, but close enough that if we see Brookins coming or going, I'll be able to see his aura."

"You're the boss, Boss."

He counted the house numbers as they slowly made their way down the street. As they approached the house, it was apparent that something was going on because almost a dozen cars lined the driveway and the street beyond.

"Do you think they're having a party?" he wondered aloud.

"Nothing like a party to mask a stake out," she chuckled. "I can't believe our luck. They certainly won't notice an extra car on the street, that's for sure."

"No, but what are the chances we're going to see Brookins if he's holed up inside with his guests?" he asked.

"That's a good question," she replied, turning the car around at the end of the street and heading back in the direction of Wayne Brookins' house. As she put the car in park, he saw another pair of headlights coming down the street.

"Oh my God, Mia! Get down!" he yelled, ducking down below the dashboard.

She laughed aloud. "You really aren't cut out for this line of work, are you?"

"No. Mia, get down. Whoever it is will see you."

"They won't. They've already parked up the street in front of Brookins' house and gotten out. It's three men. I'm having trouble seeing their auras. Maybe when they get closer to the house lights I'll be able to see them better."

He sat up and watched the men walking up the steep driveway to the front of the house. The house was unlike any he had seen before. He estimated the row home he shared with Mildred would fit into this house ten times over.

"Nice place," he said.

"Really nice."

"What kind of job affords you a house like this?"

"Who knows? Based on what you told me, it sounds like for this guy there's a good chance whatever it is isn't legal."

He was uncomfortable. The voice inside his head began to caution him that something bad was about to happen. He could feel his anxiety levels rising and something deep inside his gut was screaming for him to get away. He typically listened to his instincts whenever he felt unnerved and yet, with Mia beside him, he couldn't.

"Can you see them yet? The auras?"

"Not yet. When they get in the light I should be able to." She paused and pressed her nose against the glass of the window. "Dark. All three. Very dark. I guarantee the men inside this house belong in prison."

"Well, at least you got the confirmation you needed. Guilt by association, right? If those three were dark, good old Wayne's no choir boy. I guess we can go now," he said, pulling on his seatbelt.

She didn't respond as she mulled over her next move. His internal struggle continued and he was desperate to tell her about the danger he felt was coming.

"No, Mia," he pleaded as he saw the start of a plan in her expression. "We did what we came for. These are bad guys. You saw with your own eyes. Now let's get out of here and go catch a movie or something. Anything."

She turned to face him and he saw her eyes sparkling with anticipation. "Do you have any idea what kind of rare opportunity we've stumbled on here? We've got a party of baddies all in one place. If we can get in there we might gain some insight into what's going on."

"Inside?"

She opened her door and scurried into the night.

"Hey! Wait!" he called as he fumbled with the door handle. By the time he got out of the car and closed the door quietly behind him, she was already halfway across the neighbor's yard. She was crouched behind a large oak several feet from the property line when he eventually caught up to her.

"I'm beginning to think I might not have the stamina for a relationship with you. What are we doing?" he asked.

"We're going inside."

"Don't we need a warrant or something?"

"You don't," she replied.

"I'm not going in! And even if I did it would be breaking and entering."

She glared at him and it was clear he was irritating her. "I won't arrest you."

"How considerate," he groaned.

"Look, no one is going to know we're here. If anyone asks, I'm just responding to a noise violation. But no one's going to ask. We're just taking a look around. Nothing more," she explained matter-of-factly.

He shook his head, completely frustrated with her lack of common sense. "I honestly didn't believe falling in love with a cop was going to land me in prison."

He looked up and their eyes locked as he became aware of his verbal blunder.

"First of all, you are not going to end up in jail. And secondly, did you just say what I think you said?"

"I'm in a high-stress situation and I'm panicking," he blurted. "I don't even know what I'm saying."

She leaned close, whispering into his ear. "We learned at the academy that the more stressful the circumstances, the more likely it is someone will tell the truth."

"Well I guess that's the truth then, Officer Rosetti. I guess I *am* falling in love with you. Are you happy?" he snapped, his anxiety rising with the pressure of the situation.

"Actually, for the first time in a long time, I am," she sighed, wrapping her arms around his waist and laying her head on his chest, "because I'm pretty sure I'm falling in love with you too."

His heart swelled. In that instant, he was no longer hiding behind a tree, hoping to avoid imminent injury or death - he was just standing at the exact center of the universe holding the most amazing woman in the world. And that woman, for some unknown reason, loved him back.

The magic of her pronouncement held his anxiety at bay for a moment, but the reality of his situation quickly returned and he felt compelled to move them both to safety.

"Then let's celebrate our love with dessert and then head back home. Please, don't do this," he begged.

"I can't. It's in my blood. I have to know," she said.

He sighed in resignation. She was breaking into the house and he was going with her.

"After you," he said finally, releasing her from his embrace.

He followed her to the side of the house where they paused briefly beside the air conditioning units for her to further assess the situation.

"The first floor is lit up. There's a walk out basement but the lights are out down there. That's going to be our way in," she instructed.

"If you say so."

She nodded. "Stay close."

They crept from their hidden position behind the compressors to the back of the house where she began trying the windows, one by one, to see if any would budge. The third one she tried slid open and she waved him over.

"We're in."

"Fabulous," he replied, his voice dripping with sarcasm.

"Come on," she whispered as she shimmied through the open sash. He saw her feet dangling in midair for a few seconds before she disappeared into the house.

"Are you okay?" he called.

"Yes," she replied. "Hurry up."

He followed her lead, hoisting himself through the open window. By the time he was inside, he caught only a glimpse of her as she hugged the wall around the corner of the staircase leading to the first floor. He hurried, squatting low across the length of the room, his sneakers squeaking against the travertine flooring. He began to tiptoe for fear of giving them away.

From his vantage point at the bottom of the steps, the light from the rooms above silhouetted Mia crouching behind the banister at the top. She was, from his perspective, glowing. Bathed in the light from above her, he imagined he was seeing her as she would appear to herself. He knew without a doubt she had a good soul and he stood transfixed, in awe of both her bravery and her determination.

Quietly, he climbed the staircase and sat on the step below where she was listening.

"Can you see them?" he asked in a low voice.

"Yes. There are about fifteen of them."

"And?"

"And their auras are dark. Every one of them. I need you to peek around the corner to confirm that you see the other men from Belinda's. Can you do that?"

He hesitated. "Do you need me to?"

"Yes," she replied. Her exasperation was palpable.

She was counting on him and he knew it. "Then I can," he said, surprising himself.

She carefully slid around him and he moved to the top of the stairs.

"Be careful. Make small movements," she instructed.

He peered around the corner into a spacious gathering room where all of the men were located. There were several large sofas where a handful of the men were seated. The rest were scattered around the room chatting in small groups. He immediately recognized three of the four men he had overheard at Belinda's that afternoon. He crept back to the step beside her.

"I see three of them. Wayne Brookins of course. Also, Frank Guthry is sitting on the sofa closest to us with the cigar and grey sweater vest. The last guy is on the far side of the room by the window talking to two other men. He's wearing tan khakis and an oxford with the sleeves rolled up."

Mia grabbed him and kissed him forcefully on the lips. "I'm so proud of you," she whispered.

"Good. So can we get out of here now?"

"I've only been able to hear a little of their conversations and I want to try to get some pictures first."

"Pictures!?"

"Yes. Pictures. I need to have something to give my dad, even if it won't prove anything officially. Give me ten more minutes."

He watched her venture out beyond the newel post once again. His anxiety levels began to diminish and his breathing finally slowed. He didn't know if it was her confidence or his own that comforted him, but he felt as though the danger had passed.

He strained to hear what the men were discussing but only caught bits and pieces. They were definitely talking about the women. He heard someone mention "the one that escaped."

He checked his watch. It had been six minutes since she began her 'investigation' and he was going to hold her to the ten she had requested. He watched the hands slowly ticking forward around the face. Boisterous laughter suddenly flooded the stairway and his skin prickled. He tapped her on the back.

"Let's go, it's been ten minutes."

To his surprise, she didn't hesitate. "I'll follow you," she said.

He breathed a sigh of relief when they were once again safely ensconced inside her car. Without a word, she started the engine and backed up slowly down the street. She left the lights off as they wove through the neighborhood, hoping to find a way out that wouldn't require driving past Brookins' residence. After several tense minutes, she pulled out onto the main road and quickly switched on the headlights.

Finally, he reached out to gently touch her cheek as if to wipe away an unshed tear. "Are you okay?" he asked.

"No. Not really."

He couldn't believe how shaken up she was. He had never seen her so upset. "Do you want to talk about it?"

"Not in the car. Not while I'm driving."

"Okay. Where do you want to go?"

"Will you come back to my place?" she asked hopefully.

"Of course," he replied.

They drove in silence the entire way across town.

"Chelsea's car isn't here. I wonder why she's still not home," she said as they walked across the parking lot together. He saw her checking her phone as they entered her apartment.

"Chelsea texted me while I had my phone off to let me know she's staying at Tyler's tonight." She looked at him and suddenly burst into tears.

He hurried to her, wrapping her in his arms. "Mia, what's the matter?"

"It's those men. From the house tonight."

"What about them? What did you see?" he probed. He led her into the den and sat with her on the couch.

"In all my years of being a cop, I have never seen anything like it. They were ruthless. The things they were saying about the women were unimaginable. They spoke about those women as though they weren't even human. They were acting like they were selling drugs or weapons. But Thomas, they're selling people! What sort of monsters do that?"

"The worst sort," he said.

"I've got to tell my dad about this. We have to stop these men from hurting any more women. And we have to find the girls that are still out there."

"That sounds like a good plan," he said, holding her face in his hands. "If anyone can do this, you can, Mia."

He was frightened by what he saw in her eyes. The confident, self-assured woman who chased down muggers and had no reservations about breaking into a house full of criminals was gone. Something she saw broke her spirit.

She cleared her throat and her voice wavered.

"Thomas?" she said.

"Yes?"

"I don't want to be alone. Not tonight."

He was sure she could hear his heart beating from within his chest, but he wasn't sure he understood what she was saying.

"Are you asking me to stay?"

She gazed up at him, her eyes glistening with tears. "Do you want to stay?"

"Yes," he replied without any hesitation.

"Then I'm asking."

He lowered his face to hers, gently kissing her forehead, her nose, her lips. She returned his kiss forcefully and passionately, pushing him backward onto the sofa.

Instantly, all the fear and anxiety of the night washed away, and for him, all that existed was Mia. Her hair fell into his face and he was surrounded by the crisp, familiar smell of her shampoo. She continued kissing him as if possessed by something powerful and needy. Suddenly she stopped and he watched as she quickly removed her shirt, her fingers nimbly unfastening each tiny button with great proficiency. Next, she pulled him up by his arms and wriggled him free from his shirt, throwing both into a pile on the floor.

He hesitantly touched her arms. Her shoulders. The small of her back. He was surprised by the strength of the muscles he felt beneath her smooth skin. Her body felt lean and powerful and he was overcome by a desire to know every inch of her.

He was aware that she was exploring him with the same fervor. She kissed his chest and his stomach but hesitated at the waistband of his jeans. She looked up expectantly at him, her eyes full of desire. He saw something else behind her passion. He suddenly recognized it as the love she had spoken of earlier in the evening. Love for him, a man who had been thrown away his entire life. And now, here she was loving him as much as he loved her.

He quickly took off his belt and she stood up so he could remove his pants. He followed as she led him into the privacy of her bedroom. Within seconds, what was left of their clothing was strewn across the floor and he was beside her, their bodies pressed firmly together as they lost themselves in one another's embrace.

He watched her as she lay quietly sleeping on the pillow beside him. He reached out to move a lock of her hair that was draped across her cheek. He touched her lips with his fingertips and considered how alive and secure she made him feel. For the first time in his life, he embraced the hope of a new beginning. He curled his body around her tiny frame and slept peacefully through the night.

CHAPTER

29

MIA

The alarm sounded before dawn and Mia was immediately wide awake. She was also on the floor.

"Sorry!" Thomas cried as he leaned over the edge of the bed to reach out his hand to her. "I don't know what happened!"

"Do you do that every morning when the alarm goes off?" she asked, pulling the covers around her as she climbed back into bed.

"No. That's new. I didn't mean to shove you off the bed. I guess I just didn't realize where I was. Or who I was with. It's probably left over from all the moving around when I was a kid."

"Well, remind me next time to put a pillow on the floor before we fall asleep so I can at least have a soft landing," she laughed.

She folded herself into his arms and thought about facing the day. She was dreading it.

"Tell me we can just stay here all day," she said.

"We can just stay here all day," he replied.

"You, sir, are a liar."

"Yes. Yes I am."

She turned toward him. Their faces were only inches apart. His chin was covered in stubble and his eyes were still heavy with sleep - she'd never seen him looking more adorable. She didn't know how it had happened, but Thomas Pritchett had stolen her heart.

"I have to deal with last night now," she said.

"I know. What's your plan?"

"I don't have a plan. I'm just going to wing it."

"That sounds like it is going to require coffee."

"Lots of coffee," she agreed.

"I'm on it," he said, kissing her on the nose.

She watched as he climbed out of bed, threw on his pants and went searching for his t-shirt in the other room, thankful he hadn't brought up her emotional break-down from the night before. She quickly showered, dressed for work, and was applying a layer of mascara when the smell of freshly brewed coffee made its way into the bedroom. There was also the smell of something else that drew her into the kitchen.

"French toast!" she cried as she sat down at the breakfast bar. "I haven't had homemade French toast in the longest time. I love French toast. How did you know?"

"You ordered it at Belinda's," he responded.

"You're a stalker," she replied, laughing at his observation skills. "You might have some detective abilities after all!"

"I might be observant, but I don't think I have the cojones to do what you do. Now, eat your breakfast because we both have to get moving if we're going to make it to work on time this morning."

"What happened to letting me stay in bed all day?"

"You have to save the world, remember? And Belinda needs her tables bussed. So that makes us both pretty important," he replied.

She devoured her breakfast. It was delicious and she was starving after the adrenaline rush of the previous night. When they finished eating, she cleared the dishes while Thomas showered and dressed for work.

"I hope no one will mind I'm wearing yesterday's clothes," he said as they stood together in the parking lot beside her car.

"You smell good. You look nice. No one will even notice. Are you sure I can't drive you in?"

"You'll be late if there's any traffic. The bus is fine," he said.

"Okay." She hesitated, suddenly not wanting to let him out of her sight.

"Call me. Let me know what you find out about the traffickers."

"I will," she replied, not wanting to think about any of the men at Brookins' house.

"Okay. Have a great day."

"You too." She continued to stall.

He leaned down to kiss her gently. "Bye, Mia."

"Bye," she said.

She watched as he walked down the sidewalk toward the bus stop. She slid into the car and headed in the opposite direction, toward the beltway.

On her drive to work, she forced Thomas from her mind and measured her options with regard to the traffickers. Part of her wanted to tell Jack but knew he would be upset that she hadn't called him to go along with her to Brookins' house. When she considered how furious he would be if he found out she took a civilian on the stakeout, she ruled out confiding in him before ever reaching the station.

That left her father. She decided to go straight to him with the information she acquired at the stakeout, knowing she would have to fabricate a back story which didn't involve Thomas. She found him in the briefing room with a group of senior officers, so she waited outside the door until he finished, ambushing him as he came through the door.

"Dad, I have to talk to you."

"Whoa! Good morning to you too. Where's the fire?"

"It's important. I have some information about the girl that was brought in the other day."

"Which one?" Rosetti laughed.

"The foreign girl claiming she escaped from a basement brothel. Zocha."

He eyed her skeptically. "Okay. What have you got?"

There were dozens of officers hurrying through the station. "Can we go someplace private? I don't really feel comfortable discussing it here in the hallway."

"Sure," he replied as he led her toward his office. He invited her to sit in the chair beside him at his desk.

"So, what's so important?"

"I think there's a large group of men here in the city who are trafficking women from overseas."

He rocked back in his chair. "That's a pretty big accusation. What kind of proof do you have?"

"If I tell you, you have to promise not to be mad."

He narrowed his eyes. "This doesn't sound good, Mia."

"Just hear me out," she began. "I did some undercover work last night and nothing I have will be admissible in court, so someone else will have to track it all down legally."

"Mia!" Rosetti yelled.

"You promised not to get mad," she said.

"I did no such thing! I didn't teach you to go out on your own to follow leads outside of protocol. Please tell me you had Jack with you."

"I went alone," she lied.

Her father stewed beside her, confirming their conversation wouldn't be pleasant, but for the sake of the women out there suffering, it was the least she could do.

"Dad, I have names. And photos. I've seen lots of them and their auras are all very dark. It was awful." She saw his demeanor softening. "Please, Dad. We have to stop them."

He ran his hands across his face and rubbed the back of his neck. "Show me what you've got," he said at last.

She handed him her phone and let him scroll through the photos.

"I'm not even going to ask how you got into this house," he said.

"That's probably a good idea," she acknowledged.

"And what did you hear?"

"They bring the women here from overseas. They lure them. The women don't know they are going to be sold into prostitution. Once they get here, they lock them away and sell them repeatedly to the highest bidder. The men make huge profits. We have to stop them. And we have to find the women."

He scrolled through the photos a second time. "You have names?"

"Two so far. We could probably run facial recognition software on these photos to get others. I'm sure many of them have some sort of record."

A smile spread across his face.

"You're a good cop, you know that?" he said.

"I am?"

"Yeah. You are. The girl that came in last week? I haven't had a chance to think about her since. But you? You saw a problem and took the initiative to figure out what's going on. And not because you want to look good to the brass. You did it because you honestly care. I don't know how you turned out to be such a good woman, growing up without a mother, but you did. I'm proud of you, Mia."

She swelled with pride. Her father had never been big on praise. "Thanks, Dad," she said.

"The commissioner is headed in here this morning for his weekly news conference. I'm going to let him know about this. You deserve some recognition."

She blanched involuntarily. "No. I don't think that's a good idea."

"Why not? You worried about him wanting to know how you got the pictures?"

"No. It's not that." She hesitated.

"Oh God, Mia. It's not the darkness thing again, is it? We've beaten this horse to death."

She fumbled for words, unable to form a cohesive argument.

"I'm going to go see if he's here. He needs to know about this."

She followed her father out of his office and up the stairs to the conference room. She was aware that he trusted the commissioner implicitly, but she couldn't share his confidence because of what she saw. She decided to throw a Hail Mary.

"Dad, maybe we should bring county in on this. The house was out in Owings Mills. Then we don't need to involve the commissioner at all."

Rosetti stopped sharply and turned to face her.

"Where did the girl show up?"

"Here at the station."

"You think she walked here from the county?"

"Not likely."

"Then where do you think they are holding these girls?"

She was silent. She had no further arguments.

"You wanna help these girls or not, Mia?"

"I do. You know I do."

"Well, then come on," Rosetti said as he turned on his heel and continued down the hall.

By the time they reached the conference room, Commissioner Dalton was already fielding questions from the press. She stood in the back of the room and willed the darkness she saw surrounding him to disappear. She closed her eyes and opened them repeatedly. She squinted and even tried one eye at a time. The result was always the same. Commissioner Dalton was shrouded in darkness.

When the meeting was over and the press began filing out of the room, her father made his way to the front and she watched as he shook hands with the commissioner and they shared a laugh together. Within moments, he was motioning for her to join their conversation.

She saluted as she approached. "Good morning, Commissioner Dalton," she said.

"Officer Rosetti, it's lovely to see you again. The Chief here tells me you've done a little side investigation and have turned up what you think could be a human trafficking ring?"

"Yes, Sir."

"Can you tell me what you know?"

"Yes, Sir. I received a tip that a man named Wayne Brookins and three of his companions were overheard discussing the sale of women."

"Who shared this information with you?"

"It was an anonymous tip, Sir," she lied.

"I see. Go on."

"I did some investigation into Mr. Brookins and found he had several arrests for solicitation. I decided on a whim to take a drive to his house to see if I could find out any more about his activities. I discovered a dozen or so men at his house and they all seemed to be in on the trafficking."

"That's some pretty good detective work," said the commissioner.

"Thank you, Sir," she replied.

"Would you be able to identify any of the other men?"

"I don't know. It was sort of dark," she said, not wanting to share more than she had to with him.

"Tell him about the photos," her father suggested.

She glared at her father. The last thing she wanted to do was let the commissioner know she had photographs of the men. Now she would be forced to release them to Dalton immediately.

"I took a few photos with my phone. They aren't very good," she said, shrugging her shoulders to insinuate that she was an incompetent photographer.

"I'd like to see them just the same. May I?"

She handed the commissioner her phone and he scrolled through the photos.

"I'd like to take your phone so I can get a copy of these photos for myself."

"I'm afraid they won't be admissible," she said.

"Just the same, we can use them to help us with the case to get admissible documentation."

She hesitated. "That's fine," she said.

"Wonderful. Well," he said, turning to her father, "you've got yourself one hell of a detective here. I'll put some of my best Lieutenants on the case and see if we can sniff them out. Great job, Officer Rosetti."

"Thank you, Sir."

She glanced at her father. He was beaming with pride. For an instant, she forgot that she had just given important information about herself to a man she didn't trust. For an instant, she only saw her father's joy. It had been a long time since she had seen such satisfaction in his eyes. She relished the moment. And then, it slipped away.

"Thank you for this," said the commissioner, holding up her phone. "I will return it to you shortly."

"That's fine," she said.

"Chief, I'll see you this afternoon?"

"Absolutely. Wouldn't miss it."

"Thank you both. Have a great day," Dalton said as he started walking toward the door.

"I'll walk with you," said her father.

"Goodbye," she said quietly, but the men had already left the room.

Mia remained frozen in place, alone and disquieted for several moments, not knowing where to go or what to do. The realization of how poorly she handled the trafficking situation infuriated her. Nothing had gone quite the way she planned and she was livid with herself for allowing the commissioner to get involved.

She absentmindedly reached into her pocket for her phone so she could call Thomas. When she found that her pocket was empty, remembering the commissioner had just left with her phone, she could no longer keep her anger at bay. She realized immediately that she didn't have his number memorized and would have no way of contacting him until her phone was returned.

Exasperated with the situation and with nowhere else to turn, she made her way to her office to begin her assigned daily duties. A fresh stack of files greeted her arrival but her mind was elsewhere. Visions of emaciated women, beaten and abused, kept her from fully focusing on logging the evidence from an overnight burglary. She sensed the men at the party were somehow involved in whatever was going on and was determined to find a viable connection, with or without the commissioner.

Her thoughts wandered to Thomas and she couldn't help but wonder about the apprehension he exhibited at the Brookins' estate. She wasn't used to being around someone so fearful and assumed the trepidation stemmed from his traumatic childhood. On the other hand, fearfulness aside, it was curious to her that neither the physical or psychological abuse he endured seemed to have damaged him in any significant way. There was no evidence of drug or alcohol abuse, self-harm, social disorders, or depression. He seemed genuinely happy with his life. It was almost as if something was shielding him from the effects of his abusive past.

Halfway through the list of missing items from the convenience store, she logged out of the precinct's server and typed "Sevens Prophecy" into the web browser. Thinking of Thomas reminded her about his third foster mother who was also familiar with the bizarre end-of-days prediction. She didn't think this added to its credibility but was curious to explore it more fully just the same.

A quick Google search provided pages of related articles, and she was surprised that with the wealth of information available she had never come across it before. The fourth article she clicked on was written by Dr. Margaret Mendelsohn, a name she recognized immediately as a reliable source. Dr. Mendelsohn described the prophecy, which dated back to the ancient Egyptians, in great detail, explaining what she believed to be the specific types of psychics involved in the revelation. The seven abilities listed for the good psychics included telepathy, energy healing, psychometry, telekinesis, clairvoyance, premonition, and aura reading. Upon reading the last ability, her hands were shaking above the keyboard. Her ability to read auras, one of the rarest of gifts, was listed among the seven, as was perception outside the known human senses. She wondered if perhaps this was a gift Thomas himself possessed as it could explain both his fearful behavior and lack of physical damage from his past. It did not however explain why she was unable to see his aura.

Mia was still researching the prophecy an hour later when Jack burst into the room, his face flushed from the coolness of the outdoors. She quickly shut down the browser and returned to the burglary file before looking up to greet him properly. With so much on her mind, from the trafficked women to the commissioner to Thomas to the prophecy, she looked forward to the end of her shift when she could go home to be by herself and sort it all properly.

CHAPTER

30

KATE

Kate sat quietly in her cell, examining the walls around her. Although her faith in her power had been restored after it protected her from being raped by Mr. V, she realized that perhaps she would not be able to rely solely on her gift if she was going to save her sisters and rescue the others. She would be forced to rely on her earthly abilities as well.

She touched the bruise on her face, a painful reminder of her evening with Mr. V. The bruise would heal quickly. Far more quickly than the damage the others sustained the night before.

Each had returned to the basement separately and she had been one of the first. Hours later, in the stillness of the night, Anya was brought to her cell and her bindings were released. Her eyes were dark, hollow orbs.

"Anya?" she called as soon as they were alone.

Anya did not respond. She was lying on her mattress in the corner of her cell in the fetal position, her knees pulled tightly to her chest.

"Anya, come talk to me," she pleaded.

"Go away, Kate. I just want to be left alone," she responded.

"Are you hurt?"

"Yes! Of course I'm hurt! That monster tore me wide open!"

"Oh, Anya. I'm so sorry." She hesitated to continue. "Did he beat you?"

"Does it matter? Enough, Kate. I don't want to talk about it anymore."

She honored Anya's request and retreated into her own thoughts, replaying the events of her evening until Lera arrived less than an hour later. She heard muffled sobbing before she could actually see who was approaching and quickly identified that it was Lera being brought down the stairs. Unlike Anya, who dealt with her grief by shutting herself away, Lera was desperate for consolation.

"Kate, it was so horrible," she wept through the bars. "It was like he was possessed, attacking me like I had no feelings of my own. He didn't care whether he was causing me pain. He just kept going. I think he was actually trying to hurt me."

"It's all over for now," she said soothingly. "And you are still in one piece, so you can heal. It's just your body. And your body is a strong house for your soul. It will heal."

"It feels like he's stolen my soul," Lera moaned.

"He hasn't. He can't. Not unless you let him. So don't let him. He can do what he wants to your body, but your soul is yours alone, so don't let him get to it. Do you understand me?" she asked, reaching out her hand into Lera's cell.

Lera grabbed her hand and held on to it tightly. For a long while, neither girl spoke.

"Was it so awful for you?" Lera asked her.

"Yes. He was unkind and he demeaned me. But he's just a man. A stupid man that pays money for sex. He's the one who deserves our pity, not the other way around. So I feel sorry for him because he is a wretched creature who doesn't know anything of love or kindness. And he can try to make himself feel less pathetic by using me the way he did, but it clearly isn't working because he keeps doing it. I won't let him bring me down, Lera. I won't."

"Me neither," Lera whispered. "You are right about them. They are the filth. Not us."

"Yes. And do you know something else? I'm going to get us out of here."

"You are? How can you do that?" Lera asked excitedly, reaching both of her hands through the bars.

"I don't know yet. I'm still working on it, but I feel like it's a possibility. It will take some time, so you may have to persevere for a while. Do you think you can do that?"

"I don't know. I can try."

"You must. You are stronger than you think, Lera. We all are," Kate said, loud enough for Anya to hear as well.

It was dawn before the last of the girls was returned to the basement. She watched as they each dealt with the abuse in their own way. Most were like Anya, shutting themselves away from the others to grieve the small death they experienced each time they were taken to the men who owned them for the night. Only a few cried openly and she noticed two of the women seemed unfazed by the night's events. She wondered if they had made peace with their circumstances and had chosen to rise above them or if the souls within their decaying bodies were already completely dead.

Even more determined to save them all, she spent the following day concentrating on finding a way out. After the morning's rations were delivered, she began taking stock of her assets. She was physically strong, although not strong enough to defend herself against most men. She also knew she could walk or even run for long distances if necessary. Although she assumed she had lost a few pounds, her body had not yet begun to deteriorate from lack of nourishment, which she added to her list of strengths.

After hours of racking her brain for anything she could use to help her escape, she suddenly remembered the hair pins her father had given her on the morning of her departure. She had not seen the rest of her belongings since boarding the plane that fateful day, but the tiny velvet box had made the trip, tucked carefully away under her mattress.

She slid the velvet box out from where it was hidden and stood for a moment to feel the weight of it in her hands. As if she was holding a sacred relic, she opened the lid of the box and picked up one of the pins. It was beautifully painted, made of the highest quality metal, and measured almost three inches in length.

She immediately identified the pin as a means to open the door lock. For several hours, she sat on the floor of her cell, her hands twisted painfully outside of the bars as she attempted to pick the lock. Without a word, Lera watched anxiously from the adjacent cell and even Anya stole a glance now and then from her mattress to check on her progress. However, as night began to fall, she finally accepted that it was an impossible task and she placed the pin back into its box.

As she was closing the lid, she was struck by yet another use for the pins. She held the head of the pin in her right hand and slid the length of the pin between her fingers. Next, she poked the pin firmly into the palm of her other hand. It felt sharp. And painful.

She added the hairpins to the list of assets she was tallying in her head. Should the opportunity present itself, she was sure she could palm one of the pins in her hand and force it into the eye socket of her captor. The thought brought a smile to her face.

For the remainder of the evening she concentrated her energies on thoughts of escape. Over and over she whispered to herself "I will find a way out" until she became one with her mantra. She focused on sending her desires out into the world, hoping her gift would bring her a plausible solution. When the lights finally turned off at the end of the day, she slept soundly for the first time since leaving Kiev, satisfied with the knowledge that if there was a way out of the situation, she would be the one to find it.

CHAPTER

31

THOMAS

Thomas took his phone from his pocket for the fourteenth time since lunch. There were no messages and no missed calls. He tossed the phone across the kitchen table and rested his head in his hands.

"Tommy, what is it?" Mildred asked as she placed a warm bowl of beef stew on the table in front of him.

"Ugh. It's Mia," he said.

"What about her? I thought things were going well. You promised you were bringing her over," Mildred said as she sat in the chair beside him.

"Things were great, but I think I blew it."

"Why's that?"

"Because it's been three days and nothing."

"What happened three days ago?" she asked.

He hesitated. "I told her I loved her."

"Oh." Mildred paused, observing him across the table as she ate a spoonful of stew. "And what's happened since then?"

"Nothing. Not a single thing. That's the problem. I called her that afternoon. She didn't pick up so I left a message. Told her I'd like to get together when she was free and to call when she got a chance. She didn't call me back. I figured she was just swamped at the station. So the next day,

I did the same thing. Left a message. No response. Today, I left another message asking if I've done something wrong because I have no idea what's going on."

"Why don't you just go see her?" Mildred asked.

His shoulders slumped. "I don't want to seem desperate. I already feel like such a loser."

Mildred slid her chair closer to his. "Tommy, do you like this girl?"

"Yes. I'm falling in love with her and I opened my big mouth about it accidentally. I think maybe I freaked her out a little with that. Too much, too soon."

"Well, then, if she already knows how you feel, what's the harm in going to see her so you can find out face to face why she's not returning your calls?"

He blew on a spoonful of carrots and reflected on Mildred's suggestion, admitting in the end that she was right. Mia was clearly avoiding him for some unknown reason, but there could be no harm in trying to see her to find out why.

"I wonder if she's working tonight?" he thought aloud.

"Are you heading into the city to play tonight?"

"I was going to," he replied.

"Then why don't you just stop by the station on the way to see if she's there. The worst thing that can happen is she won't be there."

"No, Ma. The worst thing would be if she *is* there and refuses to see me."

"I guess you're right about that," Mildred replied thoughtfully. "She'll see you, though. How could she resist that face?" she asked, giving his cheek an affectionate squeeze.

He rolled his eyes, ignoring her optimism, and placed his bowl and spoon into the dishwasher after finishing his meal.

He glanced at the clock on the stove. "If I leave now I can make it to the police station and still get to the hotel before the dinner crowd."

"Do you want me to wait up?" she asked.

"It's okay, Ma. I'll be fine."

223

"I know. Somehow, you always are," she said.

He wavered between subdued anticipation and full blown dread on his bus ride into the city. By the time he climbed down the steps onto the sidewalk outside the station, he'd convinced himself he would probably never speak to Mia again.

He was unsure of where to go or who to speak with when he entered the building. He was familiar with the lineup officers so he decided to start by talking to them.

Without looking up from his computer screen, the officer manning the desk addressed him. "Lineups are over for the day," he said curtly.

"I'm not here for a lineup," he replied. "I was hoping to speak with Officer Rosetti."

"The chief?" he asked, looking up from his keyboard.

"No. His daughter. Officer Mia Rosetti."

The man chewed on the inside of his cheek. "Haven't seen her today. Come to think of it, I haven't seen her all week. Is there someone else I can get to help you?"

He blanched at the information. In the pit of his stomach, he immediately felt that something wasn't right.

"Is her partner here? Jack?" he asked.

"I don't know if he's gone for the day or not. Do you want me to give him a call and see if he's at his desk?"

"Sure," he replied, unnerved by the prospect of meeting her partner. "That'd be great."

"Who can I tell him is here?"

"Mia's friend, Thomas. Thomas Pritchett."

He listened to the lineup officer's half of the phone conversation and quickly surmised Jack was willing to speak with him. He was led through a labyrinth of hallways until he finally reached the office Jack and Mia shared.

Jack stood to greet him, knocking a large stack of manila folders off the corner of his desk. Thomas stooped to help him pick them up before they formally shook hands by way of introduction.

"So, you must be Mia's Thomas," Jack said, smiling.

"And you must be Mia's Jack," he replied, returning his firm handshake.

"Nice to finally meet you," Jack said.

"You too. She speaks very highly of you."

"You too." Jack paused, and Thomas could see he was sizing him up as he sat back in his chair. "You're lucky you caught me today. Most days I'd have been out of here by now, but since Mia's been gone, I've had to stay late to get all the work done. So, what can I do for you?"

He settled himself in the chair beside him. He could tell Jack was upset by Mia's absence and it wasn't because of the additional workload. He obviously missed having her around. He was surprised that, instead of feeling jealous, he felt a sudden kinship with Jack.

"It's actually Mia I came to see, but I was told she's not here."

Jack shook his head. "Nope, she sure isn't."

"You have any idea where she is?" he asked.

"No. I don't. It's funny," Jack said laughing, "I thought for sure she was with you."

"Clearly not."

"Clearly."

"So where is she?" he asked. His mind was racing with possibilities. None of them were good.

"I have no idea. I just heard from human resources two days ago that she requested to take leave," Jack said.

"For how long?"

Jack shrugged. "I don't know. They didn't say."

"And you have no idea where she might have gone?" he asked.

"Like I said, I thought for sure she was with you."

He felt a sense of desperation closing in around him. It was obvious Jack would be of no further assistance, so without wasting another minute he thanked him for his time and left the office.

"I'm sure she's fine," Jack called out the door as he was nearly halfway down the hall. "I'll have her call you if I see her before you do."

"Thanks," he replied half-heartedly. "I'll do the same."

He was unsure of his next course of action. He was, for some reason, overwrought with concern for Mia's safety. It was unnerving to him that she would call out from work without letting the people closest to her know where she was or what she was doing. Jack's lackadaisical attitude led him to believe that she had probably taken leave without warning in the past. If that was the case, then it was possible he was completely overreacting. Just the same, he decided to go to her apartment to see if she was there.

On the bus ride out of the city, he allowed himself to hope that perhaps her unresponsiveness had nothing to do with him at all. He considered the possibility she had been called away unexpectedly by an old friend or family member.

Before he made it to her apartment, it suddenly dawned on him that he should have asked to speak with her father while he was at the station, assuming he would know what was keeping his daughter from work. He almost got off the bus to make a return trip to the station but realized there was a good chance her father had already gone home for the evening.

Resolved to stay the course, he got off at the Parkville stop, just a couple of blocks from Mia's apartment. He hoped she would greet him at the door with a wonderful story about a long lost cousin who had come for a visit. As he approached her building, he scanned the parking lot for her car. It wasn't there. His heart sank.

Desperate for answers, he climbed the steps to her apartment two at a time and then hesitantly knocked on the door. He drummed his fingers on the door frame, waiting anxiously for a response. He didn't hear any movement from behind the door to indicate anyone was inside. He knocked again, pounding the door defiantly with his fist. There was still no response from inside the apartment.

He returned to the ground floor and walked around the perimeter of the building to where he could see the back windows of her apartment. Although he doubted he was being ignored, he wanted to check to be sure that she wasn't just avoiding him. Above him, all of the rooms were dark. This was enough to convince him neither Mia nor Chelsea was home. The realization that she wasn't at work or at home only served to heighten his anxiety.

A glance at his watch confirmed his wild goose chase had officially made him late for work. He predicted that if he was lucky, he could still make it back into the city in less than thirty minutes which would leave him several good tipping hours before the crowds thinned out.

Upon his arrival to the hotel, he spent the remainder of the evening playing baroque requiems by Mozart and Faure. He doubted his selections did anything to improve his tips but his mental state didn't allow him to play anything more upbeat. It seemed only appropriate that he should play funeral masses when he felt as though he was mourning his own losses. Nonetheless, while he played, he resolved to pay a visit to her father at the station after his shift at Belinda's the following day. He was hopeful the chief would be able to provide some insight into her whereabouts. He only hoped that wherever she was, she was safe and happy. He also hoped there was some small possibility that wherever she was, she was thinking of him.

CHAPTER

33

KATE

Kate was suddenly awake, staring into the darkness of Lera's cell. For a moment, there was only silence, and she couldn't pinpoint what it was that had roused her from her sleep. Then, without warning, the overhead bulbs flickered on and the sleeping inhabitants of the basement were bathed in a harsh, glaring light. She was stricken blind for several moments while her pupils struggled to adjust to the sudden brightness of the room.

She watched as the captive women began to come to, groaning and stretching in their cells. The men had never been to the basement in the middle of the night and she surmised their arrival was an indication of bad news. For that reason, she was immediately concerned for her own safety and chose to remain motionless, hoping to avoid drawing any unnecessary attention to herself. The familiar scraping of the door latch confirmed they would soon be joined by at least one of the men, and she wasn't surprised to hear several sets of footsteps coming down the stairs.

She willed herself to lie still on her mattress although she longed to know what was causing the commotion further down the corridor.

"Keep walking, Princess," a familiar voice said.

"She's a real piece of work," said another of the men who frequented the basement. "Wonder what they're gonna do with her?"

"Who knows? She ain't our problem. All they told me was to find somewhere to keep her down here for now. I just do what I'm told."

"Quit throwing elbows or I'll rip them off!" the first man yelled at whoever they were dragging down the hall.

"If she's this much trouble tied up, I bet she put up one hell of a fight when they grabbed her. I heard somebody ended up with a broken nose."

"Hope it was Lenny. That kid had it coming."

"Who knows? You wouldn't think such a little thing would be so tough, but this bitch has claws."

She was aware the trio had stopped directly in front of her cell. The final cell, next to Anya's on the opposite side of the hall, was the only one that remained unoccupied. She listened as the metal door creaked on its hinges and the newest arrival was shoved unceremoniously into the cell.

"You gonna leave her like that?" asked one of the men.

"Yeah. Why not? The others will be here in the morning with breakfast for the rest of the whores. Let them deal with her. I don't wanna risk getting this beautiful face of mine messed up," he laughed as he shut and locked the cell door behind him.

"Whateva you say."

Without any further conversation, the two men made their way along the hallway, climbed the stairs, and disappeared into the night. They extinguished the lights and the basement was thrown into immediate darkness. She sat up on her mattress and waited as her eyes struggled again to acclimate themselves to her surroundings.

"Anya?" she called into the shadows.

"Yes?"

"Can you reach her?"

"I don't know. I can't see yet," Anya replied. She began speaking to the newest member of their group in English.

"If you can understand me, follow my voice and come stand beside my cell. I will help get you untied."

She heard the new girl shuffling along the floor in Anya's direction. She took it as a good sign that the woman understood English. Her eyes were beginning to adjust to the darkness and she could just make out the outline of the woman fumbling toward Anya's voice.

"That's good. You are almost here. Be careful. Don't run into the wall. Good," Anya said, coaching her across the cell. "Okay, now I need you to turn around so I can try to untie your hands. I can see them now, pretty well, but it might take me a few minutes, so hang in there."

She watched from her cell as Anya worked diligently on the woman's bindings. The woman was indeed small, as the men described. Part of her shirt was torn away and in addition to being bound, she was also blindfolded and gagged. Kate's heart ached for the newest arrival.

"I've almost got it. Just another minute," Anya said.

Finally, the rope slipped from around the woman's wrists. It fell to the ground and she immediately tore the blindfold from her eyes. She saw horror spread across the woman's face as she looked around the basement for the first time. The woman took two steps back and tripped on the mattress, falling to the floor. She did not attempt to stand up and instead started peeling the duct tape that was fastened securely across her mouth. She watched as the woman pulled delicately at the corner of the tape, grimacing with each tug. She was horrified when the woman began pulling firmly at one edge, and with one final yank, removed the entire strip of tape from her lips.

The basement echoed with an agonizing scream. She winced, imagining the excruciating pain the tape had caused. After several moments, the woman settled herself and walked to the edge of her cell.

"Thank you," she said weakly to Anya.

"You're welcome," Anya replied.

She detected something strange about the woman's voice. Her English was perfect. Almost too perfect.

"What is your name," Kate asked.

"Mia," the woman responded.

"I am Kate."

"And I am Anya."

"And I am trying to sleep!" called one of the women from the far end of the hall.

"Where are we?" Mia whispered.

"We don't know," said Anya.

"Where did you come from?" Mia continued.

"Anya and Lera and I are from Kiev, in the Ukraine," she replied. "But there are women here from all over. Where did they bring you from?"

"I live here. Here in Baltimore. I assume I'm still somewhere in the city. The ride wasn't that long so we couldn't have gone far."

The women were silent for several moments, and she struggled to understand why the men would choose to imprison an American woman. She had assumed that only foreign women were kept for the auctions because she hadn't seen a single American woman since her arrival. She wondered whether Mia would be auctioned off with the rest of them when the time came again.

She watched Mia return to her mattress where she sat with her legs folded beneath her. "What's going on here?" she whispered.

"It's too horrible to describe," said Lera, joining the conversation for the first time.

"Try me," Mia said, her voice both commanding and reassuring at the same time.

Kate sighed heavily. "There are fourteen of us. Now fifteen, including you. We've been brought here from many different countries. None of us were aware we were to be imprisoned when we arrived," she explained and then cut herself off because she was hesitant to continue.

"And why are they keeping you here?" Mia asked.

"To make money. They sell us at auction to the highest bidder," Anya said.

"And what does the highest bidder get for his payment?" asked Mia, quietly.

"He gets to rape you," Anya replied sharply.

She expected Mia to have some sort of visceral reaction to Anya's pronouncement, so it came as quite a surprise when instead, she didn't react at all. There were no gasps of shock or moans of horror. Instead, without another word, the petite woman lay down upon her mattress with her face toward the concrete wall and appeared to fall asleep. After several minutes, her voice echoed off the concrete walls of the warehouse basement.

"My name is Mia Rosetti and I am a police officer. I need you all to sleep well tonight. Tomorrow, I will need each of you to tell me your story. I will need you to remember every detail about the journey that led you to this basement. You will need to remember the faces of the men who lured you here, the men who enslaved you, and the men who have defiled you. I will need you to remember because tomorrow, I am going to help you all find a way out."

Kate curled up upon her own filthy mattress and appreciated at last the tremendous power of her gift. It was clear to her that the hours she spent each day concentrating on a way out had somehow brought Mia to help them. Never before had she been able to use her power to shape her own circumstances in such a tremendous way. She surmised that the reason for her increased ability was probably a direct result of the direness of her situation. She closed her eyes and found she was eager for morning and the opportunity it would surely bring.

CHAPTER

33

THOMAS

The clock on the nightstand read 4:18. Thomas had barely slept and although his mind continued to race, he was mentally exhausted. After several more minutes of staring at the ceiling, he decided to finally give up on sleep and begin the day.

He arrived early to the bistro and spent the hours before the restaurant opened in the kitchen with Belinda. He was glad for the distraction and baked dozens of scones by her side. If she noticed his lack of focus, she didn't mention it and seemed happy for the quiet company he provided.

By the time patrons arrived, the physical exhaustion from his lack of sleep was beginning to set in. He moved slowly around the dining room in a foggy daze. Dishes piled up and customers waited impatiently to be seated while he reset the tables. However, by the time the lunch crowd arrived, he had gotten a second wind and was turning over tables more quickly. As he carried a full tub of plates and glasses into the kitchen, Belinda caught him by surprise at the doorway.

"Penny for your thoughts today, Thomas?" she asked.

"I didn't sleep well last night," he said, setting the tub beside the industrial dishwasher. "I've been dragging today. I'm sorry, Belinda. I'm feeling better now."

233

"No. Now there's more to it than a lack of sleep. I can tell when something's got you troubled. Is everything okay?"

He wiped his hands on his apron. "Yeah. Sure," he replied.

She raised an eyebrow, her hand on her hip.

"Okay, no. Not really," he admitted.

"I knew it," said Belinda, joining him in front of the machine. "What's wrong?"

He felt stupid confiding in his boss but was powerless against her maternal nature. "Mia's missing."

"Missing?" Belinda gasped.

"Okay. Missing may be a strong word. But she's not returning my calls and she hasn't been into work all week. Apparently she requested time off and no one knows why."

"Sounds like a mystery."

"Sadly, I'm more of a comedy guy myself," he said, unable to laugh at his own joke. "Anyway, I'm going to go talk to her father this afternoon to see what he knows about her leave of absence."

"Good idea," replied Belinda.

"Yeah, except I've never met him before and I know he wasn't in love with the idea of us dating."

"What's wrong with that man?" she said, grabbing several orders from the service line.

"Not everyone's a member of the Thomas fan club."

She slipped past him with three plates of food on the way to the door. "Well, you're talking to the president," she said. "Don't be nervous, Hon. Once he meets you, he's gonna love you just like the rest of us do."

"I wish I could share your optimism."

"You're gonna be fine." She nodded toward the plates. "I've got to get back to the dining room, but I'll be rooting for you. Good luck, Thomas."

"Thanks, Belinda."

By 2:30, the dining room was empty and he had already cleaned the floors and reset all of the tables. He hung his apron in the workroom and clocked out.

As he rode the bus into the city, he didn't know whether he was more nervous about meeting Mia's father or about the information he might have to share with him about her disappearance. When he arrived at the station, he chose to enter through the main doors instead of the rear entrance that led to the lineup office.

"Can I help you?" asked the elderly woman at the front desk, peering over the top of her glasses.

"I was wondering if Jack was available," he said.

She scowled. "Officer Anderson?"

"Is Officer Anderson Mia Rosetti's partner?"

"Yes," the woman replied.

"Then, yes," he said, "I'd like to speak with Officer Anderson."

"He's out on patrol right now," she said dryly.

He took a deep breath and smiled genuinely at the woman. "Okay," he said, gathering his courage, "then is Major Rosetti available?"

"Do you have an appointment?"

For an instant, he contemplated lying to her but immediately thought better of it. "No, I don't," he admitted.

She returned to the paperback on her desk. "Then I'm afraid you won't be able to see him today," she replied.

He glanced at the woman's nametag which said her name was Marjorie.

"Marjorie," he said, "can I be honest?"

She glanced up from her novel. "Why? Have you been lying to me?"

"No, of course not. What I meant was there is a specific reason why I need to see Major Rosetti *today*. It has to do with his daughter, Mia."

"I see. Is this a personal matter?" Marjorie asked.

"Yes and no."

Marjorie's impatience was obvious as she rolled her eyes in annoyance. "Sir, I don't have time for this today. I'm going to have to ask you to move along."

"Please, Marjorie. It has to do with Mia's safety. I think he would want to speak with me. Could you just call him and ask if he'd be willing to see me, if only for a few minutes. It would mean a lot."

She looked skeptically at him. And then she picked up her telephone receiver.

"What did you say your name was again?" she asked.

"I didn't. It's Thomas Pritchett."

He listened as Marjorie connected to several different people before finally reaching Mia's father.

"Yes, Sir. I'm sorry to bother you," she said. "There's a Thomas Pritchett here at the front desk asking to speak with you." There was a pause. "He says he wants to speak to you about Mia... Yes, Sir. I'll let him know."

She hung up the phone and motioned to an officer standing on the far side of the room.

"Yes, Ma'am," he said.

"Gus, can you walk Mr. Pritchett here to Major Rosetti's office? He's expecting him."

"Certainly. Follow me," he said to Thomas.

He gave a hasty thanks to Marjorie for her help and followed Gus further into the station.

Carlos Rosetti was a formidable man. As solid as his daughter was small, he rose like an oak tree from behind his desk as he entered the room. The men shook hands and Rosetti motioned for Thomas to sit across from him at his desk.

"What can I do for you today, Mr. Pritchett?" Rosetti asked, making no attempt to mask the irritation in his voice.

"Sir, first, thank you for seeing me. I appreciate your time. I'm here because I haven't heard from Mia in a few days."

"I wasn't aware you two were still in communication," he snapped.

"Oh. Well. Yes sir, I spent some time with her over the weekend. I've been trying to get in touch with her this week, but I was told she's taken a leave of absence?"

"Yes," Rosetti confirmed.

"Oh. Okay. Well, I guess I just wanted to make sure she was safe. When I didn't hear from her, I got concerned something may have happened, that's all."

He could see Rosetti softening slightly. "I can assure you she's fine."

"Can you tell me when she'll be back?" he asked.

He tapped his hands impatiently on his desk. "I don't know exactly."

"Oh." He paused, unsure of how deeply Rosetti would allow him to pry into Mia's personal business. "Is she traveling?"

"I can see you aren't going to leave me alone until I tell you everything I know," Rosetti said. He pulled his cell phone from his pocket and began typing on the keypad. Mia's voice filled the room and he held his breath.

"Dad, it's Mia. I wanted to let you know I won't be coming into work for a little while. Some friends from school called and asked me to go away on a girls' retreat. I'll call you in a few days. I love you."

"That's all I know," Rosetti said, turning off his phone.

It was all Thomas could do to continue breathing. It wasn't so much the words she had spoken, but the intonation in her voice. Her voice sounded very different from someone who was getting ready to go on an unexpected vacation with a group of friends. Instead of sounding joyful or excited, she sounded petrified.

"With all due respect Major Rosetti, Mia didn't sound like herself at all," he said.

Rosetti scowled. "What are you talking about? She sounded just fine. Let's not go fishing for excuses, Mr. Pritchett. Perhaps this little trip was her way of ending things with you quickly and painlessly," he said smugly.

Strangely, hearing her message had convinced him she wasn't looking for a way out. In fact, for the first time since parting ways on Sunday morning, he was finally sure she wasn't purposefully avoiding him. He replayed the sound of her voice in his head, and he felt sick, swallowing back the stomach acid that was making its way into his throat. He suddenly comprehended what was going on.

"Sir, something happened over the weekend I have to tell you about."

"Oh?" he said as he ruffled through a stack of papers, clearly finished with their conversation.

"Yes," he continued, ignoring Rosetti's callous attitude. "Mia and I went to this house out in Owings Mills…"

"She took *you*?" he exclaimed.

"Yes, sir. I was there. Did she tell you what we saw?"

"Of course she did. Why in the world would she have taken you?"

"Like I told you, Sir, we've been seeing each other…"

"Mr. Pritchett, I've heard enough from you this afternoon."

"No… Sir… You don't understand. I don't think Mia's vacationing with her friends. I think somehow they found her. I can hear it in her voice. She was scared."

"I think you're really grasping at straws for some reason. My daughter doesn't get scared. She's a police officer for Christ's sake. And my daughter will certainly be better off without someone like you bringing her down. So I will thank you very much to see yourself out of my office and out of my daughter's life."

"But, Sir!"

"Good day, Mr. Pritchett."

Without another word, he stood from the chair and left Rosetti's office. After several minutes of wandering aimlessly through the station in search of a way out, he was finally recognized by one of the lineup officers who was kind enough to help him find the front door.

He spent the rest of the night worried for Mia and filled with anxiety about which course of action he should take. He was sure the fear in her voice was directly related to what they had witnessed at Wayne Brookins' house. He believed it wasn't a coincidence that she had disappeared immediately following her discovery of the traffickers. And the vague and frightened message she left on her father's cell phone helped to confirm his suspicions.

Without the support of her father, he would be alone in his quest to discover what had happened to Mia. Sadly though, without her guidance, he questioned whether or not he even stood a chance.

CHAPTER

34

MIA

Every muscle of Mia's body screamed as she rolled from her side onto her back. She stretched her legs and was immediately debilitated by cramping in her calves. She sat up and attempted to massage the tightness out of the back of her legs but her wrists and hands were so heavily bruised that they weren't strong enough to do much good. She decided to stand up but was overcome by a wave of nausea which brought her to her knees.

"It's dehydration," said Anya from the adjacent cell. "Here, take my water bottle. There's still some left."

A plastic water bottle rolled across the concrete floor and stopped several inches from where she was crouched in the corner. She reached for the bottle and quickly chugged all that was left.

"You should sip it so you don't throw up," Anya warned.

"I've already finished it," she replied. "But thanks."

"You're welcome. You have a nasty gash on the back of your head. You should let me look at it."

Mia's head was throbbing and she was having trouble thinking clearly. The events of the previous twelve hours swirled around in her head like fireflies on a summer night. There one second, gone the next.

She remembered leaving the station, furious with her father for alerting the commissioner to her discovery of the traffickers, worried for the women who needed her help, and intrigued by the prospect of Thomas possessing a gift of his own. In her frazzled state, she left the station without retrieving her cell phone, only realizing her mistake when she attempted to call Thomas a second time but was still unable to find her phone. By that point, she was already home.

Sitting in the parking lot of her apartment building, she beat her fists into the steering wheel of her car in aggravation. She decided to go inside only long enough to change her clothes and make a sandwich before heading back to the station to reclaim her phone.

She trudged up the stairs to her apartment, feeling sorry for herself and disillusioned with everything that had happened during the course of the day. Once inside, she took off her sidearm, as she always did, and placed it on the kitchen counter. She walked into her bedroom and took a moment to pick up the sheets that were still strewn around the floor where she and Thomas had left them that morning. Although only hours had passed since she had been wrapped in his arms, she felt suddenly as though he was merely a figment of her imagination that had never truly existed at all.

After changing out of her uniform and into her street clothes, she returned to the kitchen to settle her hunger. It was at that moment she sensed she wasn't alone in the apartment. She looked to the counter for her weapon and gasped audibly when it was no longer there. She caught a tiny movement out of the corner of her eye in the direction of the front door and called out to the intruder.

"If you've come to rob me, you are out of luck because my stuff is worth Jack. Not only that, but I'm a cop, so you've definitely messed with the wrong woman," she said confidently.

A man appeared suddenly from around the corner. He was not a large man and although he wore a black ski mask, he didn't appear to be carrying her weapon. She couldn't help but smile at him as he lunged in her direction. Without hesitation, she used his forward momentum against him as she brought her right heel up to deliver a swift kick to his groin. As he doubled over she used the opportunity to deliver a left hook into his face followed by a right jab to the stomach.

"You're going to have to do better than that," she said to the man as she attempted to bring him to his knees in order to restrain him.

An instant later she was blinded by an excruciating pain to the back of her head and her world had faded around her as she crumbled to the floor.

She came to, having no idea where she was or what had happened and realized immediately she was bound, gagged, and blindfolded. After several moments of quiet contemplation, she determined that she was lying on the metal floor of a moving vehicle. It wasn't long before the vehicle stopped and she was dragged outside by her captors. With a gun to her head, they removed the gag from her mouth and instructed her to leave a message for her father which implied that she was going to be away for an unknown period of time. She hoped the fear in her voice would be enough to alert him to the danger she was in. After the call was made, they secured duct tape across her mouth and escorted her to a basement cell.

"Officer?" Kate called from across the hall, distracting Mia from her thoughts.

"Please, call me Mia."

"Okay. Mia. How are you feeling?"

"Like I'm hung over," she replied.

"They should be here with food and water soon. It won't be a lot, but it will be enough to help."

As if Kate had summoned the men through telepathic powers, the scraping of the door lock could be heard echoing throughout the basement. She heard a single set of footsteps coming down the stairs and immediately determined what method she could use to overpower him. She attempted to stand up but her stomach churned angrily, returning her to her knees once again.

"Another big night tonight," the man yelled down the corridor as he approached the first cell. "Make sure you're all fancied up by this evening. We'll be back to get you then. Same as always, extra food for the girl with the highest bid, so do your best."

Mia watched as a man in a red sweatshirt delivered small bags of food, bottles of water, and dresses, shoes and makeup to each of the women. Although he wore a mask similar to the assailant from her apartment, she could tell from his voice that he wasn't one of the men who had abducted her the night before. As he reached the end of the hallway, he addressed her directly.

"I see you were able to free yourself." He nodded toward Anya's cell. "No doubt you had some help from your new friends here. You'll be disappointed to know I don't have a dress for you, although I think you'd bring in a pretty penny. Not my call though," he said casually as he tossed her a small bag of food.

"Who are you?" she asked, studying the darkness surrounding him.

"I can be your best friend or your worst enemy, depending on how well you behave for us," he replied.

She struggled to remember the voices of the men she'd heard at Wayne Brookins' house. She was unsure about whether the man in the red sweatshirt had been present that night. She attempted to commit the man's height and build to memory so she could identify him if necessary at a later date.

With his morning assignment complete, the man left the basement without another word to the women and within moments they were alone once again.

She heard each of the women tearing into their food rations greedily, like wolves on a carcass. She took Anya's advice, eating only small bites from her sandwich and sipping her water slowly. Within several minutes, her stomach began to feel better, although the throbbing in her head remained.

When she finished eating, she looked around the basement to take in her surroundings. She was becoming accustomed to the smell of mildew and excrement that had seemed so overpowering upon her arrival in the middle of the night. She estimated her tiny cell was roughly eight-feet square. The ceiling height of the basement topped out at just over six-and-a-half feet which made the space feel all the more claustrophobic. She was grateful for the primitive toilet in the corner of the room, but the significant lack of privacy was certainly not ideal.

Beyond the bars of her own cell, she watched the other women finishing their food. She was struck by how bright their auras were despite the horrific circumstances. Kate, a beautiful woman with delicate features and a head full of chestnut hair, had an aura which shone as bright as any person she had ever known. Because of the relative fullness of her face and glow of her skin, she sensed that Kate had not been held captive for very long. This wasn't the case for many of the other women further down the hall, whose skeletal frames and ashy complexions spoke of a far longer imprisonment.

"Have you seen the men's faces?" Mia asked her from across the corridor.

"Yes. Most all of them," Kate replied.

"What about the man who was just here?"

"Yes."

"Can you describe his face for me?"

"He's somewhat unpleasant looking. He has dark hair and a blotchy complexion. His nose is full and his eyes are small and closely set. I think he's the one with the scar on his left temple, but it might be one of the other ones."

She knew immediately she had seen the man at Brookins' estate. "Yes," she said to Kate. "He's the one. I've seen him before."

"You know him?" Kate asked anxiously.

"I don't know him, but I've seen him with some of the others that I am sure are involved in what's going on here."

"Are there a lot of them?" Anya asked, joining the conversation.

"Yes. And probably more I don't even know about."

The women were quiet for a moment. "Is that why they've brought you here? Because you know about them?" Kate asked.

Mia pondered Kate's insightful observation. She hadn't taken the time to reflect upon the reason for her capture and realized with sudden clarity that she must have been seen at Wayne Brookins' house during the stakeout.

"Oh God... they'll find Thomas," she said aloud.

"Who's Thomas?" Lera asked.

"Thomas is... Thomas is my boyfriend," she said finally. "He was with me when we discovered what the men were doing. If they found me, they'll find him too, if they haven't already."

"Oh, Mia. I'm sorry," Kate said.

She was suddenly less concerned for her own safety than she was for his. For the first time since her capture, she recognized there was far more at stake than just her own well-being.

"I have to find a way out," she said resolutely to herself.

"I've tried," Kate said. "I was unsuccessful at picking the lock and they tie our hands before they open the cell doors. I don't know if any of us has the strength to overpower them."

She remembered Zocha and the bruising on her wrists. "Someone did," she whispered.

"What do you mean?" Lera asked.

Mia cleared her parched throat before she began. "Several days ago at the police station where I'm assigned, a woman came in who claimed she escaped from a situation similar to this one."

"It wasn't one of us," Kate interrupted. "We've all been here for quite a while. No one has gotten away."

She remembered Zocha's description of where she was held. "Then there must be another holding facility close by," she said.

"Were they selling her for sex, just like us?" Lera asked.

"Yes."

"And she got away?"

"Yes."

"How?" asked Anya.

"She escaped after an auction when no one was looking," Mia told them.

The women were silent for several moments and she evaluated their situation.

"I can't believe there are more than just us," Lera mused. "How many girls are out there?"

"I don't know," Mia replied, her heart aching at the prospect. "There's a good chance this holding facility is only one of many."

"Then my sisters may be out there already," Kate cried frantically. "I thought I would know if they'd been taken because they would show up here. But if there are many different prisons, then I will never know. I may never see them again!"

"No," Mia consoled her, "don't think that way. We are going to figure something out and quickly. And if you think your sisters have been imprisoned as well, we'll find them. I promise." She paused to evaluate what her training would have her do. "Tell me," she asked, "how many men usually come when they let you out?"

"At least two. As many as four," Anya replied.

"And there are fifteen of us. So that would mean a maximum of four women for every man."

"But our hands are tied. We can't use them to defend ourselves or attack the men," Lera lamented.

"That's true, but what if I told you there's a way to free yourself from your restraints. I can teach you how to hold your hands while they're tying you so you may be able to wriggle free. We'd have to practice first though."

She thought back to her police training and felt confident she would be able to teach the others. "Maybe you can give it a try tonight to see if you're able to slip out of the ropes. If most of you are able, then perhaps there's hope for an escape. The only way it'll work though is for everyone to be involved."

"Just tell us what to do," said Kate as the others cried out in agreement.

She spent the rest of the morning teaching Anya, Kate, and Lera how to hold their hands to create slack in the rope while being restrained.

"You want to hold your wrists crossed with your thumbs facing up instead of to the side. This makes the distance around your wrists larger than usual when they wrap the rope around them. As they pull the rope tight, slide it up one arm slightly by spreading your elbows apart," she demonstrated.

"Then what?" asked Anya.

"Then, when they're no longer watching because they think you're secure, turn your wrists together like you're praying and slide the rope to the thumb of one hand. There should be enough slack to get one thumb out. Once you do that, you can pull your whole hand out and the other will come free as well."

"That sounds easy," Lera said.

"It's not easy, but it can be done," she said. "Now pass the information down the line. Teach the others so tonight everyone can give it a try."

She watched and listened as Lera and Anya explained the plan and instructed the women in the neighboring cells about how to escape from their restraints. It was encouraging to hear the women sounding strong and empowered. She hoped at least a few would be able to free themselves so they would be able to put the rest of her plan into effect.

Once everyone in the basement was schooled in the art of escaping from their restraints, she asked each of the women to recount the events that brought them into the basement. Several refused, stating they had no intention of dredging up the harshness of the past. Most, however, were eager to share their stories. Although different in many ways, she was struck by how the same lies were told to lure each of the women into captivity. Promises of work, money, and bright futures were held in front of the women, tempting them into an offer they couldn't refuse. She found herself crying with several of the women who described the families they left behind. It was especially heart wrenching to hear about Kate's twin sisters who had already signed up for the same program. She felt Kate's desperation as she described the torment and responsibility she felt for their situation.

If Mia had felt resolve toward helping the trafficked women before being locked away with them, after spending the day hearing their stories, seeing firsthand the horrific living conditions they were forced to endure, and witnessing the terror on their faces as they described the atrocities they had suffered, she now took it as her personal duty to save the life of every last woman in the room.

Knowing they would soon be taken to the auction, she used the opportunity while they prepared to give them something of a pep talk regarding her plan of escape. Teaching them to shed their restraints before uniting to overpower the men was a long shot, but it was the only shot they had.

"Ladies," she began, "I want to wish you good luck tonight. Practice what you've learned but don't let the men see you trying to free yourselves. Don't take your ropes all the way off or they'll know for sure you are up to something."

She paused for effect, to emphasize the seriousness of what she was about to say.

"You may be tempted to try to escape on your own tonight, but believe me when I say that you have a better chance of escaping as a group than as individuals, so use tonight as practice. If enough of you feel confident that you could free yourselves when the time comes, then I'll teach you how to defend yourselves against the men and we'll all escape together."

The hum of the fluorescent lighting bouncing off the concrete walls was the only sound she heard as she waited for someone to respond. Finally, Kate broke the silence.

"Thank you, Mia."

"Yes. Thanks, Mia," Anya said.

"We'll do our best, Mia," said Lera.

"We can do it," came a voice from further down the hall.

"I believe in you," said Svetlana, "and I believe in us."

The sound of the metal door groaning on its hinges signaled the arrival of the men who would take the women to the auction site. Kate threw her a conspiratorial glance. She hoped the confidence she had spent the day building in the women would survive the ordeal they were getting ready to endure.

CHAPTER
35

THOMAS

Thomas threw the bobby pin across the floor, furious with himself for his ineptitude. After spending the better part of fifteen minutes attempting to pick the lock, he resumed his search for the key in his mother's nightstand drawer. Among the hand lotions and packs of travel tissues, he finally found the keychain for which he'd been searching. He returned to Mildred's closet and placed the tiny gold key into the lock of the box on the floor. The key turned smoothly and he breathed a sigh of relief as he opened the lid.

The handgun felt wrong in his hands as he looked down the barrel and attempted to focus on an unseen enemy. He questioned whether he would have the intestinal fortitude necessary to actually use the weapon should the need arise, but he hoped he would feel more confident having it holstered to his hip for the night.

He returned the box to the top shelf of Mildred's closet and was certain she would never suspect the gun was missing. It had been his father's and he was grateful for the time Howard had spent with him at the firing range teaching him to use it so many years ago. Unfortunately, firing at a paper target was much different than firing at a human being, and he questioned whether or not he would have the ability to pull the trigger. He prayed he wouldn't need to find out. Before leaving the house, he buckled the holster to his waist and wrapped his jacket over top in an attempt to conceal the weapon.

The car keys in his pocket felt as foreign as the gun had in his hand. At work that afternoon, Belinda had happily agreed to allow him to borrow her car for the night, no questions asked. He had dropped her off at her home and promised to return the car to her before morning. He hoped it was a promise he would be able to keep.

On his way out the door, he grabbed a large bag of chips from the pantry, a soda from the refrigerator, and a mystery novel he had picked up at the library earlier in the week. He wasn't expecting to be gone for very long but wanted to take something to keep his mind occupied in case he needed to wait longer than he planned.

He drove carefully around the outer loop of the Baltimore beltway. He was thankful the rush hour traffic was all but gone as he merged onto the expressway and headed north toward Owings Mills. He didn't really have a plan. All he knew was that he had to do something. Be active. Find some way to convince Mia's father she needed his help.

As he pulled off the exit ramp, he tried desperately to remember which way Mia had turned when they had traveled together the weekend before. He felt sure they had headed west and within several minutes his suspicions were confirmed when he happened upon the entrance to the sprawling neighborhood where Wayne Brookins resided.

He turned off the headlights of the car, just as Mia had done, and when he pulled in front of the Brookins' estate, he was relieved to see there was but a single car in the driveway. He doubled back and parked the car three houses down from Brookins'. From his vantage point, he could easily see anyone coming or going and if necessary, he was poised to pursue a suspect or make a hasty escape.

Alone and unsure of what to do next, he found himself drumming his fingers idly on the steering wheel after only a few minutes. He opened the novel and began to read but worried immediately he would miss something happening. He laid the book on the passenger's seat and opened the bag of chips. Without taking his eyes from the house, he placed one chip after another into his mouth. The bag was almost empty when he noticed the garage door of the house opening slowly.

He quickly licked the salt off his fingers and turned the key in the ignition. Wayne Brookins appeared from the garage and climbed into the vehicle that was parked in the driveway. Within seconds, Brookins was speeding down the street toward the main entrance of the neighborhood. Without turning on the car's headlights, he eased the transmission into first gear and followed Brookins onto the main road.

He found it was relatively easy to keep a safe distance and still maintain visual contact with Brookins as they drove toward the city. Traffic was light and Brookins maintained a consistent speed in the right hand lane which kept him from having to jockey around other cars to keep up.

Unsure of where he was heading or what he would do once he got there, he followed Brookins, who exited off the interstate onto North Avenue. As a precautionary measure, he allowed several cars to merge between them as they traveled east, away from the city. Before reaching the historic Baltimore Cemetery, Brookins made a series of right hand turns and he found himself in a deteriorated neighborhood surrounding the old American Brewing factory.

He watched as Brookins parked his car inside of a fenced lot which surrounded a long abandoned warehouse. There were three other cars parked in the lot along with two white commercial vans. Brookins disappeared inside the building and Thomas turned off the car's engine.

He became aware, for the first time since leaving the Brookins' estate, that he was sweating profusely and his heart was beating rapidly. The voice inside his head cautioning him to drive away confirmed the involuntary reactions of his body. He had spent his entire life listening to the advice of his inner voice and it had always kept him from being seriously harmed. And now, even though he knew Mia would have immediately followed Brookins into the building, he couldn't bring himself to get out of the car.

Moments later, from the relative safety of the vehicle, he watched a small group of women, each with her hands bound behind her back, being led out of the warehouse and into the vans. He knew at once he had stumbled upon the holding facility and that somehow, Mia was involved as well.

As the vans pulled away, his instincts continued urging him to head in the opposite direction. He was in danger and the best course of action was to alert the authorities at once. However, thoughts of Mia compelled him to ignore the anxiety he was feeling and to follow the vans downtown to where they parked outside of a small renovated brownstone tucked away down a side alley.

From his vantage point on the street, he couldn't see the vans or the women contained within them. Desperate to confirm what he assumed to be the truth about what was happening, he reluctantly got out of the car. Each step toward the building caused him physical pain as an internal war raged inside of him. Nonetheless, he crept cautiously along the far wall of the building and peered around the corner into the alley where the vans were parked.

There appeared to be about a dozen women lined up beside the entrance. While a few held their heads high, most of them stared down at their feet and he was saddened by how frail all of them seemed. As he continued to watch, he was struck by how awkward and cartoonish they appeared, each of them dressed in a cocktail dress with matching heels. However, it wasn't the clothing that disturbed him as much as their faces which were painted with garish cosmetics that distorted what he assumed were beautiful faces beneath.

Without realizing what he was doing, he found himself scanning the lineup for Mia's face. He was both disappointed and relieved to see she wasn't there. As the women were led inside the building, he hesitated at the corner, questioning his own motivations. After several moments of quiet contemplation, he decided he would risk going inside for the opportunity to see the faces of the men involved even if he wouldn't be saving Mia directly.

He unconsciously touched the firearm holstered to his hip as he crept silently to the entrance. The door was warped with age in its jamb and had not shut completely when the last of the men had gone through. He pulled at the door slowly and found that, despite its weight, he was able to open it with very little effort. Once inside, he allowed his eyes to adjust to the dimness of the room. A heavy navy blue curtain was draped from the floor to the ceiling and he could hear men's voices coming from the other side.

He felt his heart throbbing in his temples and although he was terrified, he slid the curtain to the side just far enough to make out what was happening in the room beyond.

During his life, he had known evil. He had been beaten by men who were supposed to be fathers. He had felt the anger of strangers and seen the unspeakable violence that came as a result. He had witnessed the naïve being preyed upon by conmen. And yet, the evil he saw beyond the curtain exceeded anything he had ever witnessed.

A dozen men milled around the girls, examining them as though they were museum pieces or in some cases, livestock, instead of human beings. He watched as the women were groped and ogled and his stomach churned with disgust. He looked carefully at each of the men and recognized a handful who had attended the party at Wayne Brookins' home. Some were selling the women while others were buying their services.

As he stood digesting the new information, he was able to make out a conversation between the two men who had driven the vans from the warehouse. He remained frozen in place and quietly listened to what they were saying.

"Whadda ya think they're gonna do with the woman cop?" the first of the men asked.

"Walt said they're gonna keep her for a little while until somebody gets she's not coming back and then they're gonna kill her and dump her out in the mountains somewhere. No one will ever find her," the second sneered.

"I don't get why they didn't just off her from the get go. Make it look like a robbery gone bad or somethin'."

"I think the boss just needed her out of his hair right away and didn't want to have to deal with a murder investigation. I heard she was on to all of us. Had photos of us at Brookins' place the other night." The man paused to take a drag on the cigarette he was smoking. "All I know is I'm glad she can't make a big stink from where she is now and soon whatever she had on us will die with her."

Thomas felt violently ill and struggled to keep from throwing up. Between the heartbreak of watching the women being auctioned off and the realization that Mia's life was in immediate danger, he could no longer maintain his composure and quietly hurried outside.

In the alley behind the building, he crouched against the wall until the nausea finally subsided. After several moments, he attempted to stand up and steady his breathing, trying desperately to make sense of all he had seen and heard. He closed his eyes and focused on what Mia would have him do next.

And then, without warning, a wave of anxiety overtook him. It was so severe, he began to run without having any idea of the reason for his flight. As he crossed the street to where he had parked Belinda's car, the door of the building opened and one of the men who had driven the van from the warehouse emerged. He was wearing a red sweatshirt.

"What the hell are you doing here?" he called out, drawing his handgun from behind his back.

Without responding or thinking to draw his own weapon, he continued to run toward the car, aware only of the extreme danger of his situation. He heard a shot fired and instinctively covered his head with his arms as he ran to the far side of the car in an attempt to use it as a shield. He hastily opened the passenger side door, climbed in, and straddled the console to make his way into the driver's seat. As the engine roared to life, he glanced out the window to see his assailant barreling toward him, gun still pointed in his direction. He heard two more shots fired as he took off down the street. Glass shattered all around him. The next thing he saw was the blood.

CHAPTER

36

MIA

Mia picked at her cuticle. She had been alone in the basement for almost three hours and the walls were beginning to close in around her. When the rest of the women were taken to the auction, she had been left behind. She was initially relieved to not be subjected to the torment that awaited the others, but that relief soon gave way to dread, when upon further rumination, she realized there was probably something far worse planned for her in the coming days. It was a thought she could not allow herself to dwell upon.

During her isolation, she focused her attention on many different tasks. For the better part of half an hour she mulled over different ways to escape from her cell. This lesson in futility included using the buckle off her belt as a key in an attempt to pick the lock and ramming her body repeatedly against the door. Neither method proved an effective means of escape although she did succeed in bruising her shoulder severely.

After giving up on escaping, she curled up on her mattress and reflected upon the plight of the other women. She wondered if any of them had successfully wiggled free from their restraints and hoped she had empowered them to take back some control of their situation. She smiled to herself, thinking of the determination she had seen in their faces as they were led from the basement to the auction. She was anxious for them to return.

When she could no longer stand to worry over the women, she hesitantly reflected upon her own situation, recalling all of the events that had transpired since Thomas called with news of the traffickers. She had been careless in her pursuit of the men, and she cursed at herself for her lapses in judgment. Her first mistake had been searching the precinct's database from her home computer, especially given her wireless connection. She also realized she had likely been seen at Wayne Brookins' estate and therefore, so had Thomas.

Her heart ached as she thought of him. By throwing herself into the case on the morning after the stakeout, she had not allowed herself the luxury of reflecting on their night together. However, as she cataloged the unfortunate circumstances into which he was placed because of her poor decisions, she finally allowed herself to think of him.

He had been kind and tender toward her, respecting her needs and addressing her desires as if they were his own. If he had been unsure of himself or insecure in any way, it hadn't translated into his lovemaking. He had said all the right things, telling her she was beautiful and in his words, 'amazing.' With his image in her mind, exhaustion finally took over, and she drifted to sleep.

An hour later, hungry, cold, and utterly alone in the warehouse basement, she woke. The warm feelings that lulled her to sleep had abandoned her and fear and anxiety set in. She was overcome by a sudden realization that she was only in trouble because of her inflated sense of self-confidence. She wished she had called Jack to join her on the stakeout instead of placing Thomas' life in jeopardy unnecessarily. She was well aware that if she had told Jack about her plan, he would have quickly talked her out of it, and she would never have ended up locked in the basement.

Depression and isolation continued to overtake her spirit and her mind began filling with terrible thoughts, each one more horrendous than the last. As she paced the length of her cell, she was struck by a possible reason for her discovery and subsequent capture she hadn't yet considered.

She thought about Thomas and whether he had a connection to the traffickers, as he had been the one to alert her to the men from the bistro - men from the network of traffickers who he may have been working alongside from the beginning. It seemed highly coincidental that he should alert her to their presence immediately after she told him about Zocha. It was almost as if he wanted her to have just enough useful information to help him keep tabs on her level of involvement.

She wondered if it was possible that Thomas had been part of some larger scheme from the onset – a scheme that included infiltrating the police department. She thought about the timeliness of when he began participating in the lineups and realized it coincided with the commissioner's arrival. She fell to her knees as she realized that perhaps he had been planted by the commissioner to keep tabs on her because she was the chief's daughter.

What enraged her the most was realizing that she may have been right to doubt Thomas and his missing aura from the beginning. Had her lack of prudence placed her life in jeopardy? Perhaps, she thought finally, Thomas wasn't one of the seven good psychics from the prophecy after all. Perhaps, instead, he was one of the seven bad ones.

She cursed at herself for allowing him into her world and tried desperately to hold back the tears she had been carefully controlling from the moment of her abduction, but with her new suspicions, she could no longer hold them at bay.

She sat on the ground and wept heavily into her arms. She wept for the women who were forced into sexual slavery. She wept for Thomas, wondering if his love for her was all a façade, part of a carefully planned set up. And at long last, she allowed herself to weep for the desperation of her own situation.

When at last she had cried herself out, she took a deep cleansing breath and refocused her attention on her present situation and the part of her reality she could control - helping the other women to escape.

Minutes later, scraping metal and the sound of footsteps on the stairs alerted her to the return of her companions. She had already wiped her eyes on her sleeves and pushed her own worries from her thoughts as she stood to greet them. She watched the women as they returned to their cells and looked for signs of hope on their faces. Instead she saw only grief and despair. When the last of the women was locked in her cell, the evening's meager food rations were distributed and Kate received an extra portion. Before leaving, one of the men strode confidently down the corridor and approached her cell.

"Hope you're not getting too comfortable down here, Officer," he jeered, "because the boss has big plans for you tomorrow night."

"Is that right?" she responded boldly.

"Yeah, that's right. Let's just say you ain't gonna be here for much longer, if you know what I'm sayin'."

Although she felt as though she was standing in a pool of quicksand, she did not give the man the satisfaction of a response or a reaction as she stood stoically before him.

"Stupid pig," he said, before spitting into her face.

He joined the rest of the men at the end of the hall and climbed the stairs to return to the world of the living, leaving them alone once again.

"Well?" she asked, wiping her face with her sleeve as she looked around the basement with great anticipation, hoping the women would have something positive to report.

No one spoke. They were expecting her to be upset about the man's revelation of her impending demise, but for the moment, all she was interested in was helping the women escape. A few of the girls were holding back tears and many hung their heads so she was unable to read the expressions on their faces.

"Was anyone able to slip free of the ropes?" she asked.

"I think I almost had it," Anya said finally, "but it was too tight. I couldn't wiggle my thumb free."

"What about you, Lera?" she asked.

"No. I couldn't get out. I tried so hard, Mia. I must have done it wrong."

"Kate? Svetlana? Anyone?"

"No, Mia. We're so sorry. None of us was able to get free," Kate said.

She held tightly to the bars of her cell and sighed heavily. "Really? No one?"

"No," said Kate.

She quickly shook off her disappointment. Seeing her frustration wouldn't help them but a positive attitude would do wonders for their esteem.

She laughed feebly as she slipped her arms through the bars, reaching out to the others in a gesture of solidarity. "Do you know how long it took me to learn how to free myself at the academy?" she asked. "Weeks. I'm not joking. It took me weeks of practicing and even then it was a struggle. So don't feel bad. We'll keep trying."

"But we'll never get out before tomorrow," Lera lamented, tears streaming down her cheeks.

"No," she said truthfully, "I'm afraid we won't."

Lera reached out across the space between them, unable to touch her hand. "Then tomorrow it will happen. They will rape us again and they will take you away. We'll never see you again," she cried.

"I'm so sorry," she replied. "I'm working on it. I will figure something out in time, you'll see."

Her empty promises were not enough to console Lera's desperate soul and she wailed unabashedly.

"I can't do it again!" Lera screamed, pulling at the bars of her cell door. "I have to get out of here! Please, help us get out! There has to be another way!"

She thought for several minutes while Kate worked to soothe Lera. Finally, she spoke candidly with the group.

"Here's what we're going to do – you need to practice on your own, without having to wait for the men to bind you. That way, with or without me, you stand a chance of being able to free yourselves when they least expect it. If you all work together, you can overtake them. But to practice, you'll need something to practice with. A rope or maybe strips of fabric."

"We can use our clothes," Anya said.

"We'll freeze," replied Kate smartly.

"And we will raise their suspicions if they see we are tearing our own clothing," Svetlana added.

"That's true," she agreed. "What else can we use?"

"How about our mattresses?" called a woman from the far end of the hall. "They wouldn't see if we used the material from underneath."

"You're right," she agreed thoughtfully. "That's actually a great idea."

She lifted her mattress off the floor and propped it up against her cell wall. The aging springs were wrapped entirely in faded blue and white striped mattress ticking. She searched the material for signs of wear. Surprisingly, there were no holes she could use to begin ripping a strip of fabric for binding.

"I need to make a hole in the mattress. Does anyone have anything I can use?" she called.

"I do," Kate said immediately.

She watched as Kate fished underneath her own mattress to retrieve a small velvet box, which she slid across the hallway toward her cell. When Mia opened the box she was surprised to see a set of ornamental hair pins. She carefully removed one of the pins and began using it to tear a hole in the mattress fabric. Once the hole was created, she easily ripped a long strip of material that she used to bind Anya's hands behind her back. She repeated the process several times and handed strips of fabric down the corridor to the others. When she was finished, she returned the hair pins to Kate.

"They're beautiful," she said as she slid the box back across the hall, "but they're a strange thing to have brought with you."

"They are a family heirloom," explained Kate. "My father gave them to me. For luck."

They exchanged a smile and Kate let out a sarcastic laugh. "I guess they aren't working."

"Don't give up on them yet," Mia replied.

After watching the women struggle for close to an hour with their makeshift restraints, she could see the majority of them were making very little progress.

"Unfortunately, I don't think we'll be ready to overtake our captors any time soon," she announced sadly, "so you will have to endure being delivered to the men tonight. And by tomorrow, it sounds as if I may no longer be here to assist you. But I want you to keep trying. Keep practicing. When you are all ready, you'll know it's time for your escape."

The timers on the lights clicked several times, signaling that they were about to turn off for the night. As the lights flickered off, she stumbled to her mattress and curled up with her thoughts. Strangely, she was less concerned for her own life than she was for the helpless women she had come to know and admire.

"Kate?" she called.

"Yes," Kate replied.

"I have a favor."

"Yes. Anything."

"When you get out…"

"If we get out," Kate interrupted.

"No. When you get out, I need you to find my father. His name is Carlos Rosetti and he's the chief of police."

"Okay. How will I find him?"

"Any police officer here in the city should be able to find him for you. So, when you do, I need you to tell him what happened here and that I was with you."

"Okay."

"And also, tell him I love him."

"Okay, Mia, but you will figure something out. You will get away too."

She could hear Kate crying now. "Maybe I will, but if I don't, there's one more thing. I need you to tell my father to search for a man named Thomas Pritchett."

"Thomas? Your boyfriend?"

"The man who I thought was my boyfriend. But now... now I just don't know what to think anymore. There's a chance he is involved in all of this in some way and I need my father to get to the bottom of it. If he's involved, he needs to be held accountable for his crimes."

"And if he's not involved?"

Mia shuddered to think of it. "Then he will need my father's help, if it's not too late already."

CHAPTER

37

THOMAS

Thomas continued to check his rearview mirror for signs that he was being followed. He was having difficulty driving with his left hand while he applied pressure to his bleeding shoulder with his right, and he was relieved to see the police station just down the block.

Adrenaline continued to course through his veins as he parked the car haphazardly and got out, scrambling across the street and into the station. The elderly gentleman at the front desk looked at him cautiously.

"Can I help you, Sir?" he asked. "Looks as though you need a hospital, not a police station."

"I need to speak with Officer Anderson or Major Rosetti right away, please."

"Major Rosetti isn't here at the moment, but I can check to see if Officer Anderson is still in the building. Can I ask what this is about?"

"Just tell him I think I know what's happened to Mia," he replied.

He tried to ignore the shooting pain radiating through the left side of his body as he listened to the desk clerk attempt to locate Jack. He couldn't shake the images of the women he had seen at the auction and he was overwhelmed with worry for Mia. He wanted nothing more than to run screaming through the hallways of the station to find Jack on his own, for he felt as though every moment that he wasn't looking for Mia was a minute something catastrophic could be happening to her. However, both blood loss and the early stages of shock were having a disabling effect on him, and he was unable to move from the spot where he was standing. He was more than a little relieved when after only a couple of minutes, Jack himself appeared in the lobby.

"Jesus Christ, Thomas! What the hell happened to you?" Jack exclaimed as he hurried to his side.

"It's kind of a long story. Can we talk about it in your office so I can sit down? I don't feel so well all of a sudden," he said, overcome by wooziness.

"Of course, but what in the world happened to your arm? Did you get shot?"

"Only sort of," he replied with a half-hearted chuckle.

Once they were safely ensconced in Jack's office, he took a few moments to compose himself and control his breathing. Without thinking too much about the emotional toll the night had taken on him, he quickly recounted all of the events that had transpired since they had seen one another just after Mia's disappearance. Jack sat in contemplative silence for several moments when he was finished and Thomas sat quietly with his head in his hands.

"So what do we do now?" he asked. "We've got to find her, Jack. I know they've got her somewhere. And we have to save the other women too."

"As much as I hate to say it, I think we need to bring in her father. He won't hesitate to send officers to the warehouse for the women. In fact, I bet he'll have people over there tonight. I don't know if he'll buy the fact that these people have kidnapped Mia, but once he sees what's at the warehouse, it might be enough to change his mind. Meanwhile, I can find someone to take you to the hospital."

"I'm not going anywhere, Jack. Not until you find her."

Jack shook his head. "Then let me at least call around and find someone here at the station to take a look at it.

You've lost a lot of blood. You should probably eat something too."

"I'll be fine. Just call the chief, get those women, and go find Mia."

"You really think they've got her?"

"Yeah. I do."

"I hope you're wrong," Jack said.

"Me too."

CHAPTER

38

KATE

There was a crack, like the sound of a firework exploding. At first, Kate was positive it was a part of the dream she'd been having. When she heard the noise a second time, this time fully awake, she sat straight up on her mattress and called into the night.

"What was that? Did you hear it?"

"I heard it," Anya replied.

"It was a handgun being fired," Mia answered.

"A gun?" cried Lera.

"Yes. And it sounded close," said Mia. "Depending on what part of town we're in, it may be gang or drug related. We should be safe down here."

The irony of Mia's words wasn't lost on Kate. "Funny, that this is the safe place to be," she remarked.

Suddenly, she heard another gunshot, but this time it was louder and closer, causing her to cover her ears. The basement was thrown into chaos as the women began crying and calling out to one another.

"They're right above us," Mia said cautiously. "It sounds like they're inside the warehouse."

"Who do you think it is?" Lera asked.

"I don't know. But whoever it is could mean trouble for us," Mia replied. "During my life I've observed that people who do bad things tend to hang out with other people who do bad things. A lot of times they end up turning on each other. If that's what's going on then we need to be ready in case they bring whatever is going on up there down here."

Kate was petrified and felt more than ever like a caged animal. "What should we do?" she screamed. "We're trapped in here!"

"Get down low. Make yourself small. Cover your head and your ears."

"Do you think they'll come down?" Lera cried hysterically.

"I hope not," Mia answered.

Kate lay silently thinking of her sisters. During her imprisonment, they had been her sole motivation for survival and escape. She imagined them, lost and afraid, perhaps separated from one another and she knew she had to be strong if she ever hoped to see them again. She would have to survive whatever was about to happen.

"We're going to be okay," Kate said aloud, in an attempt to bend the universe into her submission.

"You can't honestly believe that," Anya whispered.

"I have faith," she replied. "We're going to get out of here. I can feel it."

Two more shots were fired in the warehouse above her. Kate drew her arms over her head and curled into a ball in the corner of her cell.

And then, she heard the door opening at the top of the stairwell.

It was agonizing, listening to Lera quietly whimpering in the adjacent cell, knowing there was no way to console her. Kate waited for the men, whoever they were, to turn on the lights and descend the stairs, but the basement remained pitch black.

She focused on her breathing and the conscious thought that they were all going to be okay. The mood in the basement had changed and the initial chaos had given way to silence as the women prepared for what was coming. After what felt like an eternity, she saw a shaft of light piercing through the darkness at the end of the corridor. She didn't dare to uncover her head, but she managed to peer between her arms as the light grew closer. She couldn't yet see the men but the sound of their footsteps grew louder with every breath she took. Finally, the beam of a flashlight swept across her cell and the men stopped just outside her door.

"Clear!" called the man into the night. "Can someone try and find a light switch?"

"We're working on it," came an unfamiliar voice from the top of the stairs.

"Derek?" she heard Mia say.

"Who's there?" the man said, swinging the beam of his flashlight into Mia's cell. "Mia?"

Kate watched as Mia sprang from the floor and reached for the man from between the bars of her cell. "Yes! Oh my God, Derek! You've found us!"

"Mia! What the hell are you doing down here? I thought you were on vacation or something! What's going on?"

"There's too much to explain, but right now, you have to get the other women out of here. Some of them have been here for months! Please! Hurry!"

Kate struggled to make sense of what was happening. Only moments before, she'd been contemplating death and the possibility that her dreams of escape and of rescuing her sisters would die with her. But now, as she watched Mia and the man she called Derek talking across the hall, she couldn't help but feel excitement building in her soul.

"Mia?" she called.

"Yes?"

"What's happening?"

"We're getting out of here, Kate! Somehow the police found us and we're going to be out of here in no time!"

"Can this be true?" Lera asked, tears streaming down her face.

The overhead fluorescents suddenly came to life, bathing the basement in harsh light.

"Oh God, Mia! You're hurt!" Derek exclaimed when his eyes finally adjusted to the light.

"It's nothing. I'm fine. Leave me, just get the others out."

Derek took off down the corridor and the basement was thrown into a state of pandemonium once again. She heard the other women screaming and crying to be let out of their cells. The voices of other police officers could now be heard from the far end of the hall and after several moments, she heard the sound of the first lock being cut off.

Kate and Mia stood across the hall from one another in a state of utter disbelief. "Is this really happening?" she asked.

"Yes. It's happening. Somehow, they found us. I don't know how, but they did," Mia replied.

"It's a miracle," she said, unable to believe the reality of the celebratory hysteria surrounding her.

"It really is," Mia agreed.

Slowly and methodically, the officers made their way down the hallway, cutting the locks with bolt cutters to free each of the women from their cells. She watched as Anya and Lera's doors were finally opened and they frantically scrambled into the hallway, throwing themselves into one another's embrace. As the officer approached the final two cells, he turned to Mia.

"Kate first," she said.

The man, who was dressed in a navy blue uniform, his badge clearly visible on his chest, took the bolt cutters and easily broke through the lock which held her cell door securely shut. As the lock fell to the ground, the door swung open and she stepped into the hall. Suddenly, she remembered the box hidden below her mattress and went back into the cell to retrieve it. By the time she returned to the hallway, Mia had been released as well.

Lera nearly knocked her over as she gathered her in an unexpected embrace.

"Thank you," she whispered into her ear.

"For what?" Kate asked.

"For being my friend and taking care of me. And for saying all those prayers. I heard you, you know."

"I didn't do anything special."

"It was special to me. It gave me hope," Lera said as an officer wrapped her in a blanket to escort her from the basement.

Kate looked down the corridor. Lera and Anya were the last of the women being led up the stairs by the officers. Mia stood beside her and took her by the hand.

"So now what?" she asked, her mind reeling from the night's events.

"Assuming they're following protocol, everyone will go to the hospital where you'll be treated for injuries, dehydration, and malnutrition. They'll take rape kit samples and you'll give your statements. INS might get involved."

"And then?"

"And then I don't know. But we'll figure it out together, okay?"

"You'll stay with me?"

"I will."

"Okay. But, Mia? What about my sisters. I don't know where they are. They could be here in America already."

"We'll find them. I promise. You have my word on it."

Kate walked with Mia out of the warehouse and into the brisk night air. They were surrounded by ambulances and police cars with their lights flashing. She watched as a gurney was loaded into one of the ambulances with what appeared to be a dead body. The left arm of the victim fell limply off the side as the paramedics hoisted the stretcher into the back of the vehicle. When she saw the corpse was wearing a red sweatshirt, she felt strangely conflicted, knowing she should never be happy about the death of another human being.

With all fifteen women safely out of the basement, the officers began to load them into ambulances two and three at a time. After spotting Lera and Anya huddled together under a blanket just outside the entrance to the warehouse, Kate crossed the parking lot and approached them hesitantly, unsure of how to behave with her friends now that they were no longer bound by captivity. It was a surreal situation and she struggled for just the right words to adequately express all she was feeling. However, before she could say anything, Anya began to cry.

"Kate," she said, "if someone had to be with me through this nightmare, I am glad it was you."

"Me too," Lera added.

Lost for words, she shed tears of her own as they were helped into the back of an ambulance. They were being escorted from the warehouse to the hospital, and as they drove out of the lot, she spotted Mia through the window embracing one of her fellow officers.

Kate smiled to herself, knowing it was because of her gift that Mia had become an instrument of change, facilitating both their discovery and release. Somehow, her gift chose to bring Mia into her life as the means of ending her imprisonment. With that knowledge, she closed her eyes and used her gift to send yet another message into the universe. This time she made sure to speak the words aloud.

"I'm going to find my sisters," she said.

"You know the drill, Officer," Detective Donna Switzer, a member of the crime lab, said to Mia as she entered the examination room of the hospital. "Clothes in the bags and I'll be back in a few minutes with the nurse to get your statement and to process hair and nails for DNA sampling. If we're lucky, we might be able to get a match on your abductor from the system."

"Thanks, Donna," she replied.

As soon as the door clicked shut, she removed all of her clothing over the collection sheet, folded each piece neatly, and placed everything into the large paper bag on the table. She redressed in the clothing that was provided and sat down to wait for Donna to return. After he cleaned and stitched the wound on her head, the doctor had thoughtfully brought her a large cup of lukewarm coffee and a package of peanut butter crackers which seemed like a gourmet meal in light of her situation. As she munched on the crackers, she wondered how the other women were adjusting to their new realities. They would be alone and frightened and she longed to finish with her own statement so she could be with them in their time of need.

She also couldn't help but feel conflicted about Thomas. Although she continued to wonder if he was somehow

274

involved in her abduction, there was also a part of her that was very concerned for his well-being. As she tried to wrap her head and her heart around the complexity of her situation, Donna Switzer knocked on the door.

"How are you holding up?" she asked as she entered the room with one of the nurses.

"I'm surprisingly okay. I don't think I'd hit the point of utter desperation, so I was still running on hope and adrenaline. Can't say the same for some of the other women though."

"I saw. A few of them were barely alive. What a travesty," Donna said shaking her head. "Let's do hair and nails first, then I'll take your statement."

She waited while the nurse combed meticulously through her hair for fibers or DNA that may have transferred during her ordeal.

Mia wondered about what had transpired in the outside world while she was being held captive. "I assume my father knows I'm here at the hospital," she asked cautiously.

"He does. But he's back at the station dealing with the fallout from the raid. I'm sure he's doing his best to get here to you," Donna replied sympathetically.

"I know," she said, suddenly desperate to see a familiar face.

She thought again of Thomas as the nurse moved onto her fingernails, carefully scraping samples from beneath each of them into envelopes labeled with her name.

"What I can't get over is how they found you," Donna commented casually.

"How *did* they find us?" she asked.

"No one's told you?"

She couldn't believe she hadn't thought to ask already. "No!" she replied.

She shook her head knowingly. "Then I shouldn't be the one to fill you in. If you aren't already aware then your account will be more accurate without the bias of that information."

"You can't do that to me, Donna!" she exclaimed.

"I just did," she replied with a smile as the nurse finished her nails. "Now, about your statement. Why don't you start from the beginning and as soon as we're done, you can head back to the station to get the answers you're looking for from someone who was there firsthand, okay?"

"Fine," she pouted.

She began her story with Thomas' revelation about the men he overheard at Belinda's Bistro. She described in great detail what she and Thomas discovered at Wayne Brookins' estate and how she was ambushed in her apartment the following night. Donna asked her many questions about the women in the basement and she recounted what she could remember of each of their stories. At long last, Donna pushed her chair back from the table and asked her one final question.

"How do you think these men knew you were involved, if you had to speculate?"

"Honestly, at first I assumed they'd seen me and Thomas at Brookins' house and traced me to my apartment because of that. But now I'm wondering whether Thomas Pritchett may have had something to do with it."

"Hmm. Okay. Well, I'll make a note of that then."

"Am I free to go?" she asked.

"For now. If we need something more, I think we know where to find you," Donna laughed.

She gave Donna a hug and ventured into the hallway. As she wandered through the hospital, she was surprised to see Thomas, sitting without an aura, in a chair beside the nurses' station. There was a large bandage wrapped around his left shoulder.

"Thomas!" she called, surprising herself with the excitement in her voice.

He rose immediately from his seat and began running toward her. "Oh, Mia!" he cried. "Thank God."

She stood, frozen in place, unable to choose whether to be elated or furious.

"I can't believe you were there in the warehouse with the others! It's a miracle," he declared, wrapping her in his arms. Despite his enthusiasm, she couldn't bring herself to return his embrace. "Mia, what is it?" he asked.

"Somehow, the traffickers found me," she said.

"I know."

She glared at him. "But they didn't find you."

"No. Thank God. Why are you angry? What's this all about?"

Before she could reply, her father appeared from around the corner looking uncharacteristically disheveled.

"Mia!" he called to her from the end of the hallway.

"Oh, Daddy!" she cried, racing past Thomas toward her father.

They held each other for several moments and she allowed her frustration to escape in the form of silent tears.

"Why are you crying?" he asked at last. "The story had a happy ending, thanks to your friend Thomas here."

She dried her eyes with the back of her hands and looked from her father to Thomas and back again. She couldn't understand why her father was beaming at Thomas when only weeks before he had warned her never to see him again.

"What do you mean 'thanks to Thomas?'" she asked.

"Hasn't anyone told you how we found you?" replied Rosetti.

She shook her head vehemently. "No! No one has!"

"You should be the one to tell her," he said to Thomas, giving him a wink. "I only have a couple of minutes before I have to get back to the station, but let's go into the waiting room and sit down."

She allowed Thomas to take her hand as they sat beside one another across the table from her father.

"Well, go ahead, Son. Don't be shy. Tell her what happened."

Thomas began, smiling at her, "So after we went to Brookins' house last weekend, you never called me the next day..."

"The commissioner took my phone! He never gave it back!" she interrupted.

"Let the man speak, Mia," her father warned.

Thomas continued, still holding tightly to her hand. "So when you didn't call me after a few days, I went to the station to look for you. Everyone told me you'd taken leave so I went to your house to see if you were holed up there for some reason."

She glanced curiously at her father. "I wasn't."

"No. You weren't. Anyway, I couldn't imagine why you weren't returning my calls after that night we were together, so on Thursday I decided to go back to the station to ask your father if he knew where you were. He let me listen to the message you left him and you sounded really scared to me."

"I was really scared!" she said, remembering the terror of being abducted.

He brushed a lock of hair from in front of her eyes. "I know. It scared me too, and so that message got me thinking the reason you weren't answering my calls was because of the stakeout and not because of something that happened between us."

"Is that what you thought? That I was ignoring you?"

"Yes."

"And you kept after me anyway?"

"Yes."

"Oh, Thomas," she said, suddenly realizing where the story was headed.

"Let the man finish!" her father exclaimed again.

Thomas smiled at him and continued, "I borrowed Belinda's car and drove to Brookins'..."

"You did what?!" she roared.

"I know. It was stupid. But I didn't know what else to do. I sat outside his house and eventually he came out. I followed him to the warehouse and saw him leaving with the rest of the women. I didn't see you leave with them so I assumed you weren't there. I followed the vans because I thought maybe they would lead me to you, but I ended up at the auction site instead. I was able to sneak inside to see what was happening, but I couldn't stand to watch for very long. When I left, one of the guys came out the door and saw me..."

"Oh, God, Thomas. Your arm," she said.

"Yeah. He shot me. Grazed my shoulder. The bandage makes it look a lot worse than it is, so don't feel too sorry for me. Belinda's car has seen better days though." He winced as he adjusted his arm on the table. "I guess I should have gone to the hospital, but I drove to the station in case they were following me. Figured they wouldn't try and kill me there. Luckily, Jack was still on duty and was willing to see me. When he heard what I had to say, he called your dad at home right away. Your dad sent a squad to the warehouse within the hour and that's when they found you. I just can't believe you were there the whole time. If I'd known, I could have gotten you out sooner."

As he finished, her father's phone rang. After a brief conversation, he announced that he was needed back at the station. He stood up, giving her a kiss on the forehead and patting Thomas on the arm. "This guy's a hero in my book. You're lucky to have him," he said genuinely, and with that, he was gone.

Alone together for the first time in a week, she was reeling from his account of what had transpired during their time apart. She was furious with herself for having judged him so poorly.

"You were so brave, Thomas," she said, crawling into his arms. "You aren't dark after all," she mused.

"What do you mean?" he asked skeptically, holding her at arm's length. "Do you see darkness around me? I thought you said my aura was light?"

She immediately realized her slip. Her gut reaction was to backpedal or try to play off the comment as a joke, however, when she looked at the sincerity in his eyes, she had to tell him the truth about how she saw him.

"I have to tell you something that may be hard to hear, but it's important for me to be honest with you."

He bit his bottom lip. "You're scaring me, Mia," he said.

She paused for a moment and gathered her thoughts. Finally, she took his face in her hands and told him the truth.

"Thomas, the very first time I saw you, it was during a line up. There was something about you that caught my attention right away and to this day I have no idea what it means."

"It was my fabulous fashion sense, wasn't it?"

"No," she laughed. "Thomas... I can't see your aura. It doesn't mean you don't have one, because I'm sure you do, it just means for some reason, I can't see it."

"Why not?"

"I have no idea. But I can't see any light. Or any dark..."

"And you can't trust what you can't see," he said.

"Sort of. It's hard for me. Every other person in the world has an aura I can use to make my initial judgment about the quality of their character. I didn't have that luxury with you."

He studied her face. "So you just had to trust."

"Yeah. I've never had to do that before. Not once in my entire life."

"But you did for me?"

She thought about the selfish nature of her initial interactions with him. It made her cringe. "I did. Mostly. Except for at the warehouse. In the basement. I started to doubt you. I began to think that maybe you were involved in some way." She stared regretfully at her lap. "I didn't know. I'm so sorry, Thomas."

"It's okay, Mia," he said, bringing her face to his and kissing her gently on the lips. "Stressful situations bring out the worst in all of us. And besides, it's better this way. Now you know for certain you'll never have to doubt me."

"But I can't understand why I don't see your aura when it's clearly so bright." She hesitated before deciding it wasn't the time or place to confront him about a possible psychic ability.

Thomas shrugged his shoulders. "I can't either." He paused and when he spoke again, she could hear the agitation in his voice. "Mia, I don't mean to change the subject, but I think there's something more important than my lack of an aura that we need to discuss right now. I've been doing a lot of thinking while I've been sitting here waiting for you," he began, looking beyond her into the hallway.

"Yes?" she prodded when he didn't continue right away.

He began again, barely speaking above a whisper. "Mia, someone realized you knew about the trafficking and they didn't like it. Whoever it was had you imprisoned, but for some reason, they didn't do anything to me, even though I knew about it too."

She thought for a moment about the implication of his realization. "I assumed while I was in the basement that if they'd found me, they'd found you too. But they didn't," she said.

"No," he replied.

"Then obviously, they didn't know about you," she said.

"And if they knew about you but not about me, then we weren't discovered at Brookins' house," he continued. "So that begs the question, who knew you knew but didn't know that I knew?"

She stared at him, impressed by his clear line of reasoning that was pointing at just one person. The revelation she'd had in the basement about the commissioner using Thomas as an informant came rushing back to her and the reality of the commissioner's involvement was clear.

"Did you tell anyone at the station besides your father about what we found?" he asked finally.

"Yes."

"Who?"

"Commissioner Dalton," she replied grimly.

CHAPTER

40

KATE

Kate had already been seen by a physician and, after submitting to a rape kit and medical examination, was given a clean bill of health. As soon as the medical staff left the room, a police officer arrived carrying a large stack of files and a bowl of hot vegetable soup which he placed in front of her. While savoring each delicious spoonful, she recounted the story of her capture and imprisonment for the second time as the officer took detailed notes. The last thing he asked her to do was look through a series of photographs to see if she recognized any of the men who were involved in her abduction.

Once the officer left the room, she was completely alone for the first time in many weeks. It was unnerving, sitting by herself with nothing but her thoughts. She was growing impatient for the questioning process to end so she could concentrate on finding her sisters. Her annoyance turned to joy several minutes later when Mia entered the room with an attractive young man. Suddenly, she felt hope return.

"Oh, Mia!" she exclaimed. "I'm so happy to see you!"

"Me too," Mia said as she crossed the room to give her a hug. "Kate, I want you to meet my boyfriend, Thomas."

"*The* Thomas?" she asked, taking his hand in her own.

Mia blushed. "Yes. *The* Thomas. And Kate, we have him to thank for our freedom. He led the officers to the warehouse."

She threw her arms around his neck. "You are a hero," she said. "Thank you so much for finding us."

"I'm no hero," Thomas replied, smiling at Mia. "Just a man who won't take no for an answer."

Mia motioned for them all to take a seat and began barraging her with questions. "How are you holding up? Have they given you something to eat? Did they do a physical examination?" she asked.

She took a moment to digest Mia's litany of questions. The entire situation was overwhelming and she was having difficulty thinking about anything other than whether or not her sisters had been abducted as well.

"I'm okay, I think. I had a bowl of soup, but to be honest, I could eat ten more. They combed my hair and cleaned and clipped my nails. They also took my clothes and swabbed me even though I told her I didn't need it. Oh, and I also looked at a bunch of pictures of men to see if I recognized any of them."

Mia scribbled feverishly into her notebook. "I'll see if I can get you more soup, or at least some crackers or something. As for the men, how many did you recognize?" she asked.

"Six."

"That's amazing, Kate. I'm so proud of you. Any chance you might be up for looking at a few more photographs?"

She didn't understand what more there was to do. "But I just told you, I already looked at all of them."

"The photos you looked at were only of the men who the police think may be involved based on their prior criminal activity," Mia explained. "Thomas and I are doing a little side investigation and I need your help. We're trying to see if you can identify any of the other men you may have seen at any point during your ordeal. I need you to think back all the way to Kiev. Do you think you're up for that?"

"Yes. Of course. Whatever you need."

Mia took the photographs from her hand and spread them out on the bed.

"All I need you to do is point out anyone you recognize. That's it."

Kate looked carefully at the portraits of the men. She had never seen the first two before, but the third photo was of a man who was present at the first auction. He hadn't been one of the bidders. He also didn't interact with any of the women in any way. And yet, he had been there. She was sure of it.

"This man," she said, pointing to the third photo, "was at the auction. He stood to the side. He didn't talk to us. Didn't touch us. In fact, I only saw him speaking to one other man. But I definitely remember him being there."

"You're sure?" Mia asked, glancing at Thomas.

"Yes. Positive."

She saw a look pass between them she interpreted as excitement.

"That's wonderful, Kate. Thank you," Mia said as she scooped the photos off the table. "I'll talk to the nursing staff to see about getting you something more to eat, and I think maybe you should stay here and rest for a while."

She grabbed her wrist firmly. "Actually Mia, there's something else before you go."

"Name it. Anything at all."

Tears welled in her eyes at the thought of the unknown. "It's my sisters. I need to know if they are here in the United States. I need to call my parents to find out. Please," she begged.

"I'll get you a phone right away."

Within fifteen minutes, Mia and Thomas returned with a cell phone. As Mia handed it to her, Kate tried to maintain her resolve. The handset felt heavy in her hands and she was suddenly unable to dial the extension. During the days of not knowing, hope had remained. As soon as she spoke to her family, she would either be overcome with joy or ravaged by despair.

"Would you like me to call them?" Mia asked.

She shook her head decisively. "No. I can do it. But I can't tell them the truth. Not just yet. Please don't think less of me for it."

"This is your life, Kate," she said. "You do as you see fit."

"I just don't want to cause them undue pain. Especially if my sisters are still at home. They don't need to know what has happened to me. At least not yet."

At last, she found the courage to dial the familiar digits of her family's phone number. Her body was shaking and she had to steady the phone with both hands. She closed her eyes, willing someone to answer the call. After the third ring, she heard her mother's voice.

"Hello?"

"Mama!" she cried.

"Yekaterina? Is that you?"

"Yes, Mama! It's me. I am here. I am fine!" she replied.

"It has been such a long time. We were so worried for you. Why have you not called us sooner?" her mother scolded.

"This is the first opportunity I've had to use the phone, Mama. I just wanted you to know that I am fine."

"And Tetyana and Natalya? Are they fine as well? Can you put them on the line?"

She stopped breathing and nearly dropped the phone from her hands. Mia was immediately at her side, holding her steady to keep her from collapsing onto the floor.

"Yekaterina? Where are your sisters?" her mother asked again.

"They aren't here with me right now, Mama, but I will let them know you send your love when I see them, okay?"

"Okay. We love you all. We are excited for you to return home. Your father is lost without you girls. And so am I."

"Me too, Mama. I have to go now. I love you and I will call you again soon."

"Goodbye, my Katerina."

"Goodbye, Mama."

She handed the phone back to Mia and could no longer keep herself from crying. She sat on the bed, buried her face in her arms and sobbed uncontrollably. Mia rubbed her back in an effort to soothe her aching heart, but it did little to ease her pain. She wouldn't feel better until the day she saw her sisters safely back to Kiev.

"They're here?" Mia asked after Kate finally dried her eyes.

"Yes."

"We are going to find them," Mia declared.

Kate saw the compassion and concern in her friend's eyes, and knew Mia would work tirelessly to find Natalya and Tetyana with every tool the police department had in its arsenal. However, she also knew they would benefit from the use of her power if they had any chance of finding her sisters before it was too late. "I want to help you with the search," she said.

Mia glanced hesitantly at her and then to Thomas and back again. "I think you've already given us the information we need to take down the entire operation. With any luck, we'll find your sisters in no time."

"Really?" she exclaimed, amazed at how quickly her gift had provided a solution for finding her sisters. "You really think it will be that simple?"

"I think we may know who is behind the entire trafficking ring. With any luck, when we find him, we'll also find the location of the rest of the women that have been imprisoned," Mia explained.

"We don't need any luck to find my sisters because we have you, Mia. You were brought to me. I asked for a way

287

out of the mess I was in and the universe delivered you into my life to correct everything that had gone wrong," she said.

She fished into her jacket pocket and pulled out the velvet box, handing it to Mia. "I want you to have them," she said.

Mia held up her hands, refusing the box. "I can't take those!"

Kate placed the box gently on the bed and slid them toward her friend. "You came into my life just when I needed you. It was no coincidence *you* were the one who came to save us."

"But I didn't save you. Thomas did," Mia replied.

"No, but you did. You saved our souls. You gave us hope. You kept us going when most of the girls didn't care to go on. And let's be honest, if *you* hadn't been imprisoned with us, Thomas would have never set out on his search. And I'd still be in that basement. So please, I want you to have them so you will always remember that you may not know why you are where you've been placed in your life, but there's always a reason you're there."

Mia picked up the box and slid the hair pins into her hand. She wound her hair onto the top of her head and carefully slid the pins into place.

"I will wear them proudly."

"Good," she said. "Now let's go find my sisters."

CHAPTER

41

THOMAS

After the women were released from the hospital, Mia and Kate were escorted to the police station while Thomas was tasked with finding them more food. Their eyes lit up as he strolled into Mia's office carrying a bucket of fried chicken and container of pasta salad from the corner market. Kate ate ravenously while Mia helped herself to a drumstick.

Jack rushed into the office with a stack of files in his arms and collapsed into his desk chair.

"I just finished interrogating the guy we picked up at the warehouse," he said.

"I thought he took a fatal shot to the chest," Mia said.

Jack shook his head and laid his sidearm on his desk. "There were two of them standing guard when the operation went down. One survived and we have him in custody at the hospital. I just spent the last 45 minutes pumping him for information before the doctor kicked me out. I didn't realize how much I rely on your bad cop persona until you weren't there, Mia," he said, smiling at her.

"Yeah... I don't think you want me anywhere near that guy right now," she said. "Bad cop would be an understatement."

"Agreed. For his sake, I won't tell you where he is," he said, giving her a wink. "Anyway, I wasn't able to get the name of the man he's working for. He claims he doesn't know him and has never seen him."

Mia pursed her lips tightly. "He's seen him," she said.

"Maybe, but unless I'm willing to inflict bodily harm, he's not giving him up. Whoever is running this whole thing has the guys under him wound tight."

"So did you get anything from him?" she asked.

"Are you doubting my abilities?" Jack laughed. "Of course I got something. I had to trade him some leniency with the district attorney for the info, but he gave up the location of a second holding facility."

He saw Kate's face light up at the news of a second facility.

"My sisters could be there," she said.

"Maybe, but don't get too excited yet," Mia told her before turning her attention back to Jack. "So what's the plan for the second place? Is my dad going to send a group over?"

"Yeah. They're talking about sending Tim's squad within the next hour or two."

"I want to go with them," Kate announced.

"We can't let that happen Ma'am," Jack said. "It's far too dangerous to send a civilian into a situation where we know men will be armed."

Kate was dogged in her insistence. "If my sisters are there, I want to be there when they find them. I need to know they are safe."

"Kate, it's way too dangerous. You should probably just stay here to wait and see what they find," Mia said.

Thomas empathized with her desperation and couldn't help but feel compassion. He remembered all too clearly how helpless he had felt searching for Mia and felt compelled to speak on her behalf.

"What if she just drove along and sat in the squad car a block or so away? That way, if they find her sisters, she'll already be there and can see them right away."

"That wouldn't be following protocol," Jack said.

"Since when are you a stickler for protocol?" Mia asked, her resolve clearly waning.

Jack sighed, outnumbered and defeated. "Fine. I'll talk to Tim and see what he thinks. But no promises."

Thomas wanted to do something to seal the deal for Kate. "What if I go along too? I'll stay with her, if that's okay with you, Kate," he said.

She nodded, offering him a nervous but relieved smile.

Mia took his hand. "You're the best," she said, planting a kiss on his cheek.

"I'll go find Tim," Jack said, rising from his chair and shaking his head, clearly unconvinced about the plan.

"No, wait. Sit down. There's something else we need to discuss," said Mia.

"There's more?"

"Yeah. There's more," she replied urgently. "Jack, who all knew about my little stakeout operation with Thomas last weekend?"

"No one I know of. I didn't even know about it until they found you. Why?"

"Think about it - there was obviously a reason I was taken. Someone was aware of who and what I saw at Wayne Brookins' house that night. I'm convinced I was kidnapped so I wouldn't talk. But nothing happened to Thomas, so whoever knew about me didn't know about him. I think that's because I never told anyone he was there."

"Who did you tell you were there, besides your dad?"

"Dalton," Mia replied flatly.

Silence filled the room as Thomas watched a look of understanding and horror pass between the partners.

"Oh, God," said Jack as the reality of the situation sank in.

"Yeah. 'Oh, God' is right. And it gets better. Kate just picked his face out of a photo lineup. He was at an auction."

"I'm guessing he wasn't making arrests."

"No," Mia said.

"Oh, God," Jack said again, rubbing the back of his neck with his hand. "Now what?"

"Now we do what we were trained to do," Mia replied resolutely.

"What do you have in mind?" Jack asked, his voice laced with skepticism.

"I think we need to go pay a special visit to the commissioner's house."

"Under what pretense?"

"Well, we know he's extremely interested in human trafficking, right? Hasn't he shown a great deal of concern here at the station? I think it would be irresponsible of us if we didn't head there right away to let him know about all the new developments in the case. I'm sure he wouldn't want to hear about it tomorrow morning after the operation is finished," she explained.

"We can't use anything we get from him unless we have a warrant," said Jack.

"Then go get us a warrant. Stella will help us out on this one for sure."

"And what about your father?"

"What about him?"

"Are we going to let him know what we're up to?"

"Are you still going to go along with it if we don't?" she asked.

Jack looked up at the ceiling as if he was looking for counsel from above. He closed his eyes and exhaled through his teeth. "Yes," he replied at last.

Mia was visibly relieved. "Good, then we leave him out of it. He's made it very clear to me that he believes Dalton is clean. He'll never give his permission for us to barge in on him at home about this. If my dad has a chance to tell us no then we'll be disobeying a direct order. At least if he doesn't know we are only guilty of not obtaining permission."

"Stella might have to say something to him," said Jack.

"As long as she waits until we're already there, I'm okay with that," replied Mia. "We might need some backup anyway."

Thomas listened in awe to the easy back and forth of Jack and Mia's conversation. It was clear to him there was great respect and friendship between them, but when she mentioned their mission possibly requiring backup, he grew leery of their plan. He couldn't stand the thought of losing her a second time.

"Maybe you should rethink this, Mia," he entreated. "Perhaps someone else would be better suited for going with Jack to see the commissioner." He looked into her eyes for some glimpse that she understood his concern for her safety stemmed from his affection for her. He was saddened he saw only fiery resolve.

"Thomas," she replied, smiling genuinely at him, "everything will be fine. He's the commissioner for crying out loud! What's he going to do to us?"

Before he could stop himself, he grabbed her by the shoulders, forcing her to look him in the eye. "He was desperate enough to have you kidnapped from your own home and we have an idea of what his final plans were for you. I can only imagine what he might've done if they hadn't gotten to you when they did. You don't know what he's capable of or what lengths he's willing to go to secure his anonymity," he pleaded.

She shook free of him and kissed him playfully on the nose. "Thomas, really, it's going to be okay. We do this kind of thing every day. Right, Jack?"

"Right," Jack agreed, although Thomas felt his anxious expression betrayed his true feelings.

"Then it's settled," she continued. "Thomas, you and Kate will ride along to the second holding facility with Tim's group as long as he approves. Meanwhile, Jack is going to coerce Stella into getting us a warrant to search the commissioner's house and as soon as we get it, we'll head right out."

"Yes," said Kate and Jack in unison.

He remained silent, still completely uncomfortable with allowing Mia out of his sight.

"I'm going to go get a shower and change into my uniform. Kate, why don't you come with me and I'll make sure we find you a proper set of clothes," said Mia, reaching for Kate's hand.

Thomas watched as Mia led Kate across the room. Before reaching the door, she stopped to kiss him passionately on the lips.

"Everything is going to be fine," she said, wrapping herself in his arms. "Have a little faith. I'll see you tonight and then maybe you can make me some more French toast in the morning."

He couldn't help smiling at her infectious optimism, and marveled at the fact that even though she'd just been released from her imprisonment, she was already prepared to do whatever was necessary to bring about justice.

"Who's the cautiously optimistic one now?" he asked.

"Guess you're starting to rub off on me," she replied.

He couldn't believe he was about to let her go. "I love you," he blurted out.

She winked at him. "I love you, too."

And with that, she headed out the door.

He and Jack sat awkwardly together in the office.

"She's something, isn't she?" Jack said, breaking the tension.

"She's pretty great," he agreed.

"I'll take care of her," Jack said, mindful of his concern. "I won't let anything happen."

He sat silently for several moments, mulling over the situation. "Does it get easier? The police thing? The worry?"

Jack fiddled with a paperclip, unbending it into a straight line. "No. I don't think so. You'd have to ask Stella about that. But if it makes you feel any better, Mia and I take care of each other. She's practically family."

It was obvious Jack loved Mia, but Thomas doubted he could keep her from doing anything she set her mind to. "I can see that, and it does help. It was hard though, when she was missing. The not knowing part."

Jack pushed back from his desk, and threw the mangled paperclip in the trash. "Believe me. I get it. I can't imagine something like that happening to Stella," he replied. He stood up from his chair and started for the door but paused as he reached the threshold. "And Thomas, for what it's worth, I've never seen Mia as happy as she's been since she met you."

"Thanks, Jack."

"And good luck at the second holding facility. I think Kate was really glad you offered to go with her. I hope you find her sisters."

"Me too," he replied.

Although everyone else had left the office, he didn't move from the table as he considered everything that had happened overnight. Despite all that had transpired, he found the one detail he kept returning to was Mia's inability to see his aura. He wondered if his unpleasant childhood had broken part of his spirit after all. This thought made him sad, but before he was able to dwell on it for very long, Lieutenant Tim Sanders appeared at the door.

"Thomas Pritchett?" he asked.

"Yes?" he replied, rising from his chair.

"I've been told you'll be coming with us when we head to the second facility," he said.

"I think that's the plan."

"Alright. Then you're going to need to come with me. We have some information to discuss before we head out."

An hour-and-a-half later, he walked hesitantly across the parking lot beside Kate toward the police cruiser that would take them to the second holding facility and possibly her sisters. The anxiety radiating from her was as palpable as his own nervous energy. As they climbed tentatively in the car, he prayed silently their mission would be a success.

CHAPTER

42

MIA

"I'm hoping the wire won't be necessary," Jack commented as Mia taped the tiny microphone onto his chest.

"I don't think it will be. But since we know Dalton may have been planning to kill me, I don't trust that he won't do something crazy. At least this way, if something happens, there'll be proof."

"Well, I just hope he backs down at the sight of the warrant Stella got us."

She tacked the last piece of tape across his back and pulled his shirt carefully over the wire. "Me too. But if I've learned anything in the last week, it's that I can't be too careful," she said.

As the partners finished their preparations, they received notice that Thomas and Kate had left with the group heading to the second holding facility.

"You think her sisters are there?" Jack asked as he retucked his shirt.

Mia grunted. "I don't know. They could be anywhere. I have a feeling we're only looking at the tip of the iceberg with regard to this trafficking operation. I just hope if they aren't there, we'll be able to get enough information from Dalton to find out where else they could be."

"Do you think Dalton is the top of the food chain?"

"Maybe. It would make sense, given everything we know about him. I guess time will tell." She adjusted her sidearm. "Are you ready?"

"Ready as I'm gonna be," he replied as he walked out of their office and into the hallway. "I sure hope you're right about Dalton, Mia."

"I'm right about him. You just have to help me prove it."

The drive to Commissioner Dalton's house was far shorter than she anticipated. She assumed she'd have more time to compose herself and wasn't even close to being mentally prepared when Jack parked the cruiser in front of a large corner row home in the historic section of Federal Hill.

"We're here already?" she said.

"Want me to circle the block again?" he asked.

"No," she replied, unhooking her seatbelt, "let's get this over with."

She followed Jack up the steps to the century-old door of Dalton's home and after ringing the doorbell, a teenage girl with the brightest of auras answered. Mia smiled at how goodness could blossom in spite of where it was planted.

"Are you here for my dad?" his daughter asked, leading them into the foyer.

"Yes, please," she replied.

"Is he expecting you?" the girl continued brightly.

"No," Jack frowned. "I'm afraid not."

Without any further pleasantries, the girl disappeared up the steps to the second floor, and moments later Roger Dalton appeared at the top of the staircase dressed in his robe and slippers. As he descended the stairs, she observed a momentary look of dread on his face when he recognized who she was. Although undetectable to Jack, it was obvious to her that he'd assumed she was still tucked safely away in the warehouse basement and was shocked to see her standing in his foyer.

"To what do I owe this Sunday morning visit?" he asked, composing himself and smiling broadly as he extended his hand in greeting.

"Good morning, Commissioner. We're here because there have been some developments overnight in the human trafficking case that we thought you needed to be made aware of," Jack began cautiously. She hoped the commissioner was unable to detect the anxiety in his voice.

"Oh really?" Dalton replied, glancing in her direction as he spoke.

"Yes, Sir," Jack continued. "We received a tip about the location of one of the facilities where women were being held captive, and at 0200 hours, a team led by Lieutenant Derek Rodriquez rescued fifteen women out of the basement of an abandoned warehouse."

"Rescued?"

"Yes, Sir. All fifteen are alive and well," Jack replied.

"That's... well, that's fantastic news." His voice dripped with phony enthusiasm as he started down the stairs.

"Yes, Sir. It was a good night."

She could see Dalton's anxiety level rising with the knowledge that women who could identify him had escaped with their lives.

He shifted nervously in his slippers. "I assume there were guards at the facility?" he asked.

"Yes, Sir. Two of them."

"And?"

"And one was mortally wounded during a volley of gunfire at the time of the infiltration and the other was apprehended without incident."

Dalton narrowed his eyes. "So I assume he's in custody now?"

"Yes, Sir. I questioned him myself overnight and he gave us the location of a second holding site."

"Nothing more?"

"No, Sir. Nothing more."

He tightened the belt on his robe as he reached the bottom step. "And are there plans to infiltrate the second facility?" Dalton asked.

"Yes, Sir. A team left half an hour ago."

There was a pause in the conversation as the commissioner ran his fingers through his hair. It was clear to her that he was on the verge of becoming unhinged and it was time for her to become involved in the conversation.

"It's interesting to me, Commissioner, that you haven't asked about the well-being of the women who were found. You know, the women who you are so passionate about protecting."

"Yes. Yes. How are the women?" he asked, unable to make eye contact with her as she spoke directly to him.

"As a matter of fact, most of them are doing pretty well, thanks for asking. I actually got to spend quite a bit of time speaking with them."

Dalton ran his fingers nervously over the mahogany of the railing. "Oh. Really?" he replied.

"Oh yes. You see, this funny thing happened to me. I was in my apartment last week, minding my own business, and these two thugs showed up and knocked me out. I ended up in the basement of an abandoned warehouse with fourteen other women who were being auctioned off for sex. Can you imagine such a thing?"

He gasped audibly, placing his hand to his chest. "No. I certainly cannot. How… dreadful."

"Quite dreadful," she agreed. "I couldn't have imagined it either. And you know what else I couldn't imagine? I couldn't imagine why in the world I was there with them. It was the strangest thing. Especially since you and I had just spoken about what I had seen the night before at the little stakeout I conducted at Wayne Brookins'. It was almost as if someone saw me at Brookins' house and tracked me down."

Dalton nodded thoughtfully. "That must have been what happened," he agreed.

"Yeah, I thought so too for a while, but I'm pretty sure it didn't happen that way."

"Oh?" He finally looked directly at her, daring her to continue. She watched as a bead of sweat made its way down his forehead and was absorbed into his eyebrow. His left eye began to twitch and he licked his lips nervously. She smiled.

"Nah. No one saw me at the stakeout."

"How can you be so sure?" he asked.

"Because I wasn't alone that night. And the person who was with me was never approached in any way." She shrugged nonchalantly. "Wouldn't make any sense to lock me away and leave the other witness walking around on the street all week, would it?"

The commissioner fell silent and reached for the newel post at the foot of the stairs for support.

She continued, taking a step closer to where Dalton was standing.

"Did my father ever tell you about this funny little quirk I have?"

Dalton didn't respond as he attempted to regain his composure, wiping his brow and readjusting his robe.

"I have this gift. I was born with it. It's kind of cool. Comes in handy on the job."

"What are you babbling about, Officer?" he demanded angrily, standing up straight and returning himself to full height.

"I see people's auras. They're like windows into people's souls. It might sound a little cliché, but good people are surrounded by brightness. Bad people are surrounded by darkness. The first day I met you, I knew."

"You knew what?" he spat at her.

"I knew you were capable of every atrocity known to man. And now I know that includes selling innocent women for sex on the black market to the highest bidder."

"You have no proof of any such thing! That's a huge accusation and I will have you fired immediately for slander and insubordination!"

"You can try," she said, venturing another step closer to the commissioner, "but first, you might be interested in taking a look at this."

She handed him a copy of the warrant from the district attorney giving the police permission to search his home and vehicle for information regarding the trafficking ring.

"What the hell is this?" he yelled, his composed façade slipping away.

"I'm surprised you don't recognize a warrant for search and seizure of property, Commissioner," she responded sweetly.

"I'm quite familiar with what it *is*, Officer," Dalton responded, his words slicing the distance between them. "What I'm interested in is how you were able to obtain this. On what grounds was this issued?

"It's funny you should ask," she replied, smiling broadly at him. "We happen to have an eye witness who observed you at an auction."

"An eye witness account?" he spat, unable to mask his contempt for her. "From whom? Some cracked up whore living in a brothel? Who do you think a jury is going to believe? Her or me?"

"The thing is, I only needed the eye witness to obtain the warrant and it was obviously sufficient enough for a judge to grant it. Now I'm hoping what we find in your personal files will put you away for a lifetime. So if you'll excuse us, we need to begin collecting evidence. Can you point me in the direction of your personal computer?" she asked sweetly.

Enraged by her coyness to the point where he was no longer able to maintain self-control, Dalton snapped, throwing himself at her in an uncharacteristic display of anger. Before she realized what was happening, he quickly pinned her arms behind her back and secured her in a painful headlock. Across the foyer, Jack had already drawn his weapon.

"Let her go, Commissioner. You don't need another nail in your coffin," Jack said reasonably.

"I simply cannot believe the audacity of you two," Dalton began, his voice suddenly calm, "coming to my home under the assumption I've done something wrong. And if that wasn't bad enough, you believe the commissioner of the Baltimore City Police Department would allow himself to get caught in something as tawdry as human trafficking? It's laughable!"

She winced as the commissioner's fingers began to tighten, bruising the flesh of her neck. The pressure he was placing on her trachea was extraordinary and she concentrated on filling her lungs with much needed air.

"Dad?" said a frightened voice from the top of the stairs.

"Not now, Pumpkin. Daddy's dealing with some insubordinate employees. Just go on back into your room. Tell your mother and sister to stay up there too," Dalton said with a level of confidence that belied what he was doing.

"Do you want me to call 911?" his daughter asked.

"Yes, please!" cried Jack.

"No. No, Honey. Just go to your room and lock the door. Daddy's got everything under control."

She struggled to breathe. With each gasp of air, Dalton tightened his grip around her neck. Her field of vision began to darken around the edges as her brain began to suffer from the effects of oxygen deprivation. She watched as Jack took a step closer to the commissioner, still pointing his gun in their direction.

"Commissioner, I need you to let her go or I will be forced to shoot you. Please don't make me do that," he pleaded.

Slowly, slowly, she could no longer focus on Jack's face and was unable to control the urge to breathe. Her body began to spasm wildly as her respiratory muscles shut down. The last sound she heard was the commissioner's voice whispering in her ear, "The end is coming, Mia. Soon the prophecy will be fulfilled."

And then, without a single thought as to the significance of her own life or death, Mia Rosetti stopped breathing altogether.

CHAPTER
43

THOMAS

"Even if they don't find them here, at this facility, they will find them," Thomas reassured Kate as he slid across the back seat of the police cruiser. "Mia won't stop until she finds your sisters. You can count on that."

"I can feel it," said Kate, as she eased in beside him and fastened her safety belt. "I just know we are going to find them today. What a wonderful birthday gift it will be."

"Is today your birthday?" he asked.

"No. It's actually not until next week."

"My birthday's next week too," he commented. "I was born on the seventeenth."

"Me too!" cried Kate. "What are the chances of us having the same birthday? How old will you be?"

"Twenty-five," he replied.

"As will I. That's very strange, Thomas," said Kate as she turned to look out the car window at the sea of abandoned row homes passing by. After a moment, she turned back to face him. "It's funny, but I feel almost as if we are supposed to be together for some reason. That we were destined to meet. It's stupid," she said, shaking her head.

"No," he replied. "It's not stupid. You never know why you're on the path you're on. You just have to trust that you are where you're supposed to be I guess."

Kate nodded but was silent for the remainder of the trip to the holding facility. He studied her as she fidgeted nervously with a strand of hair that had worked its way loose from her ponytail. It was difficult for him to imagine how she was feeling. Her devotion to her sisters and the obvious lengths she was willing to go to protect them was something foreign to him. Having never had a sibling, he imagined the love he felt for Mildred would most closely approximate the love Kate felt for her sisters. He admired her tenacity and determination and as the police car parked at their destination, he realized he too would do whatever it took to see her safely with her sisters once again.

The officer from the front seat of the cruiser turned to face them, speaking to them in a tone most people reserved for small children.

"I need for you both to stay in the car. The rest of us are going to head into the house from around back. You need to wait until one of us comes back here and gives you the 'all clear' before you will be allowed out of the vehicle. And, if for some reason the operation doesn't go as planned, whatever you do, don't get out of the car until backup arrives. Are we clear?"

"Yes, of course," he replied.

He watched as both of the officers exited the vehicle, made their way down the block, and joined with the other two officers from the second car.

"I can't do this," Kate cried suddenly, as she pulled frantically at the handle.

"Can't do what?" he asked, reaching for her arm.

"I can't just sit here, waiting for them to get back. What if something happens? What if my sisters need me? I don't want to just be stuck here in the backseat of this car!"

He laid a protective hand on her shoulder. "Kate, it's not safe to go with them. And you know firsthand what those men are capable of. We need to stay here. You'd be no good to your sisters if something were to happen to you. And besides, this is a police car - the doors won't open from the inside even if we wanted them to."

She fell silent and drummed her fingers nervously on the seat beside her. As she stared blankly out the window, his mind raced, searching for something to say which would bring solace to her aching heart. Sadly, he couldn't think of a single phrase that didn't sound trivial or cliché.

And then, seemingly out of nowhere, he noticed a man crossing the street, heading in the direction of the police cruiser. It was as if he was being drawn to the car by some unseen force.

The sound of gunfire shook Kate from her trance and she began crying out.

"They're shooting them! I have to get to my sisters!" she screamed, pounding on the window and motioning to the man who was now only inches from the car.

"No, Kate! No!" Thomas pleaded.

The door to the police car swung open as the man released the latch from the outside. At that moment, the police scanner crackled to life and Kate froze in place, already halfway out the door.

"We've got an officer down in the 200 block of Rose Street. Requesting emergency services and immediate backup."

Their eyes locked for a split second. In that flickering moment, he felt her desperation and knew there was nothing he could do to keep her from the house or the hope of her sisters.

He heard more gunfire and anxiety began to grow inside of him, deep in the pit of his stomach.

"We have a second officer down," the scanner reported. "Requesting immediate backup."

And then she was gone.

"We can't help them, Kate!" he called to her as she took off down the street in the direction of the house.

For a moment, all he could do was watch her running down the sidewalk. The fear inside him, which manifested itself as gut-wrenching anxiety, kept him safely seated in the back of the car. And yet, he couldn't stay behind.

As she disappeared out of sight, he mustered the courage to slide across the seat toward the open door, and although certain danger awaited him, he was prepared to confront it. Determined to ignore the voice in his head that was screaming for him to stay put, he stepped out of the car. He took off at a run down the street and as he approached the house, watched in horror as he saw Kate repeatedly throwing herself against the front door in an attempt to get inside. He scrambled beside the stoop and without thinking of the consequences, kicked through the blackened glass pane of the basement window. Carefully, he reached his arm inside and felt for the latch to release the lock. When she realized what he was doing, Kate joined him at the window and one at a time, they squeezed through the tiny opening and entered the house.

He recoiled at the scene before him. The stench of human excrement was overwhelming and he was surrounded by almost a dozen women, each shackled to the floor by short lengths of chain. A few cried out in anguish as they passed through the room. At first he didn't understand why most of the girls were lying motionless on the floor. And then, in a state of utter disbelief, he realized all of the women had been shot. Recently shot. He tried desperately to keep from throwing up as he scanned the room and saw every woman lying in a pool of her own blood.

"Do you see your sisters?" he called to Kate who was consoling one of the women clinging to life at the far end of the room.

"No! They're not here! Perhaps they are upstairs," she called back. He watched as she knelt beside the woman at her feet and asked, "Have you seen twins? Girls who are the same?"

"Yes! Yes!" the woman replied. "They are here!"

Kate was halfway up the stairs before he could advise her against going any further. He followed behind her as she burst through the door and emerged into the eerie stillness of the main level.

"There's no one here," she whispered from just inside the empty room.

"No," he agreed. "Not even the police. They must still be outside."

The deafening sound of a gunshot pierced through the silence. A second shot rang out before either one had time to react. By the time the third shot was fired, he had pulled her onto the floor where they huddled together in the corner.

"We need to get out of here," he urged. "Please, Kate. We can't help them anymore."

"This is all my fault," she wailed. "I *wished* for this. I wanted it. But it was never their dream, only mine. And I can't let them die because of my short-sightedness. I have to try," she wept, the tears streaming down her face.

He had never felt so torn in his entire life. Every fiber of his being screamed for him to leave the building as quickly as possible because he knew beyond a shadow of a doubt he was in mortal danger. However, as he looked at the woman sitting beside him, he also knew he couldn't just leave her and that she wasn't going anywhere without her sisters. And so, he took her hand in his.

"Come on," he whispered. "Let's go find your sisters."

Together, they climbed the staircase to the second floor of the row house. The windows were boarded shut and the space around them was dark and cold. As they reached the landing, he could feel danger close by in the form of another human being. He quickly scanned the hallway and chose the room that felt the least threatening. Kate followed him inside.

There was no furniture in the room. Nothing covering the floor. Slivers of daylight shimmered through the cracks at the edges of the window's plywood covering and struggled to illuminate the darkness. He could barely make out the room's occupants, two women, who were crouched on the deteriorating hardwoods in the far corner of the room. Like the others they discovered in the basement, both women before him were shackled to the floor. Curiously, instead of looking to see who had entered the room, the girls buried their heads under their arms as he quietly shut the door behind him.

"Tetyana? Natalya?" Kate called into the darkness.

"Kate?" both women replied in unison, as they lifted their heads from beneath their arms.

He saw her descend upon her sisters in one swift motion, a chaotic mass of limbs and hair and tears. She immediately began pulling wildly at their chains and he watched in anguish from beside the door as she acquiesced to the tightness of the restraints.

"I hear someone walking down the hall," he whispered to the women.

"Perhaps it's the police," Kate replied hopefully as she continued working to free her sisters' hands.

He looked upon the women in their frenzied desperation and felt strangely envious of them, realizing that no one had ever felt about him the way Kate was feeling about Natalya and Tetyana. His heart ached with longing to be loved as they loved one another.

He was pulled from his thoughts by the sound of the door on its hinges, and the subsequent motion of it being thrown open elevated his anxiety to new heights.

However, he found, for the first time in his cautious life, he was able to shut down the voices in his head and persevere.

The man who entered the room was brandishing a semi-automatic handgun and he took aim at the women immediately. Out of the corner of his eye, he saw Kate collapse on top of her sisters, shielding their bodies with her own as the first deafening shots rang out. From his vantage point behind the door, he remained unseen by the shooter, and his only chance of saving the women was to use the element of surprise to his advantage. With all the strength he could muster, he threw himself against the door, ramming it into the man, but not before he had the chance to fire off a second round of shots.

He found himself face to face with the gunman who was still clearly surprised that he was confronting a more dangerous adversary than the shackled women he'd been murdering throughout the house. Without a moment's hesitation, Thomas threw his shoulder into the man's gut using the entire weight of his body. The man took several steps back into the hallway but was quickly able to regain his balance and level his gun at Thomas' head. He was fully aware that the intensity of hatred he saw in the gunman's eyes was reflected in his own with an equivalent level of fear. And yet, in that moment, he willed himself into action, hurling himself once again at the man who teetered for an instant at the top of the staircase before pulling the trigger one final time and tumbling headfirst to the foyer below.

CHAPTER

44

KATE

There was darkness, but also a clarity Kate could not ignore as she struggled to remain conscious. The initial pain of the bullet wounds had subsided and she was finally able to concentrate on something beside her physical state.

As her hold on consciousness continued to slip away, she saw the path of her life spread before her like photographs, a series of snapshots beginning with her childhood and continuing through her desperate search for her sisters. She assumed the images would end there, however, as her breathing slowed, they continued.

At first, she saw the faces of the women who had been imprisoned with her in the basement. They were smiling. Happy. Free. As their faces faded, there were still more to replace them. The faces of these women were unfamiliar to her. There were dozens of them. Maybe even hundreds. And they too were smiling.

In that moment, the world seemed to stop on its axis, and she knew who they were. These were the women who would never be defiled, mistreated, abused, or assaulted because of the path her life had taken. They would never know what it was to be tortured by a man. They were the women who had been saved because of Kate and the power of her gift.

As she had always suspected, her gift had never been about providing for her own needs. Its purpose had been far greater - bigger than she could have ever imagined.

In a moment of unexpected clarity, Kate saw that she had been given her gift to assure that Mia would be led to her destiny. Without even knowing it, she had called Mia to fulfill part of what was to become her legacy.

As the women faded, a second image rose to the surface of her consciousness, like a ship sailing out of the fog. It was of Thomas Pritchett, a man who spent his entire life hiding from danger who had now been inspired to overcome the power of his inner voice so he too would begin to understand his true purpose. She saw that his newfound courage would be instrumental in the journey that lay ahead.

Like Borromean rings, linked each with the others to form a Brunnian link, so too it had been for the three of them. None of the three could have been brought to their destinies without the existence of the other two. As her heart slowed, Kate's last vision was of four other souls whose lives would soon be linked to Mia and Thomas just as she had been. She saw the end was coming – not just for herself but for all of mankind and that Mia and Thomas would play a major role in deciding the fate of mankind.

She acknowledged the world was in capable hands, and with that final thought, slipped peacefully out of her life and moved into the light.

CHAPTER

45

MIA

On her first day back to the office in over a week, Mia spent most of the morning thinking about when she would be able to return to the hospital. She sat at her desk across from Jack and unconsciously touched her neck. What remained of the bruising had begun to change from black and blue to pale green. Just three days after being admitted for the injuries she sustained at the hands of the commissioner, the doctors released her with a clean bill of health. They were convinced her trachea was healing appropriately and that she would have no lasting brain injury, thanks to the quick work of the paramedics on the scene.

Physically, she was recovering and had been cleared to return to work. Unfortunately, the emotional repercussions of her ordeal still kept her from being able to fully focus on what needed to be done.

"Thanks, Jack," she said as he closed the folder on his desk.

He cocked his head to the side and scowled at her. "Mia, you already thanked me fifty times. Enough already."

She threw a pen at his head. "You saved my life, Jack. You shot the Baltimore City police commissioner, for crying out loud. I'll thank you a million times if I want to."

"Fine," he said, smiling, "but it will be your own fault when my head is so big I can't fit through the door."

"That won't happen," she replied. "Just wait until you're stuck changing diapers when the baby arrives."

She returned absentmindedly to the inventory on her computer screen and several minutes later her father appeared in the doorway with a frosted cupcake in one hand and a manila envelope in the other.

"I searched the station for a candle but couldn't find one. You'll have to make your birthday wish without it," he said, handing the cupcake to her. "Happy birthday to my beautiful daughter."

"Thanks, Dad," she replied, tasting a bit of the chocolate frosting with her finger. "You know I'll only be wishing for one thing today."

"I know. I think we're all hoping for the same thing." He held up the manila envelope. "In other news, I just got the initial reports from the evidence they found at Commissioner Dalton's."

"And?" she asked expectantly.

"I can only hope and pray he's going to prison for the rest of his life. So far they've been able to track down over three dozen other holding facilities in fourteen cities here in the US. They found records for hundreds of women from nineteen different countries on his personal computers. This operation has been going on for many years right under our noses. Dalton has made a lot of men very wealthy, but we are going to find each and every one of them to make sure they serve hard time for the crimes they've committed." He tossed the envelope on Mia's desk. "The bad news is that Dalton doesn't appear to be the top of the food chain – someone else is pulling the strings. And on top of that, specific laws are working against us, especially with regard to citizenship. We may have to lobby to write new legislation. It's going to be a long, drawn out process I'm afraid."

"We'll do whatever it takes, Dad. I've seen too much to ever give up without a battle."

"I know you have, Honey," he said, sitting on the corner of her desk and taking her hands in his. "I know I've said it before, but I am so sorry I ever doubted you, Mia. I will never be able to forgive myself for my shortsightedness. I can't believe I almost lost you to him."

"It's okay, Dad. Who would have thought a man could rise to the rank of police commissioner with a soul like his? I don't blame you for not believing me about him. No one in their right mind would have."

There was an awkward pause as he stood up and adjusted his belt. It would take time to mend their relationship, but she was certain they would find a way to trust one another again.

"You know," he began, changing the subject, "I was so proud of how you handled yourself with the Ukrainian girl's family yesterday. What you were able to tell them about her time in the basement - I think it meant a lot to her parents and her sisters knowing what an inspiration she was to the other women."

The reality of Kate's death was an open wound that had not yet begun to scab over and she found she was still unable to suppress the urge to cry every time she thought of her. Unapologetically, she wiped the tears from her eyes with her sleeve.

Her father placed a comforting arm around her shoulder. "What happened to her, the choices she made... it wasn't your fault, Mia."

She sniffled into the tissue Jack handed her. "I know it wasn't, but Kate was... She was an amazing woman with such a bright spirit. The world was a better place with her in it. I just can't believe she's gone."

"At least she was able to save her sisters," Jack chimed in.

She folded the tissue mindlessly in her hands. "I know. It's something of a miracle that Natalya and Tetyana walked away unharmed. Kate would have been so happy to know they're safe. Protecting them was all she ever really wanted to do," she said.

Unexpectedly, she felt the vibration of her cell phone. She fumbled awkwardly to yank it from her pocket and glanced at the number on the screen.

"Oh, God," she said aloud, her heart sinking inside her chest. "It's the hospital."

Less than fifteen minutes later she was running through the hallways of the intensive care ward at Bayview Medical Center. She bypassed the nurse's station and headed straight for room 3265. She slowed to a walk as she crossed the threshold and took a deep breath in an attempt to maintain what little composure she had left.

And then he was there. Sitting upright in the adjustable hospital bed, his head still heavily bandaged. But unlike all the other days she'd seen him since the shooting, for the first time, he was wide awake. He smiled brightly when he saw her standing in the doorway.

Unable to contain her excitement, relief washed over her as she ran across the room and threw herself into his arms.

"Gentle," he murmured, burying his face in her hair.

"I'm sorry, but Thomas… you're awake! When did you come out of the coma?"

"In the middle of the night. For some reason, I guess I just woke up. I've spent all morning with the doctors and nurses evaluating my condition. They think I'm doing pretty well, all things considered."

She brushed the gauze wrapping his head with her fingertips. "It's a miracle you even survived and yet, here you are. If that bullet had hit you half an inch to the left…" She shuddered.

"I know. I'd be dead. The doctors told me." He adjusted himself to make more room for her on the bed. "Guess I caught a lucky break," he said with a half-hearted smile.

AMALIE JAHN

"I'd say that's more than a lucky break. It's a miracle, Thomas."

He sighed heavily and she could feel him studying her. "What in the world happened to your neck?" he exclaimed suddenly. "It looks awful!"

"Hey, Buster," she snickered in an attempt to redirect his attention, "have you taken a look at yourself recently?"

He didn't return her smile. "Seriously, Mia. What happened?"

She shrugged her shoulders nonchalantly, not certain whether Thomas was ready to hear what had caused the bruising. "Let's just say you aren't the only one who's been doing hard time here at Bayview."

His face fell. "Oh, God, Mia."

"Yeah. Dalton wasn't so happy with me when I confronted him about the trafficking. He got me in a pretty good chokehold. Luckily, Jack is a man who is more than happy to shoot a criminal to protect the life of his partner. Even if it meant shooting the police commissioner."

Thomas' jaw clenched involuntarily. "Please tell me he killed the bastard."

She shook her head. "No. He's under arrest over at Union Memorial. He'll stand trial as soon as he's able. We've found tons of evidence against him. Enough to get a conviction, I hope. My dad thinks it's going to be a battle though."

"A battle worth fighting considering what he did to Kate and the others." He stopped and his eyes grew wide. "Oh my God, Mia, what happened to Kate? I think she may have gotten shot. Is she here?"

She forgot that he knew nothing of what transpired during the week he'd been lying in a coma in the wake of being shot in the head. After spending three days in the hospital herself, she kept a vigil for the remainder of the week with Mildred at his bedside, willing him to return to them. She didn't relish the fact that she would have to be the one to tell him about what happened to Kate.

318

"No, Thomas. She's not here." She paused, unable to keep herself from welling up. "She didn't survive. She died at the second holding facility. She was shot twice and both bullets hit major organs. Her internal bleeding was significant and by the time the paramedics got to her, she had already passed away. Her sisters, however, are fine. At least physically. Their parents arrived here in Baltimore two days ago. I was able to meet with them yesterday. Talking to them about Kate was one of the hardest things I've done in my life."

She watched as Thomas struggled to maintain his composure, holding back tears on the verge of spilling over.

"I should have stopped her from going into the house. I should have dragged her back to the car," he said, tears streaming down his cheeks.

She took him firmly by the shoulders, holding him at arm's length in hopes that he would see the truth. "No, Thomas. I've gone over what happened in my own head at least a hundred times already. Nothing could have kept her from her sisters. You know it and I know it. And even if you had been able to stop her, the Malinov's would be burying Natalya and Tetyana instead. And think what that would have done to Kate, knowing she hadn't done everything she could to save them. It would have ruined her life."

He rested his chin on his chest. "I can't help but feel responsible," he said.

"There's only one person responsible for Kate's death and his name is Roger Dalton."

"But I didn't save her."

She took his hands in hers, empathizing fully with his pain. "Neither did I."

She held him tightly and they wept together for Kate and the tragedy that ended her short life. If there was any comfort in their misery, it was the gift of being able to mourn her loss together. She knew too well that the bullet the surgeons removed from Thomas' head could have just as easily added him to the growing death toll.

When the last of their tears had been shed, he surprised her by asking for the date.

"It's April seventeenth. Why?"

"That's what I thought," he replied solemnly. "It's my birthday. I turn twenty-five today."

"I know," she replied. "I'm twenty-five today too."

He eyed her skeptically. "You're kidding." he said.

"I'm not. We have the same birthday. I've known we were born on the same day for a long time. Since the first day I saw you in fact." He shook his head. "What? You don't think I did my homework on you?" she said, a tiny smile forming on her lips.

"I would have expected nothing less. But do you want to know what's weirder than you and I having the same birthday?"

"What?"

"Today would have been Kate's twenty-fifth birthday too. She told me on the car ride to find her sisters last week."

They stared at one another and she suddenly remembered the commissioner's ominous warning about the prophecy. She could only assume he was referring to the Sevens Prophecy in which 14 psychics would be born on the same day. Although all three of them sharing a birthday was highly coincidental, she was beginning to think the circumstances surrounding their chance encounters was no accident.

The only problem was that Thomas and Kate weren't psychics.

"That's weird," she said finally.

"Really weird," he agreed.

As she stared at his IV, mesmerized by the rhythmic drip of the saline into the tube, she thought about the strangeness of the situation and recalled one of Kate's many bizarre comments.

"What if I told you our shared birthday might be the least weird thing about us?"

"It wouldn't surprise me," he teased. "You're pretty weird."

She ignored him, adjusting herself on the bed so she could see his full reaction to what she was about to suggest. "Kate said something strange to me after we were rescued from the basement. Do you remember when she said I was "brought" to her and that she had asked for me to come into her life to correct everything that had gone wrong? It was almost as if she thought she had some sort of a superpower."

"A superpower like seeing auras?" he asked, raising an eyebrow.

"Maybe," she shrugged. "If I have my gift, why couldn't she have a gift too?"

He nodded thoughtfully. "It would make sense," he said. "You *were* born on the same day."

She hesitated and took a deep breath, finally ready to ask the question she'd been curious about since the day she noticed his missing aura. "You were born on the same day too, Thomas. So what's your superpower?"

He gazed out the window and she sensed his reluctance. "If I tell you something, do you promise not to think I'm crazy?" he asked.

"I think it's a little late for that," she laughed.

"I'm serious." He paused briefly before continuing, still entranced by whatever was holding his attention in the hospital courtyard. "Before the shooting, I'd been thinking about why you can't see my aura."

"Oh, really? You shouldn't let it bother you."

"It does bother me, and I figured there has to be some reason it's not visible to you. Almost like I have some sort of shield around me that keeps you from seeing it."

"Okay…" she said, somewhat perplexed by his line of reasoning.

He finally turned from the window and met her gaze. "I know. I told you it was going to sound crazy, but stick with me."

"Like glue."

He smiled again. "So if I have this shield around me that keeps you from seeing my aura, maybe the shield also protects me from stuff."

"It didn't protect you from the bullet they pulled out of your brain."

"No, but it kept the bullet from killing me."

She looked at him skeptically, unsure of where he was headed with his self-analysis.

"You said yourself a while ago that you didn't know how I survived the foster care system. You said most kids who are in my situation end up a mess. But not me. I had horrible experiences, and yet somehow, I always managed to avoid getting seriously hurt and I remained emotionally undamaged, for the most part I guess."

"And this is because of your shield?"

"Yeah. Maybe. And there's something else too. Sometimes, when something bad is about to happen to me or if I'm about to put myself into a dangerous situation, I know it. I can sense that I have to get away. I can't ignore it. It forces me to listen. And to act. It's how I've managed to keep myself out of harm's way for so long. A voice in my head tells me what's coming."

Mia worked to steady her breathing. Thomas' revelation confirmed for her that the prophecy was real. It was happening and they were a part of it. "If you have a power too, then all three of us were all born on the same date and all seem to have an ability."

"Something like that," he agreed.

She thought about his disclosure and found she had no trouble believing it was true. However, there was one inconsistency she was having difficulty reconciling.

"So if a voice inside your head tells you when something bad is about to happen, then why didn't you feel the danger at the holding facility with Kate?"

"I've never felt it stronger in my life. I knew exactly what was coming before I ever saw it."

She looked at the man before her, his head wrapped in layers of gauze and his face swollen from medication, and in that moment, she had never seen anyone more perfect. Thoughts of the prophecy faded into the background as she considered how she truly felt about him. There was no doubt she was deeply and powerfully in love because she already knew how he would answer her next question.

"So, why didn't you just leave if you knew you were going to get hurt?"

He shifted uncomfortably under his sheet. "Because I couldn't. I couldn't leave Kate there to fight alone. I had to help her."

"Even though you knew you might take a bullet for it?"

"I was hoping maybe I could avoid that part with my awesome Kung Fu moves. I guess I could use a few more lessons, huh?"

She couldn't keep herself from smiling at him. In that moment, it felt as though one chapter of her life was ending but that another was getting ready to begin. She briefly considered telling him what she suspected about their involvement in the Sevens Prophecy but decided he'd dealt with enough excitement for one day. Especially since convincing him of its validity, given his time with Madame Freakshow, would take some finesse.

It would be another conversation for another day.

"So what now?" she asked, resting her head against his chest.

Thomas took a deep breath and exhaled loudly. "I guess now I get better, you make sure Dalton never hurts another woman, and we live happily ever after."

"That sounds like a pretty optimistic ending."

"Cautiously optimistic," he corrected her.

They lay quietly entwined together on the tiny hospital bed. Thomas had been asleep for almost an hour when Mildred appeared at the door with a small chocolate layer cake.

"They called and told me he came to overnight," she said, her voice full of panic. "Has he fallen back into the coma?"

"No," Mia murmured, "he's just sleeping. But we should wake him. He'll want to know you're here."

When Mildred found out it was Mia's birthday as well, she insisted they both blow out the candles on the cake together. As the flame disappeared, she closed her eyes and sent her birthday wish wafting into the air with what was left of the candle's smoke.

"What'd you wish for?" Thomas asked.

She kissed him gently on the lips. "I can't tell you or it won't come true. But don't worry," she said, smiling at the aura-less busboy who won her heart, "I think my wish may have already come true."

What if a group of psychic strangers came together to save the world?

Please enjoy this sneak peek of

gather the sentient

book two in the sevens prophecy series

CHAPTER

1

JOSE

The hospital was as quiet as hospitals ever can be, which is to say there was still a modicum of chatter from the nurses' station and muted clicks and beeps could still be heard coming from patients' rooms if you listened carefully. Beyond that, the halls were silent, as no visitors were allowed in the ICU overnight.

Jose passed through the ward on his way to the ER and gave a nod to Selma, one of the nurses also working the graveyard shift. The two had been out together several times but no relationship had ever developed. This bothered Jose if for no other reason than he had always been drawn to the warmth of her smile. She waved to him, barely making eye contact, and quickly returned to her conversation with the others.

He slowed his pace once he was past their line of sight and scanned the patients' names on the doors as he strolled through the hallway. He was familiar with all but two, who he assumed had been brought in since his shift the night before. Their files hung on wall hooks just outside their rooms, and after glancing back down the corridor to be sure he wouldn't be seen, he snatched Chloe Hall's clipboard from the wall and stepped inside her room.

The lights were off except for a dim overhead light in the doorway. He peered into the darkness and could barely make out the shape of a figure asleep under the sheet. Chloe appeared tiny and her chart confirmed that she was only 17 years old, hospitalized as the result of traumatic head injury – a horseback riding accident was listed as the cause. Jose crept slightly further into the room until he could see the steady rise and fall of her chest and the green halo of the ventilation machine. Wisps of hair peeked out from beneath the gauze around her head and he imagined what she'd looked like the day before, atop her horse soaring across the Sonoran desert, the wind chasing her down.

Without a word, he reentered the hallway, cautiously replaced Chloe's chart, and entered the room of the other newcomer to the ward, Matt Mulhaney. A quick scan of his chart revealed the reason for his admission – a front end collision with a dump truck first early that morning. He'd spent all day in surgery having his arms and legs bolted back together, and while there was only a slight threat of internal bleeding, the doctor's notes indicated he remained in the ICU because of his lethally high blood pressure. Framed by the light from the hallway, Mulhaney appeared to be a sort of prehistoric arachnid, his limbs suspended around him as if he was caught in a web of his own construction. Jose wondered if the man's family was waiting somewhere in the building or if they'd relented and gone home after a full day of weeping and praying. He envisioned the man's small children climbing over waiting room furniture, no longer satisfied with broken crayons and daytime TV, unable to comprehend just what 'critical condition' really meant.

Jose left the second patient's room more confused than when he entered, and after confirming that he hadn't been seen, made his way through the double doors and onto the elevator which delivered him to the emergency room where he was expected for work. The glaring brightness and cacophony of the ER was a stark contrast to the intensive care unit on the second floor. Vanessa, the head nurse, spotted him cutting through triage on the way to the break room and stopped him before he even had a chance to drop off his bag.

"Have you clocked in?" she called, pushing an elderly man in a wheelchair through the waiting room.

"I was just on my way," he replied, motioning toward the door.

She shook her head. "I'll have Gloria swipe your card. I need you to take Mr. Fletcher here to the restroom to get washed up. It seems he's had a bit of an accident."

The stench coming from the man indicated what kind of accident he'd had and it wasn't the type that involved a motor vehicle. Although he initially balked, Jose quickly remembered his job as an orderly was a means to an end. Changing the old man's pants now was the only way he would have access to the others later, and so with that in mind, he left his bag behind the triage desk and hurried Mr. Fletcher to an unoccupied observation room.

He cleaned the man quickly and proficiently, redressing him in a pair of standard issue scrubs while avoiding both eye contact and small talk. When he began working as an orderly right after high school, tasks involving bodily fluids often made him consider other career options, but six years later, he knew he could never leave. The access it gave him to complete his life's work was unsurpassed, so he quickly learned to overcome his squeamish tendencies.

After returning Mr. Fletcher to his wife in the waiting room, he was immediately called to help restrain a new arrival who was hopped up on hallucinogens and threatening to tear an examination room apart.

"He thinks we're trying to kill him," one of the shift nurses told him. "And he's seriously strong, so be careful. Dr. Unger's already in there and has been calling for back up, but I didn't know where you were."

Without the slightest hesitation, Jose hurried past the support rooms toward the treatment area where he heard the man screaming obscenities and threatening the staff. The room's curtain was no longer closed for privacy and exposed the scene inside as he approached.

"Listen Wes, no one is trying to hurt you," Unger was telling the patient when Jose rushed up behind him. "Just set down the scissors so we can find out what's really going on."

Wes, a formidable looking teenager, stood against the far wall wielding a pair of surgical scissors he'd obviously scavenged from another treatment room. The terror in his eyes convinced Jose that the kid truly believed his evasive actions against hospital personnel were necessary for his survival and that there would be no reasoning with him. Mascara stained the cheeks of a pretty brunette pleading quietly from the corner of the room for him to stop, while Vanessa and Gloria stood behind Unger, positioned to flee if necessary.

"Come on, baby. Just chill out, okay? Please?" the brunette begged. "Let's just forget any of this ever happened and I'll just take you home."

"NO!" he screamed at her, "you're in it with them! All of you together! You're all trying to kill me but I won't let you!"

Jose immediately wished there was another man in the room. He knew with Unger's help he could restrain Wes, but the adrenaline surging through the kid's veins made him unpredictable. There was no telling what he would do if they provoked him further.

Unger turned to Vanessa. "Has security been called?"

She appeared poised, but did not take her eyes off the boy. "Yes, of course, but someone said they were outside dealing with a fight in the parking lot. Who knows when we'll see them."

Wes's eyes darted around the room and Jose sensed he was planning to make his escape. Lives would be in jeopardy if he was allowed to leave the room and there was no telling what type of chaos would ensue. He took a step closer to the teen.

"Hey, border bandit," Wes sneered. "Stay away from me. I'll kill you if I have to! Nobody will care if there's one less Sanchez in the world!"

The words sliced a nick in Jose's composure – no one ever cared that he was a fourth generation American of legal descent, but it wasn't enough to provoke him into action prematurely. He ventured another step forward with Unger by his side.

"Ready?" Unger whispered.

"Yeah," he replied.

The men tackled the boy in one fluid motion, Unger on his left side and Jose on his right, pinning him against the wall. Vanessa fumbled for a set of zip tie cuffs in the bottom drawer of a cabinet as Wes wrestled to free himself. Once found, she ran to Unger who quickly strapped his left hand into the tie while Jose continued to restrain Wes as best he could, cautious of the scissors which were dangerously close to his body.

"Get off me, Chalupa!" Wes spat as he thrashed his head in sheer defiance. "I'll kill you, I swear it!"

After securing the boy's left hand, Unger slid behind him in an attempt to reach his other side, but as he lessened his grip, Wes seized the opportunity to lunge forward, stabbing the scissors into Jose's thigh. He cried out but didn't release the boy, jamming his shoulder securely into his chest. Within seconds, Unger slipped the tie over Wes's right hand and pulled tightly on the restraint, forcing him to the ground.

"Oh my God, Jose," Gloria cried out, noticing the blood pooling in a ring on his jeans.

He brought his hand to the wound, testing to see how deeply he'd been pierced. "It's nothing," he replied, as she hurried to his side. "I don't think it even needs stitches."

Security arrived as the police were being called and Gloria led Jose into an adjacent room to look at his injury.

"Seriously, it's fine. I'll just change my pants and put on a band aid," he said.

Gloria slipped on a pair of latex gloves. "Nonsense," she replied as she carefully began cutting a hole in his pants to expose the wound. "Just let me make sure that little punk didn't do any serious harm."

He allowed her to examine him as it gave her peace of mind, but he knew there would be no lasting damage. As she cleaned and dressed the puncture, prattling on about how they didn't get paid enough to deal with crazy people, he allowed his mind to wander to the new ICU patients. It was always hard when he had to make a choice and tonight he could only choose one person on the floor. To choose more than one would be far too risky. He couldn't chance exposing his intent. By the time Gloria finished, he'd weighed all his options and made his decision. He hoped it was the right one.

The police were escorting a subdued and restrained Wes out of the ER as Jose sought out Vanessa to tell her he was going on his break. He slipped unnoticed through the lobby to where the elevators carried him back to the second floor.

It was still peaceful there as he crept down the hallway, hugging tightly to the wall so he could duck into an alcove if one of the nurses made an appearance. When he arrived at the room of the patient he'd selected, he wasted no time getting straight to work.

Chloe Hall lay before him, sleeping soundly as she'd been when he first looked in on her earlier in the evening. Selecting her out of all the possible ICU patients wasn't an easy decision, but he knew in his heart she wasn't going to make it and that he was the only one capable of putting an end to her suffering. He gently brushed the wisps of hair across her pillow, whispering a simple prayer for her soul, and then Jose placed his hands upon her chest and surrendered himself to what he knew needed to be done.

Dearest Reader,

When I decided to write *Among the Shrouded*, I knew I wanted to give a voice to the thousands of women living in our world who have been forced into sexual slavery. Please know that although I've written a work of fiction, there's nothing fictional about the real-life human trafficking occurring all over the world each and every day.

According to The Global Initiative to Fight Human Trafficking:

"An estimated 2.5 million people are in forced labor (including sexual exploitation) at any given time as a result of trafficking.

The majority of trafficking victims are between 18 and 24 years of age.

43% of victims are used for forced commercial sexual exploitation, of whom 98% are women and girls.

Estimated global annual profits made from the exploitation of all trafficked forced labor are $31.6 billion US.

In 2006 there were only 5,808 prosecutions and 3,160 convictions throughout the world which means that for every 800 people trafficked, only one person was convicted in 2006."

I implore you to learn more about what you can do to increase awareness or help stop this form of modern day slavery by taking a few minutes of your day to read the information on the following websites:

www.ungift.org
www.unodc.org
www.unglobalcompact.org
www.fbi.gov/about-us/investigate/civilrights/human_trafficking

In the words of the great 18th century abolitionist William Wilberforce,
"You may choose to look the other way but you can never say again that you did not know."

Sincerely,
Amalie Jahn

Source:
(http://www.unglobalcompact.org/docs/issues_doc/labour/Forced_labour/HUM AN_TRAFFICKING_-_THE_FACTS_-_final.pdf)

Discussion Questions for Among the Shrouded

1. Thomas' power gave him the ability to avoid danger. How did his character learn to overcome this instinct throughout the course of the book? Would it have been better if he had continued to shy away from danger?

2. Mia is torn throughout the book between trusting what she sees and what she believes to be true intellectually. She initially dismisses the implications with regard to Thomas' missing aura and the commissioner's dark one. How would the story have been different if she had trusted in her abilities from the beginning?

3. Kate's path in life was predetermined. In what ways did she epitomize classic Christian martyrs?

4. The book is written from three rotating points of view, allowing the reader insight into each of the character's unique perspectives. Why do you think the author chose this technique?

5. Do you think it's possible for a person in a position of power to be as corrupt as the commissioner? Are there real-life examples in our world?

6. Kate's journey into slavery is fictitious, but thousands of real women and children are enslaved each day. Read Jillian Mourning's story at http://www.xojane.com/it-happened-to-me/sex-trafficking-in-the-us. How is Jillian's story similar to Kate's? How is it different? What lessons can young women learn from both girls' stories?

7. Thomas has close relationships with many of the women in his life. How do you think being an orphan affected his relationships with Mia, Mildred, and Belinda?

8. How did Mia compensate for not having a mother figure in her life?

9. If you could have dinner with one of the characters from the book, who would it be and what would you like to ask them?

About the Author

Amalie Jahn is the author of *Among the Shrouded*,
The Clay Lion Series, and many, many to-do lists.
Visit her online at www.theclaylion.com.